SAVIOR OF AMRODEL

"Whether or not this 'Aren' has done a fair job of uniting his people means little, I'm afraid, Fareth," said Shaen. "He's still a Norskman, and they have ever been treacherous. If he could wield the Dragonfly Sword, which even Madawc doubted, he's as likely to be seduced by its power as to use it for our defense. And I just don't see what he could do against the Dark Tide, anyway. I think it is unreasonable to place our trust in him, despite what he was able to make Damir and Eliana believe. They were, after all, the only Woodlanders to meet this boy, and considering how tense the situation was, their judgment may well have been flawed."

"I saw him once," said Cahira quietly. The others stopped to stare at her. "He had ventured into the Woodland on some kind of 'Norsk trial of manhood.' Eliana caught him, and they became friends."

She remembered him well, a boy with almost unnatural beauty. He had pale golden hair that fell around an angelic face, and bright eyes the color of amber….

Other books by Stobie Piel:

STRANGE BREWS
LORD OF THE DARK SUN
THE RENEGADE'S HEART
RENEGADE
MISTLETOE & MAGIC (Anthology)
BLUE-EYED BANDIT
FIVE GOLD RINGS (Anthology)
FREE FALLING
THE WHITE SUN
THE MAGIC OF CHRISTMAS (Anthology)
THE MIDNIGHT MOON
TRICK OR TREAT
MOLLY IN THE MIDDLE
THE DAWN STAR

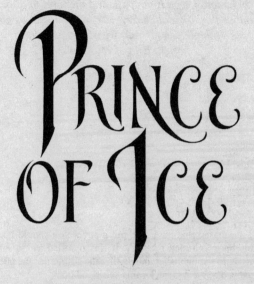

PRINCE OF ICE

STOBIE PIEL

LOVE SPELL NEW YORK CITY

*To my best friend, Carol Weymouth,
in honor of good times past, and those yet to come;
and for Peacock and Shelley, who are still with us now,
I thank you for your friendship and the
bright light of your soul.*

LOVE SPELL®

May 2006

Published by

Dorchester Publishing Co., Inc.
200 Madison Avenue
New York, NY 10016

ISBN 0-505-52651-4

Printed in the United States of America.

There was a Being whom my spirit oft
Met on its visioned wanderings, far aloft
In the clear golden prime of my youth's dawn.

—Epipsychidion, *Percy Bysshe Shelley*

Prologue

OLD FRIENDS

"I am two days past the anniversary of my seventh year—it is wrong to send me to my room!" Cahira Daere glared up at her father. "I am a Mage Child and a warrior. You cannot tell me what to do!"

"I am the king of Amrodel and your father, and you are going to bed. It grows late, and even a Mage Child needs to sleep." She sensed he was repressing a smile because his eyes twinkled suspiciously. Cahira placed her hands on her hips.

"I refuse."

The king arched an eyebrow. He wasn't a forceful man by nature, and most often, Cahira could worm around his orders. Tonight, he appeared steadfast as they faced each other at the top of the palace staircase. Cahira glanced down at the guests milling around. Mundanes and Mages alike had gathered for the solstice celebration honoring a long-past Woodland queen, the greatest Mage the people of Amrodel had ever known.

"But Eliana isn't here yet! She promised that next time she came to the palace she would teach me to explode mushrooms!"

The king issued an exaggerated groan, then aimed Cahira at her room. "Reason enough to send you to bed early."

Despite his noble heritage, her father had not been born with a Mage's *ki,* the magical energy inherent to their nature that gave a person power. Of his children, only Cahira had inherited that power, and already she felt it stirring within her soul. She shot one final glance at the door, in hopes she might spot Eliana's arrival. If she couldn't convince her father herself, Eliana certainly could.

Below, Cahira saw Damir ap Kora, a young and handsome Mage. Two women flitted around him, to whom he paid sporadic attention, but he seemed to be watching the door. Cahira wondered if he was hoping to see Eliana, too. If Damir caught Eliana first, Eliana would be distracted, and would soon be engaged in bickering with her handsome nemesis, and Cahira's chances would be lost. She sighed miserably and her shoulders slumped from their defiant posture.

"Very well, sire. I will retire to my room, where I will work on a spell that will speed up my growth."

Her father eyed her suspiciously, as if he considered her likely to succeed—though so far, her magical endeavors had failed rather dramatically. But both Damir and Eliana were tutoring her, separately because they fought so much, and even the Elder Mage Madawc had taken an interest in her education.

Cahira left the king and made for her room, and he rejoined his guests below. She glimpsed him as a pretty young woman called Shaen maneuvered to his side. Shaen looked shy, and the king greeted her kindly. Cahira's stepmother had gone with Cahira's sisters to the port city of Amon-Dhen, so perhaps he was lonely.

Cahira went into her room, fiddled with a half-finished bow of yew, added brown feathers to a few arrows, then flopped down on her bed. "Nothing ever happens to me. I will grow old, fat, and die, and still be locked in here with nothing to do."

She got up, paced around a bit, then crept again from her

room. If her father didn't see her, she could at least spy on the guests. Maybe Eliana had arrived and was fighting with Damir. That was usually interesting. Once, Eliana had tried to turn him green and his hair had caught fire instead!

Cahira slipped furtively down the hall and peeked over the balcony, but the guests had moved into the ballroom. She heard the music of harp and flute, and Rhys the Bard was singing. From the corner of her eye, she caught movement almost as furtive as her own. Her heart leapt, and she spun around.

She saw Eliana dart beneath the staircase. But why was Eliana hiding? Cahira started to wave, but as the young woman disappeared, another shape emerged behind her. Cahira stared in amazement as a boy, little older than herself, popped out from beneath the stairs. He looked up at her and her heart caught in her throat. He looked like an angel; only wilder, more beautiful. His hair was the color of pale gold, and his eyes shone like amber in a face so fair that he seemed sculpted by adoring gods.

No Woodland child was this, for all Woodlanders were dark-haired. Surely this had to be a Norsk boy, sworn enemies of her people from the icelands to the north, but clearly he had won Eliana's favor. Cahira contemplated racing to her father with the news, but as she looked at the boy, her heart moved strangely and a feeling she didn't recognize took shape in her mind.

The Mage Eliana peeked back around the corner and saw Cahira looking down from the balcony. She held her finger to her lips, and Cahira nodded in delight at this adventure. Eliana slipped away, but the boy lingered, his fair face lit with wonder as he looked up at her. To her surprise, he winked. Then he disappeared after Eliana. Cahira stared after him, her heart moving in erratic pulses. And then she knew the words that had formed in her thoughts when she saw him. . . .

"I've missed you."

1

THE LAST MAGE

"The Dark Tide has crossed into the Woodland realm." Cahira entered the King's chamber, clutching her bow in one hand, ready to fight though she knew their opponent was impervious. "It is coming this way."

Damir ap Kora, the king of Amrodel and her old friend, looked out from the open door of his balcony. There, in the garden below, water rose and fell in ancient fountains with statues carved in the images of Mages past. A host of gossamer dragonflies darted through the afternoon sunlight, its last rays glistening through the darkening forest. The light gilded his wife Eliana's beautiful face, and he gently touched her hair. "The time has come, as we have long foreseen," he said.

He turned to face Cahira and smiled. She had known him since her childhood, when he had tutored her in the magic arts. Cahira loved him like a brother. Eliana was like her sister—and soon they would all fade into darkness together.

Damir and Eliana's three children gathered around Cahira. The two boys looked calm, and both wore small swords at their sides, crafted by their father who knew no rival in the creation of magical weapons. "This is not the end," said the oldest boy. "We will rise again and become great warriors. I am not afraid."

"Nor am I," said his brother. The child paused. "Do you think we will be able to practice swordplay in spirit form, Papa?"

"I'm not sure," said Damir. "Take a few last practice swings, just in case." The two boys nodded simultaneously, then smacked each other with their swords. Eliana directed them to two small beds.

"You will be able to fight in spirit form. But not here. You must take your places now."

The two children seemed almost eager, as if this dark fate were as welcome as a new adventure. They flipped themselves onto their beds, laid the swords on their chests, and closed their eyes.

Damir's daughter, Bronwyn, eyed her brothers with misgivings, then reached for Cahira's hand. She held a stuffed cloth frog tightly, and she was trembling. "I do not care about fighting in spirit form," she said in a tense voice. "I want to be with Mama and Papa, and to play with you, Cahira."

"You will do that, too," said Cahira. The children's bedding had been brought into their parents' room so they could all face the darkness together. At least they wouldn't be alone. Cahira held Bronwyn's hand and tried to smile. "I will stay with you."

Damir laid his hand on Cahira's shoulder. "No, Cahira . . . Another task lies before you."

Cahira looked up at him. "What can I do? This tide of evil energy has come from the Arch Mage. His power is so great that, even as he lies undead beneath the eastern mountains, he can reach us here. No one can stop him now if you and Eliana cannot."

"There is still hope," said Damir.

His wife Eliana glanced toward the door. "Where is the Elder Mage Madawc? He was supposed to meet us here with you."

"He sent me alone," said Cahira. "Madawc has placed himself in a trance of some kind. He said he wouldn't let the Arch Mage have that last power over him, so he did it himself first."

"That is odd," said Damir, and his brow furrowed. "Perhaps Madawc is planning something that he hasn't shared with us."

Eliana looked hopeful. "It might be so, Damir!" She glanced at Cahira. "Did he tell you anything?"

Cahira shook her head. "He said it was between himself and our enemy, but I didn't get the impression he expected to change what is to happen today."

"No," agreed Damir. "That would be unlikely." He paused. "Well, I will leave that to Madawc's judgment, and go on with my own plan."

"What plan?" asked Cahira.

"Ten years ago, Eliana and I fought against this same evil force, and we defeated it. Yet we all knew it would rise again, and we knew that when it returned, none of us would have the power to stand against the great wizard."

"We know his methods and his intentions," added Eliana. "With this great force of evil energy he has mustered, the Arch Mage will immobilize all the Mages of Amrodel. We know he needs the energy passed on from our relative, the Woodland queen, to realize his resurrection—and that only you and I share that energy, Cahira. My daughter is still too young for his purposes, and since I have become a mother, I am also useless to him. He needs you, because you have the *ki* of a Mage, and because you are related to the woman he once loved, the woman who chose death rather than submit. He will not stop until he succeeds." Eliana paused, then gently touched Cahira's cheek. "I remember what it was like to hear his voice in my head. I know what you're going through."

When Cahira first heard that voice in her head, she had thought she was going mad, until Eliana had told her of the Arch Mage's relentless call. "In the last weeks I have heard him even in my sleep. His tone is mocking now," she said.

Her eyes warmed with tears, but she refused to allow them. "He says there is nothing I can do. He knows he has won."

"No," said Damir. "Not yet, he hasn't." He lifted a glittering white sword and held it before Cahira, and the energy trapped deep within the blade reflected in his eyes. "This sword has the power to withstand him . . . but not in my hands, nor in those of anyone here in Amrodel. . . ."

"Damir speaks of a prophecy that came to me during that dark time past," said Eliana. "It was delivered by the dragonflies—minions of the great queen's spirit, or so we believe."

"She warned us then that we could not defeat the Arch Mage, but a time would come when another would rise who had that power," continued Damir. "Our hope against darkness lies in one who carries 'pure light. . . .'"

A sharp cry from outside the palace interrupted. Damir glanced out the window. "The darkness comes even quicker than reported. It advances with malice and fury. Come quickly, Cahira. This deed must be done now, before it's too late."

"What deed?" Cahira rose from Bronwyn's bed, and looked between the king and queen, and she sensed that this moment had been long planned. Even the children seemed to know what was coming.

Damir set aside the white sword and faced Cahira, and Eliana stood back to give him room. Without explanation, the king placed his fingers on Cahira's temples, then spoke in a low chant. Cahira recognized but did not understand the language of his father's people, the dark people of the land of Kora far to the south of the great sea. His eyes closed, and as he chanted, Cahira felt herself drawn inside his words as if a mystic cloud enveloped her. She felt safe and warm and protected. As Damir poured the power of his *ki* into the force around her, she felt his own strength weakening.

Dimly, she heard Eliana's voice, and knew the queen, too, was afraid for her husband. "Damir! Stop! It is enough . . ." But he didn't stop. Around and around, energy swirled, and

Cahira felt as if a suit of armor had been placed upon her, but far stronger than any metal. Damir had shielded her before, when she was a child, just after her father, the previous king, was murdered. She had felt a brief warmth and a sense of safety then, but this shield felt different—far greater and more powerful. It sought out her inner defenses and connected with them.

When the chanting stopped, Damir stumbled back, then lowered himself onto his bed, his energy exhausted. "I have shielded you, Cahira, with all that I have to give."

Cahira stared at him in disbelief. "Why me? I have never been as strong as either of you! What can I do?"

"He had the power to shield only one of us," said Eliana, her voice breaking, but she smiled and touched Cahira's arm. "We know you are the one."

"My shield will protect you when the darkness tries to overtake you," said Damir. "No attacker can harm you, but you must be wary in choosing those in whom you place your trust, for the shield cannot protect you from those you allow close."

A cloud of darkness entered the room as Damir spoke. It curled over the western balcony, and moved over the two boy children like a snake swallowing prey, and their expressions faded into stillness. The little girl Bronwyn looked to Cahira, and before the dark energy claimed her, the child smiled and whispered, "Good luck."

" 'Pure light must face the darkness, and win, in order to defeat the Arch Mage.' " Damir paused, his voice weakening. "Remember, it may not be as it seems, Cahira. Darkness is ever deceptive."

"The Arch Mage will never trick me," she vowed. "I know his evil voice too well."

"But darkness might. Never forget." Damir gestured toward the white sword. "Take my sword . . . Take it . . ." The darkness advanced upon him and stole his words.

His wife threw herself over his body as if to protect Damir from the evil force, but it shifted and engulfed her, too.

Eliana's eyes shifted to Cahira and her lips parted as she tried to fight the darkness that was claiming her.

"What do I do?" Cahira's voice came out a whisper. "Where do I take it?"

Eliana's lips quivered, and with her last breath, she whispered a single word. It was a name Cahira knew: *"Aren."*

The darkness stole over Eliana, and Cahira watched transfixed with horror as the defiant queen fought against it. Angry, it drove her away from her husband, and her lovely face contorted with the pain of separation. A tear slid down Eliana's cheek and at last her body stilled.

Cahira backed away, but the dark energy turned and approached her. Relentlessly, it moved forward. She felt its awareness; she knew that it recognized the power of her *ki*. An evil voice laughed in her head. *"I have you now. There is no resistance. No hope. No future, but to serve me."*

She placed her hand on the hilt of the white sword and stared into the midst of the darkness. It rose around her and moved inward with a force like, yet opposite to, Damir's shield. It struggled and it loomed, but it did not penetrate the king's shield. It froze, then twitched with rage. At last, it relented and slid away. But the voice lingered in her head: *"Little fool! You refuse the inevitable. But my power over you will soon be complete. In time, you will come to me. There is no future but to serve me. All paths lead to darkness. . . ."* Cahira heard the echoes of his mocking laughter as the energy receded.

She looked down at Eliana and Damir. Damir's face was turned toward his wife, and her hand reached out for his. Something about this image burned into Cahira. The Arch Mage's magic destroyed all in its path, all to serve his evil ends. So Eliana and Damir, who had loved each other so desperately and for so long, lay frozen, unable even to hold each other.

Cahira took Eliana's hand and laid it gently in Damir's outstretched fingers. A strange echo rose in her mind, like a far-off child's voice. For a brief instant, that echo overwhelmed the Arch Mage's voice. *You will never separate us . . . We will always find each other again, and one day, you will fall before us!* A vision formed in her head, as if her own spirit rose above the two lifeless forms, and she saw herself looking down over a windswept desert amidst a tide of dark fury and swirling sand.

The vision abated, and she had no idea what it meant. Then she went to the window and watched the darkness recede through the trees. It had come as far west as it needed to go—all the Mages except Cahira now lay insensate from its power. It slid away into the east, and Cahira knew its destination. It returned to its source and its core, the evil heart of the Arch Mage. She picked up her bow and raised her fist to the east. "You will not defeat me. I will find the power to face you, and when I do, all you have torn asunder will be mended. And it will be you that flies before me!"

"The Age of Darkness has returned. None can escape it now." A woman spoke, and Cahira, standing in the tavern's shadowy hall, recognized Shaen, her late father's mistress. Though not a Mage herself, Shaen had won a place of esteem in the realm, and the Mundanes at the Hungry Cat Tavern gathered around to hear her words. If she gave up, the others would find no reason to hope, for Shaen was closer to the inner workings of the Mage Elite than any other Mundane in the Woodland of Amrodel.

Like a harbinger of doom, a small brown bat swooped through the tavern door and into the front room where the Woodland people gathered. It angled awkwardly, then circled as if seeking a spot to land. Shaen gasped in surprise and disgust as the creature flitted over her head.

Fareth the innkeeper swatted at it, but the bat evaded him and settled upside-down on a beam. "Doom is at hand . . ." Fareth said as he sank into a deep chair and bowed his head.

"We have known this was coming for a long while," said Shaen. Her voice was even, almost a drone, as if the peril of their situation had enervated her. "All the Mages have fallen.

I was with the Elder Mage Madawc when he set himself to sleep." She paused, and her brow furrowed. "He actually set himself in a trance before the darkness descended upon him, though I could see no point in that, when it was going to take him anyway. The palace guards say the king and queen now lie in slumber, not alive, not dead. . . ."

Fareth shook his head and, beside him, his young apprentice Alouard began to weep silent tears that ran over his round cheeks. "All the Mages . . . trapped like that, forever. It's the worst fate I can imagine. And what's to become of us, those left behind?"

"We must stay and await our fate, each in our own way," said Shaen. She looked around. "All the Mages are accounted for and Mundane guards are protecting them—for all the good it will do. But no one has reported Cahira's location. I intend to watch over her personally, as her father would have wanted."

Fareth glanced up. "Wasn't the lass with the Elder Mage? She's lived with him since her father passed away."

"Maybe she chose to spend her immortal confinement with her stepmother and sisters," suggested Alouard.

Shaen shrugged. "They live on the far side of the forest, and I saw Cahira only this morning. It is important that we find her."

Cahira moved from the shadows of the tavern's front hall and stood before the inn's desperate crowd. She had lingered too long, listening to them with no idea what to say. The tavern patrons appeared too stunned by her presence to speak. "I am here."

Shaen picked her way through the crowd and hugged Cahira in a warm embrace. "Cahira! I'm so relieved. But how is this possible? We were told the Dark Tide was certain to immobilize all the Mages of Amrodel, that none would be left awake or able to defend us."

"Damir shielded me before he fell into the sleep, so that I can take action against this fate."

Alouard eyed her doubtfully. "Why you? Why not Damir himself or his wife, who were able to beat back the darkness before?"

Shaen cast him a dark look. "I'm sure the king knew what he was doing when he chose Cahira." She touched Cahira's arm gently, adding, "He and Eliana have always believed in you."

Fareth rose from his chair and studied Cahira. "If Damir ap Kora and The Fiend . . ." He stopped and coughed. In the ten years since Damir and Eliana had become king and queen of Amrodel, Fareth had never been able to forget Eliana's former title, the name given to the gifted herbalist in response to her many acts of youthful mischief. "Meaning, of course, our queen . . ." He coughed again. "If those two chose you, then you're the one to save us."

"But I don't know how," said Cahira. When she had vowed to defeat the Arch Mage earlier, she had meant it. Now, her task seemed insurmountable, and she felt so alone.

"Didn't he give you any direction before he fell into his trance?" asked Fareth.

"I'm sure Damir didn't have any real idea of what Cahira can do," said Shaen, and she paused to sigh. "I'm afraid it was a desperate attempt, born of hopelessness rather than any real strategy. Perhaps Eliana talked him into it. Though she is certainly a gifted Mage in her own right, we all know how impulsive she could be." The woman bit her lip and gazed at her feet. "I will miss them so much."

Alouard thumped a full tankard of ale onto the bar counter, his face reddened with emotion. " 'Miss them?' How can we be talking this way? Without the Mages, there's no way we can protect ourselves! Without them, we're doomed. I don't understand what's happening. Why couldn't Damir and The Fiend stop this? Didn't they beat back this Dark Tide once before? They were strong then. Why aren't they strong enough now?"

Shaen cast a commiserating glance at the young man, then

gently patted his thick arm. "I know, Alouard. It's so hard to accept, especially for those of us born Mundanes, without magical energy. How could their strength fail?"

"Because the Dark Tide comes from a greater *ki* than any we have known," said Cahira. "It has grown in power since Damir and Eliana drove it back ten years ago. It receded, but it was not destroyed. The Arch Mage has gathered strength in that time, and now no force can stand against him."

"I don't even know who he is!" said Alouard. "Some long dead Mage who fought in a battle that even our Elders can't remember? What does he have to do with what's happening now?"

"The Arch Mage isn't dead, Alouard," said Shaen. "Long ago, in the shadows of the eastern mountains, there was a great battle between the Elite Mages of Amrodel and the Dark Mages. Their leader was an exile from the desert realm of Kora, and his power was insurmountable. But the Arch Mage fell in love with the Mage who was then our Queen, and she betrayed him."

" '*She* betrayed *him?*' Ha!" said Fareth. "As I heard it told, he wanted to sap all her energy into himself and take control of all the lands of the world!"

"Of course," agreed Shaen. "But in his mind, it was a betrayal. We know the Queen only did what she had to do. But because she refused him, he was trapped in a spell from which he cannot be released without the return of her *ki* to his cavern."

"She gave up her life," said Cahira quietly. "She must have been a brave woman." She stopped and sighed. "We are never truly free of the past. It's an ongoing river, forever to the sea. Eliana and I are her relatives, though not in direct lineage. Because of that, the Arch Mage requires my energy to regain his life. He is seeking me. All his will is bent on bringing me to that dark cavern." An involuntary shudder ripped through her, and Cahira closed her eyes.

"Like he sought out The Fiend before she wed Damir!" said Fareth.

Alouard looked pained. "Dead people can't just resurrect themselves."

"As Shaen said, the Arch Mage isn't dead," said Cahira. "When the queen gave up her life rather than submit to him, the battle turned against him, so he buried himself deep in the caverns beneath his mountain kingdom and there he lies, trapped in a spell of his own making."

Shaen nodded. "Apparently, he believed his followers would soon resurrect him using the energy of the queen's younger sister, from whom both Eliana and Cahira are descended. But a secret lover impregnated the sister, and that division of her energy rendered her useless to the Arch Mage."

Fareth's brow angled. "So pregnancy shuts down his plans?" He shifted his gaze to Cahira. "So get yourself a lover and get to business!"

Cahira glared, and Shaen laughed. "I don't think we can make such a demand of poor Cahira! No man has yet won her heart, Fareth."

"No man has dared," said Alouard. He spoke under his breath, but Cahira heard him.

"And no man had better!" she said. She shook her head, adding, "If it would work, I would do it, however disgusting. But do you forget? Eliana and Damir have a daughter, and she also shares the queen's lineage."

Fareth looked stubborn. "Well, we wait until she's old enough to mate, and then we'll set her up with a suitable male, too!" He paused. "Of course, I don't know if she'll age or not, pickled in a slumber as she is now. . . ."

"We could just kill them all," suggested Alouard.

Shaen gasped, but Cahira sighed. "If it were only me, I might choose that over what awaits us if we fail. But if we kill a child—are we not as dark as the Arch Mage ever was?"

"I suppose so," agreed Alouard. He shook his head and clamped his hand over his eyes. "Of late, I've been thinking evil thoughts like this. I don't know why."

"It is the effect of the darkness," said Cahira. "Madawc

the Elder Mage told me it would be this way. Whatever darkness we have within us will be fanned, and we all have some shadow inside—we must fight it to survive. You are not alone, Alouard."

"Then what do we do?" the young barkeep asked. "What did they expect of you?"

Cahira didn't answer. She walked to the front door and, with effort, lifted a sheathed sword from where she had left it propped against the wall. "Damir gave me this," she told them. "It is the white sword he crafted to fight the dark force ten years ago."

"The Dragonfly Sword!" Shaen gasped, then stared at the sword. "But what can he expect you to do with it? Your skill is with the bow, and you've had such a hard time collecting and manifesting your *ki* . . ."

Shaen bit her lip as Cahira turned away. This was a sore spot. Such power, Cahira felt inside herself! And yet, as easily, it would vanish and leave her weak. In all these years, Madawc hadn't been able to train her to focus or hold it. She could shoot a leaf in the wind with her bow, but she couldn't hold the power. No one had ever understood why.

"For this reason, I too doubt Damir's decision to shield me," she said. "But it is done. Before he faded into slumber, he bade me take his sword."

"And do what with it?" asked Alouard. "You can barely lift it! I don't rightly see you facing off with the Arch Mage, not with that thing, no matter how powerful it is."

"What did he tell you to do with it?" asked Fareth.

Cahira met the bartender's eyes. "He told me to take it and give it to one who can wield it."

"Who?" asked Shaen in surprise. "Only a Mage with power equal to Damir's can wield the Dragonfly Sword—and no such person exists. If a lesser man should touch it, it would sear his hand. If he tried to wield it, it would destroy him."

"He must have intended someone," said Fareth.

"He lost consciousness before he could finish," said Cahira, and Shaen sighed in defeat. "But Eliana told me what to do." She paused, knowing the reaction to her news wouldn't be positive.

"What?" asked Fareth, clearly suspicious.

"She told me to give it to a man called 'Aren.'" She paused again. "It is the name of the chieftain of the Norsk."

Fareth groaned. Alouard hurtled his tankard of ale against the wall, and Shaen slumped into a chair, her head in her hands. The other Hungry Cat patrons behaved likewise, some banging tables, some moaning. More than a few cursed their headstrong queen.

"I knew it!" Fareth groaned again. "With 'The Fiend' as queen, there had to be trouble down the road. Now she wants us to trust our land's greatest weapon to one of those vile, savage, ice-hewn devils? What would a Norskman know about a sword, anyway? Don't they prefer war-axes— and probably their own brawny fists—to bash in their enemies' heads?"

"It was Aren who wielded the Dragonfly Sword against my father's killer," said Cahira. "He is not a typical Norskman."

Shaen rose and addressed Cahira, a kind and patient expression on her face in contrast to the others. "Cahira . . . I know Damir and Eliana claimed this Norsk boy wielded the white sword, but even they admit he had no magical energy, no *ki*."

"If the Norskman was able to wield the sword, he has some kind of power."

"I wish it were so," said Shaen. "But I doubt very much that's the case. I've always felt that Damir's energy must have somehow spread to the boy and allowed him to touch the sword—and I know the Elder Mage Madawc suspected this as well. As I understand it, the Norsk boy didn't really wield the sword. He simply caught it when Damir threw it to him, then hurled it at the rogue Mage, killing him. It was pure chance, and Damir's power, I'm afraid, not any mysterious power of this Norskman's own."

"I don't know. . . ." Fareth tapped his thumb against his

lip and looked thoughtful. "Damir and The Fiend had faith in this lad, and Cahira says he's now chieftain of his people. For once, the Norsk tribes aren't warring against each other, or raiding the Guerdians, or sending out war parties on our borders. A Woodlander can travel to the seaport of Amon-Dhen in peace, and even pick up a few good items. Not that I've done so myself—never left Amrodel and never will—but Alouard here has picked up a few good items for my inn, and sold some of my best ale for a good price, too."

"Whether or not this 'Aren' has done a fair job of uniting his people means little, I'm afraid, Fareth," said Shaen. "He's still a Norskman, and they have ever been treacherous. Even if he could wield the Dragonfly Sword, which even Madawc doubted, he's as likely to be seduced by its power as to use it for our defense. And I just don't see what he could do against the Dark Tide, anyway. It is beyond the reach of mortal combat. I think, in any case, it would be unreasonable to place our trust in him, despite what he was able to make Damir and Eliana believe. They were, after all, the only Woodlanders to meet this boy, and considering how tense the situation was, their judgment may well have been flawed."

"I saw him once," said Cahira quietly. The others stopped to stare at her. "He had ventured into the Woodland on some kind of 'Norsk trial of manhood.' Eliana caught him, and they became friends."

"At that time, 'The Fiend' wasn't too popular around here," said Fareth. "A Norsk warrior boy must have been about the only friend she had, until Damir ap Kora conquered her heart and tamed her."

Cahira frowned. "It seemed to me that it was Eliana who conquered Damir, not the other way around."

"You were but a sprite at the time," scoffed the innkeeper. "We remember how it was. But go on. . . ."

"Eliana helped him sneak into the Palace—for fun, I suppose—but I saw him." Cahira paused. She remembered him well, a boy with almost unnatural beauty. He had pale golden hair that fell around an angelic face, and bright eyes the color of amber that glittered when he saw her. He had winked—annoying, true—but she had blushed furiously. Strange words had formed in her head when she saw him, words she had not forgotten in all the years since. "He hardly seemed a savage to me," she said.

"He was a child then, and under Eliana's care," Shaen reminded her. "He will be much changed by now. We've all seen Norskmen—"

"I haven't," interrupted Fareth. "But I've heard tell enough of their brutal ways to keep me safe in Amrodel forevermore!"

"They're bad, even now," agreed Alouard. "Every one I've seen in Amon-Dhen has been huge—and supposedly, I've just seen the small ones, the traders. The warriors are giants and brutes by all accounts. They're drunken and dangerous, living for a fight at every turn. Best our kind stay far away from the Norsk. They're not civilized like we are in the Woodland, you understand."

"I have to agree," said Shaen. "There is nothing the Norsk can do to help us."

Cahira closed her eyes and fought against hopelessness. Even now, she heard his voice—the Arch Mage was calling her as if to an inevitable fate, telling her there was no choice. Yet she also sensed her enemy's frustration. His dark energy had conquered all the Mages but not her—not the one he had to have to restore his life. He had expected someone to bring her immobilized body to him in his distant mountain cavern, to wake him with her presence. Damir's shield had thwarted that attempt.

She looked out the open door of the tavern to the shadowed grounds beyond. In the center of the small clearing, a fountain churned endlessly, a product of the Elder Mage Madawc's inventive skill. A final ray of sunset pierced the heavy clouds. It cut through the trees and glanced off the spiraling water.

Above the fountain, its lavender wings glistening in the

light, a dragonfly flitted back and forth. It circled one way then the other, then hovered, then flew away with the oncoming night. It flew north. *"This way . . ."* Cahira heard—a whisper softer than her own thoughts, and it was not the dark voice of the Arch Mage but a tiny glimmer of hope instead.

She turned back to the crowd. "I will go to the land of the Norsk. I will take the sword to Aren."

Silence met her words, but slowly, one by one, the tavern patrons nodded. A man came through the door behind her. He was tall and handsome, his dark hair loose around his face, and his eyes were wet with tears. It was her sister's young husband. "I will come with you, Cahira."

"Elphin . . . What has happened?"

"My son. We weren't sure if he had the Mage's gift . . ." His voice grew ragged and he stopped to collect himself. "It didn't seem possible with us both Mundane. All this time I've hoped he was—I thought a Mage would have the most wonderful life. But now . . ."

"No." Tears swarmed Cahira's vision as she thought of her bright, rambunctious nephew.

Elphin nodded. "He fell into the slumber an hour ago. I watched the darkness as it filled our house, and it took him. He lies there unmoving. Alive, but not alive." His words trailed off, and Cahira took his hand.

"We will go together, then."

Fareth watched them with a strange expression on his round face. "This isn't right. We can't let this evil Mage conquer us this way. Not our king and queen, not our children. What does he want with us?"

"What the Arch Mage always wanted," said Cahira. "Power over all. Ages ago, he was a high priest in the desert realm of Kora, but he tried to usurp their prince, and was driven away. After his exile, he built a great palace in the mountain east of the Great Sea, and made the little Guerdian people who lived to the north his slaves."

Alouard shook his head sadly. "It seems especially cruel to

make the Guerdians slaves," he said. "They're short, but they're proud. Must have been hard on them."

"Many died," said Cahira, and she sighed. "You're right. They are proud, and at one point, they tried to rebel against the Arch Mage. They failed."

"The Guerdians have long been our friends and allies," said Fareth. "They might not have magic, but they make the best armor in the land, and they're to be trusted . . ." He paused. "Unlike the Norsk."

Cahira ignored his intimation. "The Arch Mage exploited their skill at building, and forced them to craft his palace. Evil Mages were drawn to his power, and they formed a dark and dangerous alliance, which was only destroyed by the last blood of our own Elite Mages. He wants to regain that—but we will stop him."

"How?" asked Shaen.

"I will fight him—with my bow, with all that I am. And I will give this great sword to a warrior with the strength to wield it. Together, we will face the Arch Mage. And we will destroy him."

Complete silence met her vow. Shaen bowed her head as if grieving. Fareth glanced at Elphin, who stared at Cahira. She understood their lack of faith in her abilities. It was a doubt she shared. Ten years before, her father had been murdered, and when she might have saved him, she'd run. "I failed once," she said softly. "I will never fail again."

A slow smile grew on Elphin's face. "I am with you."

Fareth gulped audibly, but he, too, stepped forward. "And me."

They all gaped at him, astonished.

"But Fareth," said Cahira. "You've never left the Woodland. And you just said you never would!"

He met her gaze, and she felt humbled by the great courage of the Mundanes—they had no magical energy to wield, no force to defend themselves. And yet, Fareth would go with her to the land of the Norsk, people almost as feared as the Dark Tide that now engulfed them.

"Alouard here will keep the bar until my return," said Fareth. His voice was a little shaky. "I know he'll do right by it, whatever happens."

The young man straightened, and for the first time, he seemed to carry his bulk with pride. "I will, sir. You have my word."

Tears filled Cahira's eyes. "Thank you. I don't think I could do this alone."

Elphin clasped her shoulder. "You won't have to. We'll help you in any way we can."

"If nothing else, I can cook us some good meals on the way north," added Fareth.

"That will be welcome," agreed Cahira. Her heart felt lighter, and hope found its way to her soul. "The journey to the Norsk is long—the chieftain has moved his tribes even farther north since the last battle, and though it is spring here in the Woodland, it will still be frozen and cold in their land."

"Damir and Eliana had traveling clothes—they'd want us to use them," said Elphin. "That way, we won't have to go to Amon-Dhen first for supplies. We can just ride north." He paused. "I'll get the ponies ready for the three of us."

"Make that four." Shaen moved to stand beside Cahira.

"Shaen?"

"I'm coming with you." The woman smiled, and Cahira gaped at her. "You'll need me, for support and friendship. I can't let you face this alone."

"It will be a difficult journey," said Cahira. Shaen seemed more likely to slow the party—she wasn't a warrior, and her abilities in the wilderness were certainly dubious. "You are kind to offer, but I don't think you should accompany us."

Shaen clasped Cahira's hand tight. "I *must* come with you, Cahira." She paused, and her dark eyes shimmered with unshed tears. "I know it's what your father would have wanted. Please, let me do this for you, for his sake. I couldn't live with myself if anything happened to you!"

"I can defend myself," said Cahira. "But you'd be placing yourself in danger if you come with us."

"Fareth has never been out of Amrodel," Shaen pointed out. "And Elphin isn't a warrior."

"I can fight," said Elphin.

"And I can cook," added Fareth, offended. "The young Mage is right. You're too delicate to go on such a journey, Shaen. Stay here where you're safe, and we'll take care of this trouble."

Shaen glanced between Elphin and Fareth. "But I vowed to the late king that I would always look after Cahira," she insisted. "My safety can't be a concern, not with so much at stake." She paused. "And there's another matter to consider."

"What's that?" asked Cahira.

"Do any of you know the layout of the Arch Mage's domain?"

Cahira glanced at Elphin, who fidgeted, and Fareth shrugged. "We'll figure that out when we get there," said the innkeeper.

"What do you know about his lair?" asked Elphin.

"Not as much as Madawc, of course," admitted Shaen. "But during the time I studied with the Elder Mage, he instructed me to study the archives relating to the Arch Mage's palace." She stopped, and a sad smile formed on her face. "I was always trying to please him. But fortunately, I have a good memory for images, and I committed several maps to memory." She paused again. "I believe I could guide you effectively once we reach his domain. Otherwise, it might you take many days to find the correct passageways that lead to his tomb."

"Couldn't we just bring a map?" asked Elphin, echoing Cahira's thoughts.

"I'm afraid that's not possible," said Shaen. "The map I studied was lost in a fire—the same fire that Eliana started when she tried a mischievous spell on Damir, years ago."

"I remember that," said Fareth. "The Fiend had Damir

cornered in one of the Elder Mage's back rooms, and as I recall, it was indeed part of his library."

"Was this when she tried to turn Damir green, and set his hair on fire instead?" asked Cahira. Clearly, love sometimes took a long and winding road to fruition.

"I believe it was," said Fareth.

"With my help, the Elder Mage was able to salvage most of his scrolls," added Shaen. "But those particular volumes were lost, unfortunately."

"So you remember the layout of the Arch Mage's Palace?" asked Fareth, and he glanced at Cahira. "Might be useful, after all."

"I do remember," said Shaen. "There are many passages throughout the ancient domain. You could be lost there for days without accurate guidance. There were majestic suites and grand halls high in the mountain palace, and countless servants' quarters, as well as stabling for horses and even a shipyard. Besides that, there were vast catacombs below the palace, cut deep into rock. His tomb lies within those, but it will be very difficult to locate on your own."

"What did he need such a big palace for, anyway?" muttered Elphin.

"I'm sure he expected his reign to continue," replied Shaen. "Though he didn't reside there long, he had already accumulated the allegiance of many other Mages, who took up residence there. At the time of the great battle, his palace had only just begun to take shape. Had it been completed, the Arch Mage would have created a city grander than anything our world has known—greater than the Guerdian city, even greater than the magnificent cities in the desert land of Kora."

"It would have been a city of darkness, no matter how vast and grand," said Cahira. "He had many slaves." She eyed Shaen. "But I don't know . . ."

Shaen smiled at Cahira sadly. "I know I'm not a Mage, Cahira, and I am weak compared to you." She paused and laughed. "Compared to most people, I'm afraid. But I took my studies with Madawc very seriously—I desperately wanted to earn the confidence others had placed in me. I'm sure I can direct you through the Arch Mage's palace. Please, let me do this for you. Don't deny me the opportunity to be of some use, after all that has happened between us."

Cahira endured a tug of remorse. She had often discounted Shaen's abilities, though she had easily accepted Fareth and Elphin's offers. And the idea of wasting days while hunting for the Arch Mage's secret tomb was, indeed, daunting.

"I'm thinking she might be right," said Fareth, and Elphin nodded. "We don't want to get to the Arch Mage's lair, and find ourselves lost."

"And Shaen will be good company for us all," added Elphin. "She's always been a good friend to everyone."

Shaen beamed at Elphin's praise. "My friends are more important to me than anything. And Cahira . . . I've always thought of you as a sister. Please, let me do this for you."

Cahira hesitated. Shaen had always been kind to Cahira, and had tried to be her friend. Even so, as a child, Cahira had disliked her intensely, and made no secret of her contempt. As an adult, she had discounted Shaen as uninteresting and weak. Yet here, when all the other Mages were immobilized, the courage of the simplest Mundane Woodlander had risen to the fore. How could she refuse such an offer now?

"I know I'm not as strong as you, Cahira," said Shaen, as if she'd guessed Cahira's thoughts. "But I am a good judge of people, and I can help you in other ways besides deciphering the Arch Mage's domain. I'm sure I can help you when it comes to dealing with the Norsk."

Shaen's capacity for dealing with the Norsk seemed limited at best, but Cahira relented. "Thank you, Shaen. You've made a courageous offer, and I accept."

As they spoke, the little dark bat swirled around the room again. Fareth huffed. "Where did that creature come from? Never had bats in my tavern before! See that you clear them all out, Alouard. Can't have them terrorizing my customers while I'm gone!"

"I'll get rid of 'em, sir," said Alouard. He swung at the bat, but it easily evaded him. "Agile little creature. And smart, too. Look—he's perched just out of my reach. But don't worry, sir. I can handle this!"

Shaen eyed the creature nervously. "Can't you shoot it with your bow, Cahira?"

Cahira looked up at the small bat. Troublesome, indeed. She seized her bow and set an arrow to the string, then took aim. *I can shoot a leaf in the wind, a nut from a tree* . . . The bat didn't move. It seemed to be looking back at her as if it knew what she intended. She heard a dark voice inside her head. *"Use your power, destroy it. It is worthless. It is in your way. Destroy everything that is in your way* . . ."

Cahira drew the arrow taut. Darkness swarmed around her. Anger filled her. *This, I can do. I can kill one troublesome pest.* Her breath held, her *ki* rose and she focused on the bat . . .

Then Cahira lowered her bow. "I choose . . ." She defied the darkness and the voice of the Arch Mage in her head. "The bat has done no harm. Leave it."

Shaen eyed her with misgivings, then patted her arm. "Of course. You've been under such a strain. Maybe we should take the night to rest before our journey."

Cahira glanced back at the beam, but the flying pest had disappeared. "No. We will leave as soon as our gear is packed. I want this over."

2

THE CHIEFTAIN OF THE NORTH

"My lord, we are under attack!" A young guard stumbled toward the chieftain's seat, out of breath, his voice distinctly higher than usual.

Aren opened one eye, but his head remained comfortable on the back of the tall chair. "Attack? By who?"

"Evil!"

This was unexpected. Aren opened both eyes, sighed, then sat up. " 'Evil?' " He eyed the guard more closely. "Thorleif, I know the winter has been long and is slow to pass now that spring is here, but if you've taken your share of ale before the dawn is half past—"

"My lord! I do not jest, nor have I taken ale. We are under attack!"

Aren studied the young man. Like all Norsk warriors, Thorleif generally welcomed even a skirmish, and revealed no fear when true battle threatened. But he looked terrified.

"Who assails us?"

"The worst of the worst, Lord Chieftain. The Mages of Amrodel!"

Aren stared. Then he rolled his eyes and leaned back in his

seat. "That hardly seems likely. For one thing, we count the king and queen of Amrodel as our friends and allies. For another, the journey from the Woodland is one a Mage is unlikely to take, even after the passing of winter."

"It is true, my lord! Our scouts saw them advancing from the west wood."

"How many?"

"Five, at least."

"Five?" Aren paused to groan. "And you consider this an onslaught?"

Thorleif's eyes narrowed to slits. "For a Mage, it takes only one."

"What makes you think they're Mages at all?"

"Because they're led by a woman!"

"Ah. The worst of the worst." Strange, that of all things Norsk warriors feared the females of the Woodland most. "Where were they seen?"

"A furlong south of the gates."

Aren pondered the matter. "Then, by my count, I have at least a half hour's peace before they arrive at my door." He closed his eyes and yawned. "Wake me when they're here."

Ten minutes peace at most. Horns sounded outside Aren's Great Hall, and men shouted as if tribal warfare had begun anew. Aren remained in his seat, listening as weapons clashed against shields in an ancient rhythmic defensive signal. No . . . in times past, no attack from a rival clan could have produced this panic. Only one slight, black-haired woman had this effect on the Norsk's mighty warriors.

He didn't welcome this meeting. He sensed why they had come—the old darkness that had once consumed his brother had returned. Stars knew how it affected the Mages this time, but his people had thus far escaped its menace. Aren had sensed its shadow on the outskirts of his land, and he had moved his people northward until the midsummer sun melted the snow from the ground. The darkness didn't seek his people, it barely acknowledged the Norsk existed at all, since his brother had failed to become its vessel. It wanted the Mages. But the Mages would bring its fury back to the Norsk.

Not if Aren had anything to say about it. He took a swig of flat ale from a tankard left half full the night before. If the king and queen of Amrodel had forgotten their past agreement, he would soon remind them. Battles between Mages should stay between Mages.

The commotion outside his Great Hall intensified, and the wide wooden doors burst open. Aren's warriors fell back as if before an invincible army. Their axes were poised in defense, but none seem to have engaged the enemy. Aren sighed, then sat upright, more or less, in his seat. He refused to stand as the group from Amrodel entered.

"My lord! Take cover! She's armed!" Thorleif stumbled back toward Aren's seat, gripping his axe in shaking hands.

"Is she?" Aren surveyed his assailants. Two men, and two women. Four. Not five. The two men positioned themselves on either side of the younger female. One man was distinctly fat, and obviously terrified. Aren squinted to see what metal object the man held—it appeared to be a skillet. The taller man had the lithe build common to the Woodland folk, and though he carried a sword, he hardly appeared formidable.

Both women were slight of build and dark-haired, but there was no question which one Aren's warriors feared. She stood at the center of her little group, taller than the other woman, her back straight, her hair loose but kept in place by small braids amidst the dark mass. Her body was clad in dark leggings and a snug bodice, and she wore a old shearling coat that seemed overlarge for her body—it looked like the coat Damir ap Kora had worn ten years ago when he rode into the Norskland. Even across the dimly lit hall, Aren could see her blue eyes glimmering with challenge. He was not a Mage himself, but experience had taught him to read their energy. Her power seemed subdued and uncertain, unlike what he had known in the king and queen of Amrodel. But it was obvious that this woman was the Mage his men feared.

She shoved her way forward through the astonished Norskmen and presented herself before Aren. But she didn't speak. She just stared at him, and her mouth drifted slowly open. Aren waited. The woman glanced back at Thorleif, who stood frozen as if waiting for the final blow. "This is *him?* Your leader?" Thorleif nodded, then froze again. Her gaze turned slowly back to Aren. "It can't be!"

Aren allowed himself to return her attention, though he almost dreaded what he would see. She was worse than his darkest imaginings. The Mage of Amrodel was the most beautiful woman he'd ever seen, bar none. Her face was small with delicate, fine features, her lips curled expressively, and her eyes glittered like a jewel of the sky. He had known she would come. He had known it all his life. He had seen that face in his dreams.

Aren rose to his feet, placed his hand on his chest, and bowed. "I am Aren, son of Arkyn, chieftain of the Norsk. I bid you welcome."

She recoiled, and her face revealed abject horror. "You're . . . hideous!"

Aren scratched his unkempt beard, then angled his brow before reseating himself. He leaned back in his chair and crossed one leg over the other. "So much for the fabled graciousness of the Wood. Did you travel all this way to comment on my appearance, or does this invasion serve some other purpose?"

She studied him through narrowed eyes as if she couldn't believe what she saw. Her lips curled to one side. Then she puffed out a decisive breath. "Speak the name of Eliana Daere's mare!"

Aren retrieved his tankard of ale and took a long drink. "A strange question. Why do you make such an odd request?"

She took a step toward him. In her hand, she clutched a finely crafted wooden bow, and her knuckles appeared white from her grip. "You will answer." She paused. "To prove you are, in fact, the Norskman called Aren, who once befriended our queen, Eliana."

Aren rolled his eyes. "The mare's name was Selsig. That means 'Sausage' in the language of your people, and was a name, as I recall, fairly appropriate to her appearance. Is that sufficient to prove my identity?"

The woman didn't answer—perhaps because she didn't want to believe it.

"And you, Lady Mage, I guess to be Cahira Daere, cousin of the queen, daughter of the late king of Amrodel, whose magical energy extends to her bow and little else, and whose strident nature has made her the dread of every suitable Woodland male since she first came of age six years ago."

"How do you know that?"

Aren shrugged. "Word gets around."

"You've been listening to the gossips of Amon-Dhen." Cahira appeared deflated and depressed, and she sighed heavily. "It *is* you." She paused, then shook her head. "You are much changed from the boy I saw in my father's palace."

"I was nine years old," said Aren. "You are also changed."

"I was seven." She still sounded depressed. "Perhaps the memory plays tricks."

"Boys grow and become men."

She glared. "But not"—Cahira waved her hand absently at him— "*this.*"

"I'm sorry to disappoint you." He wasn't. Disappointing the image Woodlanders held of him was the one thing he'd intended. "But tell me, who are these people in your company? Not Mages."

"How would you know that?" asked the thinner man.

"Just a hunch."

Cahira turned to her companions. "This is Elphin, my sister's husband, and Fareth, innkeeper of the Hungry Cat Tavern in Amrodel." She paused, then indicated the second woman. "And this is Shaen. She has studied . . . matters pertaining to our quest. They have come with me to persuade you to join our mission."

"And they're doing an exemplary job," added Aren.

"What is your mission, that you decry my ragged appearance before declaring your intentions?"

Cahira took another look at him, then sighed again and shook her head. "I guess it doesn't matter what you look like. You'll have to do."

"Do what?"

Cahira started to answer, but something squirmed inside her pack, then squeaked as if entangled in her belongings. Shaen recoiled and pointed at the bag. "Something's in there!"

Cahira spun around, then ripped the pack off her back. A small, round head with pointy ears emerged from beneath the flap, and as all watched in horror, a fat brown winged creature pulled itself out of the bag. It perched awkwardly on the rim of the pack, but when Cahira screamed and flung the bag aside, the bat tumbled to the floor. It righted itself and looked distinctly disgruntled, facing Cahira.

"What in the name of the gods is that?" asked Thorleif, and he grimaced in disgust.

An older warrior, Bodvar, once a guard of Aren's brother Bruin the Ruthless, stood near the door of the Great Hall, and his normally stoic face contorted in horror. "It's an omen, my lord. These Woodlanders bring great evil here!"

"It's said that witches take animal companions," said Aren, "creatures that carry the spirits of past Mages. Dragonflies followed Eliana, and gave her messages. I do not think this bat is evil. But I had pictured such companions as somehow more . . . dignified." Aren felt sure the bat frowned.

Fareth the innkeeper eyed the creature. "It looks like the same fat brown bat that pestered us back at the Hungry Cat!"

Elphin glanced between the bat and Cahira. "Could it be some kind of emissary sent by the Arch Mage?"

Cahira studied the creature. "Its presence is no coincidence, but I don't believe it's evil." To Aren's surprise, the creature seemed to understand her and to take her words as an invitation. It moved toward her in a friendly fashion, then looked expectantly up at her face.

"If you have intended to prove to us the similarities between our races," said Aren, "you have failed."

Cahira frowned, but her attention remained on the bat. "It has chosen me." Her back straightened as if she had made a decision. "I accept." She stretched out her hand, then bent low, and the bat jumped onto her wrist. From there, it scrambled onto her shoulder and perched like the pet birds kept by the Koraji sailors.

"This is odd beyond measure," said Aren.

"Its presence is a sign," replied Cahira.

"Of what?"

"That my quest here is right, of course!"

"Amazing I should misread that," said Aren. "It couldn't be that this fat creature found the crumbs in your pack appetizing?"

"Of course not!" She glanced at the bat. "I wonder how I missed it in all our days of travel? It is small, but it must have been deliberately hiding to escape my notice."

The Woodlanders accepted the bat's presence as if it weren't an oddity, but the Norsk looked between each other as if they'd only heard a tenth of their western neighbors' peculiarity.

"It is time." Cahira gave the bat and her pack to the fat man beside her. Fareth eyed the creature doubtfully, but it took up residence on his shoulder and looked expectant. "Give me the sword, Elphin."

Elphin pulled out a sheathed weapon that seemed heavy, and Cahira took it. She lifted it with effort and presented it to Aren. He looked at the hilt. Buried in the pommel, he saw the amber stone engraved with a dragonfly. It was a jewel he had made himself and presented to Eliana long ago—then later, used in the completion of Damir ap Kora's greatest creation. "You offer me Amrodel's most powerful weapon, the Dragonfly Sword of the king. Why?"

"You wielded it once before. You can wield it again."

"I have an axe, the favored weapon of my people. I don't need a Mage's sword."

"An axe isn't good enough. You'll need the power in this sword if you're to defeat the Arch Mage."

Aren stared. Then he laughed. This woman looked so sure of herself. And yet, beneath the surface of her conviction, he sensed her doubt. Aren set aside his ale and then rubbed his forehead. "It may be I should take less ale—"

"We don't have much time," she interrupted.

Aren eyed her, then turned his attention to her followers. The two men looked a little uneasy, as if, like him, they doubted her sanity. The woman standing behind Cahira looked concerned—and watchful, as well as disgusted by the squalor of her surroundings. She placed her hand on Cahira's arm.

"This is not the man Eliana and Damir spoke of—it is as I feared."

"Appearances aren't everything," said Cahira, and she pinned her bright gaze on Aren. "He can do this."

"Can I? I am honored by your confidence, if not the tasks you assign. So, you would have me take up this white sword and issue challenge against a long-dormant but still evil wizard deep within his grave? How could I refuse?"

"He is no longer dormant," said Cahira. "His energy has risen and infected all Amrodel."

"Your king and queen drove that energy back once. They can do it again."

"They can do nothing!" The young Mage's voice quavered, and the chill around Aren's heart increased its grip. "The darkness has claimed them and the Mages of Amrodel, even the youngest among us. Unless we face and destroy the Arch Mage in his domain beneath the mountains, they will all die."

Aren bowed his head and remembered Eliana, the lonely but kind woman who had befriended him when he'd ventured into the Woodland. He remembered Damir, facing an army of Norsk warriors alone and fighting against the demon that had overcome Aren's brother. And he remembered the dark energy they had all felt that day, harsh and relentless even as it was dealt a temporary defeat. "What would you have me do, Lady Mage? March my warriors beneath the eastern mountains? And what? Stab at something that appears as less than a cloud?"

"He won't be a cloud if we go there," said Cahira.

"'We.'" Aren paused. "I take it you're going with me."

"It's necessary." She hesitated and looked uncomfortable, as if she guessed he wouldn't accept the logic of her argument. "Like Eliana, I am related to the ancient Woodland queen, to whom the Arch Mage was once bonded. If the energy of her relative, a female Mage, should enter the cavern where he bound himself in a deathless spell, then he will rise again."

Aren leaned forward and braced his arms on his knees. "Then here's a suggestion: Don't enter the cavern!"

A brief sidelong glance from the fat innkeeper, Fareth, indicated that Aren wasn't alone in finding this a sensible alternative, but Cahira shook her head. "If we do nothing, those he has imprisoned will die. You are our only hope."

"Why me?"

"Because Eliana told me to bring this sword to you. Damir said the sword can defeat the Arch Mage—in the right hands."

"And you think mine are the 'right hands'?"

"You did it before."

"I caught it in midair and threw it," said Aren. "It was Damir who directed its force, not I."

The other woman, Shaen, shook her head sadly. "I feared this was so. This man has no power other than what Damir gave him on that fateful day."

The words grated, but Aren didn't argue, though he knew she was wrong. His power was far greater than they knew— but not great enough to accomplish what Cahira asked.

Cahira issued an impatient huff, then shoved the heavy sword onto his lap. "Take it!"

Shaen caught her breath. "This Norskman is a Mundane, Cahira! Without Damir's energy protecting him, the Dragonfly Sword will sear his hand if he touches it, and kill him if he tries to wield it."

Thorleif and the other Norsk spluttered amongst themselves, insulted enough to forget their wariness. "There's no Woodland craft that's stronger than the chieftain of the Norsk," bragged Thorleif, braving a step in Cahira's direction. "Whatever spell a Woodland witch might think to cast, she's come up against the wrong man!"

"Never trust a spell-caster," added Bodvar. "We all remember what they did to our last chieftain, Bruin the Ruthless. No such harm will come to his brother while I have breath in my body!"

"I am not a spell-caster," said Cahira impatiently.

"You're a Mage," replied Thorleif. "We can all see that!"

"Indeed," said Aren. "And as such, how is it you escaped the wizard's darkness, if it is as powerful as you say?"

"Damir shielded me, so I could bring his sword to you. He knew the only hope we have is to face the risen enemy and defeat him." She paused, impatient. "Take the sword!"

"If he does, he will die," warned Shaen.

"Maybe you'd best not, my lord," said Thorleif. "No need to get entangled with some magical weapon that might fry your hand."

Aren looked among them. Cahira was holding her breath—for all her purported confidence, she had as much doubt as the woman beside her. The Norsk looked tense, but their faith in him was strong. Even the bat seemed eager to witness Aren's decision. It leaned forward from its position on Fareth's shoulder, and the innkeeper adjusted his head away from the creature.

"Don't do it, my lord," said Thorleif. "It might put a spell on you, or some such Mage-like devilry."

"He's touched it before," argued Cahira. "It responds to what he carries within, not what we would put upon him."

Shaen clutched Cahira's arm. "Therein lies the danger.

What he carries within will respond to the power of that sword. As we have seen too often, the Norsk are ruthless and take what they want. Given this weapon's power, we have no idea what he will do—if he even survives its touch. A man of his type could too easily be perverted. Our cause would be lost."

Fareth glanced between the women. "What if she's right? What if this Norskman proves worse than the Arch Mage himself?"

This was too much for the Norsk. Thorleif raised his axe angrily. Bodvar seized a halberd from a door warden, who followed him through the angry crowd.

Aren had had enough. "Let us see, shall we?" He lifted the sheathed sword and placed his hand on the hilt. Slowly, he drew the blade from the scabbard, and it sang as he held it up. Those watching gasped, but Aren's focused on the weapon he had held only for one second, ten years ago. It felt cool in his hand, but a warmth grew within the blade and spread to the hilt. A light seemed to kindle in the jeweled pommel, in the stone he'd wrought as a gift for the Woodland witch who had become his friend. For a fleeting moment, the image of a dragonfly flickered before his vision, then disappeared. The pale silver blade began to shine until it glowed white, and as he looked up, he saw that light reflected in Cahira's bright eyes. Her face lit in a smile, and she closed her eyes as if in prayer.

When she looked at him again, he saw tears. She opened her mouth to speak, but another voice, small and gruff, cut in before her. "Who would have thought it? I thought that sword would fry the Norsk creature to a crisp!"

Fareth screamed and jumped, eyes round in his broad face. From such a stout man, the scream was unreasonably high-pitched. Everyone in the Great Hall turned slowly and stared, not at Fareth, but at the fat brown creature on his shoulder. Here was something even the Woodlanders didn't expect: The stowaway bat had a voice.

Cahira stared, then approached it, leaning close to look into its scrunched face. "Did you . . . *talk?*"

"Well, it wasn't a chirp!" The bat shook its head and body, then issued several, scratchy coughs—or barks, as if clearing its throat for further speech. "It's not something I'm accustomed to—wasn't sure I could do it, quite frankly, but it appears I do have some gift for the art."

"'Some gift,' indeed," said Aren. "May I suggest that no art is appreciated when overused?"

The bat cranked its small head in Aren's direction. "No, Norsk creature, you may not issue such a suggestion! Rude, it is!"

"This is not good," said Bodvar. "It is unnatural. The witch has placed a spell on this animal, and it speaks in the tongue of demons!"

"I speak the same tongue as you, brute!" said the bat. "Big, but still no room for brains! If you consider how large my brain is in comparison to my body in contrast to your own, it is almost tragic."

As the bat chattered, Fareth stood utterly immobile, his face pale, his breath noticeably held. The bat eyed him. "What's the matter with you, innkeeper? Breathe!"

Fareth sucked in air once, then held it. The bat huffed. "Never underestimate the magic of the Woodland!"

Cahira beamed. "You have come to assist me!" She paused. "Haven't you?"

"I am a guide of sorts, yes," said the bat. It sounded proud.

"Are you, indeed, as legends tell, harboring the spirit of a Great Mage?"

The bat hesitated. "You might say that, yes. An adequate explanation."

"What do we call you?" she asked, reverential.

The bat smacked what presumably were its lips. "Not sure, exactly. A fitting name must be chosen at some point. What about 'Graitus'—meaning 'great guide,' in the ancient language of your elders?"

Cahira's lips twisted. "I'm not sure I like that. What about 'Blossom?'"

The bat braced. "Certainly not! For one thing, besides being silly, it sounds female. I, quite obviously, am a male of my species."

Cahira looked doubtful and somewhat surprised, but then she nodded as if the bat's masculinity should have been apparent. "Well, we'll decide on a name later."

"Indeed. Now that you've nabbed this Norsk creature, you don't have much time to waste."

Aren frowned. *Norsk creature . . .* Clearly, the bat shared the Woodlanders' bias against their northern neighbors.

Cahira glanced over at him. "When I first saw you, Aren, I was sure Damir and Eliana were wrong. But it's true." She sighed as if the weight of the world had been lifted from her slender shoulders. "You are the one who will face the Arch Mage, the one said to have 'pure light.'"

"'Said' by whom, my lady?" asked Aren. "We Norsk do not put much value on vague prophecies."

"The prophecy was delivered to Eliana by the Dragonfly messengers . . ."

Aren arched a brow. "Ah, well, if insects instructed you thus, who am I to argue?"

Cahira ignored him and glanced at the bat. "Were they also guides, like you?"

The bat shifted weight from one short leg to the other. "Not exactly. Somewhat."

"Because, as I recall, Eliana's dragonflies didn't talk. They communicated with her thoughts, and their messages were very brief and somewhat mystical—they were beings of divination rather than practical advice, it seemed to me. You seem more direct, less prophetic." She paused. "And wordier."

"I am not a prophet, young Mage," said the bat importantly. "I am a guide. There's a difference."

"Ah," said Cahira. "I see," she added, though Aren suspected she didn't understand any better than he did.

Aren looked between the Mage and her bat. "Again, odd beyond measure." He glanced at his nearly empty tankard of ale. "Perhaps a dream from which I soon will awaken?"

Thorleif shook his head. "If it's a dream, it's one we're all sharing. Shouldn't we just make war on this crazy Mage and her talking bat, lord? Be done with them once and for all?"

The bat stiffened. "Try it and see your flesh seared from your bones, boy!"

Thorleif recoiled, but Aren considered the creature's powers limited at best. He sensed energy in or around the bat, but it seemed more inherent to the creature's nature than a prospective weapon.

Cahira ignored Thorleif and studied Aren. "I don't see any evidence of 'pure light' in you, but nonetheless, it must be true. You've proven that you can wield the sword, and that's all that matters." She clapped her hands in delight. "We shall start tonight. I suppose you'll need provisions, but don't take too much. We must hurry if we're to reach the eastern mountains in time to save my people."

"You assume too much," said Aren. He slid the sword back into the scabbard, and the light vanished. For a moment, in its absence, he felt blind.

Cahira's eyes narrowed. "What do you mean? You held the sword. Not only did it not burn you, but it glowed!"

"I have to admit," said Fareth the innkeeper, "I figured it would fry him like a fish in a pan, but it looks as if The Fiend was right after all. He can use the sword, and put right all that has gone wrong."

Elphin nodded. "There is hope after all. Our journey was not in vain."

"It was, if you think I'm going to accompany you into the mountains and resurrect the most powerful and evil wizard the world has ever known," said Aren. He set the sword aside and sat back in his seat. "I will not do it."

"I knew he'd be trouble," said the bat, who settled comfortably atop Fareth's shoulder to witness the argument.

Cahira's brows knitted in anger. "If you refuse, Eliana and all the Mages will die. She befriended you. Damir saved your people from the dark energy that consumed your brother. How could you refuse now, and let them die?"

Aren fought pity and looked her straight in the eye. "You say the Mages are not dead, but engulfed in this darkness. It is reasonable to believe that the wizard who inspires this tide cannot hold on forever. He expects you to come to him—and with astonishing simplicity, you seem bent on doing just that. Tell me, Lady Mage, what do you expect to happen if this demon arises and your unlikely plan to defeat him fails? Will he leave your friends safe? Will he leave these lands free as he reclaims his own existence?"

"Of course not! Given free rein, he would seek to enslave everyone—probably even your people, though I can't imagine what value this frozen land would be to him. But we won't let him get that far."

"Again, 'we.' But I have not agreed to this, and I see no reason I should. There must be another way to free the Woodland Mages from his grip and yet leave him in his eternal slumber. Marching headlong into the pits of the mountain to confront him, armed only with a pretty sword, does not seem to me a good plan."

"It is the only plan!" Cahira sputtered angrily, then clenched her fist tight. "We're wasting time! You will do as I say, because there's no other way, and you're the only one who can."

"If you can give me a better reason . . ."

"*I'll give you a reason . . .*" Before he could answer, Cahira whipped out her bow, set an arrow to the string, and aimed it at his heart. "Do as I ask, or meet your fate here, Lord Chieftain!"

Aren opened his mouth—to laugh or gasp, he wasn't sure—but her arrow flew and pierced the back of his seat not a hair's breadth from his neck. The Norsk cried out and drew their axes, but Cahira's hands moved faster than sight, and before he saw what she'd done, she'd rocked a fresh arrow. "Nobody move! This is between me and your leader!" The Norsk hesitated, and her little face glowed.

"You really are crazy," murmured Aren. She heard him.

"I am no spell-caster, but I am not without magic or

power." Without preamble, Cahira aimed her arrow at some unseen target and let fly. It burst into flame and darted around the hall, bouncing off walls, and as it passed, torches leapt to life. The arrow lifted and spun, glittering sparks in its wake, then plunged into the low burning fire at the center of the Great Hall. That fire flared blue then green. "Before you react, I could pierce the hearts of every one of you! But I cannot fight the Arch Mage alone. I need you and that sword. So you're coming with me, Aren, whether you want to or not."

The bat leaned forward from its position on Fareth's shoulder. It looked intent, as if expecting a revelation regarding a long-pondered mystery. But surprisingly, it said nothing.

"You are a formidable archer, Lady Mage. Until now, I believed Woodland witches practiced their arts only in potions and noncombative ways."

"I am unique," she replied.

"I see that." And beautiful. "But you're also crazy. Clearly, you are a woman who acts first, thinks later. You are doing exactly as the dark wizard desires—flinging yourself headlong into his domain!"

Maybe it hadn't been wise to criticize her. She snatched the slender blade of Elphin, then swung it without warning. Only instinct prevented a serious gash—Aren seized his war-axe and thwarted her blow from his seat, but the little spitfire came at him again. She wasn't strong, but she was quick and determined. He stumbled up from his seat, cursed himself for that last draught of ale, then fended off her next attack. She beat wildly against the blade of his axe, then spun to attack lower. Suddenly, Aren found himself in a serious fight for his life—or at least his limbs.

The others backed away, astonished as the delicate Woodland Mage assailed their leader, but Aren met her blow for blow. He was too surprised by her skill to stop her, and too moved by her passion to assert his own power. He felt her wild, raw energy as she battled. He felt her desperation, her anger, her pain, and all her frustration. She fought like a wild animal—but not to kill, or even to wound. She fought against fate, against the darkness that had followed her into his frozen land. And Aren allowed her attack, because he knew her rage had to go somewhere or consume her.

She fought and fought until she'd backed him against the fire, the flames of which now reflected in her wild eyes. Her blade against his axe, she pressed all her strength against him, and Aren knew her fire was the more dangerous. "You will do as I say, or I will turn this hall to cinders, and you and everyone else with it!"

"My lady, I cannot."

Cahira reeled back as if his refusal cut deeper than any blow, and a wild cry erupted from deep inside her. She screamed, and if the Norsk hadn't been afraid of her before, they were now. Energy more powerful than mere fire spun around her, visible and swirling like a whirlwind. Her hair was tossed by the wind, and her cry grew in power until it seemed she became part of the cyclone. The bat held itself rigid and gaped in wonder. The other Woodlanders stared at Cahira in amazement, as if they, too, were astonished by what they saw, as if this strange manifestation of inner magic was remarkable among even the Mages of Amrodel.

Aren looked into the swirling power that circled the woman, and he saw himself. *All that power, and we can do nothing to save the ones we love. It is never enough.* If he refused, she would go on without him—or kill them all in a fit of rage. If he agreed, she would lead them all to their doom. But in the energy that burned around her, Aren saw that doom was at hand, either way. If he agreed, maybe he could direct her on a wiser course, and thwart the darkness of the evil wizard in a manner that didn't involve direct confrontation.

He would pretend to surrender to her greater power, then go along with her on her quest—until he found a way to dissuade her, or take control of her in some other way. He hesitated a moment. Aren felt a connection to this delicate, fiery woman, and his judgment might be altered by that fact, even more than by her display of power. Yet, if he gave in to what he sensed about her, or his perception that there was passion between them, then in so doing, he might risk what he had fought his whole life to preserve: his people.

Yet if the Arch Mage woke to torment the land again, the Norsk people would fall prey to his villainy. He would make them slaves. Aren's heart hardened against this possibility. *I will not see my people as slaves* . . . The vow struck deep into his core. He did not know the true origin of his brave, reckless people, but whatever their beginnings, they had risen to something greater, and in the last generation, the warring tribes of the Norsk had united. For their sake, it would be wisest to surrender to Cahira now, and to seek his own solution to the renewed power of darkness.

"You have won, Lady Mage. Such power as yours, I cannot defy." Aren spoke softly, but Cahira heard him. She slumped to her knees, then looked up.

"You are my prisoner?" she asked.

He smiled. "I am."

3

TWO HORSES

"He's not quite what I imagined." Elphin seated himself beside Cahira on a long, low bench at the edge of the Great Hall and peered around at the gathering Norsk. He took a bite of bread, and seemed to find it adequate. Both Cahira and Shaen eyed Aren with misgivings.

"He's utterly repulsive," said Cahira. She broke off another section of the loaf and ate, though she was too tired to be truly hungry. Her new companion, still unnamed, maneuvered closer, and she passed him a small piece. The bat ate it greedily.

"I can't imagine how Eliana ever termed that Norskman 'angelic,' even as a youth," said Shaen with a shudder. "He looks like he hasn't washed since he visited her—and that had to be fifteen years ago."

"Looks can be deceiving," said the bat, speaking thickly around the bread.

"You should certainly know," replied Elphin. He reached over and patted the bat's round head, then said, "We need a name for your guide, Cahira. What about 'Dryw,' for 'wise?'"

"'Cadyryeith?'" suggested Fareth. "It means 'well-spoken,' which this creature certainly is."

Cahira shook her head. "Too long, and too complicated. The words of the Old Tongue are hard to pronounce."

"'Dall' also means wise," suggested the bat. "It seems appropriate to my station."

"I don't really like any of those," said Cahira.

"It is to be *my* name," the bat reminded her, but Cahira's attention was diverted to where Aren stood speaking with his advisors. Several older males joined their circle. The young, more vocal warrior, Thorleif, gestured excitedly, but the older warrior, Bodvar, seemed most set against the mission. A tall, beautiful blond woman stood with them, garbed like a warrior, and she seemed to be awaiting a decision.

"I suppose they're trying to change his mind."

Fareth shook his head. "They're all hulking brutes from what I've seen." He paused and patted Cahira's knee. "But you put the terror of Amrodel into them, and set them in their place, to be sure. I don't think they'll dare refuse you now!"

Elphin gazed at Cahira. "I've never seen anything like that, Cahira. What did you do?"

She hesitated. "I'm not sure. It just . . . happened."

Shaen smiled. "The Elder Mage once said it often 'just happens' for you. If only you could control that power!"

"It has never happened like that before," said Cahira. "I was so angry! I don't know where the energy came from, but I felt as if I could destroy the Arch Mage himself."

"Let's not get carried away, girl," said Fareth. "You were a mite scarier than anything I've ever seen, but he's by far and away worse than you could ever be. And I haven't seen anything in our erstwhile 'hero' to say he can stand up to that devil any better."

"You saw him with the sword, Fareth," said Elphin. "He may not show it, but he has some kind of power even Damir ap Kora didn't understand."

"Maybe, but it doesn't look to me like he's keen to use it."

"At least, not for our purposes," agreed Shaen.

Fareth glanced at her doubtfully. "What do you mean? Do you think that brute has something else in mind?"

Shaen hesitated, then drew a breath. "As I said before, although I have been reluctant to press my case in deference to Damir and Eliana, that has been my concern all along. If this Norskman is able to handle the sword—and that appears to be the case—then I worry what he'll do with it once he realizes how much power it gives him."

"The power arises from a symbiosis between the sword and its bearer," said Cahira. "In a sense, Aren is already part of the sword, was part of its making because Damir placed in the pommel a jewel Aren made. The prophecy Eliana spoke of referred to a being of 'pure light,' and I see no reason to fear what Aren will do with it when the time comes."

"Perhaps the inclusion of that jewel explains why he can hold it when others cannot, though he has no magical energy of his own," said Shaen. "But surely you can't believe that filthy brute is 'pure light?'"

"Light begins at the core of one's soul. Appearances are often misleading, as Damir told me before he fell into slumber." Cahira looked around the room. "The prophecy said that the one of pure light would face one who is total darkness, and so, defeat the evil of the Arch Mage. But it is said that the Arch Mage himself was impossibly handsome—so beautiful that to look upon him was to become spellbound. Beauty can be misleading, can conceal darkness within."

"Ancient scribes record that he was an attractive man," agreed Shaen. "His virility and prowess with women were legendary."

Cahira huffed. "Well, if the women were spellbound, I can't imagine their legends were very accurate!" Both Elphin and Fareth laughed, but Shaen sighed.

"Perhaps he never encountered a woman who understood the passions within his darkness."

The bat looked up at Shaen, its small face scrunched and thoughtful. "Humans who are disconnected from their own hearts always want what they can't have, Mage and Mundane alike. They want what they lack. A woman of darkness wouldn't interest him at all."

"I'm sure that's true," said Shaen.

"And he is dangerous, Shaen," added Cahira. "As we draw closer to the Caverns of the Arch Mage, his will and his power will also increase. It may become hard to resist."

"He's aiming it at you, not me," replied Shaen with a smile, "fortunately for me!"

"Darkness is ever stealthy," said the bat. "Its voice whispers softly, until it finds a heart in which to reside. We should all beware—even you, mistress."

Shaen eyed the bat doubtfully, then smiled. "I know the perfect name for you! 'Gair.'"

The bat's eyes narrowed. "That means 'short and small.' Stout, in essence. *No.*"

"What about 'Felix?'" Aren suggested from behind Cahira. She startled, and her cheeks flushed unexpectedly.

"Felix? Why Felix?" she asked. And why did Aren make her nervous? She held the balance of power between them; he was, as he had agreed, prisoner to her will.

The bat looked at Aren in surprise. "It is the name of a great Woodland Mage of old, one who mastered the language of animals and could communicate with them! How do you know that, Norsk creature?"

Aren smiled. He was almost . . . not entirely repulsive when he smiled. "I spent time with Eliana, if you remember. She told me many of the legends of Amrodel, and I always liked that one."

Cahira glanced back at the bat. "What do you think of the name 'Felix?'"

The bat considered the matter. He twisted his leathery wing around and actually scratched the underside of his chin. "Felix . . ." The bat straightened, then hopped back onto Fareth's shoulder, perhaps to get closer to Aren in height. "That is a name which honors both me and the great Mage. A perceptive choice, Norskman."

Aren's amber eyes twinkled, but he didn't comment on the switch from 'Norsk creature' to 'Norskman.' Cahira sighed. If Aren continued with this level of charm, he'd be 'My Lord Chieftain' within two days. Well, his personality had no power over her. "Are you ready yet?" she asked.

"We can leave within the hour." He paused and yawned. "Though you have seriously disrupted my day, Lady Mage, and I cannot be said to await our journey with any pleasure."

"Indeed? Well, I'm not offering you a journey of pleasure."

"I would think you owe me no less, what with the trouble you've already caused." His gaze traveled with deliberate ease from her eyes to her lips, then lingered on her breast. "I'm sure you could provide an interesting diversion. However, as long as you agree not to disrupt me with orders and threats . . ."

Her mouth drifted open. "You can't be serious!"

He scratched the side of his beard and shrugged. "No? It might serve to while the hours of this tiresome and foolhardy journey. Give it some point, from my perspective."

Cahira chewed her lower lip—he sounded so casual. "You are talking about romantic intimacy, are you not?"

His brow angled. "I'm not sure I'd term it 'romantic,' but yes, that was my hope. Sadly, it appears you're too hell-bent on mayhem to appreciate the invitation."

Elphin and Fareth rose at the same time, dislodging the newly named Felix, who scrambled back up Fareth's shoulder. The bat then assumed the same position as Cahira's defenders. Elphin faced Aren, who appeared amused, and though Aren was far stronger and much taller, Elphin looked ready to fight. "This journey we are to undertake is for the survival of my people." Elphin paused, and his green eyes were intent. "For my *son*. We will do what we must to free them from this darkness, but don't think for a second we'll let you harm Cahira."

"I wasn't thinking of harming her," said Aren. "I was thinking of sex." He paused. "It might be amusing . . . at least, for a few days. Make the journey more interesting, since you're not giving me a choice in the matter."

Fareth pulled out a skillet and aimed it at Aren's head, which Aren noticed with a repressed smile. Cahira stared at him in amazement. He was baiting them, deliberately. Maybe he was just amusing himself at the Woodlanders' expense, but Cahira sensed something deeper. His words spoke of casual delights, but she knew he wasn't truly offering intimacy—by his words, he was assuring himself it would never happen, and proving to her that he wasn't a man to be considered from that perspective. Which was all good and fine, because she had no interest in him romantically, either.

Aren held up his hands and drew a mock sigh. "Since you're so dedicated to her preservation, I'll have to restrain myself. But I would think you might consider offering me something rather than the questionable allure of certain death."

Elphin's eyes narrowed to slits. "So . . . you want a reward."

Cahira stood up and moved around the table. Facing Aren she said, "You can keep the Dragonfly Sword if we succeed."

"As I've said before, Lady Mage, I prefer my axe. What else do you have?"

She paused. "What do you want?"

"I assume you came north on horses."

"Yes . . ."

"Are any sired by Damir's stallion from the Koraji herd?"

"My horse, Pip, is one of that horse's sons. . . ." Cahira frowned. "But you can't have him. And didn't Damir send you a nice colt years ago?"

"He did, and that one is busy servicing mares. Not much use as a riding horse, when his mind is thus occupied. And I don't want to risk my people losing him if we don't return from certain death. At least I will have left a good legacy of horses in my stead. Let me see this Pip."

Cahira led Aren outside to where the Woodlanders' four horses stood waiting. She gestured at Pip, who appeared to be sleeping. Aren's eyes widened and he descended the stairs of the Great Hall to assess the beast. Pip was a tall bay—

dark brown with a black mane and tail—and a white stripe down his face that formed a coil on his forehead. He was the most impressive horse sired by Damir's stallion, to Cahira's thinking, and her favorite.

Aren turned to look at her. "What do you need with such a tall mount? This horse is even taller than Damir's stallion."

"I fit him perfectly!" Cahira paused. "And he's friendly."

Aren patted Pip's nose, and Pip nuzzled him pleasantly—traitorously, Cahira thought. "I'll take him."

"You will not!" Cahira marched down the stairs after Aren and placed herself between them. "You must have your own horse."

"I do, but it just seems wrong to me to accept your demands and get nothing in exchange. Besides being warriors, the Norsk are also traders—it's in my blood."

"Plunder is in your blood, you mean." Cahira paused. Maybe it was his pride that made him issue such demands—or maybe he wanted to see if it was in her nature to yield for the greater good of her quest. "Very well—as long as you treat him well, and I approve of the way you handle him." Cahira paused. "But what horse shall I ride?"

Aren motioned to Thorleif. "Bring Zima."

Something in his tone, and in Thorleif's veiled chuckle, told Cahira there was in a catch in Aren's suggestion. "If you fetch me an old nag, you'll be sorry," she warned, but Aren smiled.

"I think you'll find her most impressive."

"A mare. Of course. Mares can be testy."

"Her temperament suits you."

"Well, I don't want a mare . . ." Cahira's words stopped as Thorleif led a tall, dappled gray mare from the opposite stable. Cahira caught her breath. "She's magnificent!"

"I thought you'd like her," said Aren. Then why did Thorleif chuckle, and why did Aren look like he'd just won a small battle? "She's a product of the stallion Damir sent to me, and one of our strongest Norsk ponies."

Thorleif tied the mare next to Pip, then moved Pip's gear

to her back, and the source of their amusement made itself known. Zima's ears flattened to her head in dire warning, and she stomped a front foot in agitation. Pip eased aside and looked in the other direction. Cahira eyed Aren suspiciously. "She doesn't bite, does she?"

"No . . . not really. And we broke her of kicking."

"How?"

"Every time she tried, we tossed a bucket of ice water on her. You might say she was a difficult foal—but spirited. She can be . . . moody."

Cahira gazed heavenward and sighed. "I see." She glanced at the mare, who had managed to seize a portion of the hay Pip was eating. "Still . . . she is pretty." She hesitated. "Does she have any other bad habits?"

"She likes to go first."

"So do I!" Cahira went to the mare. Zima stopped chewing. They looked at each other. Cahira held out her hand, and Zima sniffed it. "I will treat you with respect, and you will always go first," Cahira said.

The mare went back to eating Pip's food, and Thorleif returned with three other horses, each saddled with a thick woolen blanket and ready for travel. "What are those three for?" asked Cahira.

"My companions," said Aren, casually. "You don't expect me to travel without them, do you?"

"What companions? I didn't approve any companions!"

"I didn't ask," replied Aren.

Thorleif leaned toward her. "If you think we're sending him off in your clutches with no one to back him up, you've got another think coming, witch!"

"I take it you're coming with us," guessed Cahira, and Thorleif nodded.

"I am," said the youth. "I was too young to take part in the last battle. I'm not going to miss this one!"

"I missed it, too," remained Cahira, somewhat sadly. Maybe things would have gone differently, better, had she been there. "Though I begged Damir and Eliana to take me with them, they felt I was too young and said I had to stay behind."

Aren looked at her in surprise, then smiled. "No doubt the Norskland was safer for your absence."

Thorleif seemed inoffensive enough—rather highly strung for a Norskman, but certainly alert. But Felix the bat sighed heavily. "We won't get a wink of sleep with that Norsk youth jabbering! I noticed he talks a good deal more than is necessary."

Thorleif glared at the bat. "I was just thinking the same thing about you!"

"Who else are we taking?" asked Cahira, trying to change the subject.

To her dismay, the hulking warrior who had objected most strenuously to her presence seized the reins of the largest horse. "I am Bodvar, son of Bodolf," he told her, his voice full of scorn. "Bruin the Ruthless was a great leader, until wizardry slew him. I will not let his brother meet the same fate."

Cahira frowned. "As I understand it, Bruin wasn't called 'Ruthless' for nothing! His end was cruel and tragic, but had he not been so eager for power and gain, he might have avoided such a dark fate."

Bodvar glared, and Aren sighed. "My brother wasn't without flaws, but Bodvar speaks the truth. There was good in him." He paused and his expression turned sad. He had loved his brother; that was clear. "It was Bruin who first united the warring tribes of our people."

"And who pillaged the borders of Amrodel!" countered Elphin while mounting his horse. "Among our people, his name is still spoken with fear."

Fareth shuddered as he adjusted the packs on his saddle pad. "The Norsk legions are the stuff of nightmares. Never seen so many people carrying weapons!" He glanced at a group of small boys who played just off the steps of the Great Hall. "Even the children are armed!" A little boy waved a wooden club at Fareth, and Aren laughed.

"Can I hit him, just once?" asked one boy. Fareth recoiled, then climbed hastily onto his horse.

Aren furrowed his brow. "What challenge is there in that?" he asked. Fareth frowned but didn't argue. The little boy sighed, so Aren grinned and slung his large battle axe from his heavy belt. "But against your chieftain, honor might indeed be won."

Cahira watched in astonishment as Aren readied his weapon. The boy whooped with glee, then bounded toward him. With an innate grace and ease that seemed impossible, the Norsk chieftain gently deflected the boy's blows, yet allowed himself to be driven back. They traded blows, but then Aren deftly dislodged the club from the boy's grip.

"You're getting better, Frode," he offered, and the boy beamed.

"Don't be gone long, my lord. We'll miss you awfully here. Don't let that witch put a spell on you or anything."

Bodvar turned a dark glare on Cahira. "I will be watching her. There will be no spells."

Cahira rolled her eyes. "I told you. I don't do spells. Especially not possession spells. I have channeled my energy into the use of my bow. I have no interest in altering the natures or minds of others."

"The last witch that came here had erased her own memory with a spell," countered Bodvar.

Cahira winced. "That was a mistake. And it was a potion, not a spell. But I am not an herbalist, either." She looked around. "Who else is coming?"

The tall, beautiful woman who had been in Aren's council came out from the Great Hall carrying a heavy pack. She stopped to face Cahira. Cahira noted the disparity in their respective heights, and tried to straighten herself upward.

The woman said, "I am Rika of the Eastfold, daughter of Rognvald. I am the eyes and ears of our chieftain. I will not let him battle alone." She held Cahira's gaze, and Cahira felt every unspoken challenge a warrior could issue. Despite his appearance, Aren must inspire loyalty and admiration in females, if he could win the affection of so strong and beautiful a woman as this.

A small boy followed Rika from the Hall, and she spoke to him quietly then left him with an older woman. Cahira watched them doubtfully. "She's leaving her child?"

"Rika is a warrior," said Aren. "When her mate fell in battle, she took up his axe and avenged his death. Her son knows her task, and will follow her courage in battle when his time comes."

"Yours is a violent society," said Cahira.

Aren sighed. "We are now. What other people could live in a world so cold as this?"

"I suppose you're right—but it still seems strange to me that your culture places warfare in such high regard."

Aren mounted Pip, waking the horse, and checked the braided-rope reins. "We know little of our origins, nor where we came from, but in this world, without the magic that benefits your soft people, or the comfort of the warm forest, courage is all we have."

Cahira hesitated, then mounted Zima as respectfully as she could. She sensed the mare valued respect. Though she didn't admit it, it was convenient to have a slightly shorter horse, and the fit between them was undeniably better. Zima was light to the bit and responsive, and Cahira relaxed.

"For one as warlike as yourself, it would seem you'd welcome a battle with a dire wizard," she said. Aren shook his head.

"I have seen the wizard's strength. Not courage, but magic will be required to stand against him. There is no way to fight a phantom."

"He won't be a 'phantom' once he's resurrected," Cahira reminded him.

Turning Pip down the road that led from the Hall and from the hamlet, Aren said, "I feel so much better knowing that."

*   *   *

"In mere seconds, you have managed to offend both myself and my mare!" Cahira trotted up beside Aren, then edged her horse forward into the lead.

Aren watched her ride by and smiled. "I meant no offense."

"You were trying to antagonize Zima by taking the lead, and in doing so, annoy me."

His intention exactly. "Not at all."

She glanced back at him. Her long dark hair coiled over one shoulder, and the light from the melting snow glittered in her eyes, bluer than the sky above. "I didn't mention it, but as it happens, Pip prefers to follow."

"Then why didn't you let one of us lead on the journey up here?" asked Fareth from his position behind Aren and Pip.

Despite her unpredictable temperament, Aren noted Cahira's comrades didn't seem afraid of antagonizing her. In fact, they seemed to treat her like a child—protective, but not entirely respectful—though it was clear they'd placed all their faith in this last remaining Mage. Leadership had been passed to Aren young, he had left his childhood behind on the day his brother died. But Cahira had faced no such challenge until now. He could imagine her doubt that she was ready for the task.

Cahira's hesitation validated Aren's insight. "I am leader, and it is appropriate that I go first." She sounded as if she were trying to convince herself. "Zima is more agreeable to the position, true, but it was Pip's duty as my mount."

The bat, Felix, sat perched on Cahira's shoulder. "For creatures of servitude, it is important they accept their tasks. Of course, horses, like other herd animals, naturally choose a leader, whose duty it is to protect the rest. For this reason, the lower animals in a pack constantly test the leader, to be sure he remains in form. Most often, there's a top male and a top female." The bat paused to draw a quick breath. "The females, it can be said, are particularly aggressive in maintenance of their leadership."

Thorleif glared at the bat. "Is he going to talk like this the whole way?"

The bat glared back. "You could learn from my wisdom, Norsk boy! Just a few logical words meant to enlighten your perspective seem a great trial for you now. But after a few weeks—"

"Weeks!" Thorleif turned toward Aren. "Is it really going to take weeks, my lord?"

"Probably," said Aren. "It is a long way to the caverns south of the Guerdian Hold in the mountains."

Cahira looked back at him suspiciously. "From my calculations, it will be two weeks, at most, if we ride straight."

"But, of course, we can't ride straight, as I'm sure you must have considered," said Aren. "For one thing, we can't head straight south to the sea and then turn east—which would appear to be the most direct route on a map. The passage eastward would be impossible, even on foot. There's a treacherous marsh that goes onward almost to the mountains. Our only course lies south but a short way, then east to the land of the Guerdians, and after that, we will have to pick our way slowly along the foothills southward."

"You're trying to delay us!" Cahira accused.

"Not at all." If geography worked to that end, who was he to deny its benefit?

Cahira's lips twisted in thought. "I don't know much about the Guerdians, except those few I've encountered in Amon-Dhen. Will they be agreeable?"

"Not if they know your purpose, but I assume you mean to keep that quiet. Though how you'll explain our southward journey, I can't guess. But that—since this is your idea in the first place—will be your problem."

He watched as she considered. "We will have to come up with some other explanation. One that doesn't mention waking the Arch Mage," she said.

"Good idea. I doubt they'll take kindly to having the wizard who once enslaved them resurrected as a neighbor."

"Well, we won't put it that way!" Cahira puffed out an agitated breath, then urged her mare faster. Pip lengthened his stride in order to keep up. Odd, the horse hadn't seemed the type to care much where he stood in relation to others. Maybe that's what had drawn Aren to him—he and the quiet horse were much the same.

"They won't allow us to pass through their land without an audience with their king," Aren mentioned. Of course, Cahira's party could slip by unnoticed if the three Norsk used their skills to avoid detection, but Aren had no intention of missing a chance to slow their progress.

Thorleif's brow furrowed. "Now, my last scouting party avoided . . ." Aren shot him a dark look and Thorleif winced. Cahira looked back suspiciously. "Avoided even going into their territory, because, as everyone knows, you cannot elude Guerdians in their own land." The young man paused, somewhat breathless. "And should we tell her about the rogue bands, my lord?"

"Go ahead."

Cahira's eyes narrowed to slits. "What 'rogue bands?' We haven't heard of anything like that in Amrodel. This land has been remarkably peaceful, despite the Norsk taste for drunkenness and brawling, since you became chieftain."

"Thank you," said Aren.

"It was Damir's doing, really." She blushed, and Aren offered a knowing smile. She snapped, "What about this 'rogue band' issue?"

"It's no wonder you wouldn't have heard of them," answered Thorleif, eager with the story. "They keep mostly in the land between ours and the Guerdians', and then on down toward the seaport of Amon-Dhen, where they ambush and plunder traveling merchants. In the last year, maybe thanks to this 'darkness' your evil wizard is pitching out, these bands have gotten worse—more reckless, and crueler. Many of them were banished for various misdeeds. But they are skilled fighters, and you don't want to run across them unless you're in a well-armed party."

Felix issued a loud whistle. "Name of the Gods, we understand your point, Norsk boy! In fact, a single word, *rogue*, conveyed quite enough. And before you say anything more, I think we all gather that these bands pose a significant physical threat, and therefore, this party must be ready to defend itself."

Thorleif's eyes narrowed to slits. "I don't believe I was done. I hadn't yet mentioned that there are also exiled Guerdians among them. And because the Guerdians are beyond compare in the design of armor, they are quite difficult to battle."

"There's no armor that magic can't pierce," said the bat. "I'm not worried."

The young Norskman took umbrage. "There's no warrior that Aren, son of Arkyn, can't match and defeat in battle without your witch for protection. Apparently, she's the one in need, bat, given that she came crawling to beg for his aid!"

Felix tensed and looked as if he might launch himself at Thorleif, so Aren eased Pip between them and held up his hand. "Shall we discuss this after our respective skills have been proven in battle? We're in little danger of an ambush until we leave the southern borders of the Norskland. But when we reach the foothills, it would be wise to take care."

"I am not afraid of ambush," said Cahira, "except if it delays our progress." She paused. "It might be interesting to prove myself in real battle. Since you brought about this peace, there hasn't been much for a warrior like myself to do except study my art and hone my skill."

Rika overheard Cahira's comment from the rear of the column, and spoke disparagingly. "You do not resemble a warrior in any way. You are slight of build, with no discernable muscle, you could barely lift the sword you presented to our chieftain, and I do not believe you could even hold your own against a Guerdian child. Not without the benefit of your witchcraft."

Cahira jerked Zima to a halt, whirled the mare around, and in the space of a breath, had drawn her bow and set an arrow to the string. "This bow doesn't require a spell to aim, wench, so hold your tongue lest I put an arrow through it!"

Cahira's companion Elphin looked proud. "Mind yourself, indeed, Norskwoman. I've known Cahira since she was born—her sister is my wife. I've seen her pin down older boys twice her size and four times her weight with the strength of her fury alone. I wouldn't challenge her if I were you. She may not be large, but there's not a Norskman alive"—he gestured at Aren—"including this one, who can hold their own with her for long. I think she proved that in your Great Hall."

"Only because our chieftain didn't resist," replied Rika icily.

"Looked like he fought back to me!" said Fareth. "And got beat, too."

"You Norsk boast overmuch," added Elphin.

"Not half so much as a Woodlander!" retorted Thorleif. "We fight with skill and courage—we have reason to boast."

"We don't rely on a witch's spell to win our battles," said Bodvar.

"We rely on the strength of our bodies," said Thorleif.

Shaen glanced back and forth between them, then shook her head sadly. "Please, don't fight about this. There's no need to be unkind to each other, despite our differences."

For once, Aren agreed with Shaen, but the bat leaned forward to involve himself in the squabble. "'Strength of your bodies?' I don't know what you see when you peep into a looking-glass, Norsk boy, but from my viewpoint, you're one of the puny ones! How those ropey little arms of yours can even lift an axe is beyond me!"

Aren cringed. The bat was treading now in dangerous waters, where Thorleif's pride was concerned. "Thorleif is seventeen years of age, Felix. The Norsk grow late into manhood. I was much smaller at his age."

"Seventeen? I was at my full height and weight at seventeen!" said Fareth.

"You were just as rotund?" asked Rika. "That is nothing

to boast of. It simply requires little activity and too much food."

"It's all muscle!"

Aren groaned. "We are all shaped differently, just as we have individual gifts and weaknesses—though at this point, we seem to share an argumentative nature. Since we're on this journey together, might I suggest we set aside the differences inherent to our peoples, and attempt to ride in peace?"

His words brought about a sullen silence, but Cahira looked back at him thoughtfully. She said nothing, but her expression softened, and Aren's heart stirred unexpectedly. She was hotheaded and impulsive, but there was something in her that begged to be explored.

"If it's acceptable to you, Lady Mage, we will ride until nightfall, then take our rest at the Snow Pony Inn in the hamlet of Eddenmark. From there we will begin our more dangerous journey eastward, so it would be wise to eat well, sleep, and add to our provisions while we can." He paused. "A shame we won't be traveling farther south."

She peeked at him again, suspicious. "Why? You're the one who suggested the eastern road."

"There's another pleasant inn—the Lusty Boar, it's called. You might enjoy it."

Her lips curled into a sideways frown. "Ha! I know of what you speak." Her frown deepened. "Eliana and Damir take yearly holidays to that place, and they are not shy about declaring their reasons. I assure you, I would not find a visit interesting." She paused. "It only holds fascination for them because they . . . fomented their feelings for each other in that inn."

"Gave in to their passions," corrected Aren.

Cahira rolled her eyes. "He probably got her drunk."

Aren laughed. "You are so cynical for a maiden. Why is that?"

She shrugged and returned her gaze to the path. "Oh, I know they love each other. That was always obvious, though

I didn't pay much attention when they were tutoring me. Eliana and Damir seem stronger together than they were apart. But that would not be so for me."

"Why not?" Aren paused. "And how do you know?"

"It is hard enough to summon and hold my *ki* without having to worry about another person."

"To love means to protect," said Aren quietly. "It is hard enough to fail those we were born loving. To add another by choice into that circle . . ."

Cahira turned slowly, her blue eyes wide with surprise. Aren watched her swallow and draw a tight breath. They looked at each other for a long moment, and their companions and the frozen landscape through which they traveled seemed to disappear. Then a small and sorrowful smile gentled her expression. "Yes," she whispered.

Aren smiled, too, and spoke so no one but Cahira could hear his voice. "I knew you would agree."

4

THE SNOW PONY INN

They rode through a long day, and Cahira maintained her position in the lead where Zima seemed doggedly determined to stay. Cahira often had to ask Aren for direction. Felix the bat had declared the weather unendurable, and had retreated into her pack. Occasionally Cahira felt him squirm into a more comfortable spot, and every so often, she heard a faint snore.

They were riding south now, but all the Norsk lands looked alike to Cahira. Where spring had come in full to the woodland of Amrodel, winter still lingered here, though in places the snow gave way to dull grass and rocks. Mounds of fading slush dotted the landscape, gray and receding before the faint warmth of the distant sun.

"This is a bleak land," Cahira said. She hadn't spoken much after Aren's unexpected comment about loss and love and failure. For a painful instant, she had felt as if he looked inside her soul and seen everything she was and had ever been. His words had pierced her loneliness. *"To add another by choice . . ."* He couldn't know, not fully, what it meant to have great power within and yet know also that when the time came for that power to serve others, to save lives, how bitterly it could fail.

She peeked back at him. Maybe he did know. His brother had died. Maybe Aren blamed himself, though Bruin the Ruthless had made his own fate by allying himself with the minions of the Arch Mage. Her father had earned no such responsibility for his demise, other than his too-trusting nature. She could have saved him, and she had run away instead. Age was no excuse. Though she had been only twelve at the time, she had had her bow, and even then the skill to wield it.

Aren met her gaze and smiled. "You witness the dawn of spring in our land, Lady Mage. The beauty that will soon spring forth exceeds anything you've ever seen, I promise you. Beautiful, because it is fleeting but still dares to rise." He paused. "It reminds us, I think, to live in the moment that is presented to us, and to not linger overmuch on what might have been or what might yet be."

Cahira halted Zima and stared at him. "How do you know what I'm thinking?"

Aren rode up beside her, and Pip stopped. Zima's ears edged back in displeasure, and the horse started forward without Cahira's permission. Pip started again too, and casually kept stride with the mare. "Because I was thinking the same thing."

"That doesn't mean I had any such thought," said Cahira.

"Didn't you?"

She chewed the inside of her lip. "I suppose we must all be thinking similar thoughts."

Aren's brow elevated. "Do you think so?" He glanced back. "You there—innkeeper! What occupies your mind?"

Fareth started and looked confused. "Wondering how I'd get my cooking gear together and feed this group, if you really need to know."

"And you, Thorleif?"

The youth blushed furiously. "Well, my lord . . . I was

wondering if this venture we're on would qualify as a 'hero's quest.'"

"It does, indeed," said Aren. "Your participation ensures your reward in the Hall of Ages."

"Good, my lord!" Thorleif paused. "Whether I live or die?"

"Absolutely." Aren looked knowingly at Cahira. "Shall I ask the others?"

She sighed. "No need."

They rode in silence for a little while. Cahira glanced at him, but he gazed out over the little mounds of snow and upturned rocks, and again seemed lost in thought. "Of course, it doesn't mean anything—even if we were thinking the same sort of thing," she said.

"No," he agreed, but he didn't look at her.

Cahira fiddled with Zima's reins. They were made from a fine, braided rope, softer than the reins woven by her people. "I suppose it's interesting, in a way. But not meaningful."

"Not at all."

He still didn't look at her. Cahira studied his face. She didn't like his beard. It wasn't trimmed, which might have been a passable improvement, so she couldn't see the shape of his face. He might have had a strong chin, and his lips appeared well-formed. His nose was straight and well-designed, as if the sculptor had lacked the imagination to give it quirks and simply designed the subject to a standard of perfection. His cheekbones were wide and strong, but also too perfect. His forehead was clean and unlined, broad with the suggestion of wisdom. But his eyes intrigued her most, amber-gold, and like amber itself, filled with ancient memory. Odd, because by her count, he wasn't much older than herself.

"You seem old," she said.

Aren looked surprised, but he laughed. "I would ask you to refrain from insulting my appearance further, Lady Mage, but it seems to delight you. Still, you need not go on. I understood from your comments earlier that you find me lacking in good looks."

"I do," she agreed with special emphasis. "But that's not it. It's your eyes. They have the look of a very old person. Ancient."

"And in your eyes, Lady Mage, I see the blue of the world's first dawn, so it might be said that you, too, have an element of the ancient."

Cahira just stared. A chill coursed along her nerves. "You say such strange things for a Norskman." She paused and shook her head. "You are flattering me."

"But I do not lie, Lady. Nor, I think, do you. Tell me, does it not surprise you to find that people do?"

She nodded. "Yes, because I do not understand why they bother, though I confess I will sometimes lie if I dislike someone intensely—as a sign of defiance and disrespect."

"An honest confession," he said with a laugh. "Yet, you have not lied to me."

She fidgeted. "I've had no reason. I don't know you well enough to dislike you. In general, I have found no cause for deceit. I suppose people lie because they want something and must hide their intent in order to get it. For me, it has never seemed worth the effort."

"Aye, for treasures won by trickery are treasures no longer."

"That is true," she agreed, and she repeated the phrase inwardly so as to remember.

"Cahira, when I tell you that you are beautiful, that your eyes shine with wisdom, do not think that I lie, for we feel the same about that, at least. It's not worth the bother to say words I don't mean, or to seem to be something other than . . ." Aren stopped and lifted his hand slowly to touch his face. "Never mind. Perhaps I am not always as honest as I would wish."

He slowed Pip and rode once again behind Zima. Cahira didn't ask what he meant. Aren didn't converse like other men she knew, and thus it seemed strange that she understood him. Worse was that, when he spoke, his words resonated deep inside her. Of course, she wasn't sure what his last comment meant. Perhaps he was planning to deceive her, and was honest enough not to claim complete candor?

Cahira slowed Zima, much against the mare's will, until she rode alongside Aren. "I have found that people who make unsolicited declarations about their virtues tend to have the opposite traits. If they boast of honesty, they can be assumed to lie frequently."

"I have seen that also," said Aren. "But my declaration wasn't unsolicited. You said I flattered you. Flattery is a lie, a manipulation. I simply corrected you."

"I suppose that's true," she agreed.

As they rode along, Aren absent-mindedly stroked Pip's neck, a gentle communication. He clearly had a way with animals. Before they'd left his village, Cahira had seen him stop to pat a dog, and he'd made sure it was safely placed with a small boy before leaving.

He was an exceptionally tall man, taller than any Woodlander or even any Norskman she had seen, and the Norsk were virtual giants among her people. But he wasn't bulky, and he carried himself with true ease. He wore a leather jerkin that fitted him well and adhered closely to the powerful lines of his body. He kept the Dragonfly Sword sheathed at his side, and his Norsk axe hung ready at his belt, as well as a richly carved horn. Cahira's attention maneuvered from his wide shoulders down his body to where his strong leg lay against the horse's side. He was well-formed, no question. But also relaxed.

Aren cleared his throat, and Cahira realized to her horror that he knew she was studying him. She felt her cheeks warm, and tried to look casual.

"Is there anything else?" he asked. His amber eyes twinkled.

"No . . . I just didn't want you thinking I am easily swayed by flattery or lies."

"Given that I am here, as your prisoner, riding to a destination I consider certain death, it seems unlikely I'd consider you easily swayed by anything."

"Good." She paused. "And since I am expecting you to

wield our greatest weapon, and to save my people, it seems reasonable that I get to know your character a bit before the time comes."

"What would you like to know?"

She considered. "Well, what matters to you, I suppose."

"The soul of my people, the joy taken in life, the welfare of those I represent—my people, our creatures, our land, our culture."

"I meant personally!"

"Oh?" He sounded overly knowing, so she fixed her gaze ahead. "But those things *are* personal, my lady. What else would you ask of me?"

"Do you have close friends?" She paused, her voice light. "A sweetheart?"

"Many friends," he agreed, then paused. "Many 'sweethearts.' What an odd term!"

Though he wasn't the brave young hero she had once imagined, Cahira's heart fell a little at his declaration of many sweethearts. But she kept her expression even and said, "It's an odd term when applied to 'many.' It generally refers to one special person."

"Ah, but all are special in their own way."

Cahira frowned. "Never mind."

"I am not in love, and I am not mated, if that's what you mean."

"I couldn't care less," she insisted. She hesitated, fidgeting. "The term 'sweetheart' means to be in love."

"To me, it means a desirable woman with whom I can share a pleasing activity."

"That's not about the heart!"

"It involves affection, which comes from the heart."

"I suppose your behavior is common," Cahira scoffed. "Damir used to toy with various females before he won Eliana."

"I recall that. But it seems to me that the Woodlanders lack skill in separating the sport of the body from the bonding of the heart, and too often confuse the two. For us, there is a clear difference."

"What if it creates a baby?"

"A child is special of its own right, and not by the circumstances of its birth."

"You evade the issue."

"I am also adept at preventing conception."

Cahira cringed and held up her hand. "Say no more!"

"This is a practical conversation—if we are to become lovers." He spoke evenly, as if discussing the weather. "Or 'sweethearts,' if you prefer."

Cahira's hand stayed in the air as she turned slowly to face him. Zima sensed her surprise, and slowed the pace as if awaiting further instruction, then moved on when she noticed Pip edging ahead. "What would ever make you think there is any possibility, under any conditions, *ever,* that you and I would become lovers?"

"'Sweethearts,'" he corrected, and now his lips curved in a teasing smile. Cahira fought the desire to strike him. "Your interest in me seems obvious, despite my hideous appearance."

"My interest in you is professional!"

"You wonder where my power comes from," he added in a low voice meant only for her. "You wonder if it's the same as yours, or different, and what it would feel like blended with your own. And you are curious, because you're young and have denied yourself any exploration, because you are afraid you are too passionate and will love too deeply." He paused and looked thoughtful while Cahira just stared at him, too stunned to argue. "For this reason, I think it best that we refrain until you have better control over your heart."

Cahira sputtered incoherently, struggled to think of something truly cutting to say, and failed. All she managed was a trembling growl.

"I don't want to disappoint you," Aren said as her growl died down. "I know it will happen sooner or later." He paused to sigh. "Maybe when you calm down a bit."

"You are repulsive in every way! I will not be engaging in any intimate encounters with you, ever, of any kind!"

From behind them, she heard someone chuckle. She glared back and saw Thorleif repressing a grin. Was he expecting his chieftain to conquer her? "Ever!"

Fareth exchanged a look with Elphin, as if they were debating the strength and authenticity of her denial, and both appeared somewhat skeptical. Bodvar eyed her as if she'd threatened Aren in some way.

Aren gestured to the path ahead. "We are approaching the ice meadows that lead to the hamlet of Eddenmark and the Snow Pony Inn. Here the road splits, and those routes that seem most direct are often longest. It is necessary that we pay heed." Cahira scowled, as he made it seem as if she were diverting him! "If my Lady Mage allows, it might be wise to let me pick the path, or we will waste hours where we need to spend only one."

"Fine!" Cahira whirled Zima around and directed the horse to the rear of the column, where she placed herself beside Shaen, whose mount was slower than the others and tended to fall behind. Shaen wasn't accomplished on horseback. In fact, the woman was nervous and had already slowed their journey from Amrodel with an abject fear of the faster paces. Zima wasn't pleased to take the new position, but apparently respected Cahira enough not to battle over the issue.

Shaen looked at Cahira kindly. "You must be wary of the Norskman, Cahira."

"Lest I kill him before he serves his purpose?"

"Lest he seduce you, and destroy your usefulness to the Arch Mage."

Cahira gaped. It wasn't like Shaen to be so blunt. Shaen pressed her lips together as if she, too, realized she'd sounded harsh. "I'm sorry, my dear. But we must face facts. We both know the Norskman resists this task—it may be that he's surmised a pregnancy would destroy your energy for the Arch Mage's purposes."

"He's just trying to annoy me." Cahira paused. "And he's succeeding admirably."

"You mustn't trust him, or lower your guard."

"I don't intend to!"

Shaen smiled. "I do understand, Cahira. He has a brutal, primal masculinity that promises an encounter that any woman might consider."

"Not me!" Cahira shuddered. "And that's not what I find intriguing about him," she added, before realizing how much her comment revealed.

"What else is there?" asked Shaen, and the woman sounded genuinely baffled.

Cahira gazed ahead at Aren. He was talking with Thorleif, laughing. Though Fareth and Elphin tried to maintain some distance, she could see them listening intently, and occasionally, Elphin also laughed. "He says the most unusual things—things I've been thinking myself, but he gives words to my feelings, shapes to the images I see. He has a wisdom I've never encountered before."

Shaen laughed. "Oh, Cahira! You must be smitten, to credit him with wisdom or insight!" She patted Cahira's knee again, fondly. "I understand completely. When you first meet a new man, everything he says seems interesting and totally unique. Young women like yourself always feel that way. It's perfectly common and normal, I promise you. But really, you must face that your reaction to this Norskman has more to do with his broad shoulders and animalistic lure than any 'wisdom' you might see."

"That is not all I see in him," said Cahira. Then again, she *had* noticed his shoulders, and that his eyes were strikingly beautiful. He certainly had an allure which affected her like tiny shocks along her nerves—and worse, he seemed to know it. Maybe he meant to make her look foolish. Cahira considered this and felt small. "You are right. I should avoid him," she agreed.

"I'm glad you see it that way," said Shaen. "I just don't want him to take advantage of you. He may be primitive, but those types are often wily. He knows how you react to him, and as a warrior, he'll be quite prepared to use that against you. Think what he could do if he could harness both you and the Dragonfly Sword!"

"I doubt that's his wish. He doesn't even want the sword."

"That's what he's told you, of course," agreed Shaen. "But he accepted it, didn't he? You mustn't take things just as they seem on the surface, Cahira. I don't have a Mage's *ki,* but everyone says my intuition about people is amazing. I imagine that a Norsk male would prefer a different type of woman. One like Rika, for example."

Rika rode behind the two Woodlanders and occasionally commented disparagingly on something Elphin said. He especially seemed to antagonize her. Her hair flowed like a river of pale gold, and loosed from its braids it caught the sun like white fire. She was tall and strong, a woman who could handle anything, including the passions of a Norsk lord. "She is beautiful," admitted Cahira. "She looks more like a warrior than I do."

"I'm afraid she does. But you have your *ki,* which gives you power she lacks," Shaen said. "That is a blessing the gods have seen fit to bestow on very few."

"Some have called it a curse," said Cahira.

"You mustn't think of it that way! It's a blessing, however randomly it's bestowed. I'm sure you will learn to use it eventually." Shaen studied Cahira's face for a moment. "What's the matter, my dear? You seem so down."

Cahira fought the urge to reply, *"I am now,"* and instead sighed. "I'm not sure. We're facing such an evil power. At times, I feel helpless against it."

"Our opposition is tremendous, I know," agreed Shaen.

Felix the bat stirred in Cahira's pack, and she started as he emerged. "I forgot you were in there!"

"Get used to it," he replied. He sniffed at the air, then issued a small growl. "It's cold, and getting colder still. I would think it might snow before nightfall, if it weren't spring."

"It will snow," pronounced Rika. "Not heavily, but there is no mistaking the gray skies to the north."

"How much farther to our destination?" asked Felix.

Rika nodded to the southeast. "Past yonder crest, down a shallow valley, and to the top of the next we must travel, and there we shall find the Snow Pony Inn. It is an hour's ride—maybe less if the snow falls light."

Felix groaned, and Cahira felt tempted to join him. "Ride up ahead, lass, and tell the chieftain to move faster!" the bat said.

"She's better off back here," said Shaen. "I'm sure we're going as fast as we can."

"Are you going to take the sage advice of your guide or not?" the bat shrilled. "Get up there and tell him to move out before we freeze!"

"It's not that cold," said Cahira. The bat glared in response, so she sighed and obeyed his command. Zima pushed eagerly past Rika's mount and those of the two Woodlanders, then jogged past Thorleif, who frowned.

"Pushy witch," he muttered.

Bodvar cast Cahira dark look. "She does not leave him alone."

Cahira gritted her teeth but ignored the Norskmen, instead riding up alongside Aren and Pip. As they approached, Felix began to shiver violently, but the effect seemed forced.

"My guide has requested that we move faster to our destination," she said. "He is cold."

Aren eyed Felix doubtfully. "I see that. You'd think a bat's fur would be more beneficial against the weather."

"I was getting my summer coat in Amrodel!" said Felix. "Just went through my spring shed. This frozen wasteland will be the death of me. Get us to an inn and fast—and there'd better be a substantial meal for all travelers, including myself."

"What would you have me do, Lord Bat?" asked Aren. "Unlike yourself, horses don't have wings. Perhaps you'd like to fly on ahead?" He gestured southeast, but Felix emitted a disparaging squeak.

"And what? Be swatted as a pest? I expect you to introduce me properly, and see that I'm treated as an honored guest." The bat shot a dark look at Fareth. "Almost got swatted in my own homeland. That is not to be repeated here!"

Fareth winced. "Didn't know you were an honored one. Thought you were a pest."

"You might have spoken up then," added Cahira. She paused. "Why didn't you?"

Felix swelled with self-importance. "I had my reasons, and as an Elder of my species, I fully intend to keep those to myself."

"He likes shocking people, I'd say," said Thorleif. "Pompous little creature!"

The bat craned his small head around and glared at the young Norskman. "I'll shock you, all right, boy! Just you wait. When you least expect it . . ."

Thorleif's eyes widened, but then he smiled devilishly. "Hope you don't wake me all suddenlike, because I might think to swat you with my ax before I recognize you."

Aren groaned. "I think you're right, after all."

"What do you mean?" asked Cahira.

"Anything is better than listening to these two for another hour." He glanced at Cahira, his eyes gleaming. "Another thing I failed to mention about Zima . . ."

"What's that?"

"She's fast."

Cahira felt a rush of delight. "Is she? I sometimes wished Pip were faster. He never seems to hurry."

"He may hurry when Zima stretches the distance between them." Aren laughed. "In our language, 'Zima' means 'Breath of the Wind,' in honor of the goddess of wind. That horse was well-named, as you will see—if you can handle her."

"Ha! Watch me!" Cahira tensed, and Zima responded with eagerness for the race. Cahira glanced back, then sighed heavily. "I'm forgetting Shaen. She's uncomfortable with horses. Though Elphin picked a quiet and aged gelding for her, I suppose we can't just gallop off."

"He'll follow. She'll be fine," said Aren without interest. He turned to the others. "The Snow Pony Inn awaits. Let us shorten the distance, and find a hot meal and warm beds in a time well spent."

"What are you talking about?" asked Fareth, but Rika had already passed him.

"He means we race, innkeeper!" Rika's horse leapt forward, bursting into a gallop. Elphin cried out in challenge, then galloped after her. Fareth held his horse back as he adjusted his packs, then edged his large body into a forward position. Slowly and methodically his big-boned old horse moved from a trot to a canter, then rumbled forward in ever-increasing solid strides.

"Faster than he looks," said Thorleif. "But I will leave them all in a wisp of snow!" He shouted to his small but restive horse, and it bounded off after the others.

Bodvar laughed, and for a moment, Cahira thought he looked young, despite the scar on his brow and his hardened expression. "When a boy thinks he can outrun a man . . ." He shouted to his horse and galloped after Thorleif.

Shaen choked back a panicked scream. Her horse had whinnied at the others, rearing slightly. "Just let him run," advised Cahira.

Trembling, Shaen obeyed, and the horse started off at a brisk trot then broke into an easy canter. "What do I do?" the woman cried.

"Hold on," advised Aren, but he shook his head as she crumpled forward and clung to the horse's mane. "What possessed you to bring that woman?" he asked Cahira.

"During her time studying with the Elder Mage, she memorized the layout of the Arch Mage's palace," Cahira explained. "When we reach the mountains, she should be able to guide us to his tomb."

"Couldn't you have brought a map instead?" he asked.

"Unfortunately, all the maps were lost in a fire."

"So we're trusting the information in her head?" Aren eyed Cahira doubtfully. "And you consider this reliable?"

Cahira hesitated. "She does have a good memory. Without her, we could be floundering for days trying to locate the Arch Mage's tomb. It lies within vast catacombs."

"Then have her draw us a map, and we'll leave her at the inn."

"I can't leave her here!" Cahira paused. Shaen had grown more difficult over the past few days. "Could you find someone safe to escort her back to Amrodel?"

Aren looked unconcerned with Shaen's safety. "Easy enough. Yes."

Cahira watched as Shaen's horse cantered on ahead. Shaen clung to the horse's mane desperately and bounced unsteadily, even at the easy gait. Zima's whole body trembled with indignation at being held back. Pip closed his eyes as if happy to have peace. "I'll consider your suggestion," said Cahira.

"You'd be wise to do so," Aren replied.

Felix watched them go, peered up at Cahira, then issued a small wail. "I know what's coming," he said. He dove back into her back and buried himself deep within, but she heard his muffled voice. "Tell me when it's over."

"We've given them a fair start, wouldn't you say?" Aren smiled, then nodded. "But this race is between you and me."

Cahira trembled in unison with her mare. "Then victory will soon be mine!"

"I cannot believe you beat me. It's not possible." Cahira charged up behind Pip just as Aren dismounted at the inn. Zima appeared equally shocked, and deeply offended. Pip rubbed his head against Aren, and Aren scratched the horse's ears. Cahira hopped off, patted Zima's neck, then turned to wait for the others.

Aren was just as surprised. "I didn't think this fellow had it in him. Zima has a stride like no other, and she loves to race."

"You did take a shortcut I didn't see," said Cahira. "And you know the land."

"One must seize one's advantage," said Aren. "I triumphed over Damir in just this spot once before. I have raced ponies over this ground countless times since I was old enough to crawl onto a horse's back."

"I wish I'd had a friend like you when I was growing up," said Cahira. "Woodlanders don't like physical competition. They like wagering, but our focus tends to be on music and, of course, the magic arts. None of my sisters favored sport, either."

"My people mostly prefer ale and tavern games," said Aren. "Our sport generally involves war, but I prefer the companionship of horses. To work alone, that is a challenge. But to blend with another, that is a rare art, and a greater gift."

Cahira looked up at him in surprise, and fresh blood crept into her flushed cheeks. "I s-suppose so," she stammered, and Aren laughed.

"It is different with a lover," he informed her. She caught her breath and frowned, but he continued teasing her. "A man and a woman are the same species, after all. But to understand a horse, you must learn his ways and his nature, what is different and what is the same. He must learn to trust your judgment as he would trust the leader of his herd." Aren paused. "For this reason, Zima has been difficult for many. She is a leader by nature, so to surrender that position, she must sense a spirit of equal skill."

Cahira frowned. "You thought she would pitch me off and dominate me utterly."

He didn't deny it. "I thought she would challenge you more than she has, it's true. As a foal, she was skittish and shy, and it took a while to tame her. She makes you earn her trust."

Cahira touched Zima's soft nose. "I didn't really do anything."

"You fling yourself headlong at life, and you want to go first, perhaps to place yourself in danger. Horses sense what others cannot see. She knows your strength better than you do."

"I won't let anything happen to her," Cahira promised. "I suppose we can't take them into the caverns, anyway."

"The passages are narrow even on foot, and delve deep within the mountains. We must leave them with the Guerdians. They themselves keep only donkeys, but they will happily house horses."

"You've already thought of this?" Cahira gazed up at him, looking surprised and pleased. "And if anyone in our party wishes to stay behind, they can stay with these Guerdians, too."

"If you allow it," agreed Aren.

"I would not stop anyone who fears to go farther." She paused. "Except you."

"My fears mean nothing to you then?"

She looked at her feet, and for the first time, he saw a shadow of guilt cross her face. "You're the only one who can save us. Damir, Eliana, and all the Mages of Amrodel—they need you."

"If we could find another way, would you heed it?"

"There is no other way, and we have no time."

The others approached. Oddly, Fareth was first, followed by Thorleif and Bodvar riding neck and neck.

"Where's Rika?" called Aren. "We passed her only a short ways back. Her horse starts fast, but wears out sooner than most," he added to Cahira.

Thorleif swung his leg forward and jumped off his steaming horse. "She and Elphin got into some kind of battle, trying to drive each other aside. I think I saw her swinging an axe when I went by."

Cahira cringed. "Oh, dear! She won't kill him, will she?"

"I wouldn't put it past her," said Fareth. "That woman's a terror, out for blood."

"I see them, there," said Aren. "Both are alive."

Cahira breathed a sigh. "Where's Shaen?"

"Oh, she's a ways back, but plugging along," said Thorleif. Bodvar looked back at Shaen and shook his head. "Such a woman is not meant for a dangerous journey. She is too weak and unprepared for hardship."

"She's clinging like a spider," said Thorleif with a laugh. Then he turned to Cahira. "I have to say, miss, I didn't think you'd last a minute on Zima's back, but here you are, coming in right after the chieftain! That's a feat, and no mistake!"

"Probably due to some spell she places on beasts," said Bodvar. While Thorleif's attitude toward her had softened, the other Norskman's suspicions obviously remained intact. Cahira frowned.

"It is due to my skill with horses!"

"So you say," said Bodvar. "But a witch who can make a flying rat talk would find taming a troublesome mare easy."

Elphin galloped into the courtyard, flung himself off his horse and issued a wild string of curses directed at Rika, who rode beside him. "The Norsk are ever-treacherous, and this she-wolf is the worst of all! Tried to trip my horse, she did, and nearly succeeded! Cahira, I must insist that we leave her here when we journey onward."

Rika coolly dismounted, assembled her horse's reins and faced Aren. "The Woodlander's inability to control his mount is his own fault, and his penchant for cutting in front of me nearly led to a fall."

"Your penchant for charging through me, you mean!"

A tiny curve of Rika's lips convinced Aren that neither was innocent, and both best left unchallenged. Felix squirmed from Cahira's pack and looked around. "What about food?"

"We should wait for Shaen," said Cahira.

"Fine for you!" retorted the bat. Without warning, he hurled himself from Cahira's pack to Aren's shoulder. "Bring me inside, Norskman, and make suitable arrangements for our stay." He twisted his little head around. "We'll set things up right, and then call you in."

"Uh, maybe I should do this alone," suggested Aren. "My people aren't used to talking creatures."

"He could consider not talking," suggested Thorleif. "But I don't suppose that's possible."

"No, it is *not* possible!" said Felix. "Why should I silence myself to assuage the fears of simpler life forms? They can handle it! And it's the only way I'll be able to give directions for my preferred meal."

"He's going to start a war right here," said Thorleif. "They'll think the witch has enslaved us, and kill us for sure!"

"They will not kill the chieftain," said Rika.

"Maybe we should gag the creature," suggested Thorleif. "Just to be safe."

Cahira motioned to Elphin. "If you would wait here for Shaen, then get the horses stabled, please . . . It is my place to assure our accommodations."

"You don't trust me?" asked Aren.

"No, I do not."

He led her to the front door and held it open for her to pass. "At times, you remind me of your guide, Lady Mage."

She paused in the threshold of the door and looked up at him. "What do mean?"

"He's paying you a compliment, lass!" said Felix, who hopped back to Cahira's shoulder. Aren nodded.

Cahira accepted this, lifted her chin, and marched through the door. Before Aren could catch up with her, he heard the gasps and astonished cries from the patrons within. He sighed, then followed her into the Snow Pony's gathering room. As expected, several Norsk warriors were already on their feet gripping axes. A tavern maid had dropped her tray of ale, and had seized a knife from a trader's plate. A group of traveling Guerdians huddled together in a protective group.

"What's the matter with these people?" asked Cahira in disgust.

Aren entered the room behind her, and the group relaxed with a collective sigh. "If you didn't barge in like an ambush, with a talking bat perched on your shoulder, bow slung across your back . . ."

"Don't be ridiculous! Felix isn't talking, and I just walked in!"

"Lady Mage, from what I've seen, you don't 'just' do anything. Every step you take is an assault."

She considered this, then looked proud.

"That wasn't a compliment," he said, but she still smiled.

The crowd gaped nervously at Cahira and her bat, then turned to Aren. "Has the Lord Chieftain taken a Woodland Mage prisoner?" asked one of the traders.

"No," replied Aren. "The Woodland Mage has taken your chieftain prisoner." He paused, and smiled. "Calm yourselves—we're here for the night and a good meal. Despite her combative nature, the woman is no threat to you."

An older warrior Aren knew, Gunnolf, stared at Cahira, then at Aren, then back to Cahira. "'*Prisoner?*'" he asked.

Cahira straightened, and her small face looked extremely smug and self-assured. "I have convinced your chieftain to lend his assistance in connection with a task my people have undertaken, which would be of no interest to you, I'm quite sure."

Aren eased her aside. "She's wrapped the equivalent of a magical noose around my neck, and intends to thrust herself into the cavern of the Woodlanders' ancient foe, the evil phantom that enslaved my brother and resulted in his death. This will resurrect the dark wizard, whom she then supposes I will battle to certain victory with this pretty white sword she has generously provided." Aren laid his hand on the Dragonfly Sword, and the amber jewel in its pommel glittered in the firelight.

Cahira spun around and faced him, her cheeks glowing with anger. "Are you crazy? I thought we were going to keep these matters private!"

"From the Guerdians, Lady Mage, not from my own people, to whom I have sworn protection, as well as the Norsk code of truth."

Every Norskman in the gathering room fingered their various weapons and moved to surround Cahira. Lacking good sense, she whipped her bow from her back and took aim at one.

Aren sighed, placing himself in front of her. "Put away your weapons," he said. He paused and glanced at Cahira. "*All* of you." The Norsk complied. Cahira did not. Her fingers twitched, which caused the taut string to shudder. "Lady Mage, I suggest you respect the honor of your fellow warriors and set aside your weapon, as they have done."

Her lip curled, and for reasons Aren couldn't imagine, he found the expression tempting. *I may have to kiss her, just once.*

Cahira lowered her bow, but her combative posture remained. "I am not to be trifled with," she said.

"No one ever imagined you were," he replied. And he found himself admiring her spirit. *Liking* it.

At his request, the Norsk returned calmly to their benches and resumed their meals. The Snow Pony's innkeeper emerged from the kitchen carrying a large portion of roast mutton. "What's all the commotion out here?" he asked. "I just picked up after the last brawl . . ." He took one look at Cahira, squealed, and dropped the tray. "Not again!"

Gunnolf nodded to the innkeeper, then elevated a tankard of ale in Cahira's direction. "This witch has enlisted our Lord Chieftain, intending on raising that evil wizard so she can take over our lands and make slaves of our people. It looks like the chieftain has her under control, though."

"*What?*" Cahira marched toward the warrior, but Aren caught her by the shoulders and drew her back. She struggled, but he held her firmly.

The innkeeper relaxed. "Well, then, if Aren son of Arkyn has her nicked, there's naught to worry about." He smiled and bowed once to Aren. "Bring you ale, lord?"

Cahira's mouth slid open, but she seemed too shocked and offended to speak. Aren eased his grip on her shoulders, which slumped slightly.

"Allow me to introduce Ranveig, known to your king and queen from their previous visit to the Snow Pony. He also took part in the battle where the wizard was driven back, and his minion destroyed."

"I did," agreed Ranveig. "I am known as Ranveig the Fat, like my father before me." He paused to pat his large stomach. "I'm not a fighter, as such, but when Aren son of Arkyn calls, his people answer!"

The tavern door opened behind them, and the rest of Cahira's party entered the hall, led by Fareth. "What manner of place is this? Ice falling from the sky outside, and enough fumes inside to knock a man down!" He looked around in disgust. "By the way, it's commenced snowing again out there. Isn't it spring?" He caught sight of the fallen mutton and gasped. "I knew it! These brawny devils eat from the floor!" He paused to sneer, "What is that? Not *mutton?* Don't you people know how to cook?"

Elphin and Shaen came up beside him, both horrified by the sight. Thorleif shoved past them, retrieved the tray and mutton, then tore off a section and ate. "Tastes fine!" he said.

Ranveig snatched the tray away, then flung the meat out a side door to several dogs. "It was an accident," he said.

Felix sputtered on Cahira's shoulder. Mercifully he'd remained silent, but Aren's hope that that might continue faded. "What did you do that for? I could have lived on that for weeks!" the bat complained.

Another tray dropped—Aren didn't see whose this time. He held up his hand to silence the burst of forthcoming questions. "I neglected to mention the Woodlanders' bat. It talks. So far, that's all it does, but it appears harmless."

"Haven't seen my teeth and claws in action, have you, boy?" Felix flared his leathery wings in warning.

"Bring the bat a plate of food and water, and we can be assured of its good will," added Aren.

"For the time being," warned Felix, though he seemed appeased by the promise.

A serving maid darted off and returned with a plate laden with more food than twenty small animals could eat. Felix hopped down and dove in, while the Norsk at the table eased away. The girl gave him a goblet of water, but he plunged his small head into an abandoned tankard of ale instead. Thorleif cringed, then seized a fresh tankard and drank from it at a safe distance.

Rika entered the hall, walked past Cahira and took a seat at a table beside the other warriors. Bodvar joined her. Gunnolf eyed them both doubtfully. "Did the witch set a spell on you, too, Bodvar?"

"None that we know of," said the warrior ominously.

Rika took a drink of ale and shook her head. "We ride with the chieftain. No spells."

Gunnolf looked to Aren. "Shall any of us join you, my lord?"

"I need my warriors here more than at my side," said Aren. "I can handle the path ahead."

Gunnolf accepted his word and returned to his meal, but Cahira looked at him suspiciously. "What do you mean, 'handle the path ahead?' Are you planning something?" she asked.

"If I was, I wouldn't tell you, would I?"

"I hope you haven't forgotten my power!"

"I have not."

"Then you understand planning something would be futile."

"Of course."

Her blue eyes narrowed to slits. "I don't like this at all! You are obviously planning to trick me!"

"I wouldn't dream of it."

Ranveig disappeared into the kitchen, then emerged again with a large plate of food, meat, and bread. He nodded to the tavern girl. "Bring the Lord Chieftain ale—enough for his guests, too." He paused. "You do want me to feed them, don't you, my lord?"

"That seems fair," agreed Aren.

Ranveig eyed Fareth. "Looks like that one's had enough already!" He paused to whistle. "Got a girth on him, doesn't he?"

"Not so wide as you!" said Fareth. "And mine's all muscle.

No one attached 'The Fat' to my name! I'd say you earned yours fair and square."

"It's a title merely to honor my sire!" Ranveig's wide face flushed. "I don't suppose *you've* been in any battles?"

"Too busy cooking food people can eat—food not meant for the dogs," said Fareth.

Ranveig slapped his tray onto a table, seized a knife, and stared at Fareth. Aren cast his gaze heavenward and sighed. "Try the meal, Fareth, before assailing it. You may remember that your own queen found our taverns welcoming—"

"And ate more than her share at every meal," added Ranveig.

"'The Fiend' always had her own ways," said Fareth. "Never was quite normal."

Cahira eased from Aren's side and sat down at the table. "Eliana was perfectly normal. She just loved food." She took a bite of the bread, and her eyes widened. "It's quite good!" she said. She spoke thickly, and stuffed in more before swallowing. "You should try some, Fareth."

Aren seated himself across from her—a better angle to watch her delight in the dinner—and Fareth placed himself beside her. Elphin sat beside Aren, and Thorleif hurried to his other side, as far from the hungry Felix as he could get. Shaen seated herself beside Cahira, though she ate only bread and tried nothing else of the Norsk meal. "My stomach is too sensitive for ale," she said sadly. "Is there wine?"

"No wine," said Ranveig, with obvious disgust. "Rots your gut, that. Got some tea, though. Been a favorite of my customers since your queen got us started with it. I have to admit, I've developed a taste for the stuff myself."

"That will be fine," said Shaen. Ranveig brought a small iron pot and poured hot water into a cup, but Aren noticed that Cahira went straight for the ale.

"No wonder you're so fat!" declared Fareth to Ranveig after a long draught of ale. "Woodland ale has a lighter touch than this hefty brew." He took another drink. "Can't compare to ours, of course." Another "sip" drained the tankard, and Aren repressed a grin, then refilled Fareth's pint to the brim.

"And how do you find our ale, Lady Mage?" he asked.

She looked up, a small froth mustache dotting her lip. "Very good! Eliana was right—it warms every part of me!"

He arched his brow, but she returned to the ale. Aren passed her another piece of bread. "Maybe you should balance your draughts with food."

She seized a fork and stabbed at a bowl of cooked roots, and it occurred to Aren that she ate with a Norsk warrior's vigor. She sliced off a piece of meat, focusing on the crispy parts that he also favored, and munched happily. "We'll have to bring some of this on our journey."

"Ranveig can prepare some dried meat of surprisingly good flavor," said Aren.

When Fareth huffed, the Norsk cook said, "I can do better than that!" He paused to administer the other man a scathing look. "I think I'll come with you."

Aren liked the idea, but Fareth stood up, aghast. "We do not need another cook! And our party's as large as it needs to be anyway."

"Maybe cooking up squirrels and herbs is good enough for your people, not having a taste for anything better," said Ranveig, "but warriors need substantial fare to keep up their strength!"

Fareth turned to Cahira, whose mouth was full of food. "My Lady, we do not need the addition of another Norskman! There are too many as is."

Felix looked up from the his plate. Oddly, he used his wing tips as fingers and ate like a human, which Aren guessed wasn't the norm. "I say trade the puny Norsk boy for the cook, and we have a good deal."

Thorleif sprang up, indignant. "I am not leaving the party! The Lord Chieftain needs me!" He paused and nodded at Aren. "Don't you, my lord?"

"I do," agreed Aren. "If we run across any of those rogue bands, you know the territory better than anyone."

"I see no need to swap anyone," spoke up Cahira, after swallowing. "I don't see what harm another cook would be, Fareth. You might even enjoy working together." Clearly, she was enjoying her meal.

Fareth sat down and turned his head. "This is an offense," he muttered.

Cahira shrugged. "Well, you can cook for us, and he can cook for the Norsk. But you might have to share pans and fires."

"I'll be bringing my own pans," said Ranveig. "Now that that's settled, how do you want us to put you up for the night, my lord? You could all use baths, so I'll have those readied, too. Got plenty of rooms open tonight, but I'm thinking you'll want to keep an eye on the witch."

"*I* am guarding *him!*" Cahira snapped. She took a quick drink of ale, wiped her mouth on her sleeve and stood up. "But I would prefer my own room."

Shaen smiled. "I'll share with Cahira—you don't want to be alone. I wouldn't feel right leaving you unprotected."

"What about you?" asked Cahira, looking at Aren.

Aren shrugged. He looked pointedly around the room, fixing his gaze on a pretty tavern girl. "Since you're not interested in guarding me this cold night, I'll find other accommodations."

She caught the line of his gaze and, for a moment, appeared shocked. But then she shook her head in disgust and looked away. "Do whatever you want, but see that you're up at dawn. I want to leave early tomorrow."

5

VOICE IN THE DARK

Aren son of Arkyn, chieftain of the Norsk, was awfully calm for a man who willingly admitted he was a prisoner of a woodland witch. Cahira watched him maneuver casually among his people, all of whom clearly adored him. Especially the young females. An extremely pretty blonde flitted nearby, and her loose top revealed an ample bosom. A quick downward glance reminded Cahira that her own physique might be termed fit but never ample.

As Cahira watched, Aren stretched, spoke to Ranveig, then left the gathering room. She hopped up and started after him, but Ranveig caught her arm. "I don't think you'll be wanting to follow, Miss."

Cahira twisted away. "Why not?"

"He's going to the private chambers, to bathe." A wry grin appeared on Ranveig's beefy face. "Then again, maybe you do want to tag along."

"Certainly not!" She paused. "He could use a bath. I hope the water is very hot, and much soap is available. He could use a shave, too, for that matter, or at least a trim. Woodlanders do not wear beards."

"Probably because they can't grow them," said Ranveig. "But I'll pass along your request."

"It's not a request!" Cahira's teeth ground together as Ranveig headed off after Aren. "It's an order!"

She heard the innkeeper chuckling as he disappeared. Turning back to her table, in the distance she felt sure she heard Aren laugh, too.

"I cannot believe how annoying he is!" She seated herself next to Shaen, then noticed that Felix had fallen asleep, on his back, beside his empty plate. His little legs were splayed apart, and his wings flopped out on either side of his suspiciously rounded body.

Thorleif gaped at the bat and grimaced. "That beast is snoring!"

"Leave him be," said Cahira. She paused then added, "I think he should sleep in your room."

"Why?" asked Thorleif, clearly horrified.

"Because he's male, of course." For some reason, this ended the youth's argument, and Cahira relaxed.

Elphin and Fareth sat together and watched the Norsk. Bodvar surveyed Cahira with an expression of dislike that she began to find tiresome. Rika had abandoned them utterly, and sat with the tavern's other warriors. She never once looked their way. Elphin glared at her. "That woman is pure devil. Like as not, she's planning to stick us with one of those Norsk pikes just as soon as we get out of here."

"I'd rather have her behind me than that oversized innkeeper," said Fareth. "Don't like the look of him one bit."

Cahira thought the two men resembled each other to the point they might be brothers, despite Ranveig's full beard, but saying so wasn't likely to please either Fareth or Ranveig. Thorleif eyed the two Woodlanders and a small smile appeared on his lips. "Think you could take me in a game of Fulthark?" he asked.

Elphin's eyes brightened; then his expression shifted to innocence. "I don't know anything about the game," he said. "But I guess learning would serve to while the hours."

A quick glance passed between Elphin and Fareth, and Fareth nodded. "Don't know nothing about it, either," he added as he got up and followed Thorleif to another table. "By the way, how do you Norsk feel about placing a few bets . . . ?"

Cahira glanced at Shaen, and they both smiled. "I think Elphin has been practicing Fulthark for this very moment, ever since Eliana came home and taught him how to play."

"It would seem so," agreed Shaen. "I see Fareth has already placed a bet." She paused and shook her head. "I never did feel comfortable about the practice of wagering in Amrodel, but at least it's not over personal matters this time."

The Woodlanders had a taste for gambling, specifically regarding the romantic escapades of others. Cahira herself had won a good deal on the outcome of Eliana and Damir's romance, though she'd had to split her winnings with the Elder Mage Madawc. But since Shaen had been the subject of a wager involving her relationship with the late king, it made sense the woman was sensitive about the practice.

"Are you feeling all right, Cahira?" she asked. "You look a little tired."

"I'm fine," Cahira answered, but inwardly, she knew something was wrong. She could take a long day's ride, she could take fighting or any other physical challenge. But as the sun sank in the night sky, a too-familiar sensation had crept over her. She felt as if a dark cloud had sought her out and now hovered above her, moving slowly inward until it would eventually consume her. She closed her eyes to blot out the image, but as if someone whispered just beyond her hearing, she knew she was being called.

"Cahira?"

"It's nothing." It was a voice only she could hear. A voice that whispered of doom, that told her she was powerless.

"Are you sure?" Shaen placed her hand on Cahira's arm. "You need sleep."

"No!" Cahira cleared her throat. "No . . . I'm not tired. Not yet." She would ward it off a little longer. Sleep offered no rest for her, not now. In dreams, he called to her, mocking her defiance. He didn't want her, didn't care who she was, or what she wanted for her own life. He just wanted the energy she carried, the blood she had inherited from a distant relative. He would annihilate her, Cahira, and all the great deeds she had imagined within her grasp would fall to ruin as he used her essence for his own ends. "I'm not tired."

"Well, you have to sleep sometime, my dear."

"I know . . . but not yet." She didn't intend to tell Shaen about the Arch Mage's dark pull. She didn't want to admit it, let alone to someone as likely to smother her with compassion and pity as Shaen. She didn't want pity. She wanted a friend who would tell her she was stronger than the Arch Mage, that she had the power to defeat him—even if it weren't true. Madawc would have told her that. He'd had faith in her, had faith in destiny, that the light would always, eventually, triumph over the dark.

But tonight, as her people bickered with the Norsk, as Aren busied himself with the intent, she suspected, of seducing one final beauty before being dragged into a confrontation he didn't want . . . tonight, when Madawc lay in a distant slumber, she wondered if the light was always just a wish, and that darkness could never be defeated, least of all by the last Mage of Amrodel.

"I know how you feel," said Shaen gently. "There is so much weight on your shoulders, so much pressure. I can always tell when you're feeling down. So many people are depending on you!"

Like I didn't know that! Cahira wanted to say, *Thank you for reminding me,* but she restrained herself and took a long draught of ale.

Shaen squeezed her hand. "You mustn't let it bother you."

Cahira eyed her doubtfully. "Damir chose me because he believed I could do this. And I will."

"Of course you will. We all believe in you." Shaen pressed her lips together. "I don't want to add to your worries, Cahira. But . . ."

Cahira sighed. "What?"

"The Norskman . . . I just can't help feeling he has some plan—he's taking this too easily. I know it seemed as if you defeated him back at his Great Hall, but to me, it seemed as if he was leading you."

"What do you mean?" But Cahira knew Shaen was right; Aren had given in too easily.

"I wonder if he planned this, somehow. Could he have convinced Damir, or more likely, Eliana, that he could be of assistance when the time came? After all, it has been no secret that the Arch Mage's energy would return at some point."

"You think he planned for us to seek him out? That hardly seems likely. And if so, why not simply agree?"

"To throw us off, so we don't suspect his real plan," said Shaen. "After all, we've given him great power in the Dragonfly Sword."

"Why would he go with us, then? Why not just take the sword and stay?"

"I'm not entirely sure what he hopes to achieve," admitted Shaen. "The Arch Mage possesses great power. Maybe the Norskman has plans in that regard."

"Like what? The Arch Mage wasn't known for negotiations or forming alliances," said Cahira. "If he rises unchecked, he will make slaves of Aren's people, just as he once did to the Guerdians."

Shaen shrugged. "Would it hurt him if the Norsk fell into slavery, if he could benefit personally by aiding the Arch Mage's awakening? History shows that the Arch Mage was generous to those who served him willingly."

"History shows he gathered together those likewise bent on evil. Aren isn't evil."

"We can't be sure of that," argued Shaen, "no matter how

much you want to believe. I don't trust him, and I don't like the way he's toying with your emotions."

"He isn't doing that."

"Oh, Cahira! He is. And please forgive me for being blunt, but it's for your own good—it's working, too."

"It is not!" Cahira paused. "In what way?"

"You can't take your eyes off him. I've noticed, my dear, though I confess I don't see the appeal. He's so unkempt and insensitive, like a ragged beast, and you have absolutely nothing in common. Really, if you just look at him, you'd see . . ."

Cahira opened her mouth to speak, just as Aren entered the room. Cahira glanced his way, and he turned toward her. Her mouth stayed open, but no words came. He had washed. As she might have guessed, his blond hair was indeed a shade or two lighter after a good scrubbing. It hung past his wide shoulders, unbraided and loose around his face.

He had trimmed his unkempt beard, revealing a masculine beauty beyond anything she had imagined possible. Their gazes locked, and in a horrible flash, she knew he'd seen her reaction to his newly revealed good looks. She held her breath, expecting a taunting smile or a mocking laugh, but instead he looked resigned and turned away.

"Well," said Shaen. "I must admit he cleans up well."

Cahira puffed in a quick breath. "I suppose he does." She stood up too quickly, and overturned her ale. Fortunately, she'd drunk most of it, so only a little spilled. Seeing the liquid made her think ale would help. She reached over and drained the last of Thorleif's tankard as Shaen watched in horror.

"You should be careful with that, my dear. Women don't usually partake of that particular drink."

Cahira felt a little dizzy. "Well, I do." She looked around the room, allowed herself only a quick glance at Aren, enough to see he had, indeed, made his way to the pretty tavern maid, and then aimed for the door. "Innkeeper!" she called.

Ranveig came to her, but Aren didn't look her way. "What is it, Lady Witch?"

"My room. Which way?"

He gestured down a hall and to the right. "Second door on the right. Got it set up for you, the other Woodland female, and Rika."

"Very good." Cahira walked, somewhat unsteadily, to the room and went inside. She hoped Shaen wouldn't follow until she had fallen asleep. The woman meant well, but listening to her overmuch always seemed to leave Cahira with a headache. She flopped down on the bed nearest the window, then sat up again to peek out at the night. Outside, she saw a long balcony that ran alongside the rear of the inn where, in more dangerous times, the Norsk could post a watch over the endless snowy fields to the east.

The snow had stopped, and the clouds parted, revealing distant stars, and for a moment, her hope returned. But there, far to the south and the east, she saw the shadows of the mountain range rising dark purple against the indigo sky, and her heart fell. She lay back on her bed, hoping the ale had numbed her senses enough for unbroken sleep.

Dark mists surrounded her, and Cahira ran blindly through shadows. She tripped on unseen rocks, cut her hands on jagged walls. A dark shape like a dragon rose up before her, and she tried to close her eyes. His laugh penetrated the darkness and he forced her to face him. Huge and grotesque, the Arch Mage stood before her, his face hidden in a dark hood, amidst a black shadow wreathed in flame. "I called. How quickly and how well you obey me!"

"I came to kill you!"

"You came because I called you, because you belong to me."

She struggled to speak, and her words were like a soft breath. "I belong to myself."

He laughed again, and then moved toward her. "You are nothing, no one. You exist only to fulfill my destiny."

"I am someone. I am Cahira."

"There is no Cahira." He lifted his skeletal hand, fingers dripping blood, and waved it slowly back and forth. As it moved, she felt herself disappearing into the mist. . . .

"No!" Cahira shot up in bed, her skin damp, her breath coming in short gasps. Her heart slammed in her chest. She looked desperately around the room, and remembered where she was. The light of the moon as it waxed bathed the room in an eerie blue light. Shaen slept on the bed opposite her, and Rika occupied the bed nearest the door. The nightmare hadn't woken either woman, mercifully. Cahira hated to seem weak or afraid, but she was trembling as she fought to regain her breath.

I need air. She rose from the bed and slipped from the room. Peeking up and down the hall, she crept to the rear door. She eased it quietly open, then walked out along the long balcony to the point where it faced the southern fields. The night was clear and cold with no wind, and though she hadn't brought her coat, the air felt good against her face.

The balcony overlooked a long stretch of rolling hills, and she looked in the direction she guessed to be their course. Like shadows against the night sky, wild Norsk ponies moved slowly in loose-knit herds below, resting and grazing on bare patches of spring grass. There, ten years before, beyond the hamlet's gates, Damir had met and defeated the Arch Mage's minions. The dark energy had reached its high-water mark in those snowy fields, and retreated back into the secret caverns far below the eastern mountains. But it again loomed in the distance, reminding her it had not been destroyed.

"Cahira." Aren spoke in a low voice, and she turned to see him near the door. She still trembled from her nightmare, but she swallowed hard and nodded. He came over and stood beside her, still quiet.

"I needed air," she said. She wanted to sound strong and sure, but fear and dread infected her voice, which came out weak instead.

Aren looked out over the southern fields, but he didn't

question her as she'd expected. "There lies the battlefield where we last met your foe," he said quietly. "There, I saw such feats of magic and horror that I will never forget. I saw Damir ap Kora summon unimaginable power, but the Mage who opposed him called up an even greater devilry. It took control of my brother, who had already fallen to the allure of dark power, yet, until that point had maintained at least his soul. With a red dagger and a dark spell, the evil Mage controlled my brother and manipulated him against Damir. Damir nearly succumbed, and for the love of Eliana, might have surrendered all."

"Instead, he threw the sword to you," said Cahira. "And you destroyed the dark power."

He looked down at her. "Not destroyed. Drove back. But it's not gone."

She looked back across the fields, closed her eyes. "What if I'm wrong?" She hadn't meant to speak aloud, to share her fears with him, but the words had come anyway.

He didn't answer, and she glanced up at him. Here was his opportunity to chastise her, to remind her that he'd warned her from the first. Instead he said, "What does your heart tell you?"

Tears filled her eyes at his question. "That I must go on. But I don't want to." Her voice broke, and she couldn't stem her emotion. "I want to go home! I want life to return to the way it was, with the Mages practicing and boasting about new spells, with the Mundanes bickering and wagering on each other's escapades." She squeezed her eyes shut. "Why did they pick me? I'm not strong enough. And I am so afraid." She couldn't let him see her cry, couldn't let him see she was weak.

She felt his fingers gently touch her face, and she looked up at him in surprise. The kindness in his eyes pierced her heart. He cupped her face and his thumb moved softly across her cheek. "So you're not crazy, after all," he said quietly. "You are afraid. You should be, because what you're planning is beyond what any person should ever have to do.

But you haven't taken this quest upon yourself because you desire it, and that makes all the difference."

He stood close to her, and he was so strong, so unexpectedly beautiful. She looked into his amber eyes, and it was as if the sun drove away the darkness and pierced the blackest clouds. "I hear him," she whispered. "He calls to me. So what if what I think is my heart is really the voice of the Arch Mage?"

A gentle smile formed on Aren's lips, but he didn't speak. Instead, he bent down, hesitated, then kissed her. His fingers moved to her hair, then to her shoulder, and his mouth played softly against hers. So gently that she barely knew what he was doing, he tasted her lips, and her body seemed to turn liquid.

Cahira gripped his linen shirt to steady herself, and the warmth of his body surrounded her. She leaned against him and parted her lips beneath his. His arms drew taut and he deepened the kiss. The tip of his tongue slid between her lips, and she tasted it, then sucked gently. A low groan stirred in his throat, and she wanted him closer. But Aren broke the kiss and released her. They stared at each for a long moment, and still he didn't tease her or point out that he'd been right about their attraction all along.

"Do you hear him now?" he asked.

"No," she whispered. "He is gone."

"And what does your heart tell you now?"

She smiled. "That I must go on. That I *can* go on."

"Then we will go on."

He touched her cheek again, and she saw both sorrow and happiness mingled in the depths of his golden eyes. "We will say nothing of this," he told her. "It was written long ago that we would meet this way." He paused, and his words seemed to cause him pain. "I am afraid, too, because the task before us seems impossible. I am afraid that, when the time comes, I won't be able to stop this force, nor protect you, and that what might have been between us will fall to nothing before a greater power. And if I fail, my people will be left to ruin and despair, and all their raw passion and courage will come to nothing before the darkness that will reign instead."

Cahira gazed at him in amazement. "Did you know this would happen? That you would be called upon to face the Arch Mage?"

"I knew," he said.

"And . . . about me?" Her voice was smaller now.

Aren nodded. "Do you know what I thought when I saw you, long ago in your father's palace?"

She shook her head, and again, he traced his fingers along her cheek. Every nerve in her body stirred as if it recognized his touch. "What?"

"This thought formed before I realized what it meant: 'You haven't changed.' " He paused. "You were just the same as I remembered you."

"But you'd never seen me before!"

"I know," he agreed. "And I wondered at my reaction, what it meant that I should feel as if I knew you." He paused. "What did you feel when you first saw me?"

Her heart filled with a strange chill, and tears misted her vision. She did not fully understand the reason, but the words that had long ago formed in her mind came clear at last: "I thought . . . I thought, 'I've missed you.' "

They stood together for a long while in silence. Aren took her hand and held it in his. *We are safe here, together*, he thought. For a moment, a longing to stay took hold of him, one so strong that he barely breathed.

After a moment, she spoke. "If you expected me, you didn't seem happy to see me when we arrived at your hall."

He looked down at her and smiled. "Your arrival was the coming of doom," he said. "But tonight, I see that doom brings its own joys."

She bit her lip. "Earlier tonight, you hinted at other joys."

Aren laughed at her expression, and he squeezed her fingers. "It may be that I exaggerated that element of my character. It worked for Damir, after all."

She eyed him suspiciously. "What do you mean?"

"The illusion that many women were interested kept the one who mattered at bay for a long while, did it not?"

"I suppose so. I wasn't paying much attention at the time. But I guess he dallied with other females before he won Eliana's heart." She paused. "Why would a man want to keep . . . a woman—any woman—at bay?"

"If he feared he could not protect her when the time came, would that not be a reason?" Aren asked.

Her expression changed, and she nodded. "It would." She turned her attention back across the still frozen fields and her beautiful face formed an exquisite silhouette against the indigo sky. "We are both afraid to fail, you and I, when the time comes." She glanced up at him again. "I liked kissing you."

"I liked it, too," he replied. In fact, he'd liked it so much that his body still burned, though he had no intention of pressing his advantage, not while she was so vulnerable and alone.

"And I have to admit, you are much handsomer than I thought."

"Since you thought I was 'hideous,' that is a comfort."

"Woodland men don't have beards." She paused and fidgeted. "Somehow, it makes you awfully . . . masculine."

"Thank you. Your delicacy is particularly feminine," he replied. "It much belies the violence inherent to your nature."

She brightened and looked proud. "Thank you!" Then her smile faded. "I have tried hard, always, to earn the title of warrior. From my first memories, I knew I would be called upon to fight." She paused again. "Did you know that also?"

"I knew I would be tested," he answered, "though I have never been certain in what fashion. But it is probably in battle. Isn't that always the way?"

She heard his reticence. "You don't speak of battle with the same glee I've heard from other Norsk warriors."

"Ah, but I don't consider myself a warrior, Lady. I consider myself a priest, for what interests me most is the currents beneath life—the currents that move our souls, and the truth of who we really are."

Her eyes widened. "A priest? How odd, and unexpected! You don't look like a priest. In fact, no man has ever fit my image of a warrior better than you do." She paused and looked closer. "And yet, this fits somehow. Even when I found you repulsive, you seemed to me wise, as if your words reached deeper, your eyes saw further. There is something strange about you, something ancient. Even more so than the Elder Mage Madawc, and he is the wisest person I've ever known."

"Maybe a man can be both warrior and wise," said Aren. "I have fought and felt the thrill of battle, though it doesn't fire my imagination in and of itself. Instead, I admire how souls grow and change, what the battle means to them, how they reach inside themselves to become greater. How a man, or a woman, builds and creates him or herself through a lifetime. And why they fight their fate and deny their hearts. Why they lie, and why they fear the truth."

"I have wondered that, too."

"You are honest," he said. "Especially about kissing."

Cahira blushed, but she didn't deny it. "It is as we discussed. There seems little point in lying. I have never understood people who do."

"Because they want something that others would deny them, because they covet something that belongs to another. Because the only way the wolf can get close enough to the farmer's treasure is to disguise himself as a sheep."

"Your words frighten me, though I'm not sure why. The Arch Mage isn't posing as a sheep."

"That is true, but he uses others that way. He did so with my brother and the Mage who assaulted us ten years ago."

"That same Mage murdered my father," said Cahira. "He was my father's closest friend. And yet . . . I almost wish the Arch Mage *would* pose as a sheep, if only for a little while," she added with a sigh. "Then at least I might get some sleep. He torments my dreams, which is why I came out here tonight."

Aren stooped and kissed her brow. "You will sleep well tonight." He drew back and looked into her eyes. "I am with you."

"I thought you had . . . other plans."

"If you mean the tavern maid, it might interest you to know that she is my cousin and not my lover. As it happens, she wanted my advice concerning a man who wishes to marry her. He's a trader, which is deemed less honorable than a warrior, but I believe he is a good man."

"You were giving marital advice?" Cahira looked a little embarrassed. "Priestly advice?"

"The role isn't as religious as in other cultures—we are storytellers and observers, and we fight for the welfare of our brothers' souls. But when my people request my advice, it is my duty to consider their various predicaments."

"So you advised her to marry him?"

He smiled. "I advised her to follow her heart."

"What did she decide?"

"She will marry him, and he will set up a trading post near here where he will sell the wares of other traders."

Cahira sighed. "It is so easy for some."

"Each person has a path to follow, and there is no use in comparing one to another," said Aren. "If we focus on others while walking our own road, we will lose our way."

"I had not fully accepted my fate, but you are right. There is no use questioning why Damir chose me, nor why the Arch Mage is rising now—nor anything." She lifted her chin. "This is my path."

"And mine," he agreed. "If nothing else, your presence alongside mine makes the journey better, no matter how it ends."

She smiled, and her gaze shifted to his lips. She looked sleepy now, and sensual, but he fought the impulse to draw her into his arms and carry her back to his bed. Cahira lifted her hand, hesitated, then touched her finger to his lips. With his gaze locked on hers, he kissed her fingertip then drew it between his lips. She shuddered and rose up on her tiptoes to kiss him.

Her body felt warm and soft against his, and he felt her heart race wildly. He wanted to make love to her, but she was young and untouched, and though he was winning her friendship, he knew he didn't yet have her trust, not fully. She entwined her fingers in his hair and pulled him closer, and for a long while they kissed, until his body burned. Each breath was an exploration, each murmur like a shared memory.

Again Aren broke the kiss, but Cahira seemed unsteady and he held her in his arms. "Please don't leave me," she whispered. Her plaintive voice tore at his heart. "I don't want to dream anymore."

"Come," he said, and he took her hand again. "I will protect you and keep you safe. Tonight, at least, is within my grasp."

Weariness seemed to flood her, and she leaned against him. She was shivering, and Aren realized that this Norsk spring night must seem bitter cold to a Woodlander used to the sheltered cottages of Amrodel. He picked her up and carried her back into the tavern, and she didn't resist. Two traders heading late to their beds met him in the hall, and they chuckled, assuming their chieftain had made a predictable conquest.

"Where are we going?" she asked. "Are you taking me back to my room?"

He stopped by the door to the room she shared with the two other women. "Isn't that where you want to go?"

She bit her lip. "I would rather stay with you." She gulped, but her eyes were shining. "I feel safe with you. He will not reach me there. I know it."

Aren nodded, then took a quick breath. "I will keep you safe, Cahira, and tomorrow we will ride out to face your nemesis. But I don't think we should make love, however much I may want to."

"No . . . I know," she agreed, though she sounded wistful. "I can't, you see. Not if my quest is to succeed."

He carried her across the hall and into his room, setting her on the wide bed. "Why not?"

"If I become pregnant, my usefulness to the Arch Mage will be lost. It was that way for Eliana. Apparently, when a woman shares her body with a baby, it renders her energy impervious to him."

Aren's eyes widened. "Hasn't this occurred to you as a possible solution to your problem?"

"I would like a baby," she said dreamily. "And I would like to avoid this fate, if I could . . ." Before she finished, Aren began unbuttoning his shirt. She sighed and closed her eyes. "But it wouldn't be right."

"Why not?" Aren tossed aside his shirt, then moved to unfasten his leggings. They felt tight across his arousal, and the perfect solution had unexpectedly presented itself.

"Eliana has a daughter. If I am rendered useless, he will simply seek her out. She is only a small child now—but he could take her captive and wait until she grows into womanhood."

Aren refastened his leggings and slumped onto the bed beside Cahira. "That would be a grim fate, indeed." He paused, groaning. "Then we really can't make love, you and I, lest we place Eliana's daughter in danger."

"I didn't think I could endure that solution, when Fareth first suggested I simply take a lover," said Cahira, but her gaze scanned his chest and she bit her lip. A giddy expression suffused her face. "But you are a strange temptation to me." She squirmed in the bed and he imagined every sweet ache that rippled through her—and everything he might have slowly done to assuage it.

She reached up and touched his chest. "You are so strong. The people of Amrodel speak of the brawn of the Norsk, but I hadn't imagined such an exquisite . . . Every portion of your body is strong and beautiful." Her fingers trickled down along his taut stomach, and he caught her hand.

"If you go any farther, my lady, you may find that the Norsk have unexpected weakness, too, in the area of self-restraint."

Her bright gaze fixed on his arousal, and her eyes widened. "Is that . . . *you?*"

He cleared his throat. "I don't know what else it would be."

Her gaze flicked to his face, then back to his groin. Her lips parted and a soft, shuddering breath tore through her. She looked like a wild creature in his bed, tempted and alive with desire. "I know something of this, but the sight fills me with such a strange sensation!"

"Don't tell me!" Aren pulled back the coverlet, and edged her beneath the woolen blanket. He adjusted the pillows, which were soft and filled with goose down, then lay down beside her.

"Your bed is much nicer than the one Ranveig gave the rest of us," she said.

"After I became chieftain, he fitted this room for me, for I often travel this way and I have favored the Snow Pony Inn since childhood."

"For its ale?" she asked, and snuggled closer to him. Strange, that such a defiant and prickly female could become so warm and sensual.

"I like the wild ponies. We found Zima's dam among them."

"I like ponies, too," said Cahira, and she yawned.

Aren gathered her into his arms, and she rested her head against his shoulder. She yawned again, and in the fading firelight he saw that her expression was content. "To think I found you hideous," she murmured. "When now I want to taste every part of you—it's as if you were some delectable meal designed by Fareth or Ranveig . . ." Her voice trailed off.

Aren waited a moment in silence, but her breathing slowed and she was soon asleep. The dark wizard would never penetrate her slumber now, nor torment her with nightmares. But for Aren, a long night would pass with the image of Cahira's soft lips tasting every part of his body. He couldn't help thinking nightmares would have been easier to endure.

6

THE JOURNEY SOUTH

"I cannot believe you slept with him!" Shaen gripped Cahira's arm and pinched, hard. "Cahira, what happened?"

"What do you mean, 'happened?'" Cahira asked, but she averted her eyes and began fiddling with the sleeve of her leather bodice. "*Nothing* happened."

"You must tell me everything. What did he do to you?"

"He didn't do anything." She paused. "Much."

Shaen groaned and released Cahira's arm. She looked shocked, and perhaps angry, but her expression soon switched back to sympathy. "I'm not angry, just terribly worried about you. When I found you asleep last night, I was sure you were safe. I should have been more alert. This is all my fault!"

"We did nothing that would disrupt my usefulness to the Arch Mage, if that's what you're worried about," said Cahira. "We just talked."

"Is that all?" Shaen's eyes darkened, and her gaze seemed to bore into Cahira.

"We kissed." A tiny shudder rippled through her at the memory. He was so tall and so strong, and his body felt so good next to hers.

"And you slept in his bed! Oh, Cahira, I can't imagine what you were thinking."

Cahira faced Shaen, and her own anger surfaced. "I was afraid, Shaen. There! Does that surprise you? Every night, the Arch Mage torments me in my dreams."

Shaen nearly crumpled with remorse. "I'm so sorry. I had no idea. But why didn't you tell me?"

"There was nothing you could have done."

"Surely more than that treacherous Norskman! I can be trusted with your fears. He cannot."

"I felt safe with him," Cahira said quietly. "I believe he is my friend."

"No doubt he wants you to think that." Shaen clasped her hand to her brow. "You mustn't let it happen again. I'm not sure why he spared you this time . . . unless . . . Did you tell him that you would be spoiled by pregnancy?"

"I didn't phrase it that way, but yes, I told him. What of it?"

Shaen hesitated as if her words came hard. "I fear he is enticed by the promise of the Arch Mage's power, and can't risk impregnating you. That would ruin everything for him. Why else would he restrain himself?"

"That's ridiculous! He knows what we're up against—and he certainly knows that the Arch Mage isn't apt to share power. He may doubt our methods, but he wants the same outcome that we do."

"It's impossible to know what he's thinking. The Norsk are so different from our people!" Shaen pressed her lips together. "I don't want to hurt you, but I'm so afraid this will end in disaster for you, and for all those back in Amrodel. If anything happens to you, all is lost."

Cahira turned her attention to the tea Ranveig had brought. "Damir has shielded me from all harm."

"Yes," agreed Shaen. "But his shield cannot protect you from those you have chosen to trust. The Norskman knows something this shield, too, for Damir used it on Eliana during that last battle. So he'll know its limitations—and he may seek to exploit them, if you let him."

"He wouldn't harm me. I know it."

Shaen's brow knit with concern. "You have to remember that the lure of the Arch Mage calls upon the secret desires and fears in everyone. The Norsk are renowned for seizing their advantage, and this man is, after all, their chieftain. Bruin the Ruthless believed he could control the Arch Mage's energy for his own purposes. Maybe his younger brother, who admits he admired Bruin, is finding that an attractive option, too."

Cahira felt weary, and she closed her eyes. *What does your heart tell you?* "He is stronger than you know," she whispered. "I feel it."

"I hope you're right," said Shaen, and she took a sip of tea, then placed her hand gently on Cahira's. "I do understand, Cahira. Truly, I do. I had never been in love nor known a man's embrace before I met your father." Cahira shifted in her seat; Shaen's affair with her father wasn't an entirely comfortable subject, and they had never discussed it directly before. "I was about your age when he first expressed interest in me. Oh, I resisted at first, naturally. He was married to your stepmother, though everyone knows their relationship wasn't what it should have been."

"I know that," said Cahira. "She was my mother's closest friend, and they married in grief soon after her death. Instead of joining in comfort, they were just lonely together."

"He needed my support, and I was so grateful to have his attention," Shaen explained. "You may not know it, but at one time, many in the Woodland believed I had a Mage's *ki*. I went to study with Madawc for a time, but it just wasn't there. I was so disappointed, as you can imagine. So when the king invited me to become his assistant, I learned to accept my own meager talents and appreciate what I could do for others. His love was a blessing for me, though I know many people disapproved. But he was always good to me, and I know I helped him, too." Tears welled in Shaen's dark eyes, and her voice grew thick with emotion. "It is for his sake that I must protect you. You father would be horrified to think a Norskman was attempting to seduce you, his most beloved daughter, and that you might actually succumb to such a person."

Cahira met Shaen's pleading gaze. "My father would approve of the man who avenged his death," she said.

Shaen offered a light laugh and fondly patted Cahira's hand. "You really are smitten, aren't you? You've elevated him to heroic proportions already, and he's done nothing but trim the hair on his face and wash! Oh, I admit, he's got quite a body . . ."

"Aren is more than that!"

Shaen leaned forward, her brows knit and her face serious, as if she intended to penetrate Cahira's deepest thoughts. "Is he, Cahira? Or are you just telling yourself that, when the truth is that what you really want from him is sex?"

Cahira stared at her in astonishment. "How strong is that tea, anyway?"

Shaen giggled, then lowered her voice in a conspiratorial tone. "If it weren't for our quest, I'd say to go ahead and enjoy every inch of that man—but don't tell yourself it's emotional when it's obviously just a physical attraction. You have to admit that you don't know him well enough for it to truly be anything deeper. You can't possibly trust him, and a good relationship such as Eliana and Damir's is based on trust."

Cahira angled her brow in disbelief. "She tried to steal his memory with a potion, he tricked her into drinking it herself and then told her she was his wife! Trust wasn't exactly the cornerstone of their romance."

Shaen smiled indulgently. "But unlike you and this Norskman, Eliana and Damir had so much in common, as Mages and peers, and they'd known each other since childhood. I'm sure you'll agree that trust became foremost in their relationship after they overcame those initial hurdles."

Cahira didn't like Shaen's argument, but in this, if nothing else, she might have a point. For now, her own purpose varied from Aren's, and though he had been supportive during the night, she wasn't sure he had fully accepted the course she felt destined to follow. He hadn't tried to change her mind, but there was still a long road ahead.

"Should I not give him—and everyone—the benefit of the doubt unless proven otherwise?"

"What an odd concept!" remarked Shaen, but then she offered a patient nod. "I think you're blinded by infatuation and the Norskman's sexual allure. I don't think you're seeing him for what he is."

"Do we truly see anyone for what they are? Surfaces are ever deceptive." Felix's gruff voice interrupted them, and Shaen overturned her teacup in surprise. Cahira looked around, and saw the bat on the floor beside the table.

"Felix! What are you doing down there? Don't you fly?"

He peered up at her impatiently. "If I fly around this place, I'm likely to be swatted down by one of these brutes." He hopped up onto the bench, then onto the table, suspiciously close to a loaf of bread. As she feared, he stuck a wing tip into the butter and tasted it. Shaen shuddered, but Cahira quickly broke him off a section of bread and placed a large pat of butter on a plate. Felix eyed her tea pointedly, and she poured him a cup.

"I'd think you risk being trodden on, if you're on the floor where no one can see you," said Cahira as he stuck his tongue into the tea.

"I'm quick on my feet," replied the bat. "And those brawny devils aren't moving much this morning, anyway." He looked around. "Where's the chieftain?"

"He's gone to ready our gear," said Cahira. "There was some argument between Fareth and Ranveig, predictably, about what to pack."

"What about the others? Elphin—and the hulking brute, the fighting wench, and that scrawny boy?"

"Elphin is readying the horses, and I think Rika followed him." Cahira paused to sigh. "They were already bickering when they left. I'm not sure where Thorleif is, though."

"I'm here!" announced the young Norskman as he

emerged from the kitchen. "I've been hunting for this cursed creature all morning, and now I find him, as I might have known, perched on a plate of food!"

"Felix needs breakfast, too, Thorleif," said Cahira.

The boy seated himself opposite the bat and glared. "Does he? Well, it looked to me, from the footprints and tooth marks on the pantry butter, that he's already taken more than his share!"

Cahira eyed Felix. "Did you sneak into the pantry, Felix?"

The bat looked up, unrepentant. "No, I didn't 'sneak' into the pantry! I *walked* in." He paused. "Helped myself to a little breakfast, until I heard this ornery youth charging around, calling out with no respect at all. Didn't even bother with my name." He cranked his head in Thorleif's direction. "In the future, boy, understand that I do not respond to 'filthy rodent'—I'm *not* a rodent—or 'miserable pest.'" He paused. "By the way, you snore, and I expect you to sleep on your side in the future, lest you disrupt my rest again."

Thorleif's eyes widened to icy blue pools of fury. "*I* snore? You sound like a herd of fat ponies charging over the snow dunes!" He whirled to face Cahira. "I see why you left him with us! The little devil perched on my headboard—couldn't have bedded in with the Woodlanders, of course! And whenever I happened to wake in the night, I'd see that round body right over my head and those pointy little ears . . ."

"That sounds somehow comforting to me," said Cahira, but she repressed a grin at the thought Felix had chosen Thorleif's bed as his resting perch.

"Does it?" Thorleif twitched with anger. "Well, then you haven't wondered where this foul creature defecates, have you?"

Shaen set aside her bread and sighed heavily, and Cahira fiddled with her hair. "No, I guess I haven't."

Felix spat out a small wad of bread, directed at Thorleif, then straightened indignantly. "My private functions shall remain private! You, boy, are speculating on matters that are none of your concern."

"It is if you're perching over my head!"

"I didn't think bats 'perched,'" said Cahira. "I thought they hung upside-down in caves."

"I am unique," said Felix, and no one argued. He took another bite of bread, then eyed Cahira. "So what's going on with you and the chieftain? Bit of mating, lass?"

Cahira winced and cringed, then blushed furiously. "If your 'private functions' are private, then so are mine! And we were simply . . . getting to know each other."

Thorleif's brow arched and he chuckled, but Shaen looked pained. "If that's what you call it," said the Norskman.

"Nothing happened! How does everyone know about this, anyway?"

"Well, with your friend here banging on all our doors trying to find you, then screaming when you emerged from the chieftain's bedroom, it was a little hard to miss." Thorleif looked at Shaen, then paused. "By the way, I understand you Woodlanders place wagers on this kind of thing."

"*No . . .* "

"So far, the wagers are fairly predictable," Thorleif continued. "I'm betting on the chieftain, but the Woodlanders favor you."

Cahira clasped her burning face in her hands. "Madawc warned me that one day I would suffer retribution for placing bets as a child."

"And he was right, lass," said the bat, speaking thickly around a mouthful of bread. "But it's your time in the light now. The Norskman seems like a good choice for a mate, I'd say. Good, strong build, straightforward manner. You'll pop forth a fine litter with that one!"

"This seems a little premature," said Cahira, fighting embarrassment. "We only just met, and barely know each other."

"My species mate immediately after formal introductions are made," Felix said.

"Well, we . . ." Cahira stopped. "Bats make formal introductions?"

He looked at her as if she were a simpleton. "Of course."

Thorleif stared at the bat, his mouth agape, then pointed his finger at Felix and glared. "We do not want to hear anything—*anything*—more about this subject from you, ever!"

Felix cocked his head to one side. "Afraid you might learn something, boy?"

"Yes! Something that will haunt me for the rest of my days!"

"I'm almost afraid to ask . . ." a voice came from behind Cahira. Aren. She started and bumped her tea, which splashed Felix.

"Watch it there, lass! Singed my fur, you did!"

"I'm sorry." She gulped, then allowed herself a glance at Aren. She repressed a groan when she saw him, and her skin tingled at the memory of his kiss. She knew her face flushed pink. He met her gaze briefly, enough for her to know he was thinking the same thing, then looked around at the others. Cahira couldn't tear her eyes away. If the night had favored him with a stirring beauty, the morning sun streaming through the tavern windows was kinder. There was something mesmerizing about the way he moved, with such contained power. He was . . . straightforward, just as Felix said. And so handsome!

What if Shaen was right? Cahira couldn't deny her attraction to Aren, nor that her pulse sped up whenever he was near. He stood behind her, placed his hand casually on her shoulder.

"I had to relent and allow Ranveig and Fareth separate cooking gear," he said, "though it seems a waste to carry the extra items. Stubborn men, they are. I would have thought them brothers."

She glanced up at him. "I thought the same thing."

He smiled. "Let's keep that to ourselves, shall we?"

She smiled, too. "That would seem for the best."

"She doesn't *look* pregnant," observed Felix. Cahira's shoulders scrunched forward and her eyes closed tight.

Aren's hand remained on her shoulder, but she didn't dare look at his reaction.

"I think it's safe to assume she is not," he said calmly.

"Got to be a certain season, does it, my lord?" asked the bat. "That's convenient! Wish it were so for my species. A female bat can conceive at any time of the year, day or night. They're a bit *testier* during the light hours, but that's when you catch them sleeping. Good time to get a jump on them."

"I warned you, bat!" Thorleif jumped to his feet, spun to face Aren. "Do we have to take him with us, lord?"

"He is my guide!" said Cahira. "Of course we have to take him!"

"The bat might be useful," agreed Aren. "If we need a lookout in the dark . . ." He eyed the bat. "I assume you can see in the dark?"

"Of course!" Felix sounded proud. "My eyes can see where even a torch casts no shadow. Indeed, my talents will be invaluable in those caverns."

"Yes, he can help us find our way to the Arch Mage's hold," said Cahira, without much enthusiasm. "Of course, no one has been down there in an age. The way may not even be passable."

Felix hopped onto her shoulder. "Of course it will be passable, lass! Do you think that devil has sent out his dark force, knocked out all the Mages, and put every effort into pulling you there and hasn't thought to clear the way?"

"I suppose not." Cahira paused. "I wonder how he intended to get me there if his plan had succeeded and I'd been immobilized like the other Mages?"

"That's a good question, lass," said Felix. "But I'd say it seems reasonable he had someone lined up to get you there."

"And coming here must have thrown them off," she guessed.

"That might be, lass." Felix paused. "But then again, it might not."

Bodvar entered the room, and his expression darkened when he saw Aren standing close to Cahira. "My lord, the horses are ready," he said, but his gaze fixed on his chieftain's hand.

"If you've all taken your fill of breakfast, we should go," said Aren. He eyed Shaen. "I have found a trader who is willing to escort this female to Amon Dhen, where she can easily make her way back to Amrodel."

Shaen blanched, and Cahira winced at Aren's blunt disclosure. Shaen turned to Cahira, her expression plaintive. "You can't mean to leave me behind! Only I have knowledge of the Arch Mage's domicile."

Aren slapped a parchment on the table in front of Shaen, then produced a vial of ink and a quill. "Draw a map."

Shaen reached for the quill, her hand trembling, and tears welled in her eyes. Cahira endured a stab of guilt. "It does seem wisest, Shaen," she said. "Our journey will grow increasingly dangerous from here. You'd be much safer back in Amrodel."

"I understand, of course," said Shaen in a quavering voice. "It's just that I have such a hard time conveying the images in my mind onto paper. Madawc always said I'd have been his best student, if only I could have translated my thoughts into print."

Felix angled his head and eyed her doubtfully, but mercifully, he made no comment. Cahira couldn't recall any time when Madawc had issued flattery of any kind, but she felt fairly certain Shaen wasn't among his brightest students.

Shaen attempted to draw a map of the Arch Mage's domain, but it soon became apparent that her skill was lacking. She began a large square, then crossed it out and tried again. She took a quick breath, and began a long series of winding lines, which she again crossed out. Aren issued a low groan, then snatched the parchment away from her.

"You couldn't draw a map getting us out of this inn, let alone through the wizard's lair!"

Cahira frowned at Aren. "Must you be so tactless?"

He appeared unmoved. "You're trusting her to guide you

through a palace that was once the size of a city, and she can't draw even a rudimentary map?"

Shaen bowed her head. "I'm sorry. I can see it as clearly as if been there, but it's so hard to draw out as you request. When I'm there, I'm sure I can find the right passages. But I just don't have the skill to draw it accurately."

Aren frowned. "We'll have to remember to bring extra supplies for that leg of the journey, then. I don't think we can count on her direction."

Shaen straightened her back and met Aren's icy gaze. "I know you don't respect my abilities. And I know I'm not as powerful as a Mage or one of your mighty Norsk warriors. But I have a clear picture in my mind of the Arch Mage's palace." Her eyes filled with tears. "I do have something to offer the party, even if you don't value it."

Cahira eyed Shaen's attempted map, and her heart felt heavy with the weight of pity, a pity which didn't seem to move Aren at all. "We just didn't want to place you in further danger, Shaen. I'm sure your memory will be helpful."

Shaen's chin trembled. "I know *you* are concerned about me," she replied with a sniffle, but then she cast a dark glance at Aren. "Some, however, might find it advantageous to have me out of the way."

Aren didn't deny her intimation. "I did well enough last night."

Cahira looked at him in surprise, then twisted her lips into a frown. He was deliberately baiting Shaen, taunting her with his presumed success upon luring Cahira to his room. Shaen nodded as if Aren's intentions were just what she had feared. "You can't leave me behind, Cahira. I think it's obvious that you need me—for my knowledge of the Arch Mage's palace . . . and for other issues that may crop up as we go along. . . ."

Cahira hesitated. Shaen's warnings had already grown tiresome, but neither did Cahira relish the thought of wandering lost in the mountain palace. She understood Shaen's

skepticism concerning Aren—none of the others trusted
him, either. Once he had proven himself, as Cahira believed
he would, their doubts would disappear. "You can continue
with us, Shaen, if you are prepared for the dangers that may
await," she said at last.

"The only thing I'm concerned about is you," said Shaen,
but then she smiled. "And if you left me behind, I'd just have
to follow you!"

Aren's eyes narrowed as if she'd leveled a threat, but
Shaen laughed. "I'm afraid my tracking abilities can't compare to a Norskman's, so I'm relieved you've decided against
that course."

"For now," said Aren.

"We need her, and she wants to help," argued Cahira.
Aren could be a very stubborn man.

"The morning grows late," he replied, and he sounded
both sullen and grumpy. "It is time to ride out."

Aren left and Cahira rose to follow him, but Bodvar
blocked her way. "I know what you have done, witch," he
said, in a low voice so that only she heard. As much as Shaen
annoyed Aren, Bodvar irritated Cahira more.

She looked up at him, annoyed. "Is that so? Well, I've
done nothing. . . ." She started past him, but he caught her
arm and held her back.

"Deny it if you will, but know this: The Norsk lost one
great chieftain to the powers of wizardry. We will not lose
another."

They rode southeast for five days, and only the landscape
changed as they progressed. Aren listened wearily as Ranveig and Fareth engaged in another argument over the up-
coming evening meal, and Elphin and Rika bickered
over . . . something. He'd lost track of their reasons for dis-
pute after the second day. Thorleif and Felix also battled
constantly, with the bat having a slight edge, and an equal
determination to sleep in as close a proximity to Thorleif's
head as he possibly could, generally on a branch just over-

hanging the youngster's bedding. But when Aren suggested that Thorleif select a spot that didn't sprawl beneath a tree or rocky outcrop, the boy insisted there was no such place, though the rest of the party had managed to avoid obvious perches.

Shaen stuck by Cahira's side like a spiny burr, and Bodvar seemed equally intent on protecting Aren from her mystical allure. Like all Norskmen, Bodvar feared the invisible workings of magic, but his dislike of Cahira seemed particularly strong. Cahira herself had grown quieter, and he saw the doubt growing in her eyes. He knew the dark wizard called to her, and so when they stopped for the night, Aren laid his pad near to Cahira, despite Shaen's objections, and before she fell asleep, he would whisper so that only she could hear, *"I am with you."*

He battled an unseen foe, and one he didn't fully understand. Still, he refused to let this evil energy torment Cahira further—but each day, he could see it growing stronger, for she grew quieter and more withdrawn. The sun waned as the fifth day drew to a close, and he rode beside her. Pip had proven adept on the trail, picking a good path over the rocky ground. They had reached an area where the snow was all but gone, and the weather had turned warmer, though a steady wind came up from the south and howled across the plains.

"Are we near the Guerdian territory yet?" asked Cahira.

Aren gestured at the foothills to the east. "Yonder lies the border of their land, and tomorrow we will begin the winding path into their hills. We will rest tonight in the foothills, where we will find shelter from the wind, if not from danger."

"Is this the area occupied by the 'rogue bands' Thorleif mentioned?"

"Yes. From now on, we will have to beware," he answered. "It will be wise to set a watch until we reach the safety of the Guerdian Hold."

"You did that on purpose! Vile wench!" Elphin cursed at Rika, but Aren didn't bother to look back. He glanced at Cahira and sighed.

"Our group doesn't seem to be finding common ground as I'd hoped," he said.

She just gazed out across the plains and sighed. "It's not their fault."

"They could try to find the good aspects of each other. I don't understand it. Normally, Rika is as cool as . . . well, ice. No one appreciates hearty laughter like Ranveig. And in another time, I would have sworn Thorleif would have converted your bat into a pet by now. He loves animals—a talking one should be a dream come true."

Cahira shook her head. "It's the darkness, the tide of negative energy that moves in around us. As we draw closer, it grows stronger. They all feel it, even if they don't know what it is." She glanced at Aren. "Don't you?"

"No," he replied. "I've never felt the darkness of which you speak. Even when it infected my people and my brother, I didn't understand until Damir explained to me what it was."

"It never affected you?" she asked in surprise.

"No."

"He's lying!" Shaen spoke up from behind Cahira. Aren looked back, but her wide mouth formed a smile despite her angry tone. "Perhaps you don't mean to deceive us, but what you say cannot be true. The dark energy emanating from the Arch Mage reaches everyone. It comes on currents of amazing power, to Mage and Mundane alike. It has obviously infected your people, so there's no possibility that you are somehow immune."

Cahira looked between them, her brow furrowed. Aren knew she doubted him. She said, "How is it possible that you don't feel this energy? It is around us all, probing, seeking . . ."

"What does it seek?" he asked.

Cahira considered. "Our weaknesses, I suppose. Fear and doubt, anger and resentment, lust and desire."

"I have had all those emotions," he admitted. "Some more than others of late," he added with a grin.

She caught his meaning and a little smile curved her

lips—lips he longed to taste again, to savor as he learned each curve of her body. They looked into each other's eyes, and he knew they were thinking the same thing. She blushed, and he laughed.

"Perhaps he simply doesn't recognize the Arch Mage's energy," said Shaen. "If so, you're very lucky. The darkness is a weight to those of us with more sensitive natures."

"In what way does this dark force trouble you, then?" Aren asked.

"It is especially hard for me," said Shaen. "Fortunately, I don't have the more negative emotions such as anger or resentment, but of course, I have terrible fear, especially when the outcome is so uncertain."

"And you don't trust me," added Aren. "You think I'll take this sword and . . . what? Pledge the allegiance of my people to this wizard when he rises?"

Shaen bowed her head. "I just don't feel sure of anything. It's probably the effect of the evil energy, and you have no such motives." She obviously didn't intend to confront him head-on with her suspicions. "I'm afraid that nothing we do will make any difference, and our fate will be sealed in that dark cavern."

"What an uplifting companion," commented Aren, but Cahira gave him a reproachful look.

"I'm sorry to be so negative," said Shaen sadly. "But you have admitted to all of the most unsavory emotions. I am simply admitting my own flaws. I see no difference."

"But I own my unsavory emotions," replied Aren. "Every one of them. Especially lust." He paused to wink at Cahira, and she winced, but her smile remained. "I do not attribute them to some unseen force."

"Perhaps you really are stronger than the rest of us," Shaen said. "Maybe the dark energy can't get past those muscles of yours!" She sounded friendly, even flirtatious, but he recognized false flattery. He hadn't considered her one way or another, but Thorleif had mentioned her more than once, referring to her as 'pretty,' and she had been kind to the youth. And with much suspicion as Bodvar had for Cahira, he was polite to Shaen, helping her when they dismounted and setting out her gear for the night. In turn, she'd been sweet and shy with him, relying on Bodvar's greater strength for tasks Aren felt sure she could have handled herself.

It occurred to Aren suddenly that he disliked Shaen, and had from the first, and he wondered why Cahira trusted her. Apparently, there was some connection to Cahira's family.

"You're not related by blood, are you?" he asked, hoping not.

"Shaen was my father's mistress," said Cahira. He looked at her in surprise, and Shaen caught her breath, apparently unused to such blunt declarations. Her eyes flashed with irritation, but her smile remained.

"I suppose if your own relationship has been up for discussion, there's no need to conceal my own past," she replied, and she turned to Aren. "Cahira's father, the late king, and I had a special relationship. He was heartbroken when Cahira's mother died, and remarried her dearest friend in haste—a disastrous union based on grief alone. He needed me, desperately, and we became close in many ways. Perhaps it was more friendship than anything."

"Ah," said Aren. Zima had lengthened her stride as if the woman annoyed her, too, and Cahira paid no attention, leaving Aren the single focus of Shaen's reminiscences.

Shaen took note of Cahira's position, then lowered her voice; though riding just behind them Bodvar might still overhear her words. "This is a delicate subject, and I wouldn't want Cahira to think ill of her father. His death was a terrible tragedy, like your brother's, and it devastated her. I think she's taken on this impossible quest to make up for her failure when he was murdered—though of course she was only twelve, and could do nothing to save him. But sometimes she can be so blind and determined no matter what the cost to others, just as she's done by involving you and your people."

Cahira, as defined by Shaen . . . Aren shook his head. "Cahira strikes me as an exceptionally strong woman," he said. "With a rare beauty and even more unusual courage."

Bodvar huffed. "She's certainly a woman of strange power," he said. "What we saw at the Great Hall could turn a man's blood to ice. Her beauty makes her all the more dangerous."

Shaen glanced back at him, her expression sympathetic. "I am only a Mundane, with no magical energy," she said, "so I understand the fear some have of Mages. Great power, they say, breeds great temptation. But not in Cahira, of course," she added hastily when Bodvar's jaw line hardened. It was as if she had confirmed his worst suspicions.

"Is it not the lack of power which breeds an even greater temptation?" asked Aren. "The desire for more, for what we do not possess by nature?"

"But those of us who are weak are less capable of doing great wrongs," answered Shaen. "I've seen how hasty and reckless Mages can be. And . . . though Cahira's father was king, he wasn't a Mage. Of his children, Cahira was the only Mage, and he doted on her terribly. Perhaps that's why she's so used to getting her way."

Bodvar shook his head. Aren gazed ahead at Cahira, who sat straight and alert on Zima's back, her head high as she surveyed the landscape. He said, "A woman who would place herself willingly on the dangerous path Cahira has chosen is unlikely to suffer from a sense of over-entitlement, nor does she seemed spoiled by this 'doting' you mention."

"Oh, but you don't know her the way I do," said Shaen, smiling fondly. "Such a strong-willed girl, she was—and still is. You don't want to get in her way when she's set on something!" She paused to laugh. "But I guess you've discovered that firsthand."

"There's very little I wouldn't give her," said Aren. Bodvar frowned.

To Aren's surprise, Shaen nodded approvingly. "Then she's a very lucky girl." She gazed into the distance as if an old memory troubled her, and she sighed. "I wish it had been so for me. . . ."

"Wasn't it?" he asked casually. He noticed Bodvar listening with interest and unaccustomed sympathy.

Shaen glanced at Cahira and pressed her lips together. "I wouldn't want Cahira to know this, because she was devoted to her father, but I know you'll understand that as his"— Shaen paused as if shy—"as his erotic pursuits turned ever darker, my innocence was lost."

"Indeed?" Aren resisted the impulse to ask if either she or the king had come out of these pursuits with scars.

"I tried to resist, of course. But it was my duty to please him, and so I submitted." The words she spoke were clearly meant to be tragic; and yet, he knew she was trying to arouse him with her supposed weakness, and with the image of a young woman ensnared by erotic pursuits. It didn't seem to occur to Shaen that a strong woman with strong desires intrigued him far more.

Her furtive gaze shifted from his face to his body, and back again, which Aren acknowledged with a slight nod. He knew exactly where this was going, though he had never been approached in so covert a manner before. Norsk women were far more direct in pursuit of pleasure. Aren glanced at Bodvar, but the man had fallen behind and must have missed her quiet words.

Aren considered his response. "Some say the darker pleasures prove more rewarding," he said in a low voice.

She dampened her lips and drew a quick breath. "Though I gave myself to the king, he often left me unfulfilled and lonely."

Aren recognized an old reaction in himself, and it surprised him. It was the same strange rush of energy he had called upon many times in battle, when he faced an opponent whose weapon was hidden, their skill as yet unknown. He leaned toward Shaen slightly, and Pip stiffened as if sensing danger. "Then I can promise you one thing, Shaen . . ."

He lowered his voice still more, and it became darkly sensual, evenly dangerous.

She looked into his face, and it seemed to him that her eyes were like dark windows with the shutters on the inside. "What?" She sounded breathless with expectation, and perhaps the thrill of an imminent victory.

The glow of battle filled him, and his voice was sharp like a warrior's blade. "I will never leave Cahira Daere unfulfilled and lonely. You have my word."

Shaen recoiled and her dark eyes snapped with anger, but even as Aren urged Pip into a canter to catch up with Cahira, he heard the woman begin to laugh as if they had been joking all along. But Aren knew better. It had been war. And victory was his.

"Why do you trust that woman?" Aren asked Cahira. He kept Pip's pace fast, which encouraged Zima to the same, and the others in the party had fallen significantly behind.

Cahira looked back and then angled her brow at him. "What's your hurry? At this rate, we'll reach our planned campsite an hour before them."

"Not a bad idea," he admitted. "I've been thinking about you a lot today."

A little smile curved her lips. "I also have been distracted. But what are you talking about? What woman? Do you mean Shaen?"

"It seems the dark force is affecting her a great deal," he said, then paused. "Do you consider this woman a friend?"

"I suppose so." Cahira glanced back and looked uncomfortable, and a little guilty. "She's always tried so hard to be nice to me. When I was a child, I disliked her intensely, but she was so distraught over my father's murder that I began to feel sorry for her. And she never blamed me, even though I had a chance to save him."

Aren nodded, but it seemed all too likely that Shaen had reminded Cahira of that "chance" at every opportunity. "I could have saved my brother," he told her. "I carry that with me, even now. I know that Damir was right when he said Bruin carved his own fate, but had I used wisdom instead of trying to stop him in battle, I might have been able to convince him to alter his path."

"Bruin the Ruthless didn't sound like a man easily altered by wisdom," she suggested. "Even yours."

"Possibly not," he agreed. "But tell me, what is the nature of your friendship with your father's mistress?"

She looked wary. "I'm not sure, exactly."

"They can't hear you at this distance. And it interests me."

"I can't imagine why."

"*You* interest me," he explained.

A tiny smile curved her lips. "I don't want to be ungrateful to Shaen, but I've often been sorry she came on this journey. I find her rather tedious and depressing, though that may be the effect of the Dark Tide, which seems to afflict everyone but you."

"Does it affect you?" he asked. "I haven't seen much evidence of it, not like as is glaringly obvious with the others."

Her lips twisted. "I don't know. I assumed it affected me like everyone else, but I still feel hope and joy." She paused and looked shy. "And other things. The nightmares affect me, but that, I believe, is direct communication with the Arch Mage and not a result of his Dark Tide. I know it's there, almost like a fog rolling in, but it hasn't altered my mood as it has the others. I do feel doubt, but I'm not sure if that's the Dark Tide or Shaen. She never offers much insight, and always manages to confuse my thoughts."

"About me?"

"About you, yes. About everything. And when I speak with her, I tend to feel guilty. I loved my father, but he was a simple man and I felt closer to Damir and Eliana, as well as the Elder Mage Madawc. Part of my guilt from the night he was murdered is because I had run off to tell Damir and Eliana about a suspicious conversation I'd overheard."

"That seems reasonable," said Aren, but she shook her head.

"The truth is, I just wanted to be with them. And later, after he died, I sometimes felt bad because I was happier with Madawc than I ever had been at the palace."

"This old Mage understood you, I would guess."

"Yes, he did. And he was interesting, too. We had such wonderful conversations, and such fun. I feel sympathy for Shaen, but I don't find her very interesting or bright."

"She may not be intelligent, but she is crafty, Cahira. You would be wise to remember it."

She looked at him in surprise. "Why do you say that?"

He contemplated telling her about Shaen's covert attempt to tempt him with veiled references to carnal darkness. She had been seeking sexual weakness, and she assumed the hint of dark erotica would appeal to a ruthless Norskman. He knew she didn't want him, what she wanted was a conquest.

He wasn't sure why he saw through Shaen's veneer so easily, but he recognized a formidable opponent, even if he couldn't guess her true motivation. That would make itself clear eventually. But for now, Cahira had no reason to believe him. "Just take care how much you reveal to her."

"She says the same thing about you."

"I'm sure she does. And it is up to you to decide which of us speaks the truth, which of us is truly your friend. There will be a choice between us, whether you see it coming or not. Will you trust me, whom you desire yet fear, or Shaen?"

"Shaen has no reason to harm me." Cahira paused. "I can't imagine that she could, even if she tried. I am much stronger."

"A bee can bring down an ox—"

"I hope you're not comparing me to an ox!"

"You are just as direct—and as lacking in subtlety," he responded. "But far, far more beautiful."

"Thank you!" She gazed heavenward. "No one can accuse you of flattery, that much is certain."

"You believe I think you are beautiful, do you not?"

She shrugged, too casually. "Perhaps you do." She paused. "But I am taller than Eliana and not so . . . well, voluptuously shaped. And my hair is darker. I have always thought her the most beautiful woman in Amrodel."

"But you look much the same," he told her, and she brightened.

"Do you think so?"

"I do," he said with a smile. "Save the eyes. Hers are green, as I recall, and yours are as blue as the sky on Midsummer's Day. I saw that when I first met you, when you were perched like an angel above me, high on your father's balcony. You were the most beautiful thing I'd ever seen."

She beamed with happiness. "I thought you were an angel, too."

"Far from it, I fear."

"In looks, at least. You may try to hide your beauty, Aren son of Arkyn, but it shines through."

To his surprise he blushed, and he hurried to make his point. "So on the most shallow level, we approve of each other. That is good. It makes kissing so much easier."

She laughed, and bit her lip when she looked at him. "I like you," she said.

"I see that. I like you, too."

"I feel very foolish. I don't know why—as if I'm spinning and my feet haven't touched the ground. Dizzy, almost."

"Is that my effect on you, or is it time we stopped for the night?"

Her eyes glittered. "Both. But I am not so very tired."

He gestured to the lower foothills rising up before them. "Those hills are still a hour's ride from here. There's an interesting spot you may enjoy, if I can remember how to find it. I think we should shorten that distance and let the others catch up when they can."

7

THE HIDDEN SPRING

They settled the horses for the night and, as had become customary, Zima dove directly into Pip's meal, and Pip eased his way over to hers. Aren gazed at the plains below. "The others are a half hour back, at least. That gives us more time alone."

Cahira's pulse raced with excitement. "What is this 'interesting spot' you mentioned?"

He looked around, then gestured to an rocky outcrop. "This way." He took her hand and led her through huge boulders and around low, spiky shrubs. They climbed a little way, then Aren pointed. "There!"

She looked past him and saw an odd little pool adjacent to a small waterfall. "It's steaming!"

"There's an underground fissure," he told her. "It warms the water even in winter. Come . . . I think you'll find it enjoyable."

A circle of dragonflies skimmed the water's surface, and one rose up among them, larger than the rest. Cahira stared in amazement. "Look!"

"I see it," he said in wonder. "It is early yet in the season for insects."

"If I didn't know it was impossible, I would swear that is the same dragonfly that appeared to me before I left Amrodel on this journey!"

"It may be," said Aren. "These creatures have mystical powers, though until now I hadn't thought they extended beyond the Woodland realm."

Its wings were lavender, and the dragonfly circled one way then the other; then it disappeared. "It *was* the same one," said Cahira. "And it flew away south."

Aren gazed southward and for a moment looked pensive, but then he turned back to her. "Come."

She followed him to the edge of the pool, where she hesitated. "It's not big enough for swimming. What do we do?"

"It's a good place to relax after a long day's ride. My friends and I discovered this spot on a scouting party." Aren pulled off his leather jerkin and tossed it aside. He laid his axe, his Norsk horn, and the Dragonfly Sword on a boulder, then removed his boots as Cahira watched nervously. He pulled off his linen shirt, and she gulped. He glanced at her and smiled. "Come on."

Cahira stared. The setting sun glinted on his wide chest, and her knees felt weak at the sight. "Isn't it a little cold to be . . . without clothes?" Her voice sounded suspiciously high, and she swallowed hard.

"We Norsk don't feel the cold as you do," he said, and the corners of his mouth curved in a smile. "Nor are we shy about our bodies. Perhaps you require my help."

He didn't wait for her answer. He came to her, then touched her shoulders. Cahira trembled, but she didn't try to stop him. She wasn't sure she wanted to. He unlaced her bodice and drew it off, then tossed it near his jerkin. She wore only a soft cotton chemise beneath, laced with a satin ribbon. He untwined the laces and eased it gently apart.

She held her breath and closed her eyes, but he kissed her forehead softly and she looked up at him. She'd expected his desire, but the tenderness in his face astounded her. "You are beautiful, Cahira Daere," he whispered, and suddenly her nervousness dissipated and she felt safe.

"Like you, Aren son of Arkyn."

He slipped her chemise down over her arms and it slithered to the ground by her feet. The cool air met her skin and she shivered. Aren ran his hands down her arms, then untied her leggings. "I didn't remember that Woodland women wear these," he said, and his voice sounded raw and husky despite the supposed Norsk ease at nudity.

"Eliana did, when traveling," she answered. "It seems more practical than flowing gowns," she added. "I have gowns, of course . . ." Her leggings slid down around her feet, and her voice caught. "I'm *naked*. Not a little naked. A lot."

Aren's gaze shifted slowly from her head to her feet, and he drew a ragged breath. "Yes. You are." His jaw clenched, but he offered a polite smile.

"Are we going to get into the pool?" she asked. Her voice had reached a higher pitch than ever before.

"Good idea." He hesitated, then removed his own leggings. One quick glance told her he was aroused, and considerably larger in his male extremity than she'd previously imagined. He turned and held out his hand for her. "Ready?"

She stood motionless, but then she saw his gentle smile, and her confidence returned. "I am." She gave him her hand, and he led her into the water.

"It feels hot at first," he warned, "but you get used to it. Then it's incredible."

Aren sank down into the water and motioned for her to join him. The waterfall had carved a giant boulder into a bowl, which was smooth beneath her feet. Cahira puffed a quick breath, then lowered herself into water beside him.

"This is very nice!" she said. They looked at each other for a moment, then dissolved into each other's arms.

She wasn't sure if he kissed her first, or if she kissed him, but her pulse throbbed as her body pressed against his. He was warm, his skin slick, and every hesitation she had disap-

peared. He took her waist, then eased her onto his lap facing
him. She gasped, gripping his strong shoulders to steady
herself. An ache grew inside her, like a fire beneath the
earth, and a blind desire took hold of her. Aren kissed her
face and her neck, and she felt his whole body grow taut.

The sun set around them, and while the shadows lengthened across the pool, the water remained hot. Cahira tasted
Aren's lips, then his neck and the firm flesh of his shoulder.
Her hair fell loose around her, and he eased it back from her
face. He slid his hands down her arms, then slowly over her
breasts. He toyed with the little peaks, and she bit back a cry
of pleasure, then kissed his mouth again. She ran her tongue
along his lips, slid it over his. Aren groaned and pulled her
closer, and she felt his sex against her thigh. She squirmed at
the touch, and she knew where she wanted him, and at this
moment, nothing else mattered. She forgot the quest and all
she had sworn, just for the sake of drawing him closer.

"You test my restraint, Lady," he said.

"And mine own," she replied in a whisper. A languorous
sigh shuddered through her. "Didn't you say you were 'adept
at preventing conception'?"

"Aye, I said it." He sucked in a tight breath. "But there is
always a risk." He paused. "There are other ways we might
satisfy each other."

She slipped her hands between them and wrapped her fingers around his thick shaft. "Like this?" Instinct drove her,
and she moved against him so that his arousal pressed between her thighs. His breath became ragged, and he cupped
her bottom then arched so that his length moved against her
most sensitive spot.

He drew back and looked at her, and his amber eyes darkened to a rich, earthen brown. "How do you know this?" he
asked. He sounded hoarse and breathless. "You, an angel,
have the touch of a courtesan."

Cahira drew a quick breath. "I learned it in the tavern."
She kissed him again, but Aren's eyes widened.

"In the tavern?"

"I spent a lot of time there growing up, though I wasn't supposed to." She squeezed her fingers around his shaft, eased her palm along its length.

A hoarse groan tore from Aren's throat, and he leaned back against the rock wall. "Time well spent," he gasped.

"I overheard a lot there," she agreed, and she swirled her palm over his slick, hard sex and loved the feel of him. "I figured out the rest on my own." Cahira paused. "Do you like this?"

He looked at her and appeared stunned. "Um . . . *yes.*"

"Good!" She bent forward and kissed his neck, then sucked gently. She moved her hand more rapidly around him, and his hips arched. His eyes closed as he surrendered to her ministrations. A wild thrill coursed through her, centering between her legs, but filling her utterly. He was so strong and beautiful, and all that he was seemed bent to her will. To join with him would be heaven, an ecstasy beyond her most erotic fantasies.

"You have a very active mind, Lady Mage," he murmured.

She ran the tip of her finger around the blunt end of his length, then leaned forward to kiss his shoulder. "I do. And so much of it, for so long, has been centered on you."

His eyes popped open. "How long?"

"Oh, years and years," she said breathlessly. "As long as I can remember thinking of such things. Which is quite a while, actually."

He stared at her in disbelief. "You fantasized about me?"

She nodded eagerly. "I did, all the time. Eliana and Damir spoke of you often, and I imagined what you would look like as a man."

"Is that why you were shocked by my appearance?"

Cahira laughed, then nodded. "You weren't exactly what I expected. But somehow, what you are is so much more stirring to my blood than anything I could imagine." She paused and touched his cheek. "You are so strong—like a warrior-god—and yet so tender."

He appeared moved by her confession, and he ran his fingers through her damp hair. "My beautiful, sweet Cahira."

"I was so disappointed when I learned that you'd moved your people farther north! For a long while, I hoped you would visit Amrodel." She paused. "It is for that reason I do indeed keep a collection of pretty gowns, so that I could receive you to best effect."

"Had I known what awaited me, I would have ridden day and night to get there," he said, but then he drew her into his arms and kissed her forehead. "And all the while I dreamt of a blue-eyed witch who came to me in the night and made love to me until we couldn't move."

Delight filled her, and Cahira wrapped her arms around his neck. "We had the same dreams!"

"And we are sharing it now," he whispered. Again he kissed her. Happiness flooded through Cahira, and she slid her hand down his stomach and—

"Lord Chieftain!" Thorleif's cry startled them both, and Aren cursed. "Where are you, my lord?"

"Cahira! Lass, are you all right?" Fareth's voice boomed after Thorleif's. The innkeeper sounded out of breath.

Aren groaned, and Cahira hopped backward and fell off his lap. She splashed into the water, but Aren pulled her out and picked her up. He carried her out of the water, and she squealed and shivered in the cold evening air. He grabbed her clothing and tossed it to her, then dressed himself rapidly, cursing all the while.

Cahira shivered violently, and her hands shook as she tried to pull on her leggings. Her chemise stuck to her damp body and her wet hair fell in her face. She tripped and stumbled, and Aren caught her. They looked at each other, and she laughed. "Well, doesn't *this* look suspicious!" His hair fell in disheveled tangles around his face, and he'd buttoned his shirt wrong. Cahira fixed his buttons, and he fiddled with her hair. As Thorleif bounded up over the rocks, she grabbed her bodice and held it in front of her.

The Norskman held his axe in attack position as he leapt

forward, but then stopped short. He looked around, then back at Aren. "Lord?"

"Is there a reason you're swinging that axe, Thorleif?" Aren asked.

"The lady Shaen said she saw rogues!" Thorleif eyed their disheveled state, then smacked his lips. "Must have been mistaken."

Fareth charged up, panting, his round face red from exertion. He gripped a flat pan like a mace. "Where are they? Did you get the devils?"

Thorleif looked uncomfortable, and Cahira followed Aren up the crest. "We're fine, Fareth. We just got here before you and . . ." She felt her face warming but kept her voice even. "We found this little pool and washed our . . . faces and hands, and that sort of thing."

"I *see*," said Fareth. He paused and looked between them. "Didn't force you into this 'washing,' did he?"

"Of course not! No one forces me into anything."

"You got a point there, lass. Better be minding my own business, then," Fareth said. "And best get ourselves back to the campsite you laid out. Saw your horses hooked up all comfortable, but didn't catch a sight of you."

Aren glanced at Cahira and shrugged. "We're fine."

Bodvar came around a boulder from another direction and stopped short. One glance told Cahira that the older warrior was not pleased. No doubt he believed she'd used her "witch's wiles" to seduce Aren. She met his accusing gaze evenly. "Aren was just showing me this . . . interesting spot. We've only been here a minute or two."

"Enough to get plenty wet, I'd say," said Thorleif, but then he blushed furiously as he realized how this sounded. Cahira blushed, too, but Aren grinned.

"Shaen feared you were in danger," said Bodvar grimly. "It may be she was right."

"We're both unscathed," replied Aren. Cahira glared.

"If you're implying that he's in danger from me . . ."

"Implying?" said Bodvar. "No. I'm saying it outright; you

are a danger to our chieftain. You would lure him to his death—" He paused and his eyes raked angrily over her disheveled attire. "With whatever power you have."

Aren's eyes darkened with anger. "That's enough, Bodvar."

The Norskman banged his fist against his axe handle. "You've always had a soft spot for these Mages, but this one will lead you to your doom!" he snapped.

"All Mages are not the same, any more than all Norskmen," said Cahira.

Bodvar's light eyes blazed. "But a Norskman cannot enslave another's will, nor chant a spell that will make the dead rise and fight with a blood-red dagger piercing his back!"

He referred to Bruin's grim end, and Cahira looked away. This, Aren had witnessed as a boy of only fourteen.

"Evil acts are everywhere," said Aren quietly. "They are not the sole domain of either Mage or Norskman. Come, let us go."

They headed down the path from the spring, but while Bodvar reverted to silence, Thorleif chattered. "I told Shaen you could handle a rogue party on your own, my lord," said Thorleif, "but the lady was terrified. She insisted she'd seen 'shadowy shapes.'"

Aren frowned. "Shaen." He rolled his eyes. "I should have known. Next time I decide to bathe, I'm getting an hour's head start."

They returned to the campsite and found Shaen pacing nervously by the dropped gear. Rika stood by the horses, and Felix was perched on the cooking gear. Shaen clasped her hand to her breast when she saw them, but Aren faced her with a cold expression. "The rogues, it seems, were phantoms."

"I was sure I'd seen something," Shaen said hurriedly. "And we were all so worried."

"I was not," said Rika. "Even if she had seen rogues, which I consider unlikely since they are skilled at ambush and avoid detection, I knew the chieftain could defeat them." The Norskwoman paused, casting a dark glance at Cahira. "Even with no help."

Cahira frowned. "I am perfectly capable of battling rogues!"

Rika picked up the discarded bow that Cahira had left by the horses when she arrived. "Without this? I don't think you'd be much use unarmed."

Cahira's shoulders slumped, and tears of shame started unexpectedly in her eyes. Rika was right; she had been so distracted by her desire for Aren that she hadn't thought of self-defense. "You're right. I'm sorry."

"We were in no danger," claimed Aren. "Now, where are Elphin and Ranveig?"

"The Woodlander ran off in the other direction," said Rika. "I told him it was unnecessary, but he did not heed my advice, as usual. I thought the foolish man might get himself lost in the hills, which seems to be the case, so Ranveig went after him." She paused, and her expression looked even icier than normal. "It would be a shame to lose the cook."

"Devilish wench! You sent me off in that direction, and you knew perfectly well it's laced with thorn bushes!" Elphin marched into the campsite and flung down his sword, which landed suspiciously close to Rika.

"I didn't 'send' you anywhere, fool. I said I might have heard something—an animal, perhaps a hare—over that way."

Elphin turned to Cahira, his expression ripe with fury, but he appeared too enraged to speak. He shook his fist at Rika, then seated himself and proceeded to yank thorns from his leggings and coat. He muttered angrily while Rika began rubbing down the horses, a task Elphin generally assigned to himself. He eyed her bitterly. "You don't start at the haunches, woman! Start at the head and neck, so they know what you're doing!"

"The Norsk start where the horse's muscles are strained," she replied evenly. Aren glanced at her doubtfully, and Cahira guessed Rika's choice was based less on Norsk custom than on Elphin's irritation.

Thorleif eyed Felix, then issued a sharp cry. "Get out of that stew, bat, or I'll make you part of it!"

"Try it, and lose a finger, boy!" Felix flared his wings and looked ready to attack.

Ranveig stomped into the campsite and glared at the stew. "What's that? In one of my pots? I'd planned on doling out some of the salted meat tonight!"

Fareth snorted. "After the day we've had, galloping up this last slope in a panic thinking there's rogues attacking, you'd give us old slabs of meat? What else? A crust of bread? Maybe a bit of that watery brew *you* call ale?"

Ranveig braced himself and took a step toward Fareth, kicking one of the other man's pans as if by mistake. "Them 'old slabs of meat' can keep a Norsk warrior on his feet through a long day's march! Your stew just puts fat on the belly!"

Aren rubbed his forehead and started to speak, but as he did, Thorleif snatched a loaf of bread away from Felix and the bat issued a piercing whistle. "I am not letting this filthy creature soil our bread tonight!" Thorlief cried.

"It was soiled when you put your grubby paws on it," replied Felix. "Don't you creatures ever wash?"

"Wash? What do you know about washing? Water's never touched that flea-infested fur of yours!"

"My species takes dust baths," said Felix. "You ought to try it, since I'd wager fleas are a problem for you."

Bodvar seated himself separately from the others, glowering at Cahira until she felt nervous. Shaen passed by him, and his expression softened as she spoke, but his hard glare returned as Aren placed Cahira's sheepskin coat over Cahira's shoulders.

Rika picked up Zima's hind foot and examined it. Elphin stood up indignantly. "Start with the right front hoof!"

Rika rolled her eyes. "What difference does it make?"

"It's custom! It's amazing your horses are still alive if this is how you treat them!"

"Yet ours are so much sturdier—I think because we feed them rather than fiddle with silly grooming—"

Elphin seized his sword, and Cahira hopped forward and

grabbed his arm. "There's a stream running just to the south, Elphin. Maybe you and Thorleif can take the horses for water."

"I've already watered them," interjected Rika.

"We need water for dinner," said Cahira.

"The stew's ready now," argued Fareth. "We don't need water."

"Well . . . I want tea!" Cahira's voice cracked, and the tension from her thwarted encounter with Aren mingled with the bickering company burst to the surface. She smacked her hands to her hips. "All of you, if you can't get along, don't talk at all! Elphin, fetch the cursed water! Thorleif, distribute the bread. Fareth, get the stew into bowls—now!"

Apparently, her outburst did the trick. They all moved quickly and silently into their respective tasks. Aren came up beside her and placed his hand on the small of her back. He bent close and spoke quietly near Cahira's ear. "There's something I like even better than your body."

She looked up at him in surprise. "What?"

"Your fire."

Aren stood in the center of the campsite and watched Cahira order both his people and her own into various tasks. Wisely, she left Rika and Bodvar alone, but otherwise they all hopped to her commands, and, for the first evening since leaving his hamlet, he looked forward to a quiet and pleasant meal.

There were a few dark glares cast back and forth, but no one dared speak, even the bat. They all sat down around a small campfire to eat, and to Aren's surprise, Shaen seated herself next to him. He guessed there had to be a reason, so he ignored her and awaited the revelation. She hesitated until Cahira got up to refill her bowl of stew, then set her own bowl aside.

"I hope you understand my concern for Cahira," she began. "She's closer to me than a sister."

"Do you have a sister?" he asked, but she shrugged dismissively.

"I do, and several brothers. They live in other parts of Amrodel. We've never been close, though I have tried. My sister's life hasn't been as fortunate as mine, and I'm afraid she's somewhat bitter. But I have learned not to let it bother me."

"Ah."

She placed her hand on his arm, briefly, and her face puckered in a concerned expression. "It's Cahira I'm worried about."

Aren took a bite of stew and glanced at her without interest. "For what reason?"

"I can tell the pressure of this journey is getting to her."

"And I've tried so hard to relieve it." He resisted the temptation to add, *If you'd stop interrupting us, I might succeed.*

She looked at him aghast, but then laughed and tapped his forearm playfully. He resisted the impulse to swat her away like a bug. "You certainly live up to the Norsk reputation!"

"Which facet of our collective character has earned this particular reputation?" he asked. He dipped bread into his stew and swirled it around, watching Shaen intently.

"The lusty warrior with only one thing on his mind," she replied lightly, but then her voice grew more serious. "I just hope you're considering the impact it's having on Cahira. She's very sensitive."

His brow arched meaningfully. "I've noticed that."

She caught his intimation, and this time her laugh seemed more forced. "I suppose we should be grateful that she's managed to distract you in this way." She paused, presumably to let her meaning sink in. "With your mind so occupied, you can't be giving much thought to your fate. I'm sure that's why Bodvar is so worried about you. He cares about your fate, even if you do not."

Aren took another spoonful of stew and shifted his gaze to Cahira. She bent over to add another piece of bread to her plate, affording him a pleasing view of her well-formed backside. "I have to admit, the only fate I'm concerned about tonight is satisfying an ache I share with an extraordinarily beautiful woman."

Shaen's eyes flashed, indicating she realized he was baiting her, but her anger was quickly replaced with a smile. "I'm surprised that a man of your stature, chieftain of Norsk, can be so shortsighted. I suppose that's why yours is such a rugged race, living only for the moment without thought of the possible outcomes. It is said death means little to your people, and that's what makes the Norsk so fearless."

He fixed his gaze on her and waited until she met it. "It's not that death means little, but that life means more." He paused. "Death is not to be feared, but accepted when it comes."

"Is that how you intend to meet the Arch Mage?" she asked guilelessly.

"That is how I meet every foe," he replied. "Those that are obvious, and those that are not."

"Well, this is a cheerful conversation!" Aren looked up and saw Cahira standing before him. Her brow furrowed. "Why are you talking about death?"

Shaen smiled. "Aren was just telling me that the Norsk simply don't fear death as we do."

"No," Aren corrected. "I said we accept it in a way you don't."

Cahira sat down beside him and looked up into his eyes. "If I must face death, I want to face it honorably," she said. "But I am still afraid."

He reached out and took her hand, then kissed it. "Death is not the challenge we face," he told her. "The real challenge is life."

"Such poetic words!" commented Shaen. "No wonder he's swept you off your feet, Cahira!" She stood up and smiled down at them. "Eliana must have taught you soft speech during your visit to the Woodland."

"I learn by personal observation," replied Aren carelessly. "And by touch."

Shaen laughed and shook her head, then went to sit with Elphin, who was busy glaring at Rika. Cahira elbowed Aren, then took a bite of bread. "You don't like her much, do you?"

"I don't trust her, because she doesn't say what she means, and she hides her motives."

"What motives could she possibly have?"

"I have no idea. And that's what worries me." His dislike of Shaen had solidified since their journey began. But they were close now to the Guerdian city, and there, he foresaw a chance to convince Cahira to leave the wench behind, despite her 'memorized map.' No need to alert Cahira to his plans yet, however.

"She's just afraid you'll hurt me, or impregnate me, or something." Cahira paused. "At least she doesn't look at you like she wants to kill you, the way Bodvar looks at me. I can't say I like him much, either." She sighed. "But I guess they're both just overprotective."

"Bodvar witnessed my brother's death." Aren set aside his stew, and drank from a flagon of ale. "The power of Mages, good and evil, showed my people that sometimes courage and strength are not enough. Like me, he appreciates what my brother did to unite our people, and he doesn't want to see that torn asunder for the sake of a battle between Mages."

Cahira's brow furrowed, and her lips curled in displeasure. "Well, Shaen endured my father's death, when he was murdered with a Norsk dagger!"

"Wielded by a rogue Mage," Aren reminded her.

"Yes—a rogue Mage who had allied with your noble brother! Bruin the Ruthless intended to conquer my people, probably for the sport of it, and it was his lust for power that had him seeking out the 'power of the Mages' in the first place!"

"A lust that had lain dormant until awoken by the wizard's darkness," interrupted Aren. "My brother was a good man until that time."

She huffed. "I'm sure. Good at pillaging our borders! Tell me, was the title 'Ruthless' added to his name at birth, or did he do something to earn it?"

Aren fidgeted, but he refused to meet her eyes. He hadn't fully realized how infuriating Cahira could be. Shaen's description of 'strong-willed' hardly did her justice. "He was single-minded in battle."

"A lovely virtue. Axes sever necks so much better if you're truly focused!"

"I would prefer to fall to an axe blow than to have my soul sapped from me, to be manipulated like a puppet with a dagger in my back," he retorted, and his emotion soared. He took another draught of ale. "That is a fate far more grim."

"Death is death," she replied obstinately.

"The lure of the Mage's power corrupted him, and destroyed a man who once was good," Aren argued.

"If he hadn't lusted for power, there wouldn't been much of a lure, would there?"

"It fanned a weakness that he might otherwise have conquered."

"Well, we all have weaknesses, don't we?" she said furiously. "Mine, obviously, is you!"

"And my own might be said to be you, Lady," he replied, equally cold. *Infuriating!* "But my weakness doesn't include the great power of magic which rolls over everything in its path, regardless of what lies in its way."

Her lips parted for what was certain to be a cutting remark, but Thorleif coughed pointedly, interrupting them. "What is it, Thorleif?" Aren asked.

"Think we should set a watch tonight, lord?"

"This isn't a likely spot for ambush . . . ," Aren began. He stopped and glanced at Cahira, whose jaw set as she glared at him. "But a watch might be a good idea," he agreed as he rose to his feet. "I will take the first."

He'd sat there all night, on a hill overlooking the campsite. He'd intended to wake Thorleif or Bodvar, but his anger refused to cool. Unfortunately, his body still remembered the interrupted passion he'd shared with Cahira, and the subsequent discomfort in his groin had served to make sleep impossible. Maybe he'd hoped, slightly, that she would come to him and apologize, but instead she had simply curled up on her side, facing away from him, and gone to sleep. She was stubborn, as well as infuriating.

The sun rose behind him, and slanted through the mountains, casting its pale light on the campsite below. He watched as it moved slowly from Thorleif's position under an overhanging thicket—where he assumed Felix had taken up residence for the night—until the light crept over the smoldering coals of the fire and gilded Cahira's black hair as she lay asleep.

Thorleif rose and stretched, then looked around. The youth waved, and Aren half-heartedly waved back. Cahira got up, too, but she pointedly avoided looking his way as Fareth handed her a cup of what was presumably tea. She drank, took a portion of bread, then spoke to Elphin.

The night alone should have served to cool his ire. Their argument had proved that they had serious differences—differences she might perceive as a threat to her people, just as he considered the trouble with Mages a peril to his own. He cared for Eliana and her husband, deeply, and he owed Damir allegiance for succoring his people. But he still believed there must be a wiser course to end their imprisonment than waking a spellbound wizard. He hoped to find another solution in the hall of the Guerdian king, though he hadn't mentioned his intention to Cahira. For now, at least, they were riding in the right direction, albeit for different reasons.

They hadn't spoken of her "quest," partly because they'd been too busy falling for each other. At least, he was falling for her. Aren considered this. She obviously desired him, such a reaction couldn't be faked. He'd felt her desire in every pulse and every soft breath. But Cahira was new to lovemaking, if not to the passion inherent to her nature. Maybe lust was a more powerful force than she realized. She certainly hadn't diverted from her single-minded determination to march him into that dark cave and challenge the evil wizard.

If he hadn't been so preoccupied with the ache in his body, he might have given more thought to the fate she intended for him. Shaen's words echoed in his mind. Cahira seemed too straightforward to deliberately distract him, but whether she'd intended it or not, recent events had certainly served that purpose. And she had the body and the face and the sensuality to make the diversion worthwhile.

She'd told him that she had fantasized about him—he had fantasized about her, too. Though Eliana had inspired his pity, he had found the image of a mystic female Mage irresistibly erotic, and Cahira was that vision come to life. One sight of her during his boyhood had given the promise that such a being existed, and he had been well aware that she was growing to adulthood at the same time he was. He'd even kept track of her, probing the gossips of Amon-Dhen for news. What he'd heard fueled his imagination to the point where he had almost considered a visit to Amrodel, despite his vow to stay far from the land of the Mages. Cahira was headstrong, beautiful and the terror of any young man who sought to win her interest—exactly what he'd hoped.

Be careful what you wish, for it may come to pass. . . . The sage words of Norsk matrons shouldn't be ignored.

Aren rose from the boulder, stiff and sore, then made his way down the hillside to rejoin the others. "You could have woken me, my lord," said Thorleif cheerfully. He took a drink of tea, then looked into the cup suspiciously. "Not sure about this brew, but the witch says it's good for my vitals."

"Whatever that means," said Aren, grumpily. The other man's eyes widened.

"I'll just get our gear together, shall I?" Thorleif eased away and busied himself with the packs.

Elphin and Rika were already bickering about the horses, and Elphin snatched a blanket out of her hands and put it on his mount. When he turned his back, she ripped it off and put it on her own. Before he spotted what she'd done, Rika mounted. She looked at him with a self-satisfied smile, and Elphin whirled to seize another.

"This one is better, anyway!" he snapped.

"How do you manage to raise a child?" Rika asked him, "when you are so much of one yourself?"

"My children are with my wife, a woman with actual blood in her veins rather than frost."

"Frost would serve her better if she's bound to you for eternity," said Rika, and she trotted away before he could retort.

Not surprisingly, Thorleif and Felix were also arguing, but Aren couldn't hear about what. A skillet flew past his head. It was safe to say Ranveig and Fareth were at each other's throats.

"So begins the day," he muttered.

As he pulled Pip's reins from a branch, the horse sighed and Aren noticed a shallow bite mark on its shoulders. Zima stood with her ears pinned back, so the source of the wound seemed obvious. Aren found some fragrant herbs beneath the thickets, and placed them gently on the cut, then patted Pip's neck. "Sometimes it's wiser to keep your distance, my friend," he said quietly—and since Cahira was blatantly ignoring him this morning, it didn't seem too difficult to accomplish himself.

Unfortunately, she looked good. Unlike him, she'd obviously slept well, and it showed. Her face looked bright, her skin glowed like warm cream, and her eyes reflected the morning sun. Her black hair was coiled in a midnight river over one shoulder, and their evening indulgence had created loose waves and tendrils that framed her perfect face. His gaze shifted reluctantly to her body to see that she hadn't replaced her leather bodice and still wore only her light shirt. When she turned slightly, the morning light shone through the material and he caught the outline of her round breasts as she moved. The air must have felt cool on her skin—he couldn't imagine why, as it felt almost hot to him—because the tips of her breasts had hardened into little buds, just as when he had drawn his palm over that soft swell and . . .

He drew a quick breath to fight his arousal, but she caught his glance and her eyes widened. Almost as quickly, she must have noticed her exposed condition, because she grabbed her discarded bodice and pulled it on with unusual speed. He imagined peeling it from her skin and taking those perfect little buds between his lips . . .

Aren repressed a low groan and fitted Pip hurriedly for riding. He swung himself astride—less easy because of the swelling in his groin—then waited for the others. Rika rode up beside him, and waited, too.

"Well, you're in a state," she offered coolly. "What happened?"

He looked at her in surprise. "What do you mean?"

A slight smile warmed the Norskwoman's lovely face. "'What do I mean?' The two of you have been practically inseparable since we left the Snow Pony. If I'd seen you gazing wistfully into her eyes any longer, I might have had to slap you."

"Indeed?" It wasn't like Rika to comment on his romantic life, or on anything personal. "We were just . . . getting to know each other."

"One inch at a time."

He gaped at her in disbelief. "Did you have ale for breakfast? Maybe you should try tea."

"Disgusting liquid," she replied, and resumed her cool assessment. "I've never seen you make such a fool of yourself before, that's all."

"Is that so?"

She shrugged carelessly. "The most I've ever seen is a bored and perhaps lazy interest in women that, at best, could be said to lack fire or conviction. Quite frankly, I never thought you'd be much of a lover because I couldn't imagine you putting much energy into it."

"Thank you so much, ice princess!"

She looked calmly at him, a slight twinkle in her frosty blue eyes. Because she was right. Exactly right. He'd never been overwhelmed with desire before; if he'd wanted sex, there was generally a woman available who didn't ask for much more. He hadn't been passionate—except in his fantasies, which had come blazing to life when Cahira stormed into his Great Hall and challenged him to battle.

"Am I wrong?" Rika asked evenly.

He looked at her and couldn't stop a defeated smile. "No, you're not."

"You've never given yourself fully, Aren. And now you have a woman who can't look at you without going weak in the knees—before you've even consummated this tragic and restless passion! When that time comes, please get a room on the far side of a large inn from wherever I'm located—or get yourselves to a nearby hill, where there's no echo, should passion overtake you before we reach a civilized establishment."

Aren glanced at Cahira, who fiddled with her bow. Her fingers twitched in an unusually vengeful manner; though mercifully, she couldn't overhear Rika's casual and brutal comments. "That's not likely to be a worry now," he said, and he sounded more sorrowful than he intended.

Rika rolled her eyes. "Why? Because you've argued? That makes it all the worse. It was bad enough when you were looking at each other like you were answers to each other's prayer. Spitting fire and fury, you're still likely to tear into each other like hungry wolves—and be just as loud." She paused and shook her head. "Maybe you should find a deep, dark cave somewhere when the time comes."

Aren gazed at her and his brow arched. "You really are a devil-wench, as that Woodlander keeps saying. I never would have guessed it!"

"I have a son," she reminded him. "How do you think I got him?"

Aren remembered her husband, a powerful man with an

even stronger temper, and a code of honor that did every Norskman proud. "Your mate walks in the Hall of Ages among our greatest warriors," he said.

"I know that," replied Rika distantly. "I will join him one day. But not before I follow you through the Hall of Wizards, and find light on the other side."

"Do you think we have a chance?" he asked quietly.

"I don't know," she responded. "But if anyone can do what the Woodland witch asks, it's you, Aren. There is a great depth and power beneath that indolent surface of yours. I have only to look at the conviction in her eyes to believe that."

"That fire is fury now."

"And your soft amber eyes turned hard as stone when you looked at her this morning. She is more than a match for you, I think."

"I was under the impression you didn't like her much," he said.

"She is headstrong and emotional, and I believe, extremely impulsive. She doesn't think before she acts. But she is without guile, and though I question her abilities as a fighter, I appreciate her direct manner." Rika paused. "When she threatened to put an arrow through my tongue, I thought she had promise."

"That *was* endearing. . . ." He paused and saw Bodvar watching Cahira, suspicion ripe on his face as she collected her gear. "Bodvar doesn't share your appreciation, I'm afraid," he said.

"He fears for you," agreed Rika. "He rode with Bruin, and saw what Mages can do. And all Norskmen desire victory. He resents any defeat, even though Bruin's victory would have destroyed us. Still he is loyal to you, Aren, in large part because you are a better fighter than Bruin."

Aren eyed her doubtfully. "Bruin loved battle like no other," he reminded her. "Few have excelled at it the way he did."

"But you don't fight for yourself or your own glory. And

the truth is, you swing an axe better than your brother ever did." She paused. "Bodvar knows this, and he would not have you distracted by some passion for a Woodland witch."

"Apparently, Cahira's friend Shaen has similar misgivings."

Rika huffed. "If you had turned your attention to *her,* she would be boasting of a Norskman's delights and lording her conquest over everyone. I do not believe she bears Cahira the same loyalty that Bodvar carries for you. She's just jealous because you've directed this newfound passion to a prettier—and far stronger—woman."

"Maybe," said Aren. "But I can't help feeling it's more than that. Something I don't understand motivates her, and I doubt very much it's me."

"Possibly not, but for a woman like that, envy is a great force, and each conversation she has seems directed at obtaining even the smallest advantage for herself."

"That, I have noticed," he agreed.

"It was a victory for Shaen to disrupt your encounter at the hot spring," Rika mentioned. "Seeing as what you were trying to accomplish."

"How do you know about that?"

The Norskwoman smiled sagely. "I've bathed there myself."

Aren laughed, and his ill mood softened. "Then your mate was indeed a fortunate man."

"He was," Rika agreed. "His temper was short, but his passion was strong."

Aren watched Cahira sling her bow over her shoulder and so to Zima on the far side of Pip. He said, "*She* also has a quick temper."

Cahira must have overheard, but she made no response. Using a boulder, she hopped onto her mare. She then moved Zima aside so Shaen could use the same rock to mount, then waited patiently for them to begin the day's ride.

Aren addressed them all, taking special care not to look Cahira's way. "Today we ride into the foothills, and into the territory of the Guerdians. We must be alert for rogue bands, and move forward in relative silence." He paused to administer a meaningful look at Thorleif, and then at Felix who sat perched on Fareth's shoulder. "But have your weapons at your sides, and be ready for anything."

As he urged Pip forward along the upward trail, he though he heard Cahira whisper, "I am—now."

8

AMBUSH

Even his back was infuriating. Cahira rode at the end of the column, much to Zima's displeasure, which the mare displayed by flattening her ears and startling often. Here was the "moodiness" Aren had warned about, but Cahira refused to relent. She was moody enough herself.

Shaen had been right about one thing: Aren was unreasonably devoted to his brother, a man whose barbaric reputation sent chills through Woodlanders years after his death. Maybe Aren wasn't as sweet and reasonable as she had imagined. His words had been artful, but when angry, Aren became stubborn and intolerable.

He could be gratingly sarcastic, as he'd proven when she first entered his Great Hall. A tiny voice of conscience reminded her that she, too, wielded this same tactic, and generally enjoyed it. But this was different. Now that they were, or had been, romantically intimate, she had expected him to take her side on important matters. Last night he had made it clear that he didn't accept her intentions concerning the Arch Mage, and more aggravating still, that he seemed to hold all Mages responsible for creating the situation in the first place.

She especially disliked his accusation about Mages using their power to "roll over" everything that stood in their way. That comment stung, and hurt still as she mulled it over in her mind. With a dull ache, she knew it hurt because she couldn't deny that his words held an element of truth.

"Cahira?" Shaen slowed her gelding and waited for Cahira to catch up, which Zima accomplished eagerly, as if meeting the first of several challenges that would culminate in passing Pip. "Are you all right?"

"I'm perfectly fine."

"Forgive me for intruding, but it's painfully obvious that you and the Norskman have quarreled."

"You could say that."

Shaen sighed. "I'm afraid it was bound to happen, when the two of you are so different. I almost believed his feelings were genuine, and that he might reconsider the task you've asked of him. I take it he has not?"

"I don't want to talk about this now, Shaen."

"I understand. I just want you to know that I'm here if you need to. I can't stand to see you so down. You know how much I care about you."

"Thank you."

"If it helps, I think he was just trying to make you jealous this morning, by flirting with Rika."

Cahira eyed her doubtfully. "I hadn't noticed they were flirting."

"You don't have my sense of people, I'm afraid," said Shaen. "It's obvious she's in love with him. I can see that he cares for her, though he has some kind of fascination with you. Men love new and different conquests, and Norskmen seem to hold a particular fear of our female Mages. You must represent quite a challenge to him."

"Aren was Eliana's closest friend. I don't believe he looks at us the same way other Norsk do."

"Don't let it bother you. You are much stronger than he is. You've proven that by sticking to our quest, when he is afraid."

"He isn't afraid. He just doubts our chances of success."

"He may not be wrong about that," said Shaen quietly. "If only . . . if only there was another way! But I can't think of anything except to go forward with Damir's suggestion."

Cahira didn't respond. That thought had been growing in her mind, too. "If there was another way, I would take it," she said finally. "But I can see no other alternative."

"Nor can I," agreed Shaen. "I know the Norskman doubts my abilities, but you can trust my knowledge of the Arch Mage's domain, Cahira. I promise." She paused. "His voice must be getting stronger as we progress—the voice of the Arch Mage. Does he torment you still?"

Cahira gazed at the riders ahead. "When Aren sleeps at my side, I do not hear the Arch Mage at all." She paused and swallowed. "But last night, he came to me in dreams again."

Shaen's eyes widened. "What did he say?"

"He mocks me and speaks of the great power he will have when he has joined with me."

"But you only need enter the cavern where he lies to resurrect him. Isn't that right?" asked Shaen.

"I believe so," said Cahira. "But he needs something more in order to attain the true power he craves. Of course, even without it he is far stronger than any Mage now living—even Damir."

"I can't imagine why Damir believed the Norskman could defeat such a powerful Mage," Shaen mused.

"Damir once told me that, when he first met Aren, Bruin forced them to battle. He said that when his energy encountered Aren's, he felt a force like no other—as if Aren owned the light, in a way no Mage ever has. I believe Damir has legitimate reason for his faith."

"Such a brief impression formed Damir's faith?" Shaen shook her head, then stared at Cahira. "Have you seen or felt any evidence of this power?"

"No . . . Yet there is something . . . something I can't describe. He is not like other men, and it may be that a great power lies deep inside him."

Shaen smacked her lips thoughtfully. "Well, let us hope you're right. Otherwise, his end may come in the Arch Mage's cavern and our fate will rest in the hands of our enemy."

Zima's resentment at taking the rear reached a pinnacle. The horse tried to edge past Shaen's gelding, and when Cahira checked her pace, Zima stomped her hooves and threatened to rear. Annoyed, Cahira halted the mare and made her back up a few steps. Zima relented, but Cahira had not forgotten the promise she had once made. *You will always go first.*

To go first meant to pass Aren and Pip, but Cahira wasn't ready to face him yet. She let the mare pass Shaen, then ease forward more, a slow ascension. Cahira's anger had given way to sadness as the morning waned. As they all rode the winding paths through the foothills, the air warmed considerably from the open plains, and here there was no sign of snow. Green ferns grew between the boulders, and a few bushes even bore blossoms.

Cahira looked back at the plains below—a long, icy wasteland that stretched as far as the eye could see. Such an unyielding land had shaped Aren's personality, whereas her own had been carved in the secret paths and ever-changing green of the forest. Shaen was right about that much—they had very little in common.

Aren rode quietly at the head of the group, though the others spoke amongst themselves. She wondered what he was thinking—thoughts of her obstinate and argumentative nature, no doubt. She might have been kinder about the brother he had loved, perhaps. But he had been so annoying in turn!

His back looked good—strong and broad. His blond hair hung loose over his shoulders, catching the sunlight like spun gold. Thorleif too had light hair, as did most Norsk, but Aren's had special appeal. She liked the way it fell around his face when he looked at her. It softened his masculine hardness. His tenderness juxtaposed with his strength presented a powerful allure. She liked his close-trimmed beard, too; though she was almost afraid to see what he'd look like without it. He was too handsome as it was.

Growing up, she had pictured him an angelic youth, sweet and brave—a romantic and heroic figure of a young girl's dreams. Instead, he seemed as strong and as true as the earth itself, not angelic but sure; and rather than romantic sighs, he inspired a far more earthy desire.

Cahira maneuvered past Ranveig and rode up beside Fareth, who rode behind Elphin. Ahead, Rika flanked Thorleif, and Bodvar kept close behind Aren. Fareth glanced over at her. "I've ridden more in the past days than ever in the entirety of my life in Amrodel," he complained. "My backside will never be the same."

Cahira smiled. "Where's Felix?" she asked.

"He was with me for awhile," Fareth answered, "but when I let my old horse slack off a bit and we fell behind, he took off—flying for a change—and plunked himself with Elphin."

"Ah! Right behind Thorleif," noted Cahira, and Fareth chuckled.

"I believe I did hear the boy curse and groan at about that time."

Zima seemed to like Fareth's old horse, and the mare relaxed as they rode along. They ascended a steep incline, where Aren halted suddenly. The others stopped, too. He listened for a moment, then turned to them and held up his hand. "Stay here, all of you!"

"Where are you going?" Cahira asked.

"Scouting ahead," he answered. And before she could query him further, he rode Pip forward, drawing his axe.

Cahira's heart skipped a beat, then moved in fast pulses as she waited. She urged Zima forward until she reached Bodvar and Thorleif. "What is he doing?"

"Hush!" commanded Thorleif with unusual force.

Cahira started to argue, but now she heard what had caught Aren's attention—distant cries, and the echo of clashing metal. A horn sounded ahead, and her heart stirred. Though she did not recognize the instrument, the three Norsk responded immediately.

"The chieftain's call!" shouted Thorleif. "Ambush!"

Thorleif galloped off with Bodvar and Rika close behind. Ranveig charged past Cahira, his short axe already held aloft. Cahira sat stunned for a moment and a wave of uncertainty hit her so strongly that she couldn't move. Strangely, Zima waited patiently for her command. Elphin looked into Cahira's eyes, and his face was kind. "You are a warrior, Cahira Daere. This is what you were born to do. Let us go to battle. We are with you."

She stared at him, but he smiled. Fareth nodded. Cahira drew her bow and took one arrow from her quiver; then she followed the Norsk over the crest.

In a shallow valley beyond, Cahira saw what Aren had found, but it wasn't the sight she'd expected. A group of rugged warriors, some tall and obviously Norsk by birth, and a few short and sturdy Guerdians in thick, dull armor, had surrounded another, smaller group. The smaller group used short spears, while the Norsk wielded battle-axes and fought as if their weapons were extensions of their bodies.

Clearly, those of the second group were only Guerdians, for they were short and also wore armor, and their mail was brighter, as if they hailed from an upper class of the Guerdian race. Only two of these remained standing, and as Cahira watched, a large Norskman dealt one of the Guerdians a vicious blow, and the small warrior fell lifeless beside another. Near their feet lay strewn four dead or near death. The lone defender wailed, his voice a shuddering agony mingled with fury at his comrade's death. He flung himself at his attackers, but he was far outnumbered.

Aren had already engaged the nearest, drawing the Norsk rogues away from the remaining Guerdian. The rogues turned on him, but he outmatched them in skill and fought like a young god. Rika, Thorleif, and Bodvar soon joined him, and axe clashed against axe and spear as they fought.

The Norsk rogues had dismounted to fight on foot, and their horses were gathered nervously near the base of the hill. Cahira slowed Zima, not in hesitation for the task at hand, but because her senses had cleared, and her years of battle study came back to her mind. She held up her hand to stop the other Woodlanders, and they drew up beside her.

"What do we do?" asked Elphin. His voice was shaking, but he held his drawn sword ready.

Cahira thought quickly. "You can't fight them, but you might save the others if you're quick."

Elphin brightened. "We can do that! We'll sneak around while the chieftain engages those brutes, and get the injured Guerdians out of there."

Fareth gazed down at them as if overtaken with emotion. "Poor little fellows," he said in a low, hoarse voice. "Aye, we can do that, at least." As they started off, Felix hurtled himself from Elphin to Cahira's shoulder.

"Now's when *you* need me, lass."

She nodded. "Thank you." She glanced back at Shaen, who had dismounted and stood shaking with terror. "Keep Zima with you, Shaen," she said, hopping off Zima's back. "And stay here. There's no need for you to get involved. But don't let them see you. They might have bows."

Shaen took Zima's reins, then gripped Cahira's shoulder. "Don't go, Cahira. It's too dangerous!"

"I must."

"It's not our fight. Why must you go?" asked Shaen plaintively.

Cahira glanced to where Aren fought. "Because my heart is there."

She didn't wait for further argument. She set her arrow to the bowstring and sped after the others. She fired as she ran, and her first arrow struck a rogue Guerdian who had jabbed a short spear upwards at Rika's chest. Rika stumbled back, then turned in surprise to see Cahira. A slight smile touched her face, and she nodded. Cahira nodded back, then jumped onto a higher boulder and took aim again.

Aren easily deflected a rogue's reckless blow, then gazed up at Cahira as she sighted her next target. For a moment, he stood still and watched her, but then he bowed, and his eyes were shining. Their gazes met and locked before he turned back to the battle.

"Well done, lass!" observed Felix excitedly. His little claws dug into her shoulder, and she felt his body vibrating violently as he witnessed the battle.

"Thank you," replied Cahira.

Two thickset Norsk rogues charged at Thorleif at the same time. "Cowards," she murmured, and she shot one through the leg. The man yelped and staggered, and Thorleif swung his axe, and the rogue fell dead. Thorleif whirled to battle the other.

Bodvar decapitated his Guerdian rogue before Cahira had time to react. Felix shuddered at the sudden death, then tensed. "The boy's in trouble again," he cried. With his wing tip, he gestured at Thorleif, who fought against a much larger rogue, and who was now backed against a boulder. "Hurry, lass!" The bat's voice quavered with fear, but Cahira hesitated.

"He's wearing armor. I need to spot a target or the arrow won't penetrate."

"Lass, he's going to fall!"

"There . . ." Her arrow flew forward and pierced the rogue's neck. As the man howled, Thorleif drove the butt of his axe into his enemy, then felled his opponent with one final blow. He looked up at Cahira and waved, as cheerful as ever. She waved back, but her hand was shaking.

"That boy has no sense whatsoever!" commented Felix. "Look! He's taken off after another one, just as big as the last. Get after him!"

Bodvar engaged Thorleif's intended opponent, and Cahira heard the boy utter a furious cry. "That one was mine!"

"They really are crazy," said Felix.

Rika fought near Aren, and her movements were as cool and graceful and methodical as everything else she did. She quickly dispatched the final rogue Guerdian, then addressed the nearest Norsk attacker.

Still, the rogues outnumbered Aren's party, and the unexpected interruption of a certain victory—and subsequent plunder—seemed to have driven them into a rage. Four charged toward the last Guerdian defender. He wielded a richly carved spear, but his armor was already dented and blood streamed from a gash in his forehead beneath his helm.

Aren bounded to the Guerdian's defense, and placed himself in front of the little warrior. The Guerdian looked up at him in surprise. For an instant, it appeared he might attempt to battle Aren, too, unsure which Norskmen could be trusted, and probably unable to tell them apart; but Aren spoke to him in his own tongue, and the Guerdian set himself beside Aren to fight.

Elphin and Fareth appeared from behind the Guerdians' position, and together, began to carry wounded bodies out of the range of battle. Several appeared dead, and Cahira saw tears on Fareth's face as he lifted one small Guerdian in his arms.

"That hulking brute on the left, he's a good target," said Felix, but his voice sounded thick, as if he, too, grieved with the gentle innkeeper. "Got more blood on his axe than in a body, I'd say."

The rogue Felix indicated leapt forward as Elphin went to the last injured Guerdian. The rogue laughed and reached the still-moving body first. He drove the point of his axe deep into the Guerdian's chest, then howled in gruesome triumph. Elphin cried out in fury, then drew his sword and leapt toward the rogue. Cahira froze, and Felix gasped.

"No! Lass, stop him!"

Her hands shook as she draw and rocked her last arrow. Elphin swung at his opponent, but the rogue laughed and slammed a heavy axe against Elphin's light sword, shattering the blade. Elphin fell. But when he scrambled to his feet, to Cahira's astonishment he didn't run. Instead, he seized a fallen branch and raised it.

"He has lost his mind! Lass, shoot!"

Apparently, the rogue had seen her, because he moved so that Elphin was in the way. Cahira leapt forward and bounded into the battle, her last arrow drawn back. Before she could arrive, Aren defeated the two rogues before him and raced to Elphin's aid.

Elphin showed no sign of backing down, but the rogue noticed Aren and laughed again, as if he welcomed a more challenging foe. Fareth seized the opportunity and grabbed Elphin, then used every bit of his strength to haul the young Woodlander out of the fray.

The rogue swaggered to face Aren, and offered a mocking bow. "If it isn't the young chieftain of the Norsk," he said, "who sent me into exile for a petty crime! It will be a joy to put your head on a pike!"

Cahira braced, then drew back her bow. Felix hopped up and down on her shoulder. "Wait, lass!" He tugged at her hair and directed her attention at Ranveig. "That one needs you more."

"But this is my last arrow," she whispered. "If Aren . . ." She had no more time to debate. Three rogues surrounded Ranveig and, to her horror, one drew a thick crossbow and took aim.

She fired just before he could set the bolt, and her arrow struck his forearm just above his thick leather gauntlet. The rogue howled in pain and the crossbow dropped from his hand. Ranveig seized the opportunity and felled the wounded rogue, and Bodvar drove back the others just as Rika ran forward to help.

Cahira looked around desperately. "I need more arrows!" she cried.

"Find some that aren't broken," advised Felix.

She arched her brow. "There's a good suggestion. I wish I'd thought of it!"

The bat ignored her sarcasm and looked around. "One over there, and two there. Hurry!"

Cahira made her way to the center of the skirmish to retrieve her arrows. Aren had the advantage against his arrogant foe, but she herself was helpless unarmed, and if he needed her, she wanted to be ready.

Before Cahira reached the first arrow, Aren's foe stopped and backed away, hands up in surrender. The remaining rogues gave way, too, and ran through the northern trees to escape. Bodvar followed after them, but Cahira relaxed. Aren turned toward her.

"Lass!" Felix's high voice rang out, and Cahira whirled to see Aren's defeated foe seizing the fallen crossbow. He set the bolt and took aim just as Aren turned—

Cahira screamed in fury and terror, shoved the bat from her shoulder and flung herself in the crossbow's path. *"Arail 'i, Damir, nawr a am byth!"* she cried, and her body jerked back in a force of light.

Aren was safe—the bolt struck her instead.

Aren reeled, stunned, slowed in every motion, every breath. Before him, Cahira's body crumpled and fell. A cry of primal agony tore through him, and with one blow he slew the rogue who'd shot her, then dropped to his knees beside her. His tears blinded him with horror and loss unlike anything he had ever known.

She had sacrificed herself for him! Before the treachery and cowardice of their foes, she had shown ultimate courage. Rika and Thorleif came over, and Thorleif wept openly. Rika stared down at Cahira in shock, as Elphin and Fareth knelt beside her, silent. Ranveig stood quietly beside Aren and tears welled in his eyes. Bodvar emerged from the woods and looked on in surprise.

The surviving Guerdian hobbled over, and he stared in disbelief as he wiped blood from his brow. "A Woodlander and a Mage who would die for a Norskman? What manner of female is this?"

"A brave one," said Rika softly.

Shaen appeared on the hill above, then cried out in fury and grief. "What have you done? What's happened to her? Cahira! No!" She scurried down the hill path, then stopped and doubled over, sobbing.

Felix hopped to Cahira, stood silently by her head. Rather than grieve, he seemed to be waiting, as if he didn't understand or accept the finality of death.

Aren cradled Cahira's head gently, then bent and pressed his cheek against her forehead. "My angel," he whispered, and his tears soaked into her hair.

"You . . . you are so good-looking," she said groggily. Startled, he dropped her, his eyes wide with shock. He stared, mouth agape, and Cahira frowned slightly then rubbed her head and sat up. "And what a body!"

Aren sat back on his heels, astounded.

"What witchery is this?" said Bodvar, entering the clearing.

The Guerdian looked on in wonder. "The magic of the Woodland is great, indeed!"

"That bolt went right through her!" added Thorleif. "Slammed into her chest—a direct hit!"

"Apparently not," said Rika coolly.

"It did! I saw it!" Thorleif insisted.

"Look. She is unscathed. It just knocked her out. A crossbow bolt is faster than the eye."

"No." Cahira dusted herself off, then shook her head. "It hit me, all right. Though quite clearly it didn't 'go right through me,' or I'd have a hole." She gestured to her chest. "No blood." She eyed Aren doubtfully. "Didn't you notice?"

"It's impossible," breathed Aren, and he couldn't stem the flow of his tears. "I saw it hit you."

Her brow furrowed in confusion. "Yes, I know. I've just told you that." She eyed Elphin and Fareth, and shrugged. "Can one of you explain, please? I'm a little . . . dizzy."

"*Dizzy?* You take a crossbow bolt head on and you're dizzy? Cahira . . ." Aren reached for her, and she braced herself on his shoulder and stood up.

Elphin exhaled a breath of relief, but it was Felix who spoke next. "Didn't you hear the words the lass cried out before she jumped in front of that brute?"

"I heard them," said Aren. "But I didn't understand them."

"Of course not! She spoke in the ancient tongue of Amrodel, in a language generally reserved for the Elite Mages—although I speak it well enough myself. Now, bats are fluent in many languages, though as yet we've never bothered with that guttural, sonorous speech you Norsk use when drunk—"

"Get to the point, bat!" exclaimed Thorleif. "What did she say?"

"*Arail 'i, Damir, nawr a am byth,*" said Felix. "Roughly rendered, it means, 'Guard me, Damir, now and forever.' She was summoning Damir's shield—more of a formality, really, because as long as the lass didn't place her trust in that brute, which doesn't seem likely, Damir ap Kora's shield was likely to kick in, anyway. Never hurts to add the words, though. Smart lass."

Aren rose to his feet, but his legs felt weak from shock. He touched her arm gently, to reassure himself she really stood there, unharmed, before him. "Damir's shield protected you?"

Cahira nodded casually, though she herself looked a little baffled. "Of course. That's what it's meant to do."

"I encountered his shield before. The effect on me was to render me unconscious, briefly. But to stop a bolt from a crossbow . . . That is a rare power."

"The shield you encountered was different," said Elphin. "Damir shielded the Woodland so that, if an enemy—which you were at the time—entered, it would confuse his mind and cause him to faint should he instill fear in any of our people."

"The shield our king placed on Cahira is far stronger," added Fareth. "Nothing can penetrate it—even the Arch Mage himself, I'll warrant."

"Not while Damir lives," agreed Shaen. "Of course, if Damir dies the shield will fail, but not until that time."

Aren looked at Cahira closely, and his heart was moved with gratitude to Damir ap Kora. "So, nothing can harm you while you have this shield?" he asked.

"Don't know. Haven't tested it," said Cahira. And then, oddly, she chuckled.

"No, nothing can injure her," said Elphin, with a doubtful glance at Cahira. "Though, if a fellow were strong enough, and if she weren't physically harmed, she could be bound and carried, restrained, that sort of thing."

"Not if I had my bow!" Cahira looked around. "Where is it, anyway?" She paused and spluttered. " 'Restrained?' They wouldn't dare!"

Shaen eyed Elphin thoughtfully. "How could anyone restrain Cahira, shield or no? If she utilized the power of her *ki,* wouldn't that be enough to fend off any foe?"

"Possibly," agreed Elphin. "She might bring down more than just the Norskman's Great Hall, certainly. Just hope she's out in the open if it happens!"

"Let us hope there's no cause," agreed Shaen gently, and she hugged Cahira tight. "I was so shocked that I forgot all about your shield. I don't think I could take losing you—not after how I suffered when your father died." She wiped tears from her cheeks and hugged Cahira again. "I'm not going to let you out of my sight from now on. No more fighting!"

"I say put her at the fore and send her at 'em!" said Thorleif. He tossed his axe into the air and whooped as he caught it. "What a warrior you are! Not a single arrow missed! Saved me more than once, she did," he added eagerly.

"You can thank Felix for that," said Cahira. She paused and sighed as the bat and Thorleif eyed each other warily.

"A bat's vision is much sharper and quicker than a human's," explained Felix, though he sounded a little embarrassed. "Nothing to it."

"He *would* brag," muttered Thorleif, but then the boy

straightened. "But I thank you, Master Bat. Because of you, I will live to fight another day, with all my limbs and vitals intact."

Cahira looked a little odd, as if she'd taken too much ale. Aren moved close to her and placed his hand protectively on her back. She looked dreamily up at him and sighed.

"Are you all right, Cahira?" he asked.

"Oh, fine," she answered wistfully. "Damir's shield is part of me, in a manner of speaking. So it bonds with my energy and . . . boom! When the bolt hit, it was quite a jolt!" She paused and giggled, then absently fiddled with her hair while gazing at him. "Just like you."

His brow angled doubtfully, but she seemed well otherwise. "We will rest here."

"Not here," interrupted the Guerdian. "There's a better place, not far. Better shelter."

"But you're injured, and Cahira must rest," argued Aren. He couldn't go on, not until he'd sat with her, held her, and knew she was truly well.

"When I've tended to my men," said the Guerdian weakly, "we *must* go on. This party that attacked us may join with another—many rogues roam in these hills, more and more each day. And each day, the king sends more of our people into exile, for evil seems to stir from within all quarters."

"It is so in many lands," agreed Aren. He looked to Fareth. "How many survived?"

The innkeeper shook his head. "I'm sorry," he said. "There was no life left in any of the bodies we carried."

"None?" breathed the Guerdian. Elphin laid his hand on the small warrior's thick shoulder.

"I am sorry."

"This we can do, at least," said Aren. "We will lay them to rest as you see fit."

The Guerdian nodded, then bowed his head in prayer. When he looked up, he met Aren's eyes. "You came to our aid when there was no hope. If not for you, every one of the dead would also be brutalized, left on pikes for carrion fowl's sport. The chieftain of the Norsk has rare courage, and rare allies." He stopped and bowed low. "Prince Khadun, son of Kontar of the Guerdian realm offers you his allegiance, and is in your debt."

"You're a prince?" asked Cahira. She sounded cheerful, and still addled. "How nice! So is Aren, in a manner of speaking. Actually . . ." She stopped and chuckled as if surprised. "Actually, I'm a princess of sorts, too, though we don't use those titles. To be honest, they don't mean much in Amrodel." She gazed up at Aren. "But you . . . you wear the title well, my beautiful friend. *'Aren, son of Arkyn, Prince of Ice, Lord of the Norsk'* "

"Maybe she should rest, after all," suggested Ranveig. "Seems to have lost her senses a bit."

Cahira ignored him. She reached up and laid her slender hand upon Aren's face and ran her palm over his beard. "Do you know, the strangest thing happened when I was flying around there, in the light. You know, when the bolt hit me? Something else did, too."

"What?" he asked with a smile.

"I love you." She bit her lip and smiled giddily. "I really do."

His heart caught in his throat, and tears sprang again to his eyes. "Cahira . . ." He wanted to tell her he loved her too, that he had loved her from the first moment he saw her and every hour since, but she pressed her fingers against his lips and shook her head.

"It's all right. I mean, you're infuriating and stubborn and all that, but I just wanted you to know." Her brow furrowed, and she looked a little annoyed. "And now I think . . ." Her eyes spun around and she popped her lips like a bottle being uncorked. "Now I think I might faint."

She was as good as her word. Cahira collapsed and Aren caught her; then he picked her up and held her close against his body. *I love you.* Her sweet vow echoed in his head, and he gently kissed her temple as he carried her to his horse.

There he held her for a moment, then turned to the others.

"We will respect the prince's advice and go onward to the area he mentioned. He and I will return to this place after darkness falls to build a mound for his brethren."

"We'd like to come back with you," said Elphin. Fareth nodded.

"Very well," Aren agreed. "The rest will set up the camp-site and a watch. I'll carry Cahira; and Elphin, you bring Zima along with you." He paused, then glanced at Fareth. "Cahira is all right, isn't she?"

Again, it was Felix who answered, from his perch on Fareth's shoulder. "She's fine—just had her senses knocked around by the force of the shield is all."

Shaen eyed the bat with misgivings. "She's babbling and talking nonsense," she argued. "Damir's shield has never been tested in this manner before. Maybe it damaged her in some way."

The bat scoffed. "She's fine, and given how she's been slipping off with the chieftain every chance she gets, I wouldn't say her words are 'nonsense.'"

"No," agreed Elphin. "She's clearly in love with him."

Thorleif held out his hand. "That reminds me, Woodlander, pay up!"

"What?" Elphin's eyes widened, but then he yanked out a small felt bag and passed two gold coins to Thorleif, who pocketed them and nodded deferentially to Aren.

"The Woodlander wagered you'd be making the declaration first," Thorleif explained. "I put my coins on you, my lord, and bet she'd be the one."

"And when did it become habit to place bets on the private matters of your Lord Chieftain?" Aren asked.

"When we took up with the Woodlanders of Amrodel, that's when," said Thorleif. "Figured if you could do it, might as well join you!"

Aren eyed Fareth. "And you, innkeeper? Are you wagering on these matters, too?"

"Aye, but I bet neither one of you would say the words until after you'd bedded her."

Aren shook his head in disbelief. "This is a Woodland habit that I hadn't encountered firsthand, though I'm aware it frequently exasperated Damir. I can see why."

Felix chortled. "Is that so? Well, the chief offender among us, my lord, is the lass you're holding. The Mage Child's winnings almost outdid . . ." The bat stopped and coughed, but Elphin looked at him thoughtfully.

"You know more of our dealings than one would think possible," he observed, "for one we didn't know existed until you showed up in the tavern on the night we left Amrodel."

"Aye, but the bat's right," said Fareth. "Young Cahira racked up more wins than anyone save the Elder Mage Madawc—and she was closing in on him, too, before this happened."

Aren gazed into Cahira's face as she lay in his arms, sleeping. He bent low, then whispered close to her ear. "This wager I make with you, my angel. The next time one of us risks our life for the other, it will be me."

9

THE GUERDIAN KING

Cahira woke to early morning light. Aren lay close to her, his body curled along hers. She lay quietly for awhile and listened to his slow, even breaths. Then she rolled over and softly kissed his neck. He murmured, opened his eyes, and smiled. "Cahira . . ."

"I'm sorry," she whispered.

His brow knit. "For what, angel?"

"For being much less than an angel, I'm afraid. I should not have spoken ill of your brother. If you saw good in him, then good there must have been."

He looked at her tenderly, then kissed her brow. "And I am sorry to speak against your quest. You are doing what must be done to save your people. I understand that."

"Do you? I have questioned it more than once myself."

He touched her cheek gently. "If we could find another way to disable the dark wizard, would you consider it?"

"I would," she replied. "Do you know a way?"

"Not yet, but the Guerdian king may."

"How would he know?"

"The Guerdians keep detailed records, as far back in history as their own beginnings. Those records will undoubtedly contain details concerning the wizard who enslaved them. Their king is the keeper of those records. They are considered the Guerdians' greatest treasure, beyond price, even more valuable than their armor."

"Will he let us see them?"

"I will speak to Khadun, and he may be able to persuade his father."

Cahira drew a tight breath. "I am almost afraid to hope."

Aren ran his fingers through her hair. "Be not afraid to hope, Cahira. It is the star that shines on us, beyond shadows, through the darkest night. Like love," he whispered, and he moved above her, and gently kissed her mouth.

Her heart fluttering, she wrapped her arms around his shoulders and returned his kiss. She felt his tongue slide between her lips, and her nerves tingled. She grazed the tip of her tongue against his and he murmured with pleasure.

"Guess the lady's on the mend, my lord?"

Cahira squealed, but Aren rested his forehead against hers and sighed miserably. "Thorleif . . . Shaen didn't hire you to keep watch on us, did she? A few coins added to yesterday's wager, in exchange for interrupting these moments every chance you get?"

Thorleif looked confused. "No, my lord. Of course not! And I'd not take coins for such a ignoble deed!" He paused. "Actually, she sent me to check on you because you've both slept longer than the rest of us, and she feared the lady witch here might be ill—coughing up blood or some such thing, I suppose."

Aren met Cahira's gaze, frowned, then rolled over on his back beside her. "Thorleif, should you wake or disturb me again for any reason other than impending ambush—by an attacker you've actually seen with your own eyes—I will run you through with a lance."

"A lance, my lord?"

"That's what I'm thinking."

Thorleif smacked his lips, then turned to go. "Understood,

my lord." He hesitated at the doorway. "By the by, breakfast is ready. Ranveig and Fareth made it together, with only a few harsh words between them." He paused again. "Well, Ranveig shoved him once, and the Woodlander issued a few choice words in his own tongue—probably curses, from the sound of—"

"The bat may be right about you," interrupted Aren.

"How is that, my lord?" Thorleif asked in surprise, and suspicion. "Can't imagine that creature being right about anything. Now, last night, after you got back from helping the Guerdian—good deed, that, to take it upon yourself—and settled in—"

Aren growled and sat up. "You talk too much!"

Thorleif braced, sputtered, then raised his head. "As you say, my lord." He left, offended, and Cahira laughed and snuggled up behind Aren. She wrapped her arms around him and kissed his neck.

"You are testy this morning. Why is that?"

He glanced over his shoulder and smiled at her. "Because my body feels like a drawn bow, and my heart is telling me to stay right here and hold you and spend hours showing you what I feel for you. Yet if I do, I know Thorleif, or Shaen, or any one of them, is likely to stomp over here and tell me the sun is shining, or a light wind blows, and I'll never get the chance."

Cahira rested her cheek against his back and hugged him. "My heart is filled with you," she whispered, and he leaned his head back, his eyes closed.

"And mine, with you," he answered softly, but then he twisted to look at her. "But there is something I don't understand."

"What's that?"

"The dark wizard speaks to you, you say. Presumably, he hears you in some measure as well."

"I believe he does," she agreed. "Though I wouldn't call it a conversation, exactly. What of it?"

"Well, when he accessed Eliana in that fashion, she said

he was aware that her relationship with Damir was deepening—even that they drew close to conceiving a child, which would have destroyed his plans at that time, just as it would now."

"That's true. . . ."

"Then why doesn't he sense *us?*"

Cahira considered. "I don't know." She paused. A small panic budded. "What if I can't conceive, and he knows it?"

"That seems unlikely."

"No . . . No, you're right. Eliana said he taunted her about Damir—that Damir would die, that sort of thing. As far as I can tell, though he knows I resist him, the Arch Mage has no idea you exist at all. But he must know you wielded the Dragonfly Sword against him in the last battle."

"Maybe not," said Aren. "He would have felt the sword's power and hated its light, but he may have believed Damir wielded it. And I never touched his force directly, because I redirected the white sword, threw it like a spear."

"That comes as some relief," said Cahira. "He doesn't really know my thoughts. I don't think I matter to him too much. Often, he speaks as if I am only a tool to be used to gain whatever it is he expects to happen when we 'bond.'" She paused. "I wonder what that even means?"

Aren eyed her doubtfully. "There is only one way a man and woman bond, unless he means in friendship, which doesn't sound in character for the most evil wizard the world has ever known."

Cahira grimaced and shuddered. "I don't picture him as even human. He appears to me as a dark figure, wreathed in ash and blood."

"That is your image of him, perhaps, but when he resurrects, he must expect to do so as a man."

"A hideous man."

"You referred to me as 'hideous,' if you recall," he reminded her with a grin.

She kissed his ear, lightly nipped the lobe, then licked. His breath caught, and she slid her hands along his back, and kneaded his taut muscles. "I was wrong. But I suspect I may be more accurate in envisioning the Arch Mage."

"You picture him with fangs dripping blood," said Aren. "But evil is not always so clearly marked."

She massaged his strong neck, and Aren sighed with pleasure. "It will be clear with him," she continued. "He can resurrect himself, but only by the force of evil. He will hardly be pretty."

"I suppose that remains to be seen," Aren said.

She stopped her ministrations. "Not if we find another way to defeat him, it won't." She ran her hands from his neck to his shoulders, and his body relaxed at her touch. "You have given me hope that there might be another way. Perhaps I was stubborn not to consider it . . . but Damir has studied this matter since he became king, and he found no other solution."

"He may be right," agreed Aren. "But we would be wise to seek out all paths before we take the darkest."

"I will do as you ask," she agreed softly. "Whatever you ask."

He looked at her and smiled. "Does this mean I am no longer your prisoner?"

She kissed his face, then the corner of his mouth. "I think we both know you never were."

The first giddiness of love had transformed into something far more powerful in Cahira's heart. She rode Zima behind Aren and the Guerdian prince, who rode double behind Rika. Apparently, Guerdians didn't use ponies and kept donkeys only to carry burdens, and he seemed suspicious of riding despite his injuries. But Rika quietly convinced him that it was safe and would quicken their journey, so he relented.

Cahira listened quietly as Aren spoke to Khadun in the Guerdian tongue. He spoke the language easily, and treated the stout little warrior with the deference the Guerdians tended to expect. Already Khadun admired him, and she had learned that, while she slept last night, Aren had returned to the battle site and helped build the traditional burial mounds for the Guerdian's fallen companions.

Aren glanced back at her often as they rode, and silent smiles passed between them. Shaen looked on disapprovingly, but she seemed to have accepted the direction of Cahira's heart, and had stopped trying to persuade Cahira to resist what seemed inevitable. Cahira wanted to join with him, to give him all of herself, to love him fully, to go deeper into the bliss they had touched together.

The path widened, and she directed Zima up next to Pip. "How far are we riding today?" she asked.

"Khadun says we will reach the Guerdians' hold by nightfall," replied Aren. "The way is secret, save to the Guerdians themselves." He paused and glanced deferentially at the prince, who nodded.

"You've never seen it?" asked Cahira.

Aren hesitated, and his eyes shifted. "I've never been a guest of the king before, no. It's a secret and amazing realm."

Clearly Aren had, indeed, viewed the Guerdian hold—probably on escapades with his friends. Khadun did not seem to realize, but Cahira gave Aren a knowing look and he winked. *I wish I had known you then*, she thought. *What fun we would have had!*

"The Hungry Cat Tavern had the same allure for me," she said casually, "forbidden, yet everything of interest seemed to happen there. Once, Eliana put a potion in the ale that made all the men sound like hummingbirds."

Fareth glared and snorted at the memory. "We didn't call her 'The Fiend' for nothing."

"I understood that was a title bestowed upon her by Damir," said Aren.

"He might have started it, but it was well and often used by many," said Fareth. He nodded to Cahira fondly. "This one here, though a pip, became a fixture at the tavern. Kept a small keg of goat's milk on hand for her, until she convinced Madawc to let her have something stronger."

Aren laughed, but Felix spluttered on Fareth's shoulder.

"Relentless child, she was," he grumbled. "The Mage Child should not have been drinking ale!"

Cahira looked at the bat in surprise. "Did you know me?"

Felix looked uncomfortable and fidgeted, then hopped to Fareth's other shoulder. "Oh, well . . . I've been around and about for quite some time." He looked off into the distance, idly. "And my species handles ale much better than humans."

"Indeed?" Thorleif angled an eyebrow and bestowed a knowing glance upon the bat. "That's why I've found you, repeatedly, flat on your back near the ale jug, your wings splayed and your round stomach exposed, and with what appears to be a smile on your smug little face?"

Felix glared, then turned his head away and refused to answer.

"They always made it look so good," said Cahira. "Lots of froth. But I have to confess, I prefer Norsk brew now that I've tasted it. Eliana always said it was better."

"Did she, now?" Fareth huffed indignantly. Then he looked thoughtful. "Of course, I always brew it light because that's been the Woodlander taste. It might not hurt to brew up a few batches with a little more . . . kick."

Aren laughed. "Wonderful! Just what the world needs— drunken Mages."

Ranveig nodded. "Might I remind you that the Norsk build is considerably larger than that of you Woodland sylphs? We're able to handle stronger brew."

"That would explain why you just never see a drunken Norskman!" Elphin stated flatly. "In the seaport of Amon-Dhen, every Norsk I've ever encountered is the epitome of grace and culture, listening to the music of harp and flute, speaking quietly amongst his friends and quietly 'handling' their stronger brew."

Cahira repressed a giggle, but Thorleif bristled. "The Norsk constitution is hardier by far than a Woodlander's. It takes a lot to get us even *close* to drunk!"

"One tankard would lay you low, boy," guessed Felix.

"Guerdians drink wine," spoke up Khadun, "and do not

tend to drunkenness. But it seems unlikely that either Norskman or Woodlander could handle its potency."

"'Wine?'" Elphin laughed. "Only our women drink wine."

Something glimmered in Khadun's round, dark eyes, but his expression remained stoic. "It may be that I'm wrong, and some among you may sample our vintage with no effect whatsoever." His gruff voice sounded baiting to Cahira, and Thorleif responded with force.

"You can count on it, Guerdian! Your 'vintage' won't cause a ripple in my thoughts."

"Nor mine," added Elphin.

Beside Cahira, Aren sighed and shook his head. "This should prove interesting."

"Would you care to wager on that, Woodlander?" Thorleif asked Elphin. "I can put away more Guerdian wine than you, and stay clear-headed enough to string the witch's bow!"

"You stay away from my bow!" ordered Cahira. "In fact, maybe you should stay away from all weapons, if you're engaging in a drinking contest."

"Good idea," agreed Aren.

"Ha!" Thorleif turned and leaned his arm on his horse's haunch as he faced Elphin, who rode behind him. "Let us hurry on, and get started on this wager!" Elphin nodded, and the pair galloped off ahead.

Cahira eyed Aren. "I thought you said the way was secret?"

"It is secret," said Aren. "I expect we'll come across them in a few minutes, lost."

"Youth has its foibles," said Fareth. "Of course, I wouldn't have any trouble with the Guerdian drink myself, but I can handle most any brew you'd put before me."

Ranveig chuckled derisively. "You'd be under their little stone tables before you finished your first goblet. But I've built my stature on Norsk ale. It would take more than Guerdian wine to lay me low!"

Fareth's eyes narrowed. "Is that so? Perhaps you'd like to put on coin or two on that?"

"Done!" swore Ranveig. And then the two innkeepers fell back behind Bodvar and Shaen, where their argument dissolved into a clash over stew ingredients.

Aren glanced at Rika. "Are you going to fall into this, too, dare I ask?"

Rika angled her brow. "I've had Guerdian wine." She paused and nodded politely at Khadun, who sat behind her. "Not from plunder, of course—in a tavern in Amon-Dhen. Today, I'll stick to tea."

Cahira glanced over at Aren. "And you? Have you sampled this legendary drink?"

"Once only," he told her. "But that was enough."

"Why? What happened?"

"When three boys share a cask of Guerdian wine . . ." He paused and shook his head. "It's not a pretty sight."

Cahira laughed, and her heart warmed further with affection. "I hope you hadn't been helmed Norsk chieftain at that time. That wouldn't have been very dignified."

He shook his head. "No, I was younger. But the memory, as far as it goes, remains vivid."

"Maybe you should warn the others."

Aren shrugged. "Live and learn," he said. He glanced back at Shaen, then lowered his voice. "I believe Shaen professed a fondness for wine, it being 'much more ladylike' than ale. Perhaps we should suggest she sample a goblet—and get a night's peace for a change."

Cahira started to object, then stopped herself. "Good idea."

He met her gaze, and his smile turned sensual. "Then it may be, my Lady Mage, that you and I will have, at last, a chance for a conversation that lasts all night."

Aren couldn't reach the Guerdian hold fast enough. In fact, Khadun selected a path that seemed longer and more roundabout than one Aren knew, and it was all he could do not to point that out. Maybe the path he knew was rockier and a harder passage, but single file they could managed it easily, and they'd be at the hold by now.

Every time he looked at Cahira, the sensuality in her blue eyes seemed to have increased. At his last glance, she'd dampened her lips with a quick dart of her tongue, and had fallen silent as if vivid thoughts consumed her. He had a fair idea what those thoughts regarded, and it set his body afire.

The sun set over the plains in the west as the horses labored up the last slope before the hold. Khadun directed Rika ahead, and the leaders stopped at the crest to wait for the others. Aren rode up beside Cahira and watched her face as she took in the sight that he had first beheld years before. Her lips parted in wonder, and her eyes widened as she stared across the crafted riverbed to the great city of the Guerdians.

"It's magnificent!" She looked at him in astonishment. "I had no idea they lived in such a place!"

The Guerdian city had been carved, ages before, into the cliffside itself, facing west, and now the fading sun sent its last red rays over the dwellings that lined the recesses of the majestic mountainsides. A high palace had been formed at the center of the city, its levels reaching from the valley at its foot up to a peak that finally blended into the mountains above. Many rows of dwellings stretched north and south from that central palace, all crafted in the same style of golden-red clay with arched windows and doorways, yet varying greatly in size and grandeur.

Overall, the city gave the impression of unity, harboring infinite individuality in taste—a commonness within itself that allowed for all differences. A wide bridge swept from the crest where Aren's party now gathered to the entrance of the high palace. Small knights patrolled the area in ceaseless, steady motion, and the fading sun glanced off their bright armor and high, pointed helms. High steps ran upward from the bridge, and those, too, glittered in the sunset, for they were crafted of shining marble mined from deep within the northern mountains.

Khadun pointed at the central dwelling. "There lies the Palace of Amon-Daal, the home of my father, and the glory of our people."

Cahira turned to him. "The streets are paved with stones, as they are in Amon-Dhen. Did Guerdians build that port city, too?"

"Aye," said Khadun. " 'Twas founded by your own race, in ages past, when the Elite Mages spread far and wide from Amrodel, but they enlisted our builders, the greater craftsmen, to design and build the trade city by the sea."

"It's beautiful," she murmured. "I've never seen anything like it."

"I felt the same when I first saw your father's palace," said Aren.

"But we have nothing like this in the Woodland," she replied.

He smiled. "Perhaps it wasn't the palace, but the angel within that enchanted me."

"The Guerdians designed that building, too," said Khadun. "But the Woodlanders had no need for defense—not then, so it was built for art alone. This hold was crafted to withstand attack, which it has done many times in years past when the Norsk hordes were more aggressive than they are now." He gazed at Aren thoughtfully. "It is said among my people that the Norsk have finally evolved, now that the one who leads them is no mere brute, but a man of wisdom instead. I can see that is the case, and we are grateful."

"Yet too many of our people, both Norsk and Guerdian, have succumbed to darkness and cruelty," said Aren. "You may be fortunate to live in such a hold if this darkness grows."

"We feel it, aye," said Khadun. "It grows outward, and into the depths of our hearts, breeding fear and anger, hatred and discontent, though there is no reason it should be so, for my father is a generous leader. There are some among us who say this darkness foreshadows another, one that our land has not seen for an age." He paused, and his voice grew deep and low. "They say the One who Fell has returned and seeks out his minions, that those who follow his darkness are rising and will form an army in his likeness, and soon all the land will be seeped in his shadow. I do not yet believe these dire predictions."

"They may not be far off," said Aren. "The Mages of Amrodel say the dark wizard who lies beneath the southern peak is responsible for the darkness, and that indeed he seeks to rise again."

Khadun's eyes widened in fear and shock. "If this is so, a grim time awaits us. But how can he arise? He fell into darkness and locked himself there for eternity. He might reach out in thought and spirit to bend lesser beings to his will, but he himself cannot arise!"

"It appears he can," said Aren. Then he hesitated. "It is for this reason we have come to your land, to seek audience with your king. The records you keep from times long past may serve us in our quest, that we might prevent his rising and set our lands back into peace."

"Will your father allow us to see these books?" asked Cahira.

Khadun hesitated. "I know not, for our records are sacred to my people. But for this, he may allow an exception."

"I hope so," said Cahira. "With so much at stake, we need all the help we can get."

They rode into the city and dismounted. The Guerdians took the horses to the stable where the donkeys were kept, though Elphin followed to direct them carefully in proper care. Apparently, the Guerdians had the matter in hand, because the young Woodlander soon bounded up the wide stairs and rejoined Aren's party.

"Don't want Thorleif getting a jump on me in the matter of Guerdian wine!" he said breathlessly. He shoved the Norskman aside, and Thorleif pushed him back.

"If you two could wait until we make the proper introductions, this might proceed the more smoothly," suggested

Aren. "Guerdians are very formal, and I propose you respect
that."

Indeed, as they entered the massive palace, lavishly attired
Guerdian women appeared and bowed to Khadun, who
nodded respectfully back. Stout knights lined the passage to
the King's chamber, which Aren had only viewed in the dark
of night, hiding behind pillars while his friends waited outside. But with the last rays of the sun streaming into the hall
and the first lamplights set to glow, it was a glorious sight.

The Guerdians eyed Aren's party doubtfully as he passed,
and he heard whispers behind them. Khadun stopped outside the King's chambers and turned to Aren. "I will enter
alone and speak to my father. Wait here, and I will request
an audience on your behalf."

Aren nodded, and Khadun bowed, then stood back as two
mail-clad knights pulled the door slowly open. Khadun entered and the doors closed behind him. "What if he doesn't
let us in?" asked Cahira. She chewed her lip nervously and
fidgeted.

"You are impatient. He will see us."

She sucked in a quick breath. "I hope so."

"I can't imagine what you hope to gain by an audience
with the Guerdians," said Shaen as she came up beside
them. "While their craftsmanship is undeniably impressive,
they are poor warriors and have no magic. How can they
help us?"

"There are other powers besides might and magic," said
Aren. "The Guerdians maintain records of the past, for they
know it is destined to repeat itself as the generations unfold—
as indeed it appears to be doing now. Wouldn't you say?"

Shaen looked blank, but then she nodded earnestly as if
she understood. Cahira was right, Aren decided. Shaen
wasn't terribly intelligent. But she had other skills, less obvious, and was still dangerous.

Thorleif looked around. "So . . . where are the taverns, do
you think?"

Aren shook his head. "Could we attend to the matter at hand, *then* pursue the resolution of your wagers?"

"How long can it take to get permission to look through a few books?" Thorleif paused. "Better to keep records in ballads and songs as we do. More interesting that way."

"But not so effective," Aren reminded him. "The Guerdians have kept their history since a time long before the Norsk came into being." He paused. "Maybe their records contain information on our own origins, for we know little of our beginnings, save that our people moved north into the lands of snow and ice. I hope we'll have time to find our information, for the pages of these tomes are said to be innumerable, beyond the scope of one man to read in a lifetime."

Cahira fidgeted. "And how do you suggest we read the Guerdian tongue, anyway?"

"I can make out their runes, though it will take time," said Aren. "But given the Guerdian attention to order and detail, I think we can assume they'll be set out according to date, and it shouldn't be too hard to find the period when the dark wizard enslaved their race."

"I'd think he'd be worth a whole volume or two," guessed Elphin.

"How's Guerdian cooking?" asked Fareth suddenly, and he patted his stomach. "I could use a morsel besides stew and dried meat for a change. Before the wine," he added with a glance at Ranveig.

"I've tried their food when in Amon-Dhen," said Aren. "It is lighter than ours, and spiced, but I think you'll find it both filling and tasty."

"Good!" Cahira smacked her lips. "I'm hungry! And I think I'd like to try a sip or two of that wine, just to see what it tastes like."

"Not too much," said Aren. "I don't want to end up carrying you to your bed just to watch you snore."

"I don't snore," she replied, but her bright eyes glittered. "Where will we sleep, anyway?"

"I'm not sure," said Aren. "Perhaps Khadun will direct us to suitable accommodations."

"Let it be so, and soon!" said Rika. "And this night, I hope I get a room by myself." She paused and eyed Aren. "Perhaps on the far side of this cliff city from wherever our Lord Chieftain decides to bed down."

He caught her intimation and grinned despite himself. "I'll put in that request."

"I would also like to bed down alone," said Shaen, and Aren looked at her in surprise.

"Indeed? You're not going to stir up a brawl that will keep us occupied through the night, or summon us from our beds to battle some imagined cliffside phantom?"

She gazed at him evenly, revealing no anger or offense. Instead, she smiled resignedly. "I've given up on trying to keep you two apart. Though I hope you remember the great risk should Cahira . . . well, should her energy be . . . fractured."

"I'll keep that in mind," he replied.

"Don't intend to impregnate the lass, eh, my lord?" asked Felix cheerfully. Though surrounding Guerdians heard the bat speak, they merely looked between themselves and said nothing. Apparently, they expected no less from Woodland magic, and the Guerdian race had never feared the Mages as had the Norsk had, for their history together was longer and far more peaceful.

Aren cast a dark look the bat's way, and the creature whistled. "Never mind, my lord. Figure you know what you're doing."

Cahira blushed furiously, but she made no comment. Bodvar stood by silently, taking no interest in the Guerdian surroundings. Since the battle and Cahira's surprising resurrection, he had said little, and Aren sensed a darkness growing in the hardened warrior that he wasn't sure how to shift.

"Perhaps you should join the Woodlanders and Thorleif in their wager, Bodvar," he suggested.

"I have no taste for wine," the man replied darkly.

Shaen touched his arm playfully. "Oh, come, Bodvar! A powerful warrior like yourself, afraid to taste the fragrant wine of a little grape? I'll be so disappointed if you don't try just a little." She paused and giggled. "I must confess, I enjoy our Woodland wine, and I expect this will be much too strong. But still, I'd like to sample just a taste."

"The taste is light enough," said Aren. He started to add that its taste was deceptive, then stopped himself. "I'm sure you'll enjoy it."

"If not, we have ale," Ranveig reminded Bodvar. "You can have that instead, if the wine doesn't interest you and you don't succumb to the lure of our challenge."

Bodvar nodded but said nothing. Shaen tapped his arm. "I'd feel so much safer with you near," she added in a soft voice, but then laughed. "Especially if these four rogues drink too much and lose their senses!"

Bodvar glanced at her and his expression softened, though Aren caught a strange glimmer in the warrior's eyes. As the warrior looked at Shaen, his eyes darkened with attraction. Aren hadn't paid much attention to any other budding relationship besides his own, but among the rest of his company, only Bodvar and Shaen had refrained from the endless bickering. If they intended to spend a randy night together, who was he to argue?

Shaen peered at Bodvar through lowered lashes, demure, and yet . . . Aren remembered her intimation of passion and "dark erotic paths" that she had shared with the late king of Amrodel. Though Aren found no temptation in such a pursuit, Bodvar might. He wondered briefly if they would emerge unscathed the next morning, then banished the repellent thought and turned back to Cahira.

She, too, was watching Shaen and Bodvar, and seemed to sense the same attraction; though in her innocence, she surely missed the dark undercurrents. She glanced at Aren and elevated her brow, smiling as if she were witnessing the blush of a new love. Aren forced himself to smile, too, but he thought it far more likely that this new romance would leave either Bodvar or Shaen, or both, with significant bruises, claw marks, and torn clothing rather than soft sighs and gentle longing.

Khadun emerged from the King's chambers, stood back, and bowed as the king himself emerged. The Guerdian king was old but still hale, shorter than his son, but venerable and well worthy of his title. He had a long gray beard and wore thick robes that shimmered in the lamplight as he stepped forward. He waited, and Aren bowed low, then signaled that the others should do likewise. From the corner of his eye, Aren saw that even Felix managed to crumple his small body into a semblance of a bow.

"Rise," commanded the king, his voice so deep that his son's gruff tone seemed almost a falsetto in comparison. "My son, Khadun, prince of Amon-Daal and heir to the Guerdian realm . . ." Indeed, the Guerdians were formal, and long-winded, but Aren waited patiently through the king's speech. "We bid you welcome, chieftain of the Ice People of the Norskland, our neighbors, once enemies, and now our guests."

Aren bowed again. "It is an honor for the chieftain of the Norsk to visit your fair realm, my liege, and to gaze in wonder at the splendor your people have wrought."

"Ah," said the king, oddly brief in his response as he assessed Aren. "I have seen your people many times, and they all look the same to my eyes. But there was one . . . one I saw eleven years ago. A tall boy and skinny, he was, with hair the color of dawn-gold and eyes like amber jewels. There was about him a strange light, as if joy followed and grew from within him. . . ."

Aren gazed at him in astonishment. "My liege?"

"I saw the boy flit like a ghost between the pillars of this very hall," added the King. "I thought to order my guards to fetch him and give him a night or two in our dungeons, but the happiness with which he crept around—and the fact he plundered nothing save a handful of grapes—convinced me to let him pass undetected." The old king paused, and his

YES! ☐

Sign me up for the **Historical Romance Book Club** and send my TWO FREE BOOKS! If I choose to stay in the club, I will pay only $8.50* each month, a savings of $5.48!

YES! ☐

Sign me up for the **Love Spell Book Club** and send my TWO FREE BOOKS! If I choose to stay in the club, I will pay only $8.50* each month, a savings of $5.48!

NAME: _____

ADDRESS: _____

_____

TELEPHONE: _____

E-MAIL: _____

☐ **I WANT TO PAY BY CREDIT CARD.**

☐  ☐ MasterCard ☐ DISCOVER

ACCOUNT #: _____

EXPIRATION DATE: _____

SIGNATURE: _____

Send this card along with $2.00 shipping & handling for each club you wish to join, to:

Romance Book Clubs
20 Academy Street
Norwalk, CT 06850-4032

Or fax (must include credit card information!) to: 610.995.9274.
You can also sign up online at www.dorchesterpub.com.

*Plus $2.00 for shipping. Offer open to residents of the U.S. and Canada only. Canadian residents please call 1.800.481.9191 for pricing information.

If under 18, a parent or guardian must sign. Terms, prices and conditions subject to change. Subscription subject to acceptance. Dorchester Publishing reserves the right to reject any order or cancel any subscription.

dark eyes shone like warm coals in his wise face. "Strangely though, after the boy departed, I was informed that a cask of our finest wine had somehow gone missing."

Aren winced, but he had no idea how to respond. "Boys commit reckless acts," he offered weakly.

"Indeed," agreed the king. "Did you enjoy the wine?"

Aren laughed and met the king's knowing eyes. "For the first few draughts, yes. After that, my memory fails—but the waking afterward was worse than the vilest illness."

The king laughed, too, a deep rumble that echoed in the hall. "That is why we take our wine in small goblets." He stood back and assessed Aren's company. "A fine lot, you are!" he commented. "It looks as if you wear all the dirt of the foothills—and is that blood? Do any of your kind wash?"

Aren cringed, but Thorleif piped up cheerfully. "Well, the chieftain and the witch bathed a few days back," he said. "But the rest of us haven't done more than splash our faces since we left the Snow Pony Inn."

The king's brow furrowed. "'Witch?' Is this how a Norskman addresses an Elite Mage?"

"I'm getting used to it," said Cahira.

"Young lady, you are a Mage, and as such, entitled to the honor and dignity of your station," said the king sternly. "Rare are your kind, and noble their souls. We harken back to the one whose image is emblazoned on our tapestries, she who was most fair and as like to yourself as a mother to a daughter. She, whose courage and sacrifice saved our people in their darkest hour."

Cahira gazed down at the stout king in wonder. "You speak of our ancient Queen!"

"Aryana Daere, Queen of Amrodel," agreed the king.

"That's odd!" said Cahira. "I don't think I've ever known her name."

"You were lax in your studies, lass," said Felix. The king eyed the bat, but showed little surprise at the creature's abilities.

"Are talking bats common to your people?" Aren asked Cahira.

"Not that I know of," she responded.

"In the days of Queen Aryana, the Elite Mages often accomplished such transformations," said the king, but then he paused and looked at Felix again. "But I will say no more on this. The magic of the Woodland remains strong, and that gives hope to my heart."

"Then you'll let us access your records?" asked Cahira.

"Not before you've washed," said the king, but he seemed amused. Aren eyed him doubtfully, and the king held up his hands. "As it happens, the Chamber of Tomes lies above this palace, deeply embedded in the cliffside. To go there at night is to be lost in darkness. When morning comes, light slants through the long channels and illuminates the room. You should go then."

"Why don't you use lamplights or torches?" asked Cahira, and the King's brow arched as if she'd issued an impertinent question.

"The tomes are ancient and rare," replied the king. "We allow no risk of fire. Only the slanted light of the sun is allowed to penetrate that chamber—and even then, there is no direct light. Tonight, you will stay in my city as the guest of the king. Tomorrow, Prince Khadun will escort two of you—and only two, the chieftain and the Mage, for they represent their people—and you may browse our histories as you wish. There, you will find the history of the high Priest of Kora, Cheveyo."

"'Cheveyo,'" repeated Aren. "That was his real name?"

"It was," said the king. "It means 'Spirit Warrior,' and his magical energy, which the Mages of Amrodel refer to as *ki*, was said to be the most powerful ever known, even among the high priests of Kora. He was admitted into their ranks at a younger age than any before him, and like his power, his pride and arrogance knew no bounds. He challenged the priests, and for reasons that aren't fully known even to us, attempted to usurp power from the prince of Kora, that realm's highest office. The prince mustered a vast army and drove Cheveyo into exile, but Cheveyo killed many in his wrath. The Koraji people called him 'Matchitehew' which means 'Evil Heart,' and they lived in fear of his return."

"And later he was called 'Otaktay,' which means 'kills many,' " added Felix impatiently, but Aren cleared his throat to silence him. "Sorry. Go on."

The king nodded politely at the bat and continued. "Cheveyo came west and claimed the southern peak of this mountain range, where he intended to gather the power to return to Kora and rule as a god. Only the great courage of the Elite Mages of Amrodel stopped him, but they lost their beloved queen before the battle ended. Cheveyo trapped himself in a spell of his own making, and for a long while, we believed the world was free of his evil. But it was not so, and his dark energy has grown to where it affects those of my people who are exposed to its force. One day, we think, this shadow may swallow us all."

"Do you think we might find a method to stop him in your library?" asked Aren.

"There is no method," said the king, "or we would have used it ourselves when we had the chance. But you may learn more of his history, and in that, some path to his destruction. In the early years that he spent among us, he was less closed off, and he shared information with our scholars. But then he made us his slaves and ruled as all tyrants do, giving nothing and taking all. The palace he wrought in the southernmost mountain was carved and built by our people, and many died in its making. It is grand but stained with blood, and I would see it wiped from the world and forgotten."

"We will do that, if we can," said Aren, and he bowed. "I thank you, my liege. For your generosity, there may yet be hope for our quest."

"Let it be so," said the king, and he bowed, too. "But now . . ." He paused, and his nose scrunched oddly. "You and your company will depart and wash! I will have suitable clothing provided while our handmaidens cleanse and refit those you wear now."

Cahira looked at him in surprise. "Will they fit us?"

Aren cast her a warning look—the Guerdians did not react well to having their size referenced. "The Guerdians are excellent craftsmen of garb as well as armor," he offered hastily. "I'm sure whatever they provide will be fine."

10

THE GUERDIAN HOLD

"Oh, these fit just perfectly!"

Cahira emerged from a small dressing room and faced Aren, who waited in the quarters the king had provided for them. Mercifully, the lavish Guerdians had crafted what they considered high ceilings, or Aren would have spent his visit to the hold with his back bent low. His head grazed the ceiling and his body seemed to fill the room.

Khadun had taken each of Aren's party to separate dwellings abandoned by Guerdians who had either died or been sent into exile. Cahira couldn't imagine why anyone would choose to leave Amon-Daal. The palace was fitted out in a manner to make the palace in Amrodel seem like a fishing hut, the furniture carved from marble in swirls of pink, ivory, and green, with wall hangings of silk, and a few bright tapestries reminiscent of what she'd seen in the Norsk halls, yet woven with delicacy and attention to historical detail.

She looked around, still amazed by her surroundings, but Aren just stared at her. She studied his attire. "Yours really does fit!" He wore a clean brown shirt, bound with a belt at his waist, and leggings. He looked particularly handsome, his blond hair hanging soft and still damp over his wide shoulders. "The Guerdian maid told me that they collect clothing from Norsk rogues they defeat, and wash and mend it. I'm not sure why they bother, except that Guerdians don't seem to like waste. They altered some of their garments for Rika, Shaen, and me. . . ."

Aren didn't comment, seemingly shocked. "What's the matter with you?" she asked, but then she glanced at her dress. "It is rather small, isn't it?"

Aren's eyes were rounder than usual, and he nodded. "Yes. Quite small."

"I think they just took one of their little dresses and added these ties." She indicated the cotton strings at her shoulders. "It barely reaches my thighs. I can't go out in this!"

"You have the most amazing legs," he said.

She looked down in surprise. "Do I?" She paused. "You don't think this is too . . . skimpy?"

"No!" He stopped and cleared his throat. "Not at all." His eyes shifted to her legs again, and she tugged at the hem uncomfortably.

"Does it cover my backside well enough?"

"I'm not sure—turn around." Cahira turned around, then glanced back over her shoulder. "It's fine." Aren's voice sounded thick and ragged, but maybe he was tired.

"But if I bend over . . ."

"Don't!" Aren coughed. "Not yet. I mean . . . not until . . ." He stopped, grabbed her by the shoulders without warning, pulled her back and kissed her neck hungrily. Cahira shuddered, and he ran his hands down over her bare arms. "Should you grace me with any further sight of your perfect body," he whispered close to her ear, "I will grab you by the hair, bend you over, and take you to a place that even Shaen and Bodvar might see as dangerous."

Cahira squeaked and hopped away, then faced him. Her heart moved in odd little hops, and almost, she felt the temptation to edge her hem higher. But she shook her head to regain her senses. "You . . . you are not yourself!"

"Am I not?" Those amber eyes flashed—indeed, dangerously—and a feral smile formed on his lips.

"No, you're . . ." She felt odd—damp and tingly between her legs, at the apex of her thighs. "You're . . . this is just what I heard in the tavern about your kind!"

Aren's smoldering gaze locked with hers. "What is that, my lady?"

"This . . ." She waved her hand nervously. "This ravaging . . . Yes! That's what it is! You look like you might swoop through a village, plunder everything, then . . ."

He took a step toward her, his movement smooth like a Woodland cat. "Then take the most beautiful female I can find, tear off her clothing and drag my lips over every inch of her body before I bury myself deep inside her warm, wet, soft flesh? Is that what you heard?"

"Yes!" She felt strangely unsteady on her feet. "I mean, no, not exactly, not in such vivid terms. But in essence . . ." She stopped and pointed her finger at him. "You are a devil." She paused to fan herself with the end of her long sash. "I hope I don't faint again."

Aren placed his hand on her back and looked at her with concern—obviously feigned. "We can't have *that,* my lady."

"No? Why not?"

"Because I'm hungry." He paused, eyes wide and guileless. "Aren't you?"

They made their way down winding halls according to the directions Khadun had given them, but the long walk along myriad passages did little to slow the wild pulse of Cahira's heart. The way he had looked at her! Those eyes, that power that emanated all around him. And what he had said . . . she felt weak thinking about it. She squirmed to adjust her dress, then carefully ignored Elphin and Fareth's shocked stares as she entered the tavern.

Unlike those of Amrodel and the Norskland, the Guerdian tavern was neat and well-fitted with round marble tables and appropriately low stools. Fareth and Ranveig had seated themselves, and Cahira fought a giggle when she saw them, their large bodies perched uncomfortably on seats four sizes too small.

Thorleif sat opposite Elphin, with a large decanter of pale golden liquid poised and unopened before them. "Who starts?" asked Thorleif.

"We start together," said Elphin, and he poured the wine into one small crystal goblet, then into another.

"Make sure they're even," ordered Thorleif, and both men checked to see that their goblets were filled equally.

"Maybe you two should eat something first," advised Aren, but Thorleif scoffed.

"We've had bread, my lord. I'm full enough."

Aren shook his head. "Very well. But I won't expect to see either of you in the morning, nor probably in the afternoon, either."

"Think we'll be staying for a day or so, my lord?" asked Thorleif.

"Another day, at least," said Aren. "We've ridden long, and we could use the rest, as could the horses."

"I checked on them earlier," spoke up Elphin. "They're fine. Zima's bedded in with one of the Guerdians' little donkeys and has taken quite a dislike to it, but Pip's just following the little fellows in awe. They're both happy enough."

Aren guided Cahira to another table and sat across from her. He spoke in his usual low, quiet voice, but there was something in his eyes that fanned her tension and set her nerves tingling and on edge. Rika entered the tavern, and the men turned to stare at her. She wore a dress like Cahira's, though somehow she had managed to get it lower over her legs.

"Should any of you issue comment on my attire, I will dispatch you and leave your severed head tumbling around the floor." She spoke coolly, waited until the men all snapped back to their respective tasks, then seated herself at the table between Aren's and Thorleif's. She glanced at her chieftain. "I thank you for selecting a room south of the king's chambers," she said. "My own room is the farthest on the north wall."

"I thought you'd appreciate that." Aren laughed.

Cahira looked between them in confusion. "What are you talking about?" She eyed Rika and felt shy. What if Shaen was right, and Rika did care for Aren romantically? Cahira wasn't always accurate in her judgment about people, and Shaen generally picked up such matters as who in Amrodel had formed romantic entanglements. Cahira paid attention only enough to place bets. What she learned by observation, Shaen just seemed to intuit, though the woman never tested her guesses with wagers.

"Never mind," said Aren. "Rika just likes her privacy, that's all."

"I like peace and quiet," said Rika. "Something this night isn't likely to provide if I'm anywhere near you."

Cahira shifted on her small stool. "Your dress covers more than mine."

"Slightly," put in Aren, and Rika directed a dark look his way.

"The Guerdian handmaidens tried to give me a dress like to yours," she said, "but I convinced them it was in their best interest to add another swathe of fabric at the hem."

"I asked them if they could make mine a little bigger, too, but they refused," said Cahira. "They're testy little people if you question them. How did you manage?"

"I drew my axe and told them they'd be even shorter without legs."

Aren laughed. "Well, that was certainly tactful."

"It worked," said Rika evenly.

"I wish I had an axe," said Cahira. "A bow just doesn't have the same impact."

"If they'd seen you wield it during that ambush, they would obey your every command," Rika assured her.

Cahira beamed and clasped her hands together. Rika's approval meant a lot, because it was earned, and genuine. "Thank you!" she said.

Several small tavern maids sped neatly around the room, delivering large trays laden with different foods. They placed decanters of wine on each table, though Rika set out her own flagon of ale instead. Cahira eyed the wine, and Aren poured a portion into her goblet. She held it to her lips, then took a tentative sip. She'd expected something akin to fire, but it was light and almost flowery to the taste, and she took a deeper drink.

Aren clasped her hand. "Be slow with that, I warn you. Two glasses, and you'll be dancing on this table. Three, and I'll be carrying you back to our room. Four, and you'll be sick for days, so pace yourself."

"I won't be dancing on tables," said Cahira. She hesitated. "For one thing, the Guerdians didn't provide undergarments."

Aren's eyes widened and he sucked in a quick breath of air. Rika nodded. "You see why I drew my axe."

"I see why the Guerdian men are always smiling," corrected Aren.

Cahira eyed him doubtfully, then turned her attention to the meal. A loud whistle and squeal disrupted her, and she looked up to see Felix swoop into the tavern. One Guerdian maid started, but another spoke quickly—apparently the Woodlanders' bat already had been discussed—and the maid went back to her task.

Felix landed in the center of Elphin's table, and took position by the untouched tray of food. "You'd best not have started without me!"

"Felix! You're not going to drink with them, are you? I hope you remember your size," said Cahira.

He cranked his little head around and cocked it to one side. "As far as that goes, lass, even at my size, I could drink more wine than this boy. But I am a creature of wisdom, and know my limits. I'm not entering their childish contest. I'm here to judge it!"

"We don't require a judge, bat," argued Thorleif.

"After about three goblets, neither one of you is going to remember how much you've had. I'm here to keep track."

"Fair enough," said Elphin. "Keep an eye on Ranveig and Fareth, too. We've all got bets going. Last one standing—that's the wager overall."

"This should last about a half hour, tops," commented Aren.

Cahira peered down into her cup. The golden liquid shimmered with the slightest hint of pink. "Is it really that strong?"

"Yes," said Aren.

"Maybe I'll have tea instead."

Ranveig tossed her a packet of herbs, and a Guerdian maid brought steaming water. To her surprise, Aren took some, too.

"Don't you want ale? Rika has plenty," said Cahira.

"Not tonight," he replied.

"What's different about tonight?"

"Ale tends to deaden the senses. Tea, they say, makes those same senses all the more acute."

She gazed at him in bewilderment for a moment, then blushed furiously at the glint in his eyes. "Oh, good. Very well. As you wish."

Ranveig and Fareth both devoured a plate of spiced fowl of some sort, and each pronounced it excellent then turned to their tall decanter of wine. They faced off like bears in the north woods, raising their goblets at the same time. "May the best man stand tall at the night's end," said Ranveig.

"I will," agreed Fareth, and Ranveig laughed and drained his goblet in one long draught.

Khadun entered the tavern and seated himself with them. "The custom of wagering on such matters is unknown to my race."

Aren snorted but said nothing more, and Cahira eyed him suspiciously. Khadun remained focused on his guests. "My people drink wine slowly, to savor its taste. Not to learn the amount we can swallow."

Elphin held up his goblet. "Wine," he began, a little unsteadily, "is for women. You little fellows can't put away as much as we larger races can."

"That is undoubtedly true," agreed Khadun. "But it seems wrong to force my guests to drink alone."

Aren glanced at Cahira and winked, but Thorleif seized another goblet and sloshed wine into it. "He's in!"

"As a formality only," agreed Khadun.

"Formality, my backside!" said Fareth, and Cahira grimaced when the innkeeper downed his own portion. "Like rainwater," he informed them. "Flavored with little petals. Think The Fiend came up with a potion that tasted like this once. Called it her 'Wine of Truce,' she did."

"And look what it did to Damir ap Kora!" said Elphin as he took a long drink. Then he peered into the goblet to see what remained. Apparently he hadn't matched Ranveig and Fareth's impressive gulps, because he lifted it to his lips and drank again.

"Well, actually, it was Eliana who drank it," Cahira reminded them. But no one was listening.

Aren rubbed his hand over his mouth and arched his eyebrow. "I was generous," he corrected. "Fifteen minutes, at most."

"Ten," countered Rika.

"And would the ice princess care to wager on that?" Aren asked.

"Four coins," she replied. "Ten minutes before the first one falls from his seat."

"I accept," said Aren.

"If it's a matter of falling from one's seat, I would give them twenty minutes," said Cahira.

Aren's eyes glittered. "And what does my lady wager?"

"Terms of my own making, to be issued when I win."

"Dear lady, if you wager on any of them lasting twenty minutes without falling flat on their faces, I'll be the one issuing terms."

"We shall see." She glanced politely at the Norsk woman. "If Rika would teach me the rudimentary skills at handling an axe, that will be sufficient payment."

Rika laughed. "And if I win, I may just demand the same—for the enjoyment of seeing you struggle to lift it!"

"We'll see," Cahira repeated. She assessed the contestants, then turned back to Aren. "Should we bet on who will win?"

"Aye, but we'll tell our guesses to Felix alone," he suggested.

She shrugged. "Fair enough." She summoned Felix to the table and he hopped importantly toward her.

"What is it, lass?"

"We want to place secret wagers on the last one standing. I will tell you my guess first." She bent down and whispered in what presumably was his ear. "I pick Fareth."

"Good choice, lass." The bat hopped next to Rika, who considered the matter, then delivered her choice in the same manner. Cahira felt sure she saw Rika's lips mouth Ranveig's name. A fair choice, too. Then the bat hopped to Aren's shoulder. Annoyingly, Aren turned away so she couldn't see his guess.

He turned back, and the bat chuckled. "Well, this is likely to be quite a contest, I will say!" He bounced back to El-phin's table, took one look at Thorleif's face, and turned back to Aren. "How long has it been?"

"Nigh onto seven minutes for those two, four for the innkeepers."

"I'd suggest a bet on who's first to fall, but I'm afraid that looks like it'll be Thorleif," said Cahira in a low voice.

"It always is," agreed Rika.

Just as the boy seemed likely to teeter off his seat and make Rika the winner, he shook himself dramatically and re-filled his goblet. "The innkeeper's right, my lord. Rain . . . rain . . . water!" He drank more and Aren laughed.

Rika watched with a slight frown as her time estimation passed and Aren's drew closer. Cahira sat back confidently and waited.

Shaen came into the tavern, dressed in a manner similar to Cahira, though her dress was cut lower around the bust. Bodvar followed soon after. For once, he didn't stop to glare

at Cahira, though he seemed darker and somehow more
foreboding, as if his blood had been heated from ice to fire,
and she wondered if Shaen was the reason. But Shaen seated
herself next to Aren, and Bodvar sat with Rika, so possibly
she was mistaken.

Aren sat back and stretched, then nodded to Bodvar. "Care
to place a wager on the winner, my friend?" he asked.

"Wagering is for Woodlanders," Bodvar replied.

Cahira rolled her eyes. "And Fulthark is for Norskmen.
But Elphin took coins off Thorleif back at the Snow Pony
Inn, and Thorleif, in turn, won two coins on his wager
about . . . well, I guess it was about me, wasn't it?"

"It was!" exclaimed Thorleif. "What do you know, Woodlander? The chieftain's witch is right! As of now, we're tied
in winnings! But after tonight . . ."

"She's not the 'chieftain's witch,'" replied Elphin, as he,
too, refilled his goblet. He held it up to the light and shook
his head. "It's not affecting me at all."

"I barely feel it," countered Thorleif.

Aren glanced at Cahira and said, "He barely feels anything
just now."

"As I was saying," continued Elphin. "She's not the 'chieftain's witch.'"

"No?" Thorleif swayed in his seat, lifted his goblet and
missed his mouth, splashing wine down his loose shirt. He
looked surprised, but drank the rest anyway.

"He . . ." Elphin pointed to Aren with one finger while
holding his goblet. "He is the 'witch's chieftain!" Both men
laughed, and Aren rolled his eyes.

"This will be a short night for those two."

"Indeed, my Lord Chieftain," said Cahira happily. "It appears the time of your wager is almost up."

"He can't last another five minutes."

But the young Norskman continued to chatter with Elphin
about subjects that made no sense. Felix looked back and
forth between them, then glanced at Aren and shrugged his

small shoulder. "Still upright, my lord. 'Fraid the time of your guess has passed."

"Imagine that," said Cahira.

Shaen tried the wine and sipped without interest. "I'm not sure about this Norskman's sport that you've taught us," she offered, her voice light and teasing as she leaned toward Aren. "But I would think you'd have little trouble defeating any of them."

"I'd be down by this point, I promise you," he replied casually, but Bodvar's dark gaze shifted from Shaen to Aren, and he frowned. It occurred to Cahira that the woman was deliberately flattering Aren to antagonize Bodvar, though she couldn't imagine what purpose that might serve. If Shaen found Bodvar intriguing, so much the better, because it would distract her from issuing depressing commiserations to Cahira, but it might be difficult to restrain herself from pointing out that Aren's 'animalistic allure' didn't come close to Bodvar's brute force.

Shaen placed her hand on Aren's arm and laughed. "You sell yourself short, Aren. It's clear you're a man of considerable strength, in so many ways. I think you're just naturally above such silly contests. A man like yourself doesn't have much to prove."

Bodvar glowered, then got up and left the tavern, but Rika arched her eyebrow. "Then you haven't seen our young Lord Chieftain with a tankard of ale in one hand, facing off with our brawniest warriors in a contest of strength, as he pins each one's arm to the table amidst the cheers of tavern maids."

"Arm wrestling?" asked Cahira. "Eliana told me that Damir engaged in that sport!" She paused. "He doesn't like to talk about it much, though." She eyed Aren, then set her bare elbow on the table in front of him. "What do you say?"

Those amber eyes glittered, and he looked as dangerous and powerful as a god. Cahira gulped. She'd been teasing him, but he fixed his gaze upon her, then placed his arm on the table. They clasped hands and he wrapped his strong fingers around hers. But he didn't slam her hand to the table—instead, he leaned forward, never looking away, and kissed her fingers, then sucked each tip gently.

She forgot to breathe. He swept his tongue over each fingertip, and her whole body went weak. Little currents like fire sped along her nerves, centering mercilessly in her core. She shifted on her seat and he smiled. He turned her hand in his, then kissed her palm softly. His brow arched slightly as he released her hand, and he sat back. Cahira just stayed there unmoving, her elbow resting on the table, her fingers curled and tingling. The peaks of her breasts felt curiously sensitive, and she felt sure they pressed against the thin Guerdian fabric. Apparently, Aren thought so, too, because his gaze flicked to her chest and his eyes darkened to a rich gold.

She dampened her lips and drew a quick breath to clear her senses. A heavy thud startled her and she sat back to see Thorleif hit the floor, face down. He made one small utterance, a groan, then fell silent.

"Well, that's done," said Aren. He glanced at Cahira. "Twenty minutes exactly. How did you know that?"

"I didn't spend hours on end at the Hungry Cat for nothing."

"What do we do with him, my lord?" asked Ranveig.

"Leave him there," replied Aren casually. "The Guerdians will clean up later. How are you feeling, Ranveig?"

"No different," said the innkeeper as he drew his sleeve across his mouth.

"Same here," agreed Fareth.

"Truly?" asked Khadun in amazement. "I already feel quite inebriated, and I'm accustomed to our drink." He took another sip of wine, then shrugged. "That's amazing."

Again, Aren chuckled, but Felix hopped back and forth counting drinks. "The Guerdian, Ranveig, and Fareth are steady on their fourth goblet, my lord! Elphin here has just started his fifth . . ."

Elphin stood up and uttered a peculiar whoop as he, apparently, toasted the fallen Thorleif. "I knew it! A Woodlander can outlast a Norskman any day!" He looked down at Thorleif and raised his goblet high, but his eyes spun around in their sockets, and he fell straight back just as a Guerdian maid entered the room.

"Another one down, Your Highness?" she asked Khadun, whose brow puckered in confusion.

"It would appear so! Amazing, because I was sure they could hold more. Ah, but those two are frail of build, despite their remarkable height." He cast a deferential glance between Ranveig and Fareth. "You men appear much sturdier."

"That," said Ranveig, somewhat blurrily, "is because we are!"

Fareth nodded. "We are." He drank again, but Cahira turned to Aren.

"I'm beginning to guess who you wagered on—and I think this is a bet I may lose."

Aren rose and came around the table, then held out his hand. "But there is still the matter of your first wager, won fairly this night. How would you have it repaid?" She started to answer, but he placed his fingers over her lips, then leaned slightly closer to her, so that she felt the warmth of his strong body. "I know just how to repay my debt to you, Lady."

"How?" Her voice came out as a squeak, and he took her hand to ease her toward the tavern door.

"This way . . ."

Cahira didn't look back as he led her from the tavern and down the passageway to their quarters. They passed Bodvar as he stood near a balcony facing west into the night, and Aren bade him good night, which Bodvar answered with a grunt and returned to his quarters.

"He isn't exactly chatty, is he?" noted Cahira.

"He's a warrior, not a bard," replied Aren, as he held open the door to their room and stood back for her to enter.

Cahira's heart skipped a beat as she passed him, and he smiled then closed the door behind them. Lamplight glimmered lowly near the bed. "It's lucky Guerdians are so lavish, isn't it? This bed is quite big. I was afraid they'd have tiny little cots and wee pillows, but this . . ."

He caught her from behind, lifted her off her feet, and turned her in his arms. He held her up so that their faces were even, and she hung there, dangling her legs weakly as she awaited his kiss. But his amber eyes burned with a light she didn't recognize, and he smiled that dangerous smile then lowered her onto the bed.

He stood above her and pulled off his shirt, his eyes never wavering from her face. She saw the outline of his arousal beneath his snug leggings and her heart's pace sped to dizzying heights. He removed and flung them aside, then stood naked before her. Her whole body trembled.

"You . . . are glorious," she whispered. His flesh was golden, smooth and strong, perfect. She swallowed hard. "Aren't you going to kiss me?"

A slight smile formed on his lips. "Oh, I'm going to kiss you," he said, his voice husky and low. "But this stands in my way." Before she knew what he was doing, he reached down, caught the hem of her dress and tore the garment apart.

"They're not very sturdily sewn," she offered in a shrill voice, but he threw the dress aside and caught her leg in his hand, lifted it, then placed his knee between her thighs. He moved onto the bed. Cahira started to sit up, but he knelt before her, and his eyes burned like fire.

"I am going to kiss you, my angel, until you scream, and beg, and ache."

She gasped, astonished and unnerved, but Aren moved down, rather than up above her as she'd expected. She watched him in surprise as his gaze scanned her body. He touched her throat with one finger, then trailed a line down and over one breast, then the other. He bent low, then laved his tongue over one little peak, then took it between his teeth. She couldn't believe what he was doing could be real. Not the lingering kisses she expected, but something so raw and so primitive! His teeth grazed over the taut peaks, and he sucked then swirled his tongue, and she thought she would scream.

He moved his attention to the other breast as he teased the first with his thumb. He sucked and licked until her back arched and she clasped his soft hair in her fingers. Soon he would kiss her mouth and relieve her from this torturous ache—instead, he moved back and trailed lingering kisses along her skin as he made his way down her body. His long hair grazed her stomach, and she was mesmerized as he moved lower still.

She had heard of such things, in conversations overheard at the Hungry Cat Tavern, but had long dismissed them as fanciful as well as impossible. Yet the men who treated their women this way were favored, and spoken of in veiled whispers and awe by the ladies who gathered in corners sipping wine.

Aren slid his hands between her thighs, and again his gaze met hers. He smiled like a rogue, then slowly bent down. She felt his short beard against her soft skin and she froze. He really meant to . . .

His lips grazed her inner thigh, and then he found the source of her desire. She froze, held herself perfectly still in disbelief, but his mouth brushed softly over the tiny bud that she had considered secret until now. She opened her mouth to breathe, but his tongue flicked out and swept over the most sensitive spot on her body, and her breath came as shallow cry instead.

She heard him chuckle low and deep in his throat, and he took the small bud between his lips and laved it with greater force, and then greater still. His lips moved back and forth, his tongue circled the tender spot until her hips arched and she whimpered his name. He cupped her bottom in his large hands, then sucked gently, and then harder until all her soul seemed afire.

She screamed and heard her voice as if it came from a great distance. She begged him for release, and she ached with an agony she had never dreamed possible. But he didn't stop. He went on and on, gripping her hips as he teased her beyond endurance. She felt like a drawn bow, the arrow to the taut string, quivering and set to fly. He sucked rhythmically, and she flew. She flew and spun and struck the heavens and all the stars kindled as her senses reeled. He held her there as her body quaked, as her spirit raged in ecstasy, and then at last she gave way to lingering shocks of pleasure and her quaking stilled, leaving her gasping and stunned.

And then she knew what she wanted more than anything else, and that this time it would be hers.

Aren rested his face against Cahira's soft stomach, and his heart slammed in his chest. He had felt every pulse of her rapture, and was stirred beyond measure by her cries. Her muscles still trembled with the aftershocks of her ecstasy, and he waited, unable to move for the ache in his own body.

He felt her fingers in his hair, and to his surprise, she gripped tight then pulled him up. Aren laughed, then moved above her. He was too close, because his hardened length rubbed perfectly against her thigh. Apparently, she liked the pressure, because she moaned and wrapped her legs around his. Aren looked at her in disbelief, but her blue eyes burned and her little face was alive with passion and desire.

"We are not finished, my lord," she whispered in a low, ragged voice. "Not this time."

He gazed down at her, but she arched back and the blunt tip of his shaft met the soft entrance to her body. She closed her eyes and moved against him, and he bit back a cry. She was slippery and warm, and so close that he thought he would die of wanting. "Cahira . . ." He paused to groan as she moved her hips back and forth. "I can't stop this. If we do . . ."

She opened her eyes, and he was astonished by the calm reason he saw there. "I know my cycle," she informed him with stunning evenness. "It is safe, and I will have you, my lord, deep in my body, or I will die."

As she spoke, she writhed, and gave a low moan as she felt his length hard against the sweet bud of her flesh that he had worshipped. Her breath quickened—he had never known a woman whose desire flared and returned so swiftly, but then he had never really tested the matter. He clasped her shoulders in his hands and poised himself against her trembling core.

"Look at me," he said softly, and she did. Then slowly, gently, he pressed inward. Her delicate flesh opened like petals soaked in dew, and he hesitated while his body throbbed. He met the barrier of her virginity, and he moved so slowly that he thought the restraint would crush him. But she reached down and slid her hands onto his bottom, and urged him deeper. Aren accepted her plea and pressed inward until the barrier gave way, and he sank deep inside her. She cried out, but not in pain. Her face lit in wonder and joy, and for a moment they just stared at each other, amazed.

"We are two joined into one," he whispered.

"We were, I believe, one before we were two," she replied, and he bent low to kiss her.

Her lips parted, and her tongue met his in a sweet dance that mimicked their bodies. He slid his tongue over hers and she whimpered, but then her head tipped back and her back arched to draw him closer. Finally Aren's restraint shattered, and he entered her full force, withdrew, then drove deep again. She met his thrusts, and a shivering moan tore from her throat as she moved closer to rapture.

Aren's senses fled. His mind gave way to the full force of his soul, and that claimed his body. He was a ravaging Norskman and an angel, and he loved Cahira with all that he was or ever would be. His desire raged and plundered, and she welcomed every wild current, every thrust, every breath. His energy burned and soared and reached its pinnacle like an endless wave upon a great shore, and he poured himself into her, and through her, until his body went weak and he lowered himself into her arms, unable to move.

Cahira stroked his hair from his forehead, then kissed his

face and neck, and she hugged him close against her body. His heart throbbed against hers, its force pounding in his ears. "Aren," she whispered, but he couldn't move or answer her. "Do you love me, too?"

Power returned to his limbs, he looked down into her beautiful face, and he smiled as his heart filled to bursting. "I have loved you since I first saw you. I have loved you for ages and ages. We both know that. And somehow, I know it's right."

"Yes," she murmured, and smiled. "Because we were one before we were two."

11

ECHOES IN THE DARK

They lay face to face, holding hands, their bodies sated and warm. Cahira felt sleep descending around her, but she fought it off so she could watch Aren's expressions. "Nothing can part us, love," he whispered. "Nothing, ever."

"Nothing ever has," she answered. "I am with you, and you are with me. No matter what we do, no matter how far we may be away from each other, or how right or how wrong, I am with you."

"Rika was right about me," he told her thoughtfully.

"What did she say?"

He smiled. "That I'd never given myself fully." He paused and laughed. "That I was lazy and indolent, and put no energy into the art."

"That is hardly the case now!" Cahira's eyes narrowed. "And how does she know?"

"She's a woman. Women know. But we were never lovers, if that's what you mean."

"It wouldn't matter—not really," said Cahira. "Except I find that I like Rika, and I wouldn't want to cause her pain if she loved you."

"Why would you think she did?" he asked.

"Shaen said she sensed that Rika is in love with you."

Aren rolled his eyes. "Of course. Well, I trust Shaen's intuition better than that, so I will say she is lying and not wrong."

"Why would she lie?"

He flattened his brow. "For the same reason she invented phantom rogues, and has likewise interrupted us at every turn."

"She didn't interrupt us tonight. Maybe she's given up. Or found something to distract her. I suspect Bodvar was waiting for her, though I thought it was cheap and unnecessary for her to flirt with you to incite his jealousy."

"In Bodvar, jealousy would be akin to fury, so it's worse than 'cheap and unnecessary'—it's downright dangerous." He paused and his lip curled in distaste. "But maybe that's what she's after."

Cahira eyed him suspiciously. "What do you mean?"

"Despite what we've just done here, you're too innocent to know."

"If you know, I can know!" she complained.

He smiled. "Well, let's say I wish I didn't know. How's that?"

She considered the matter. Shaen had been her father's mistress. "Maybe you're right. It's best I hear no more."

"Exactly." He drew her into his arms and kissed her forehead. "We will let nothing darken this night, not when I have you here, close. Not when I feel the way I do now."

She kissed his throat, his chest, and she snuggled close beside him. "I feel safe here," she told him, "sheltered and protected with you. I almost don't want to leave."

"I feel the same," he replied. "And I like the king."

She peeked up at him. "You like him for good reason, since he didn't throw you in a dungeon for your escapade." Cahira kissed his shoulder. "I wish I'd known you then! We would have been the best of friends, you and I."

He smiled. "Not adversarial, like Damir and Eliana?"

"I don't think so, no," she answered, but her brow furrowed. "I wonder why that is? When I was small, their relationship amused me. It was as if I saw a living cord binding them, which for some reason they couldn't see themselves. And they tugged back and forth, trying to gain the advantage, until it seemed to me they both fell flat and had to pull themselves up and face each other."

"That is how it seemed to me also," said Aren. "And even though I was young—fourteen—it seemed to me that I was watching children. I knew they would resolve their fears and join together, even when they did not."

"They both gave me lessons in magery," added Cahira, "apart, because they were so competitive with each other. And I thought how much they were alike inside, though they didn't know it. I felt like an elder dealing patiently with children I loved, but sometimes . . ." She paused and sighed. "Sometimes, I so desperately longed for someone like myself, who saw farther and wider."

"A man will walk in a forest and see only the path laid before his feet, while he dwells on what he has passed so far. He will see the growth of trees and ferns, what berries he might seize, but he has no thought for the forest as it truly is, nor how it fits into the greater land—the plains, the mountains, the desert and the seas, nor the sky above, nor the stars beyond."

"But you do," she said. "And so do I, and there were times that even Madawc's vision seemed more narrow than my own. Why is that?"

"I don't know," Aren replied quietly. "But it has been this way all my life. I found I loved the small things, the play of children, of beasts and their ways, that I treasured the winter snow when it falls, and the spring when it leaps into life, and the richness of summer, and the sweet sorrow of autumn as it passes into night. Yet others passed by these things, and never saw, nor lingered in its wake."

"We are old, Aren son of Arkyn," she whispered. "So old that I cannot remember when I first knew you, except that you are the warmth in my heart and the peace in my soul. And I believe, though I do not understand, that we have loved each other always."

Tears formed in his beautiful eyes, and he smiled. "And, my love, we always will."

"Your winnings, my lord!"

Cahira shot up in bed with a cutoff scream to find Felix perched on Aren's chest. A stout Guerdian was there also, who dropped a heavy round bag on the bed, looked embarrassed, and backed away, bowing. Aren opened one eye and said nothing.

"Your pardon, Lord Chieftain," said the little man. "The bat here instructed that I should deliver this bag to you, since he couldn't carry it himself, but he assured me you would have risen by now. Forgive me."

Aren nodded, then turned a slow, ponderous gaze upon Felix, who appeared cheerful. "If you've come as instructed by the treacherous Shaen, bat, you've come too late. The deed is done." He sat up and shoved his long hair from his face, then arched his back and stretched.

Felix looked between them. "Think there'll be a little one on the way, lass?"

Cahira clasped her head in her hands, then moaned. "No, I do not." She paused for an unexpected regret. "Not this time." She peeked at the bat. "I'm not a fool, Felix."

Aren examined the bag, jingled it and smiled, then flopped back on the bed. "I take it Khadun was the last standing?"

"Standing? The little fellow was still singing and dancing when I went to my rest—where I resumed my perch over the Norsk boy, after six Guerdians hauled him and Elphin out of the tavern. Shame the others weren't alert enough to see the dancing. Don't think it was the drink, either. It seems Guerdians enjoy an active night, and take particularly to dance. The prince is apparently among the best at the art."

"I'm sorry to have missed it," said Cahira, but then she bit her lip happily. "But not that sorry."

Aren glanced over at her, and he smiled, too. Her heart fluttered, and she wished suddenly that the bat would leave. "What happened with Fareth and Ranveig?" she asked. "Was there a winner between them?"

"Flopped over, one this way"—Felix pitched his body to the right—"and one the other." He swayed violently left. "Hit the floor at the same time, as I was forced to tell them when they woke this morning."

"How are the other two, Thorleif and Elphin?" asked Aren.

The bat shook his small head, then grimaced. "Don't think you'll be seeing either of those lads 'til nightfall, and maybe later. They're in a dark place about now. The only thing young Thorleif said when I roused him—well, besides a few Norsk curses—was a plea for you not to leave without him."

"I hadn't intended to, as you're welcome to reassure him," said Aren. "A day of rest will do us all good." He eyed the bat. "Now, if that's all . . ."

"Lord?"

"You can leave!"

" 'Fraid I can't, my lord."

Aren groaned. "Why not?"

"Because I'm coming with you."

"Later!" Aren paused, then sighed miserably as he sensed defeat. "Where are we going?" he asked.

"The king has summoned you, the lass, and myself, and Khadun is waiting to take us to the Chamber of Tomes. The king suggested that I accompany you to look over these records, figuring I'm an Honored Guide and all. Apparently, there are only a few hours during each day when there's enough light in the chamber to view these records you're after, so you'd best get yourselves up and dressed."

Felix caught sight of Cahira's torn dress, then turned slowly to Aren. Aren started to speak, but the bat held up one wingtip dramatically and shook his head. "I do *not* want to know."

"For the best," agreed Aren. He paused. "But Cahira could use another garment. Just like that one." He folded his arms behind his head and closed his eyes. "That should take a few minutes, at least."

Felix soared out of the room, and from the balcony outside their quarters, Cahira heard a piercing whistle, followed by the bat's gravelly commands. Within moments, two Guerdian handmaidens swept into the room bearing a dark blue dress.

Cahira held it up in amazement. "How did you do that so fast? It isn't thirty seconds since Felix called!"

One of the small women gulped audibly. "The other female, the one carved of ice and metal, she told us to craft a dress that covered more of her body." She stopped and shuddered. "This one wasn't sufficient, so she discarded it and requested another."

"Better put sleeves on her next one," suggested Aren. "Rika likes sleeves."

The two Guerdian women huddled together, nodded vigorously, then darted out of the room. Cahira examined her new dress. "This one is a little longer. Not sure about the shoulders, though. It might be a little loose, because they altered it for Rika . . . but it should be fine with a sash."

Aren sighed. "It's probably for the best. I won't be quite so distracted while I'm trying to translate Guerdian runes, anyway."

"It's a bit low across the bust," noted Cahira. Aren's eyes opened wide and he looked hopeful, and she smiled. "Felix, turn around."

The bat did so without hesitation, as if he'd be horrified to see a naked human, but Aren waited expectantly. Cahira felt strange with the bat in the room. "Maybe you should wait outside, Felix."

He cranked his little head around and leveled a dark look at her. "I don't think so! If I leave the two of you for a minute, you'll be at it again!"

"That was the hope," muttered Aren, but then he bowed

to the bat. "You win, Master Bat. We'll go the Chamber of Tomes, and for the rest of our lives think sadly on what might have been."

"Or at least until lunchtime," said Cahira. Felix looked pointedly away, and she slipped the blue dress over her head, straightened it, then got up from bed. "This one does fit better over my thighs," she noted.

Aren appeared slightly self-pitying, but then he assessed the neckline and brightened. "It has its strong points," he remarked, and she glanced at him suspiciously. "The color suits you."

He rose and dressed, too, but oddly, the bat didn't seem moved by Aren's nudity as he had been Cahira's. "Why is it that a naked woman bothers you, but not a naked man?" she asked.

Felix hesitated, then shrugged. "It's you, lass. Seeing you in the altogether would just be . . . wrong."

"And seeing Aren isn't?"

"He's just a man. They're all the same."

"Is that so?" Aren laughed. "And I've worked so hard to keep up my looks."

"You looked like you'd just crawled up from a tavern floor when we first met you," countered Felix, "a Norsk brute after a hard night's drinking and a brawl to boot."

"That was pretty much the case," said Aren. "Well, a tankard or two of ale, maybe."

"He looks good now," admonished Cahira, and she sighed. "So good that I could taste your skin there . . ." She touched his shoulder and gazed dreamily into his amber eyes. "And your lips . . ."

"My species also nips when mating," offered Felix, and as he seemed about to elaborate, both Cahira and Aren groaned.

"Say no more!" commanded Cahira.

"Understood," said Felix. "Our courtship rituals are a bit too violent, raw, and primitive for a human to handle," he added. "Though from what I heard coming out of Bodvar's quarters last night, he might have taken it a step beyond anything I'd consider."

"Maybe he was dreaming?" suggested Cahira weakly. Aren exhaled a tense breath as if he didn't want to hear any more about Bodvar's nighttime activities, dreaming or not.

"Well, if he was, Miss Shaen was dreaming right along with him," replied Felix. "Caught her creeping out of there in the wee hours. I greeted her, pleasant as always. Gave me a look that . . ." The bat paused. "Got strange eyes, she does. Not like yours, lass, all bright and open and blue, nor the chieftain's, either, with everything you both are shining right there for all to see. Hers are different somehow."

"I've noticed that," said Aren quietly. "Like windows with no light inside, even in the bright of day—as if you were looking into a dwelling that someone owned, but the inhabitant stood outside, behind you, watching."

"That's a disturbing way to put it," said Cahira. But it was also accurate, and an unease formed around her heart. "I have felt that before," she whispered.

"What, lass?" asked Felix, his voice low and serious.

"As Aren said . . . as if Shaen is standing right in front of me, smiling or prattling on as she does, but that it's an illusion somehow, as if her real self is somewhere off in the shadows, hiding." Her unease grew, but she tried to push it away. "I don't understand why I should feel that way, though. She's always pleasant and friendly, she offers sympathy and commiserates with her friends at the tavern, listening to their problems and offering advice. She says that she can't help but put others first, and sometimes it has made her life difficult."

"Passive," said Aren, and he spoke the word disparagingly. "Or so she would like others to believe."

"She doesn't like to admit anger, though I know she feels it," agreed Cahira. "She used to get furious with Eliana but wouldn't show it. I knew, because I saw the way she looked at Eliana when Eliana wasn't aware. Maybe she's afraid to say what she really wants, or show how she feels."

"Why is that, do you think?" asked Felix.

"I'm not sure . . ." And yet, she was.

Aren answered. "Because what she wants and feels are so dark, they're unexpected by others who see only her surface."

Felix said no more, and Cahira gathered her senses and tried to smile. "Then she's found a good match in Bodvar," she said. She puffed a quick breath. "Now, shall we go?"

Aren nodded, but she saw him glance at Felix, and they both looked concerned. Aren shuffled through his gear, then selected the Dragonfly Sword.

"You're bringing that to the Chamber of Tomes?" she asked in surprise. "Are you expecting an attack?"

Aren smiled. "The king has forbidden torches and lamplights. So I thought the light of this sword might be of some use."

"Good idea!" said Cahira.

Felix hopped to her shoulder and waited as Aren affixed the sheath to his belt. "Bodvar's eyes are shaded by his anger, his doubt, and his own weakness," said the bat quietly. "But I still see him inside."

"Yes," she replied. "I know." She didn't want to think about this more, though she wasn't sure why it disturbed her so. *I don't want to see.* Why? She knew the answer. Shaen had been mistress of her father, who though somewhat weak and ineffectual, had been a good man. Shaen's darkness hadn't started on this journey, nor after the evil energy descended upon the Woodland. It had been there as long as Cahira knew her, as Shaen had looked at the prettier, stronger Eliana and whispered words of doubt in Damir's ear.

It was there now, as Shaen sought to cast doubt on Cahira's quest, and on her relationship with Aren. She didn't know how Shaen looked at her when she wasn't aware, but it wasn't hard to guess. And her father had fallen into an intimate relationship—Cahira remembered his eyes, sometimes sad and confused, as if he weren't sure what was happening to him. She swallowed hard to contain her emotion—*I am just speculating,* she thought. It might not have been so dark. Maybe Shaen had been, as she often intimated, just a kind, supportive mistress . . .

Felix touched her hair with his wingtip. "Fate unfolds of its own devices, lass," he said quietly. "We cannot alter its course, for it is a river that sweeps us along. All we can do is make a path through its midst."

Aren met her gaze, and he nodded. "And we will do that, Cahira, with all that we are, to the best of our ability." He reached out and took her hand. "And together, our ability is great indeed."

Khadun met them outside the king's chamber. He looked fresh and content, despite the bound gash on his brow. "You're looking none the worse for wear," noted Aren, and the Guerdian's dark eyes glimmered.

"Did you expect otherwise?" he asked.

"Not for a second," replied Aren.

Cahira looked between them. "How did you know he'd win, anyway?"

"I've seen Guerdians drink. And as for wagering . . . I doubt there's anyone even in Amrodel who could hold their own against that."

Cahira eyed Khadun. "You were cagey when dealing with Fareth and Ranveig."

Khadun chuckled. "All too easy." He gestured to a hall running parallel to the King's chambers. "Shall we go?"

They followed him down the hall, then up a long, narrow staircase that led to another level in the city of Amon-Daal. From there, he led them through a row of dwellings, less grand than those on the boulevard where Aren's party had stayed, but still neat and well-furnished, with boxes of flowers outside small windows and polished tools set in copper buckets, testimony to the industrious nature of the Guerdian people.

Aren looked around with interest, and Cahira glanced up

at him. "I take it you didn't get this far on your previous adventure?" she asked.

He shook his head. "Only into the main hall, as the king mentioned." He paused. "And into the wine cellar."

She laughed, but then her expression changed. "I dreamt once that I flew around like a ghost over a young boy's shoulder, and watched as he clamored up just such a palace wall. It's odd, because when I first beheld this city, I had the strangest feeling I'd been here before—but that was impossible."

A cool thrill coursed through Aren as he walked beside her, as if he sensed something he couldn't quite know. "And I recall a dream where I flew, likewise invisible, beside a beautiful girl as she . . ." He stopped and looked at her in awe. "As she crept from an old man's cluttered cottage in the dark of night, then slipped into a noisy tavern, crept from table to table unseen, then took her fill of ale while a fat young innkeeper looked the other way."

"So, skipped out on . . . on the Elder Mage, did you, lass?" Felix huffed. "I should have known. He should have kept a closer eye on you, and no mistake!"

"It was only a dream," said Aren, but his gaze remained on Cahira, and she gazed up at him in wonder.

"Then it was an accurate dream." A smile formed on her lips. "Though such events happened more times than once." She paused, and her expression softened into bliss. "You were with me . . . and I was with you." Sudden tears started in her eyes. "Whatever happens, wherever we go . . ."

Aren squeezed her hand. "We go together."

Khadun motioned them forward, and up another long staircase. Three times they passed plateaus with dwellings carved into the cliffside, and each time, the dwellings grew more sparse and fewer. At last they reached the heights of the city, and Aren stopped to look back over it and the plains beyond. The sun was still new in the sky and cast a fair light westward as it rose.

"Look there," he said to Cahira. "In the far west, you can

see the dark green haze of Amrodel, and to the north, my own land, still laden with snow."

"And there," she added, "to the south is the sea. I have visited Amon-Dhen with Madawc several times and walked along the shore. It is beautiful, but I've always felt it was sad, somehow—like a dream never to be fulfilled."

Aren looked at her with a strange expression, but he said nothing.

"It has been long since the sailing ships of Kora dared cross the sea," said Khadun, "and our traders are the worse for the loss. But the oceans have raged without mercy for many years now. It may be they will calm again one day, and make transport possible again."

"They will calm," said Felix. "Tides change, both in a day and over generations."

"We hear little from Kora now," added Khadun. "Once, it was a great land with great riches and magic akin to the Mages of Amrodel. It was said that their greatest priests, in hidden temples and secret valleys, had such power that they flew without wings, though I believe it not."

"Anything is possible," said Aren.

"Flying is nothing," scoffed Felix, but then he paused. "Though when first I tested my wings, it was a glory beyond anything I'd dreamed—until I crashed into a tree outside the Hungry Cat . . ."

Cahira looked at him in surprise. "The first time you flew?"

"Hm? Oh, no . . . not that day, not then," the bat stammered. "When I was just a new young bat, of course."

"I see," said Aren, but Cahira seemed to accept her guide's explanation and turned back to Khadun.

"The Arch Mage was a priest from the land of Kora," she said. "But even they didn't know how to stop him. It is said he killed many there before he fled."

"He must have fled for a reason," said Aren. "So there must be some power beyond his, something he feared. Perhaps the Guerdians recorded some hint of what it was."

"Not that he'd be telling them," said Felix.

"No, but oft it is seen that what is most desperately concealed is revealed in unexpected ways—by what *isn't* said."

"Great!" Cahira issued a long sigh. "Do you mean we're going to look through thousands upon thousands of books to find what isn't there?"

"If we must," said Aren. "But let us hope the time period is at least easy to find, or it will be a long day's hunt."

"We keep everything in order!" said Khadun. "Finding the right section in the Chamber will be the least of your worries, Lord Chieftain. Finding a method to destroy the Arch Mage is the real task—and I doubt very much a possible one."

They made the last climb up a lonely and steep stair. It went straight and cut deep into the mountainside. As they delved inward, light failed, and Khadun illuminated a small oil lamp that glimmered dimly ahead as he climbed. They stopped to rest, but Felix puffed out an impatient breath. "This is taking forever! I'm going on ahead to wait for you at the top!" With that, he swooped from Cahira's shoulder and disappeared into the darkness.

"I wish he'd thought of that sooner," she muttered. "After about five hundred steps, even a bat's weight feels heavy."

A piercing screech startled them, and Aren laid his hand to his sword. Before he could draw it, Felix flapped madly back down the channel, dropped to Cahira's shoulder, panting desperately. "Felix! What's wrong? What's up there?" she asked.

The bat's eyes rounded still more in the lamplight as the others awaited his explanation. "Lass! They're up there!"

"Who?" Cahira glanced at Aren, but he shook his head.

"What's up there?" he asked. "I hear nothing."

"Well, of course you don't!" said Felix, still out of breath. "They don't make noise. They just look at you with their beady little eyes . . ."

Cahira turned to Aren. "I think the climb and lack of air is getting to him. Here, I have a small flask of tea. Drink some."

She held it to the bat's mouth and he drank, then sputtered and coughed. "Thank you, lass."

"Tell us, bat, what you saw," asked Khadun. He sounded confused.

"Is there anything up there normally?" Aren asked.

"Not that I know of, no," said Khadun. "Only small insects and . . . bats."

Felix chirped, then settled close to Cahira's head, and he nodded vigorously. "Hundreds of them!"

"Ten, at least," countered Aren, then rolled his eyes. "What? Is your species territorial?"

"Not that I know of . . ." Felix stopped and looked uncomfortable. "They looked as if they might be."

"Ah," said Aren, and he held out his arm. "Perch on my shoulder, then, and I'll protect you from your brethren, should they resent your intrusion into their lair."

Felix hesitated, but Cahira arched her brow meaningfully. "Aren is armed, and I forgot to bring my bow. You're safer with him."

"Just so, lass. Don't want to leave you in the lurch, though."

"I'm fine."

Felix accepted this, and hurtled to Aren's shoulder. The group started off again, but the bat's little claws dug through Aren's shirt as they progressed. No wonder Cahira had wanted him off!

They made the final climb without any evidence of territorial bats, though Felix crouched low on Aren's shoulder as they neared the top. Khadun held up his lamp, and its light illuminated a door that reflected the dull sheen of burnished copper. The Guerdian prince took a massive key from his belt, fiddled with the door, then pushed it slowly open.

The room beyond glowed with a faint light, but that light was blinding to eyes forced to approach in the dark. Aren entered and squinted around. The Chamber of Tomes was vast beyond anything he had imagined. Scrolls and bound volumes lined the walls, higher than several Guerdians standing on each other's shoulders. He saw ladders poised neatly, awaiting use, and three long, low tables with stools where scholars might presumably sit to study.

"Where do we begin?" asked Cahira weakly.

"Where the age of the dark wizard begins, I should think," replied Khadun. "I am not a scholar like my father—my real joy is in trade—but as his son, I have had to learn about the Chamber."

"Well, find the first volume!" ordered Felix.

Khadun sighed. "Unfortunately, those particular volumes are located on the top shelf, there." He pointed to the far side of the room, the wall of which was nearly double the height of the rest of the room.

"What did you put them up there for?" asked Aren.

"I didn't," replied Khadun. "This was done many generations ago. Perhaps the old scholars considered even references to the One Who Fell dangerous, so they put them high and out of reach." He adjusted a ladder beneath a column of books, then paused and sighed. "I suppose you want me to go up there and get them?"

"Is that a problem?" Aren asked.

"No . . ."

Aren waited.

Khadun shifted his weight from foot to foot and looked off at nothing. "I don't like heights," he said.

"You live on the edge of a mountain, and you don't like heights?"

"Why do you think I prefer life as a trader?" the prince asked.

Aren laughed. "Well, we all have something." He paused and sighed, looking at the Guerdian-sized ladder. "Very well. I'll go."

Cahira turned to him. "On those little ladders, as big as you are? You won't get up two rungs! I'll go."

"No, you won't!" He checked himself, and tried to put calm back in his voice. "I don't want you to fall."

"I can get up there," said Felix. But then he waved his

wings. "However, I don't think I'd be much use lifting books and scrolls."

Cahira set aside her pack, tied her skirt between her legs—probably because of the missing undergarments—then scurried toward the ladder. Aren moved to stop her, but she jumped on and climbed quickly beyond his reach.

"Be careful up there!" he called out.

Felix chuckled. "That lass surely can climb! Used to scale the mountainside behind Damir ap Kora's old cottage—and probably the palace walls, too."

"Almost every night," she called down. "Now, what am I looking for?"

It took almost two hours for Cahira to find and distribute all the volumes and scrolls pertaining to the dark wizard of Kora. She went up and down the ladder carrying books, directed by Felix who flew back and forth as if that might be helpful. But she never flagged or wavered, and seemed excited each time she found a new book.

"This one is huge!" she exclaimed from on high. Aren leapt up from his position at the table and hurried beneath her. Each time she descended the ladder, his heart leapt into his throat, sure she would fall, and he intended to be there to catch her if that happened. But Cahira slid down the ladder, heavy book in one hand, then hopped to the floor.

"You're enjoying this, aren't you?" he asked, and she nodded vigorously.

"I like feeling useful. I can't read Guerdian runes, after all, so I might as well keep myself busy." She paused. "Have you found any mention of your people's heritage?"

"Nothing at all," said Aren, "though there is a brief mention of a race they refer to as the 'Foe-Guerdians.' I suppose that could refer to the Norsk ancestors."

"It does not," said Khadun, and a stubborn expression formed on his face.

"Then, what are they?" asked Cahira.

"We do not speak of them," said Khadun. "They do not have anything to do with this quest."

Aren rolled his eyes and glanced at Cahira, but she pinned her determined gaze on Khadun. "Do you know anything about Aren's ancestors?"

"Only that the Norsk are fairly recent additions to the north," said Khadun. "They haven't dwelt here as long as we have, nor the Woodlanders. It seems they trickled northward, though from where no one knows. Yet their manner was always bold, and their ways savage . . ." He paused and looked uncomfortable as he glanced at Aren. "Well, at least to us they seemed uncouth. It seemed to us that they fought against more than simply nature itself—they fought against some unseen bond. My people say the Norsk sought out to conquer the icelands so that they would be guaranteed a constant battle ever after."

Aren shrugged. "That seems plausible. There is, in my people and in myself as well, a desire to prove ourselves against our environment, to prove we are strong and free."

"How long do you have to go on proving that?" asked Cahira.

"Until we're sure it's true," said Aren, and he sighed.

"Maybe there's another volume up there that will shed more light on this," suggested Cahira, and she aimed for the ladder again.

"I'm sure we have enough now."

She frowned. "There's one more scroll I saw."

Aren groaned.

As she darted back up the ladder, Felix took his position on the table beside the scroll Khadun examined. "Anything of interest?" he asked.

Khadun shook his head. "There's a lot here about the building materials we used during that time. Indeed, trade with Kora was at its peak during this time. Sad to say, we don't have anything like it now. But so far I've found no references to the One Who Fell."

"Keep reading," Felix commanded. Then he hopped over to Aren. "What about you?"

Aren pored over a faded scroll, then shook his head. "This details the fashion of the sailing ships of Old Kora . . ." He paused. "It interests me, but doesn't seem relevant."

"You would do better to study up on making your way though the Arch Mage's domain," agreed Felix gruffly.

Cahira suddenly tapped Aren's shoulder, and he started. "How did you do that? I didn't hear you climb down!" he said.

"I thought I'd try coming down once without you hovering below. It made me a bit nervous, actually," she admitted cheerfully. She stood on tiptoes and kissed his cheek. "I love you."

"I love you, too." He felt young and giddy, and he bent to kiss her mouth. She sighed and kissed him back.

Khadun cleared his throat, and Aren turned reluctantly back to the task at hand. "What is it, Khadun? Have you found something?"

"Maybe. Take a look at this."

Aren scanned the preferred page of an old book, then read the next. The sheets turned like leaves in autumn, and were almost as fragile. His heart pounded as he read, but then he closed the book and turned to the others. "I think . . . I think I have it."

Cahira's eyes opened wide, and her mouth parted. He saw all her hope in her beautiful face, and smiled. "What?" she breathed.

"We can't break this spell he's put on himself . . . but another can."

"Who?" She nearly hopped with excitement, and Aren laid his hand on her shoulder.

"It won't be easy. But I think we can do it."

"How?" she asked.

Felix bounced up and down on the tabletop. "How?" he repeated.

"Somehow we have to reach the land of Kora. It says here

that the priests of the great temples there can unravel even the most intricate spells."

"Then why didn't they do it at the time?" Cahira asked.

"I'm not sure," said Aren. "Maybe it wasn't deemed necessary. And to unravel the spell means to awaken the wizard."

"Then what good will this do us?"

Aren smiled as hope returned to his heart. "These tomes have given me an idea."

She puffed out an impatient breath. "What?"

"Guerdian architecture has changed since that time, and is much improved. At the time the wizard's lair was built, there remained flaws in their design."

"What flaws?" asked Khadun indignantly.

"Not great," replied Aren. "But enough, I think, to crumble the south face of the mountain inward, and to crush the tombs below." He paused while the others absorbed his plan.

"Do you mean we would somehow unravel the Arch Mage's binding spell, then bring the mountain down upon him?" Cahira's eyes shifted to one side as she considered.

"It's a grim solution, but possible," said Felix.

"Such a being's death will bring no tears to my people," said Khadun. "At the time the wizard fell, we had no means to collapse the southern wall—but as the chieftain has said, our methods have improved since that time and it might be possible now."

"My people will aid yours," said Aren, "and it *can* be done."

Khadun looked at him in surprise. "A union of the Ice People and the People of the Mountain? These are indeed strange times—yet we are given to hope anew."

"But we can't get to Kora!" interrupted Cahira. She paused. "Can we?"

"Possibly." Aren picked up the scroll detailing the sailing ships. "I read here that the dark wizard built a vast port, and many ships docked there. The Guerdians record that though many ships washed away in various storms, a few remained sheltered—those the wizard kept for himself."

"And how do you suggest we get to these ships?"

"In the summer months, we could skirt the mountainside, for a narrow pathway runs along its length, still used by those few traders who travel north from Kora. Unfortunately, because of the season, we'll have to go through the catacombs to reach the port, but that should be possible." He paused and indicated another scroll. "I've found a map that details the passage between Amon-Daal and the wizard's lair. It looks straightforward enough, a straight cut through the mountains. It shouldn't take us more than a few days, even on foot, if the way is clear."

Cahira gazed up at him. "Then we won't need Shaen, after all, will we?"

"It appears not," said Aren; and he felt surprisingly triumphant.

"There is a door that is always barred leading to that passageway," said Khadun, "though, were the One Who Fell to arise, no door would bar his entrance. There may be fallen rocks from the shifts of the mountain, but the passage runs deeper than the frost. The mountains are old, and move little now. The way should be clear enough."

Aren indicated a spot on the map. "Here, marked appropriately in red ink, is the cavern where he lies. His tomb lies near the south end of the mountain, on the verge of a cliffside that makes the one of Amon-Daal look like a soft slope."

"Wonderful!" injected Khadun. "I can't wait to see that!"

Aren looked at him in surprise, but the Guerdian shrugged. "I am going with you, my lord. I knew that when you came to my defense against the ambushers. It is my destiny to journey with you now." He stopped and exhaled miserably. "Even there."

Aren bowed low. "Then it is my honor to accept." He paused and smiled. "And I'm sure we can find a way down to the port without scaling the cliff."

"I'd appreciate that," said Khadun.

"But, what about the Arch Mage's pit?" asked Cahira. "At

least, I think it's a pit of some sort. How do we get by it without my presence waking him?"

"He buried himself beneath the southwestern arm of the catacombs," said Felix. "That's a pit."

"How do you know these things?" she asked.

"Study, lass. Study."

"I'm sorry to question you! I had no idea bats had libraries!"

Felix didn't explain further, but nodded to Aren. "Go on, my lord."

Aren scratched his beard as he perused the map. "It should be possible to get through his lair without actually entering his tomb. It's a risk, of course, because we don't know if you have to enter that precise room, or if your energy entering his domain will be enough."

"Just the pit area," said Felix excitedly. "Sounds possible, my lord! But how do we get to Kora, and what do you expect to find there?"

"And how do we cross seas that have stopped traders from coming north for years beyond our lifetime?" added Cahira.

"They were still coming north not long before your birth," said Felix. "Damir ap Kora's sire came from that region—he was the younger brother of the reigning prince, and there was some disagreement or other, and the prince sent Damir's father into exile. He came to Amon-Dhen, where he met Damir's mother, a lovely young Woodlander." The bat sighed. "Caught the eye of many a young Mage, she did, even . . ." He paused and cleared his throat. "Even the Elder Mage."

"Madawc romanced Damir's mother?" asked Cahira in surprise. "I've never heard that! Does Damir know?"

"No, he does not," said Felix irritably. "And it's hardly important now! But as I was saying, she was a fair lass, and no mistake. Eyes like a Woodland stream, darker than yours . . ." The bat stopped and sighed. "But she took one look at that young exile from Kora, and that was it. By the time she returned to Amrodel, they had wed, and a brief season later, Damir was born. Looked like a shade lighter version of his father, but he inherited the power of both his parents—including, fortunately for you, lass, the ability to place a shield of protection around both land and person."

Cahira turned back to Aren. "So, how do we cross the sea now?"

"Sailing south would be impossible, but as I understand the currents, traveling west from the mesas beyond the southern mountain shouldn't be too difficult."

"That's true," said Khadun. "Those few bold Koraji traders who come to our land skirt the western face of the mountain to come north. They won't enter the mountain, though it would be the swifter passage by far, and the outer pathways can only be accessed in summer."

"I knew traders still appeared from Kora now and again," said Cahira. "I guess I just never thought about how they got here." She paused. "Does anyone go to Kora now?"

"None that I know," said Khadun. Then he hesitated. "Some few have tried in recent years, but none have ever returned."

"Well, that's promising!" Cahira leveled her brow and turned to Aren. "And what's to say these traders haven't taken the ships you say the Arch Mage left behind?"

"I doubt it," said Khadun. "Those used in Kora now are swifter and much larger. They'd have no use for ships of that age, and they've probably fallen into disrepair, anyway."

"We can fix them," said Aren. "The mesas are dry—little will be damaged by time, as it be would in our own lands."

Cahira chewed her lip. "How long will it take to reach Kora, then?"

"Naught but a few days, traveling west," said Khadun. "The winds carry in that direction; but there, the sea is at its most narrow as it sweeps from the southern mesas to the vast desert between, and the land of Kora to the west."

"So we'll just go, find a priest, and see if he can help?" she asked.

"It's worth a try," said Aren. "I doubt they want 'Matchite-hew,' the Evil Heart, to arise any more than we do."

"No, probably not," she agreed.

"And if these priests can do what it says here, the dark wizard may find those tombs his final resting place—and the days of his evil will end forever."

12

BETRAYAL

"She's not going to take this well," muttered Cahira as they walked back to the Guerdian tavern.

"Tell her it's for her own good. She's safe enough here," replied Aren, and he placed his hand on Cahira's back for support. "But we both agree that Shaen should go no further in our party."

"What about Bodvar? If we can get rid of your nemesis, can't we leave mine behind, too?"

Aren hesitated. "We may need Bodvar's strength if the passageway proves blocked." He paused. "And I'd rather keep him close, to be honest."

"Ah. You don't trust him, either."

"Let me put it this way—without him at her side, Shaen isn't likely to follow us."

"You think she'd follow us if she had Bodvar to help? Why? She's not that dedicated to our quest, I promise you."

"To our quest? No. But something drives her. I would do nothing to make her goal easier to attain."

"I suppose not," Cahira agreed.

They entered the tavern and found Shaen sitting with Elphin, whose head was clasped in his hands. Ranveig and Fareth were seated with Rika, eating heartily, so Cahira guessed their residual reaction to the wine was less severe. Bodvar stood near the corner of the room, fittingly in shadow, Cahira thought, and held a filled tankard of ale.

"Where's Thorleif?" she asked as she looked around.

Elphin peeked up through his hands. "Dead, or might as well be." His voice was a groan.

Rika glanced at Aren and shook her head. "He's fine, more or less. We tried to get him up, and I explained to him that eating would ease his affliction, but he informed me food wouldn't make it past his 'upper gut,' whatever that means." She paused. "Then he threatened me, if you can believe it."

"He must be really ill," said Aren, chuckling.

Cahira sighed. "Poor Thorleif. I hope he's all right."

"It wears off slowly, but the memory lingers. Which is for the best," Aren added.

"You should know!" Cahira gazed up at him, her heart full of happiness. She could picture him as a youngster, hungover and unhappy, yet full of mischief. After a moment she said, "This morning's work was tiring."

"Indeed?"

She nodded. "After we have a small lunch, it might be nice to retire to our quarters and rest."

He caught her meaning; his eyes darkened and he smiled. "As it happens, my lady, I ache with weariness. A rest is just what we need."

She drew a quick breath, and glanced at Shaen. "Then let's get this over with." She bit her lip and seated herself opposite the woman.

"There's something we need to discuss, Shaen," she began.

Shaen turned to her pleasantly. "Did you find anything of use in the Guerdian records?"

Cahira hesitated. "Possibly. I'm not sure. But we will try everything we can to avoid waking the Arch Mage, and to bring about an end to this Dark Tide that emanates from him." She paused again. "However, from here on, the way will grow far more dangerous, and we were thinking that it might be best for you to stay here, in Amon-Daal." She held her breath for Shaen's response, and steeled herself against an emotional outburst. Instead, Shaen's brow puckered.

"I take it you found a map that can guide you through the Arch Mage's palace?"

"We did," said Cahira, "so there's no need for you to take any further risks."

Shaen closed her eyes briefly, then seized Cahira's hand. "I know this is hard for you, my dear," she said kindly. "It's hard for me, too. But it's become painfully clear to me that I'm just not suited to these adventures and hardships. And honestly, I don't think there's anything I can do for you now that you've put your trust so fully in a lover. Not that I'm not happy for you. I am. But your fate is with Aren now. I'm sure your father would understand if I don't go on."

Cahira stared. She'd been ready with explanations and arguments, and now those just hung in midair, unused and unnecessary. "Well . . . that's good! I'm glad you understand, Shaen," she heard herself say.

"I understand completely. It hurts, yes, but I know you're doing what you feel you must. I can't think about myself now, only your safety." Shaen took a sip of tea, then smiled. "Please, don't worry about me. Perhaps I can enlist the Guerdians to escort me back to Amrodel."

"That's a good idea." But Cahira hesitated. Shaen's reaction was so unexpected. "If you're sure—"

"It's for the best, Cahira. You know how I care about you, but I know you'll have your handsome protector at your side. What could go wrong?"

Cahira stood up, still uncertain, but relieved. "Well, then . . ."

"When will you be leaving? Tonight?" Shaen asked idly. "I'd like a chance to say good-bye to everyone. We've all grown so close since this journey began. You all mean so much to me."

"We'll leave tomorrow at dawn," said Cahira. She glanced at Aren, who shrugged. Shaen rose and went to him, clasped his hands in hers.

"Take care of her, won't you? I know I can't go on with you, but I must know she's safe."

"I will guard her with my life," Aren promised. But his tone held a hint of a threat. Perhaps he hadn't heard Shaen's easy acquiescence, or maybe he didn't trust it. Still, Cahira was at least relieved not to have to endure an emotional confrontation.

Felix swooped into the tavern and squeaked loudly. "You have to see this! All of you!"

"What is it?" asked Cahira.

"The Guerdians are dancing—they've got drums and flutes, too," said the bat excitedly. "Even the old king is out there! They're putting on a show in the courtyard that makes our pageantry look tame. If only Rhys the Bard could be here. Come! I've already roused the young Norskman—much to his displeasure, but for his own good. . . ."

Felix flapped away, and they all followed the bat out onto the balcony, though Bodvar didn't linger to watch the festivities. In the courtyard below the palace, female Guerdians dressed in bright armor danced, and more still came spinning out wearing brightly colored dresses, followed by males in full regalia. "Of course!" said Cahira. "*Their* dresses go to their ankles!" She tugged at her own garment. "I am beginning to miss my traveling clothes."

"They're in our room, cleaned and mended," said Aren. "But wait until tomorrow, and give me the pleasure of glancing at your legs for one last day."

"You could untie your own shirt a bit more," said Cahira, and to her delight, he did. "I'll remove the rest when we get back to our room."

Shaen touched Cahira's shoulder, then hugged her fondly. "I'm going back to my room to rest. I'll see you in the morning before you leave, of course."

"Thank you," said Cahira, though she felt awkward. After Shaen left, she turned to Aren.

"That went easier than I expected. Why, do you think?"

He shrugged. "I have no idea, but let us count ourselves fortunate."

They watched the Guerdians dance, and Cahira cheered happily from the balcony as Fareth and Ranveig trotted out and joined the dancers. Aren laughed, and he looked young and beautiful, filled with the joy of life. Despite his lingering hangover, Elphin brightened at the sight of the old king dancing among his handmaidens. He turned unexpectedly to Rika. "Tell me, do Norsk females dance, or simply aim darts at their partners?" he asked.

When she replied, "We dance," Elphin held out his hand, and to Cahira's surprise, Rika allowed him to lead her down to the courtyard. Thorleif emerged looking pale and weak, but his youthful vigor restored as soon as he saw the others dancing. He seized a particularly tiny Guerdian maid, bowed low, then escorted her gracefully into the crowd.

Both Ranveig and Fareth had chosen little partners, and each seemed to be trying to outdo the other as they danced more and more vigorously. Rika and Elphin, too, had transformed their dance into some sort of competition, and Khadun again proved his adeptness and skill as he took up the central position in the courtyard. Felix swooped down over them all and darted in circles over the dancers, and some of the Guerdian maids tossed bright cloths upward as if to honor his presence.

Aren watched them with an expression of complete happiness, and Cahira remembered what he had told her truly mattered to him—the simple joys, the beauty of the moment. He looked down at her, and his amber eyes were shining.

"Would you care to dance, Lady Mage?" he asked. He held out his hand and she took it without answering, because of her own happiness. It came from being with the man she loved, among those who were dear to her; when

sweet sunlight filled the air and those who had once been enemies now laughed together, that was a joy that had no end.

Aren guided her into the courtyard, and the music of drum
and flute echoed along the cliffside, filling the sky with song.
He took her hand and they twirled together, she with one
hand on his shoulder. An older Guerdian woman shook her
head fiercely, then tapped Aren's hip. He stopped and she
motioned for him to follow, and he shrugged then obeyed.

Soon, they were all instructed in the orderly steps involved in the Guerdian spectacle. For the tall Norskmen, the
dance posed problems, because the steps were short and
quick. Thorleif's legs entangled more than once, and Elphin
was laughing so hard that tears came to his eyes. Rika and
Ranveig however, both proved surprisingly adept. Fareth
kept spinning in the wrong direction, and Cahira's laughter
made her lose count of her steps. She bumped back into
Aren, who caught her, and she looked up at him. Suddenly
she knew she hadn't missed the joys of their childhood
escapades—their adventures had just begun.

"That was so much fun!" she cried when it was done. "If
Woodlanders knew Guerdians celebrated thus, we'd be taking vacations here all the time." Cahira held Aren's hand as
they walked back to their quarters. The sun was setting, and
its final rays seemed to bid them a sweet and mournful
farewell as it lowered at last over the misty horizon.

"That might not be such a bad way for the Guerdians to
recoup their losses," Aren admitted. "If a time of peace returns, it may be that both our races could benefit from such
visits, where we all can learn of each other as well as enjoy
ourselves."

She stopped and looked at him in wonder. "And that really would be peace, wouldn't it? If we learned of each
other, celebrated our differences, and opened our hearts to
ways that are different from our own. If we did that, then
even the energy of the Arch Mage might hold no sway."

Aren nodded. "Let this day remind us of that, love, should our hearts endure doubt in the times to come."

"As they may," agreed Cahira with a sigh. "As we draw closer to his tomb, the darkness will grow stronger indeed."

"Hope will guide us past fear," Aren said, and he bent to kiss her forehead. "Just remember I love you, Cahira Daere. And I am with you always."

"Like tonight," she said with a smile. He nodded, then led her to the door of their room. He opened it, and she walked in. It was dark, which seemed strange because the sun had only just set. "Did you draw these shades?" she asked.

"No," whispered a voice. "I did."

Cahira whirled just as Aren ducked to pass through the small doorway. She started to scream, but a great shape loomed in front of her—Bodvar. The magical shield of Damir flickered around her, but Bodvar wasn't after her. He slammed the butt of his axe into Aren's head, and Aren staggered forward, then fell to his knees. Cahira choked on a scream, but Bodvar kicked the door shut behind his chieftain, then drove his axe hard into him again. Blood streamed from a gash in Aren's head, streaking his pale hair with red, and Bodvar kicked him aside.

Blinded by tears, Cahira ran instinctively for her bow, but it wasn't by the door where she'd left it. "Are you looking for this?" Shaen appeared from the shadows and held the weapon up.

"You cannot touch me!" Cahira spat, and fury pounded through her—and a grief so acute she couldn't breathe. "I will kill you all!" Her energy soared and welled within her, ten times the force of what she had displayed in Aren's Great Hall.

"And risk him?" Shaen's voice remained light and calm, even pleasant. "All that vast power of yours is likely to bring down these walls, and the ceilings, too. I would restrain myself if I were you, Cahira Daere, but that has always been difficult for you, I know. Still, with the Norskman lying there, I'd think you'd want to be more careful."

Something about that soft voice sent chills through Cahira's nerves, and she trembled violently. An explosion of her energy could indeed bring the dwelling walls crashing inward. Bodvar stood beside Aren, his face immobile but his pale eyes burning.

"How could you do this to him?" she asked. "He is your chieftain and your lord."

"Bodvar understands what you've done to Aren," answered Shaen. "He has convinced me that Aren's shortsighted acceptance of this foolish quest will be the undoing of us all."

"When the brother of Bruin the Ruthless fell prey to a witch's spell, he was no longer my chieftain," Bodvar added.

"You betrayed him because of me?" Cahira asked.

"He was great once," said Bodvar. "The greatest in battle, young and strong, as our legends tell of the gods of old. But you sought him out and conquered him—sank to your knees before him, like a courtesan before a king, pleasuring—"

"That's enough," interjected Shaen. "You reveal too much, Bodvar."

"What are you talking about? What do you mean?" asked Cahira, confused.

Shaen turned her dark eyes on Cahira and dampened her lips. "You might say I gave Bodvar a stimulating rendition of what female Mages do to their captives, to the men they seek to enslave. Though it infuriated him, I believe he enjoyed the torture. It is natural for his kind."

"*What?* I didn't do anything to Aren," Cahira snarled, "and certainly not as a prisoner. I love him, and he loves me, and I will not let you hurt him because of some vile fantasy this stupid brute now harbors!"

"Aren is young and handsome," said Shaen, and her voice was hypnotic. "A treasure of a man, even if he gives in to the corruption and temptation of a female Mage."

Cahira's stomach churned, and for a moment she thought she might vomit. But . . . *I have to save him.* Shaen held her bow, but Shaen was no match for Cahira. Cahira tensed. If she could get her bow, then shoot Bodvar . . .

"Bind him, Bodvar, before he wakes. Even injured, Aren might prove a danger." Bodvar obeyed and roughly bound and gagged Aren, but Aren didn't wake. Bodvar shoved Cahira aside, but Cahira fought against him, and with the power of Damir's shield protecting her, he was unable to return her blows.

"Stop, Bodvar!" commanded Shaen. "You can't hurt her. Don't even try."

"Ah, but *I* can hurt *you!*" Cahira lunged toward Shaen. Unfortunately, Bodvar grabbed her. His strength was enough—she couldn't free herself from his grip.

Shaen raised a short Guerdian spear, then maneuvered to Aren's side. She said, "Such a powerful man, and I am so weak! But I think, unconscious as he is now, I could pierce his throat right through."

Cahira went limp, and Bodvar dropped her to her feet. "What do you want from me? What are you going to do?"

"First of all, I want you to clothe yourself again in your traveling attire," said Shaen lightly. She fingered the spear and twisted it close to Aren's throat. "*Now.*" Glancing at Bodvar she added, "Don't you think you should look away as she changes?"

Bodvar's eyes glinted, and he turned as if the sight of Cahira's body might drive him to fury. Cahira seized her pack and yanked out her leggings and bodice, then dressed. Her hands shook so violently that she barely managed the ties. As she pulled on her boots, she turned to face Shaen. "Aren't you going to change?" she asked.

Shaen glanced down at what she wore, the short Guerdian dress. "I am more comfortable in feminine attire than you are," she replied casually. "And I have my cloak, of course, should the cavern prove chilly." She smiled, just as she always smiled, with a slight hint of compassion and condescension. "We're going to take you into the cavern passageway, you see. Bodvar has already secured the key from the little king, all without the king knowing. He was so enraptured by his dancers that it was easy. And while you've been dallying with your fanciful search through the Guerdian records, Bodvar found an apt route of escape so that he can carry you undetected as we depart."

"But what's to stop me from bringing down the whole cavern once we're away?" asked Cahira.

"The fear of your lover following you, I think," said Shaen. "For we both know he will. That's why we've chosen to leave him alive, of course. You see, after the ambush, Elphin revealed unwittingly that though Damir's shield can protect you from harm, you can still be restrained. He gave me a solution for the problem of your *ki*, too, by mentioning that a burst of your energy might shatter walls and bring an underground passageway crashing inward."

"Why are you doing this?" Cahira asked, too stunned to feel fear. "What do you want?"

"You don't need to know that," Shaen sneered, and her expression ripened with a conceit Cahira had never detected before. "Suffice to say that Bodvar has suggested a different solution to our predicament than what Damir had in mind."

"You're going to use me to wake the Arch Mage," realized Cahira with disbelief. "Why?"

"It is his wish," admitted Shaen, her voice a monotone.

Cahira closed her eyes. "The Dark Tide has infected you more than I ever imagined, if he is indeed directing your course."

"He is great beyond measure," Shaen continued. "How he calls to me in the dark of night! *'Wake me, serve me.'*"

"Those are the same words spoken by the last Mage the Dark Tide enslaved!" cried Cahira. "And he died for his efforts." She eyed Bodvar. "And you're willing to help her with this?"

For one second, the Norskman seemed to hesitate, as if he, too, doubted Shaen's sanity. But then he said, "I will not be controlled as Bruin was, nor lulled into treachery like Aren. This is the right course."

Cahira shook her head. "The Arch Mage is a demon! He's evil! If he rises from the grave, it will be with flames and blood and ash! Do you not understand that? He will kill you both and take me, and then his power will be complete! How can you two be such fools?" She groaned in agony. "*He* is doing this to you. Don't you see? As we draw closer to his cavern, his will infects our thoughts. In the name of all the Great Spirits past, Shaen, don't do this!"

Shaen was unmoved. "Bodvar, bind and gag Cahira, but gently. You'll be carrying her, I fear, for a long way. I don't think we can count on her to hasten our journey." She pressed the tip of her spear against Aren's throat. "Cry out, and I will have to kill him."

Blood oozed down over Aren's beautiful face from a cut on his forehead, but his chest still rose and fell. If someone found him in time . . .

Bodvar tore up a sheet and wound the strips into thick ties, then approached Cahira. She backed away, tears filling her eyes. She could only delay, and as blood spilled from Aren's wound, that might be the worst thing to do. It might be best to acquiesce. She strained for one last view of Aren.

"I love you so," she whispered, and then she mouthed soft words in the ancient tongue of her people. "*Arail Aren, Aryana, nawr a am byth . . .*"

She bowed her head then, and Bodvar bound her hands. He gagged her roughly, despite Shaen's instructions, and lifted her onto his shoulder.

Shaen retrieved a full pack, which presumably held food for their journey. She tossed Cahira's bow onto the bed, then carefully stepped over Aren as he lay motionless and bleeding. She drew a small scroll from the pack and opened it, revealing an old map. "You see, I told you the truth when I said I knew all the passages of the Arch Mage's palace."

"But not that you'd memorized it," added Cahira. "I suppose you stole that when Madawc's library burned."

"The maps were destined to come into my hands. Eliana's hot temper—attacking Damir as she did—simply served my ends. It was only a small fire, but I was able to convince Madawc that the maps were destroyed." She paused. "It's the only time I ever saw him angry with Eliana, though she had done so much mischief besides that. She certainly deserved his fury, either way."

Cahira hesitated, but an argument of logic would clearly be wasted.

Shaen glanced at the scroll, then put it into her pack. "And now," she said as cheerfully as if she'd begun a new morning on a spring day, "we're going to complete our quest."

He ran like a hunter, tireless, driven beyond need, thirst, or pain to find her. Blood pounded in Aren's head, his wound ached, but he refused to relent. Rika ran beside him, her loose hair streaming out behind her, her face hard and her eyes gleaming in the darkness. Khadun ran just behind them, just as quick despite his size, and he carried a lamp that illuminated the cavern passage with faint light. Thorleif and Elphin followed close behind, and then lumbering after them came Ranveig and Fareth, puffing loudly, but determined not to flag or fail as they followed Cahira's trail.

Felix the bat flew above their heads, darting in and out of shadows. He flew ahead now and again to scout out the path before them, and twice now he had found paths that shortened the distance between them and Cahira's abductors.

Blood seeped from Aren's bandage and dripped down into his eyes, but he refused to stop. He stumbled as he ran, and Rika caught his arm, then pulled him back. "Aren, we have to rest. You'll do her no good if you fall here."

He stopped, his breath coming in shallow, gasps, and he stood there, fighting weakness.

"Here, take this, my lord," offered Elphin, and the Woodlander passed him a flask of scented water.

Aren drank, then set his gaze into the darkness ahead. "We go on."

No one argued, though he knew they were nearly as tired as he. They walked now, in long swift strides, and Felix doubled back to perch on Aren's shoulder. "My lord, we may well be gaining on them, but I can't detect their sound, and I've gone a ways ahead."

"We will find her," said Aren. *I am with you, Cahira. Always.* But he had never imagined fear and doubt could be so strong.

"I'd like permission to go on farther ahead, 'til I reach them," said Felix. "I can keep hidden, and if I can get the lass's attention, I can give her hope—tell her you're here."

"She knows that," said Aren, his voice raw. "But find her. Yes, go."

The bat flew off, and Aren's group moved forward with all the speed they could muster. "I don't understand," muttered Thorleif. "What does he want with her?"

"Bodvar?" asked Aren, spitting his old friend's name. "He wants power and glory, as all fools desire—and that wench Shaen has somehow persuaded him that this is the path to it."

"I can't believe that," said Fareth. "Shaen wouldn't do this. Such a delicate woman, a Mundane! Maybe Bodvar's taken her and Cahira both captive."

"She's always been so sweet and so frail," agreed Elphin. "Never challenged anyone. She was always saying how much she cared for Cahira—like a sister, she said. Fareth has to be right. Bodvar's behind this. He's got to be."

Rika rolled her eyes. "That wench is nothing more than a snake. She bats her eyes and flatters you, and makes you think you are dear to her. You are nothing but tools she uses to get what she wants."

"But what could she possibly want *here?*" asked Thorleif.

"It makes no sense," agreed Ranveig. "She kept trying to talk the young witch out of this journey."

"And has from the first," added Fareth. "Shaen never believed this journey would work."

"But she didn't realize Damir shielded Cahira, either," said Elphin slowly. "Remember how shocked she was when Cahira appeared at the tavern, when all the other Mages were stricken?"

"But she was happy and relieved, as we all were," argued Fareth.

"Easy enough to feign," sneered Ranveig.

"Then, what exactly was her plan?" Fareth looked annoyed. Aren wrapped another bandage around his head as they walked. "To take Cahira's body up into the mountains, and to deliver her to the being Shaen considers a god."

"To the Arch Mage?" Fareth's eyes widened. "That's crazy!" He paused. "Though I do recall the lady saying something about him being 'deceived'—wasn't that it? By our great queen?" He sighed miserably. "None of us saw this, not even for a moment."

"Even so," said Elphin. "With this plan . . . How could she have hoped to carry Cahira's body from the Woodland? She'd need a cart, at least, and we'd all be keeping watch over all the Mages."

"Shaen planned to keep watch on Madawc, where she believed Cahira would be laid out," Fareth pointed out. "She told us something like that, remember? It was all there, but we didn't see it!"

Elphin hesitated. "Well, how would she get up into these mountains?"

"The Arch Mage would have guided her, I guess," Fareth said. "Or maybe there are others in the Woodland who planned to help, before the young lass took off after the chieftain."

"It doesn't matter now," said Aren miserably. "All that matters is finding her and saving her. . . ."

"My lord, you'll need to rest sometime. *They* will," said Thorleif.

"He's right," agreed Rika. "We have run for hours now. I said I would follow them into the Hall of Wizards, Aren, and I will, but we cannot go much farther without rest or food."

He looked into her cool blue eyes and saw a deep, honest compassion. She never showed it, or made emotive declarations, but there was a kindness in Rika that made a mockery of all Shaen pretended to be. At last, he nodded, and slumped down to his knees. Tears filled his eyes, but the company seated themselves beside him and he took comfort in their presence.

Rika tended his wound with help from Khadun, and Ranveig and Fareth worked together to lay out a quick meal. "We've packed enough for this journey, and beyond," said Ranveig. "So eat your fill now, my lord. You need it."

Fareth passed him a flask of tea. "Better for your vitals than ale," he said.

"That's what the witch—" Thorleif stopped and his voice softened, "—what the Lady Mage kept telling me, though I noticed she had a taste for ale herself."

"She did, at that," said Fareth, and he chuckled. "What a time that lass gave the Elder Mage Madawc! He'd storm into my tavern, tell me she'd aged him another ten years in a day, and yet every time I saw him, he seemed to look younger. The old fellow adored her."

Elphin smiled. "As did Damir and Eliana. As like to The Fiend as a sister, she is, and just as pretty. A mite less temperamental, too."

"She's a strong lass," agreed Fareth, and he laid his hand on Aren's shoulder. "Whatever they want with her, you just remember this—they can't hurt her while Damir ap Kora's shield holds. Even the Arch Mage can't hurt her, if they should get so far."

Aren nodded slowly. "I know." He felt dizzy and weak from his injury, and his emotions were raw. "But she must be so afraid."

"More likely she's furious," said Fareth. "She'll kill them if she gets a chance. Maybe not with her *ki*, but she'll do it."

"If she's afraid, it's likely for you, Aren," said Rika quietly. "You know this. And you know, too, that she senses you. She needs you to be strong."

He looked at her and couldn't answer. But she smiled at him kindly, then touched his shoulder. "Sleep now," she whispered. "Rest awhile, and we will wake you to go on."

Aren lay back, and Rika eased a cape beneath his head, then covered him with another. His eyes drifted shut almost against his will, and he fell asleep protected by the shadows of his friends.

They went on for another day at least, and Aren lost track of time in the dark cavern. The passage cut straight, and the way was mostly clear, save for a few fallen boulders that were easily skirted. Occasionally a fissure formed in the path, but none were wide, and even Khadun had no trouble jumping the gaps. But Felix didn't return, and Aren's concern grew.

The group moved silently, though their pace remained swift. Aren's head still throbbed, but the bleeding had stopped and his senses were slowly returning. A soft whirr sounded over their heads, and Aren stopped while the others gathered around him.

Felix dropped from the ceiling and landed squarely on Aren's shoulder. He seemed out of breath, because he didn't speak immediately.

"Welcome back, Lord Bat!" exclaimed Thorleif, and though his tone was light, Aren heard the relief in the youth's voice. "I was beginning to think you'd found a pretty female and abandoned us."

Felix cocked his head to one side, but ignored Thorleif's teasing.

"Did you find her?" asked Aren, his voice strained.

"They're up ahead, my lord. Not so far now," said the bat.

"Is she . . . ?"

"Looks to be well enough," Felix said, "though I didn't get close enough to speak with her. That brute is keeping a watch—probably expects me, though I don't think he knows I was near."

"You didn't talk to her?" Aren's heart fell. "Then she doesn't know . . ."

"She knows you're coming, my lord," said Felix. "In fact, Shaen seems to be counting on it, as I heard her say to Bodvar."

"Why would they want us following?" asked Thorleif.

Elphin bowed his head and spoke up. "Because it's the only thing to stop Cahira from using her *ki* to bring down this passage," he guessed miserably. "I told them as much after the ambush—even suggested a 'strong man' would be able to restrain her! I should have kept my mouth shut."

Rika laid her hand on his shoulder, and Elphin looked at her in surprise. "You couldn't know there was a traitor among us. And they might have figured it out on their own, eventually."

"Neither Bodvar nor Shaen seems all that quick," put in Thorleif. "But you're probably right. Where there's a want, the will finds a way."

"And with the Arch Mage himself directing Shaen, who knows what schemes might have been tried," added Fareth. "A devil, he is!"

"How far ahead are they?" asked Aren. "How long will it take to reach them?"

Felix considered. "They're getting close to the catacombs now, though it's a ways inward to the Arch Mage's tomb. I'd say if you run at a fair pace, you may catch them before they reach his pit—but it will be close."

"Then we run," said Aren.

"I'll fly on ahead again and keep an eye on the lass," said Felix, but he sounded tired.

"Just a moment, bat," said Thorleif. He fished around in his pack, then drew out a small portion of bread and his flask. "Take a bite first, to keep up your strength. Flying can't be easy on an empty stomach."

Felix hopped to Thorleif's shoulder, and the youth held up the bread, which the bat devoured. Thorleif adjusted the flask for the bat to drink, but Felix paused.

"This is ale!"

"You seem to prefer it to tea," said Thorleif.

"I do at that," agreed Felix, and he drank heartily. He then straightened and looked Thorleif in the eye. "You're a good lad," he said. He tapped Thorleif's hair with his wing tip, his claw got entangled, he yanked slightly to free himself, then crunched his body forward in an odd bow. "I am restored," he said triumphantly, and then the bat swooped up into the darkness and disappeared.

"Crumbs everywhere," muttered Thorleif, dusting off the shoulder of his light jerkin. "Messy creature."

Aren smiled, his heart unexpectedly lightened. Then they all took off running again, moving in even strides that echoed along the passageway.

"Bodvar will hear us coming," said Elphin as he ran.

"There's no way to avoid that now," said Aren. "And he may wish he had fallen at my brother's side when next we meet."

13

THE CAVERN OF THE MAGE

"If we're lucky, Cahira, Aren will catch up with us just as the Arch Mage rises," said Shaen. "Then you'll get to watch your lover defeated by the greatest power the world has ever known."

"And if Damir proves right, and Aren can defeat the Arch Mage . . . ?" Cahira asked. She watched as Shaen broke off a small piece of bread and delicately ate it. Bodvar threw Cahira a small portion, which she stuffed in its entirety into her mouth.

"You know how unlikely that is," Shaen answered, but then she glanced at Bodvar. "It is my intention to reach the catacombs well before Aren reaches us. We will block the entrance, so that the Arch Mage can resurrect in peace, and have forewarning of Aren's approach."

Bodvar grunted as he drank from his flask of ale. "What's your worry? I've seen that wizard's power firsthand. No white sword will hold him off, even wielded by the greatest warrior."

"We don't want to take any risks. The Arch Mage's resurrection must go smoothly. He must have time to adjust, to take in his surroundings."

"Maybe we should bring him some tea, too, to help him feel at ease!" Cahira hissed. She kicked out and knocked Bodvar's flask out of his hand. He drew his arm back to strike her, but she smiled. "Try it, and you'll find, again, that the barrier of Damir ap Kora burns rather badly."

He glowered at her, but then his hand dropped to his side and he retrieved his overturned flask. "What will he do to her?" he asked angrily, as if hoping the Arch Mage might have some dire fate in mind for Cahira.

Shaen looked thoughtful. "After her *ki* has served to rouse him from his captivity, he will seek to join with her, for that is what he desired from the Woodland queen—her power."

"He intends rape?" Cahira huffed. "He won't get far, not while Damir's shield protects me. But perhaps he intends to just sit around and wait until the life finally drains from all the Woodland Mages."

"If that is his wish," agreed Shaen deferentially, "then it will, of course, be so."

"But he will fail," Cahira said in a low voice. "Don't you think?" If she could keep Shaen talking, it would slow her progress, giving Aren more time to catch up. If she could avoid being hauled before the Arch Mage's tomb, their first plan still had a chance.

"Who will stop him—your Norsk lover and Damir's pretty sword?" Shaen laughed. "I don't think so."

"He will fail, whatever happens," said Cahira. "If Damir's shield fails—"

"Then I'm afraid you'll be at the Arch Mage's mercy," interrupted Shaen. "You will have no choice but to submit."

Now Cahira laughed, and both Bodvar and Shaen looked at her in surprise. "Do you think so, Shaen? If Aren falls, I will simply follow him."

"The Arch Mage will prevent any such act."

"I am a Mage, and an Elite. Like my ancestor before me, I,

too, can surrender my life at my own choosing." Cahira paused. "But you know that, don't you? In fact, I think that's what you're counting on."

Shaen's lips pursed as she considered this. "What are you talking about?"

"Should the Arch Mage join with me, devouring my energy until I fade, or whatever he plans to do, then his power will indeed be complete, and he will sweep across this world like a god. And if that happens, he will have no weakness, *nor any need for you.*"

A flash of anger twisted Shaen's face. "I would never hinder him in any way! I seek only to serve him, as he demands in my dreams."

"Does he speak to you? I wonder."

"I hear him constantly, as you do," responded Shaen. "I'm sure he knows that I'm here, the one person who was willing to free him from his captivity. Who understands him. Who—"

"You're in love with him!" Cahira sat back and stared. "That's crazy! He's not even human! He's a thing, a creature, and if he should ever crawl out of that pit, you will see a devil and no man!"

"He is powerful enough without you," continued Shaen. "He will tear through everything in his path, brutal in force, driving and demanding."

"No," Cahira said quietly. "It is lust and not love that you feel after all."

Shaen sneered, and yet still she smiled. "Love and lust. Are these the only options? They may be for you, Cahira, as they were for Eliana as she relentlessly pursued Damir. But I have always felt things more deeply than other women. What I feel for the Arch Mage, for *Matchitehew . . .*" She shuddered she spoke his name. "It is something far greater than you could ever know."

Cahira eyed Bodvar. "Don't you see the flaw in this plan? She's using you to resurrect a demon because she fancies him. I can't imagine that would make sense, even to you."

Bodvar glanced between them, and she saw again a flicker

of doubt, but his eyes quickly darkened. "This wench means nothing to me—I used her to slake my lust. I am not a man to fawn and fall at the feet of a woman who bends over before me, as our young chieftain has done."

Cahira grimaced, but mercifully he said no more and stood up and stormed to the far side of the cavern. He drained what was left in his flask, and Cahira glanced at Shaen. "Well, that was tender!"

Shaen didn't look at Bodvar, instead continuing with her meal. "Bodvar simply doesn't have the capacity for greater feeling. His passions are . . . limited."

"I doubt he's a legend among women," agreed Cahira. "Unlike the Arch Mage, apparently." Shaen's eyes darkened, as she presumably reflected on the Mage's great skill. "But then Bodvar at least has the benefit of having a human body—again, unlike the Arch Mage."

"He will, I'm sure," snapped Shaen, and she gazed thoughtfully off at nothing. "I understand him in a way no other woman could. It was I who first learned the method to wake him from his slumber, during the time I studied with Madawc. My discovery of an obscure scroll was completely by chance, found when I was cleaning—I believe it was hidden by an Elder long before Madawc. I believe the Arch Mage's will directed me to it."

A thought emerged in Cahira's mind, but it didn't fully coalesce. Had he been seeking someone like Shaen, or had she been seeking him, a being with all the power and menace she lacked?

"I believe," Cahira said slowly, "that you were looking for just such a power when you entered Madawc's service. You never thought you had a Mage's *ki,* but somehow you were able to make people think you might."

Anger flared in Shaen's eyes. "That is a lie! In fact, many told me they sensed I had *ki,* and I didn't believe them. I resisted until Madawc himself begged me to study."

A tiny sound caught Cahira's attention. It sounded like a miniature snort, but Shaen didn't appear to notice.

"Ha! Madawc never 'begged' anyone for anything in his life," said Cahira. "It seems to me that you got yourself placed right where you wanted to be. And when that didn't get you what you want, you made your way to my father's service, and played on his loneliness to become his mistress."

Shaen's anger grew, and it contorted her face to an expression Cahira hadn't seen before. "I see why you don't like to get angry, Shaen," she offered. "You look pinched and rather old right now. Better not show *that* face to the Arch Mage!"

For an instant, Cahira thought Shaen might actually strike out at her, and she leaned forward slightly in hope's that Shaen's brittle hand might encounter Damir's shield. But then Shaen smiled, the effect grotesque in the wake of her anger. "Your nature has always been difficult and cruel," she observed. "But I'm not angry in any way. I know you feel powerless and outmatched, and that must be very hard for someone who acts impulsively, without forethought."

"It *is* tiresome," Cahira agreed, "but I reassure myself with the thought that you will meet a dire fate at the hands of this monster you seek to raise."

"That is ridiculous. Unlike you or Eliana, I am always careful. I don't take unnecessary risks until I am sure of the outcome." She began to collect her gear, readying herself to go.

Cahira needed to keep her talking. "How did you know what to do with the scroll?" she asked, in a tone she hoped sounded impressed by Shaen's cleverness.

The tactic worked. Shaen set aside her gear and a slight smile curved her lips. "Intuition, of course. And I was smart. Once I became the king's mistress, I formed many friendships. I convinced one friend, a Mage who understood the power we could achieve, to begin, in secret, the process that would call forth the Arch Mage's energy. He failed on that first attempt, but we came close and I knew it was only a matter of time. I waited until you came of age, knowing he would finally come for you. And he has!"

"I always considered you rather stupid," retorted Cahira flatly. "But Aren was right—you are crafty. He also once told me that 'treasures won by trickery are treasures no longer'—but I expect that concept eludes you."

Shaen's anger flared again; then she repressed it into a smile. "Trickery? I have simply used my skills and talents, just as you do to get what you want, Cahira Daere. As for your weak and foolish father, do you want to know what happened to him? He began to question the nature of our relationship and even thought to banish me from the palace. Knowing how that would hurt me, my Mage ally killed your father, lest he begin to speak recklessly about . . . facets of my character."

Cahira closed her eyes. "Then he was not truly dark—"

"All men are dark when it comes to desire," snapped Shaen, and she cast a lingering gaze at Bodvar. "You'd be amazed at what arouses *that* warrior."

Cahira pinned a fierce gaze upon Shaen. "I do *not* want to know."

Shaen glanced back in surprise; then she laughed. "You are still such a child! Aren will soon tire of you, if you aren't willing to expand your imagination."

"Where he would lead, I am happy to go," said Cahira, "because he leads with his heart, and not the darkness that shadows a soul."

"You are trying to romanticize the nature of your relationship," said Shaen. "But it was obvious to me that Aren found our female Mages a sore temptation, and that the image of such a woman on her knees before him would be his undoing. You simply used that fact to your advantage."

"Here we go with the knees again," muttered Cahira. Then she shook her head.

"You fulfill his fantasies, and that is his weakness."

"As it happens, he fulfills mine as well," Cahira said. "But my fantasies stem from my desire to be as close to him as I can possibly get. That is a quest that will never end. I doubt you understand, because your motivation isn't romantic or even hedonistic in nature."

"I am deeply romantic!" insisted Shaen. "And I have always been extremely sensual."

"Are you? Do you really love the touch of a man's skin, the scent of him, or the feel of his lips on your body? Do those fires really burn in you? Do you long to join with him, to feel his pulse, to hear his heart beating close to your ear? Does the thought of his desire stir you—or does lust simply serve your purpose, fuel your own sense of power over him? I think what you feel is the thrill of victory, a simple win over another person—not the wild pleasure of joining."

Shaen's lips twitched with a frown, but she banished the expression as if she knew it revealed too much. "Intimacy is always a dance of power—just as it has obviously been between you and Aren."

"Not a dance of love?" Cahira shook her head. "I don't think it's even a 'dance of fun' to you." She paused. "I used to listen to women talking at the Hungry Cat, and they often spoke of lovemaking as an amusement, as a game. It was obvious they enjoyed the game very much, even if they didn't feel what I feel for Aren. But you . . . there's something different about you."

Shaen's eyes grew darker. "You envy me, because I understand men better than you do. Perhaps you fear I am a better lover."

Cahira stared at her for a long moment. "I don't think it's ever occurred to me to compare us in that regard." She paused. "How odd that you would! I do not believe such skill comes from practice, but from a willingness to share the experience with another person, whether for love, or for fun . . . or even just to feel close to someone. But I doubt any of that motivates you—not love, nor fun, nor even need. I don't think you give anything of yourself, and so I suspect you feel nothing in even the most heated encounter. Less, even, in Bodvar's violent embrace than I feel when Aren touches my hand."

Now Shaen flared with visible anger, and her cheeks reddened. "I feel more than you can imagine!" She paused, fuming. "Maybe not with Bodvar, or your weak father. But with the right man . . ."

"I hope you don't refer to the Arch Mage," interrupted Cahira. "Because as far as I know, he doesn't have the body parts necessary for this activity—unless you prefer a ghostly embrace."

"He will," insisted Shaen. "Once I present you before his tomb, his living body will be restored. And then he will be mine."

"What makes you think he'll want you? Isn't he more likely to head off to Kora and find a female there, one with power equal to his own?"

"Powerful women have caused him so much grief," scoffed Shaen. "Both the Woodland Queen and Eliana damaged his aspirations for power and glory. I think he can be persuaded that such a woman is a danger to him now."

You mean for him to kill me, don't you? Cahira didn't speak her thoughts aloud, but she understood Shaen's intentions now. Even if the dreaded Arch Mage wasn't so inclined initially, Shaen would manipulate him into ending Cahira's 'threat.' "I'm surprised you think such an infamously dark and evil being could be manipulated that way."

"Manipulated? What a nasty accusation!" Shaen paused and looked thoughtful. "But even the most powerful man needs persuasion, occasionally—the advice, perhaps, of a woman who has greater insight into the character and inner feelings of others. As strong as he surely is, I doubt he has any idea what you are thinking, Cahira. I'm afraid it will be a disappointment to him, especially since you have cheapened yourself by your tawdry union with a Norskman."

"What makes you think he'll care what I've done? He wants my power, not my heart."

"I know he doesn't care about you personally," said Shaen, and she sounded condescending. "But your defiance will anger him."

"And I was so hoping he'd express gratitude when my presence gives him a renewed chance at a fruitful life!"

"His gratitude will be expressed to me, not you," said Shaen, as if Cahira had engaged her in competition for the

Arch Mage's affections. "At this, my power exceeds yours, Cahira, for you are not sensitive when dealing with the hearts and minds of others." She paused, and looked particularly smug. "I will learn what matters most to him and gain his confidence, and soon, I will become indispensible to him."

"As you have been 'indispensible' to so many before," muttered Cahira, and she sighed as she thought of her father. Indeed, he had depended on Shaen, and her sly hints and whispers of doubt had ravaged his already-shaken confidence. Yet never once had Shaen spoken angrily—always, she spoke as if from the most caring heart, the dearest friendship. "The Arch Mage may not prove as weak-willed as my father," she added; but then she sighed again, and her spirits sank with a strange foreboding of inevitability. As ridiculous and implausible as Shaen's schemes seemed to Cahira, her conviction had power. "But you are relentless, aren't you? You will pry and delve until you find his weakness, as you did with my father and with Bodvar, because even the greatest man has a weakness. Then you'll pretend to accept and understand all the demons that rage within his dark soul." Cahira leaned toward Shaen, and her voice grew stronger. "And then you will wield every one of those demons against him until he is buried in his shame. All for the power it gives you."

Shaen blanched as if Cahira had struck her. "I am in *love* with him!"

"You want him, because you think having him will make you powerful," replied Cahira evenly. "You want him; therefore he should be yours, because what he wants and feels mean no more to you than the wants and feelings of anyone else besides yourself."

Shaen's hand clenched and she trembled with fury. "That is a lie! I have always cared deeply for others, and continually denied myself."

"So you would have us think," said Cahira. "But there's something more lurking beneath this dark scheme of yours. The Arch Mage wasn't just powerful—he was loved. His lover was the most beautiful and powerful woman Amrodel ever knew. And you know the Woodland Queen's spirit has guided us on this quest."

A tiny smile formed on Shaen's lips, and a chill ran down Cahira's spine at the sight. "Then the Woodland Queen will see that I am a more suitable lover for him than she was," said Shaen.

"I understand now," said Cahira. "For you, it isn't a treasure unless it's stolen from someone else. But everything about you seems stolen from someone else. You tried to look like Eliana, and you've tried to match her power, though you do not have it within you by nature."

"But I do have power, Cahira," said Shaen, and her tone turned mocking. "I had no interest in luring Aren away from you, but because of my efforts, you've lost him." Shaen sounded triumphant, but Cahira shook her head.

"If he should fall, and if I should die, too, we will not be lost, because our hearts are joined, and that is a joy you will never know. Especially if you're planning to find it with the Arch Mage." Cahira paused. "What are you going to do if he rises from that pit and isn't quite the breathtakingly handsome figure you're expecting?"

"His good looks stunned everyone," countered Shaen. "There are images of him in Madawc's library—he looked just like . . ." She stopped, as if unwilling to reveal some other dark facet of her character. "Why would he appear differently now?"

"Because he's been buried and disembodied for an Age?" suggested Cahira, but Shaen didn't seem concerned by the prospect.

"His power is beyond what you can conceive," she decided, and then she sighed. "Every woman desired him, and longed to be his consort, even the Woodland Queen."

"And you think that was because of his looks?" asked Cahira in surprise.

"As well as his legendary prowess, of course," continued Shaen evenly.

"Not that, in some measure, they were two of a kind, but too proud and defiant, too enslaved by their own power to know it?"

Shaen looked at Cahira without comprehending, and Cahira rolled her eyes. "Never mind."

Bodvar returned to the campsite, glowering as always. "We should go on," he said. "We have already lingered too long." He eyed Cahira darkly, and she leaned back.

"If you think I'm going to walk and make it easier on your back, think again, brute!"

He reached out angrily to grab her, but she issued a pert "Tsk," and he hesitated. "Careful, lest you evoke my shield," she advised. She shook her head. "Four times already you've been burned, and you don't learn a thing. Not the sharpest axe on the rack, are you?"

Dark anger flared in Bodvar's eyes, but he picked her up gingerly and slung her over his shoulder. After Shaen's denial of anger, Bodvar's overt fury was almost welcome. But the position in which she was tossed wasn't comfortable, though his shoulders were broad enough, and Cahira was tempted to walk.

"Don't let her antagonize you, Bodvar," called Shaen. "You will soon see her humbled before the Arch Mage."

Cahira twisted, which threw Bodvar off balance, and he grumbled bitterly as he tripped, then regained his footing. "I'm afraid the Arch Mage can't touch me, either," she said, as cheerfully as she could while hanging upside-down. "I'm not worried."

"Aren't you?" asked Shaen. "You should be."

"He can't kill me or even pull out a single hair on my head," said Cahira. "But you two, on the other hand . . ." She paused to catch her breath from her uncomfortable position. "I'd hate to think what he can do to *you*."

Shaen walked hurriedly over to Bodvar, eager for this coming encounter that she couldn't begin to comprehend. "He will shower me—*us*—with gratitude, and we will be the first to win his favor. Why would he hurt us?"

"I don't know—for fun?" She had more to say, but Bodvar jostled her on his shoulder, which made further speech impossible. She drew strength from her defiance, but inwardly, her fears grew. What if Aren had been too badly injured, what if he still lay helpless in Amon-Daal with his life seeping away? Or what if he was—

She closed her eyes and tried to see him in her mind, but all that came to her was the dark of her surroundings, the fear and doubt she couldn't deny. Here in the shadows, she heard a dark voice call to her, a whisper of evil: *Your resistance fails. I feel your presence drawing near. Soon I will rise, and all the world will fall . . .*

Cahira fought tears, and she steeled her will against the voice. "It is you that shall fall," she whispered, but her words felt hollow and it seemed to her that the Arch Mage laughed in response.

If Shaen and Bodvar reached the his tomb before Aren caught up with them, Cahira would have to confront him alone, without even her bow. The image in her head of the Arch Mage terrified her, and she felt sure it was far more accurate than Shaen's fanciful notion of legendary beauty. What if he rose like a skeleton, his flesh hanging from brittle limbs and sagging from his skull? Such were the nightmares of her childhood, and now they were compounded by her recent dreams, where blood dripped from his fingers and his resurrection was accompanied by ash and flame, and foul fumes.

Again, Cahira tried to envision Aren, but all she saw was his body lying crumpled on the floor where she had left him, his life draining away. She was desperate to hold him, but he lay alone, broken and in agony. Darkness engulfed her and tears dripped from beneath her eyelashes. But there, like a faint star on a cloudy night, light grew in her thoughts. A tiny image flew, its wings as barely noticeable as shadows through starlight. A dragonfly. Like an echo across a distant sea, a voice rose in her mind, as soft and kind as the Arch Mage's had been cruel: *'You have found the Light you seek,*

Cahira. It lies within you, and in the one you love. You have drawn open the veil on a power greater than any darkness. Do not fear for Aren, for I watch over him, as you requested.'

Cahira's eyes snapped open, and she remembered the words she had spoken when Bodvar dragged her away: *'Arail Aren, Aryana, nawr a am byth.'* Though a Mage's power could not be taught or copied, she had transformed Damir's spell into a prayer of her own, 'Guard Aren, Aryana, now and forever,' and the ancient Woodland queen had somehow heard her.

"Thank you," Cahira whispered, and she heard an echo of Aren's own thoughts, *I am with you.*

Cahira's hope returned, and her desperation eased. Now that Shaen had revealed herself, Cahira began to understand the enemy they faced. This was what the Arch Mage's power had created, but it wasn't invincible. Their enemy was just Shaen with a lust for "erotic pursuits," and dark glory at the side of a powerful male. She wasn't smarter or wiser because of the power he had instilled in her; nor had she gained a Mage's *ki*. She was still a weak woman who wanted what she couldn't have—the gifts inherent to another—just as Bodvar was a weak man who envied his younger, stronger leader. There was something oddly disturbing about both of them, but her fear was not as paralyzing as when their motives lay hidden in shadow.

"The catacombs are ahead!" Shaen cried out. She held up the small lamp she had stolen from the Guerdian city, and Cahira twisted around to see that the passage narrowed significantly. "We're almost there!"

"Wonderful," said Cahira. "I see you've been checking your map frequently. So much for your memory."

"I don't need the map now. I know these passageways as if I'd walked here a thousand times." Shaen insisted, "It is more a home to me than the Woodland palace ever was." She pointed toward a fork in the path ahead. "We go left and down here. The Tomb of the Arch Mage lies on the far end of the catacombs, in the southeastern wing."

"Right so far," said Cahira brightly. "But there are many twists and turns along the way—those that seem direct are often most long, so beware." She fell silent again, for those words had been spoken by Aren during the first days of their journey. *I love you so.*

Again, Bodvar jostled her position, perhaps angered by words he, too, recognized as Aren's wisdom. The walls they passed now were no longer stone, but carved rock, and then granite. Cahira recognized Guerdian handiwork, and her heart chilled as she guessed they drew closer. Vast tunnels branched off the main path, but Shaen rarely slowed to seek direction.

They reached a wide opening, then passed beneath a high ceiling. "This was the northern hall of the Arch Mage's domain," said Shaen. She spoke as if addressing visitors to the palace in Amrodel, her voice as benevolent as it had been as the king's hostess—a role she no doubt intended to fill in the Arch Mage's service.

A small column of light penetrated into the hall, and Cahira looked around as best she could. Indeed, it appeared to be the entrance to an underground castle, and the walls ended abruptly as if construction had been halted in one afternoon—probably on the day the Woodland queen died. Reliefs had been carved into the wall, and crumbling statues still stood in alcoves on either side of the quiet room. Most appeared Koraji in origin, caped figures that seemed both majestic and menacing.

"I suppose they're all him," muttered Cahira.

"They represent facets of his character, yes," said Shaen.

"Even that one?" Cahira pointed at a distinctly female carving, and Shaen frowned.

"Perhaps his mother."

"A young woman, with long, loose hair and a gown carved with wide sleeves?" Cahira clucked her tongue. "Looks like our renderings of the Woodland queen to me—the lover you're hoping to replace."

Shaen glanced at the queen's statue, then sniffed dismissively. "I never thought she was quite as glorious as everyone else did. She looked just like Eliana."

"Oh, look!" said Cahira cheerfully. "There's another one!" She flipped her arm up, deliberately striking Bodvar, and pointed at a statue farther ahead. "She looks like Eliana there, too."

Shaen walked by the second statue with only a quick glance. "Actually, that one looks more like me," she said in a taut voice. "Don't you think so, Bodvar?"

The Norshman grunted, then glanced without interest at the statue. "Looks like this wench I'm carrying," he said bitterly. "Another witch that destroyed a greater man's power."

"It's not a very detailed sculpture," Shaen decided, and she walked on, though her steps were shorter and more abrupt than usual. "This would have been the beginning of his great city," she added, as if tragedy had denied the world its greatest treasure. "From this hall, a paved road would have run northward, and another east and west. As you can see, the west road had already been started. The Arch Mage had planned many splendid dwellings in this area, which would have faced westward in a manner similar to the Guerdian city."

"Instead, it's just rock," commented Cahira.

"We'll see more of his palace as we proceed," Shaen assured her, "although I'm afraid our current destination leads down from the northern hall, and into the catacombs, which are, of course, less lavish in construction."

Shaen paused to gaze around the hall. "Here he escorted his fellow Mages, and led them into a central court, which had wide shafts open to the sunlight, yet were crafted at such an angle that the inconveniences of weather wouldn't penetrate. How glorious it must have been!"

"I can almost hear the music of flute and harp," muttered Cahira. "Or did he prefer the slow beating of drums?"

They passed through the northern hall, and Shaen checked her map again. She started toward a north passage, then cut back, and directed them beneath a small arch that led eastward. They hurried along the dark passageway, though Shaen had to stop several times to check direction. Bodvar seemed impatient and increasingly nervous as they went along, though Cahira feared they were making swift progress into the tomb area.

"Well, this is pleasant!" she commented. "Down into the midst of death and despair. Here is the real essence of the Arch Mage, I fear."

Shaen ignored her as they stopped to assess their surroundings. She directed Bodvar to a narrow passage that ran down again, and south. A faint breeze touched Cahira's face as Bodvar turned, and it bore the faint tang of the sea. Cahira closed her eyes tight. The way now was short, and the Arch Mage's tomb lay close at hand.

The passage dipped down, and the air grew dry and dull once again as the passage narrowed still more around them. Shaen stopped suddenly and looked one way, then the other. She clasped her hand to her chest and seemed overcome with emotion. Cahira hoped she'd lost her way, but instead, Shaen beamed with triumph.

"We have found the entrance to his tomb! There, ahead, where this passage meets a final crossing—beyond that intersection is the door to his cavern! We have arrived at last!"

Cahira heard a strange sound, like that of an axe being drawn. "What kept you?" she said, feeling her heart surge in her chest.

Bodvar dropped her and whipped out his axe, and Cahira scrambled awkwardly to her feet just as Aren emerged from the shadows. He stood in the dim light of the intersection, and as their gazes met, her heart felt swollen in her chest. But then he shifted his bright gaze to Bodvar and smiled.

Something whistled above Cahira's head, and she looked up to see Felix perched on a broken wall sconce. He waved his wings madly, and she hopped as best she could in his direction.

Shaen had backed against the wall behind Bodvar, and the Norskman seemed uncertain which way to turn. Felix jumped down onto Cahira's arm, chewing at her ties. The bonds were thick and his teeth made little progress, but the bat kept trying.

"The weight of one small woman slows you more than I ever would have guessed, my old friend," Aren said, his voice low and taunting. "Even with this little head wound, it was no trouble to overtake you. We've even had time for a meal while we waited."

"And a good one, at that," added Thorleif as he, too, emerged from the eastern passage. Rika appeared from the opposite direction and took her place beside Thorleif. Elphin came after her, and to Cahira's delight, she saw that the Woodlander had her bow slung over his back, as well as a new sword in his hand.

Bodvar looked between Aren and Cahira, then raised his axe as if to strike her. "Stand back, Lord Chieftain, or I'll split your wench in two."

Aren's eyebrow angled. "The magic shield that stopped a crossbow will have no trouble with your axe," he replied. "True, it left her a bit dizzy for a few moments—but that had its benefits."

"Did it?" Cahira asked. Felix peeked up at her and shrugged.

"That's when you swore him your heart, lass," the bat said. "You *were* a mite peculiar at the time, though."

"I'd suppose so."

Aren kept his gaze fixed on Bodvar, swinging his axe in an arc and then bracing it in his other hand, waiting. "I'm afraid you'll have to get through me if you intend to enter this chamber." He nodded to the heavy granite door behind him, but his gaze never wavered from his enemy.

"You'll have to get through all of us!" added Thorleif.

Khadun, Ranveig, and Fareth emerged from the two passages. The Guerdian prince held a short spear, and Ranveig his stout axe. Oddly, and bringing a soft glow to Cahira's heart, Fareth gripped his large iron skillet; and as he smacked it from one hand to the other, it really did appear dangerous.

Shaen moved up behind Bodvar, her face lit with fury. She

screamed suddenly, as if overcome with rage, then ran past Cahira and disappeared back the way they'd come. "Where's she going?" asked Cahira, but Felix shook his head.

"She won't be leaving this place, whatever happens," he told her.

Cahira shook her head, bemused. "She said it was like 'home' to her."

"I heard that. It was all I could do not to laugh and get myself found out," the bat added.

"You were nearby?" Cahira asked, surprised.

"Aren sent me on ahead, yes," said Felix. "When I reported your location, he remembered a shorter route and took that, while I came back to watch you."

"Aren is smart," said Cahira.

"But he's still wounded, lass," the bat admitted quietly. "Even if he doesn't show it."

Aren moved closer to Bodvar. "Would you care to follow the wench, Bodvar? She abandoned you with stunning speed, yet her choice to flee may be wisest."

The Norskman lifted his axe, and a menacing grin spread over his face. "This is a narrow passage for fighting," he admitted. "No more than two can fit—but once I finish with you, I'll have no trouble with the others."

Aren was undaunted. He laughed, and in his eyes Cahira saw the warrior he truly was. "I wouldn't want it any other way," he said.

Cahira saw Rika look at her chieftain nervously, and she realized that Felix's warning was accurate. As Aren drew nearer, she saw his blood-stained bandage, and his face looked drawn and tired. Fear rose in her heart like ice welling on a river, and caught in her throat as Bodvar swaggered forward.

"You deny this opportunity for great power, all for the sake of a Woodland witch," scoffed Bodvar. " 'For death and glory,' that is the true code of the Norsk!"

"But by our own power only should it be attained," said Aren. "You do not fight for the Norsk, but for yourself, Bodvar. The Hall of Ages is closed to you, for you fight for personal gain and the evil whims of another."

"It is you who groveled at the witch's feet! And for that, you will die!"

Bodvar leapt toward Aren, but his chieftain easily avoided the blow and turned and wielded his axe hard against him. Bodvar met the assault, and blade shuddered against blade as they fought.

"Can't you chew any faster?" asked Cahira desperately, looking down at Felix snapping at her bonds. "The others might not be able to help him in this passage, but if I had my bow . . ."

"I'm going as fast as I can," growled the bat.

"Well, hurry up!"

"There's a good suggestion," Felix muttered. "I wish I'd thought of it."

Bodvar backed up, then jerked to the side to evade Aren's axe. He aimed a savage blow at his chieftain's head, and Cahira bit back a scream. Aren ducked and staggered back, and she saw his bandage darken with blood. Tears welled in her eyes. *I have to help him.*

She fought her surging panic and closed her eyes, and with all her courage she summoned the power of her *ki.* She felt it swelling inside her, and she capped its energy lest it burst forth in destruction. Then she yanked her hands apart as hard as she could, dislodging Felix—and breaking the bonds around her wrist.

"Elphin! My bow!" she cried.

Elphin whipped the bow from his back, maneuvered as close as he could, then hurled it toward her. It dropped close to her feet, which were still bound, and she hopped forward to fetch it. "Arrows!" she called.

Elphin flung the quiver, but it landed closer to Bodvar and Aren where they fought, and the arrows scattered across the stone floor. Metal clashed, echoing through the passageway. Bodvar cursed as Aren drove him back. Cahira struggled closer to the fallen quiver, but Bodvar again aimed the butt of his axe handle at Aren's head. Cahira reached an arrow, fell to her knees to retrieve it. Her hands shook so much that she could barely set the arrow to the string, but at last she took aim and drew back.

Unfortunately, Bodvar shoved Aren so that they reversed positions. Aren's back was now between Cahira and her target. She held her bow poised, waiting.

A third time Bodvar struck Aren's head, and this time, Aren staggered. Yet Cahira still couldn't shoot, or she'd risk hitting him. She focused her *ki* and it seeped down into her arrow—but she had to have a target at which to shoot, even a small one.

Bodvar clearly believed he had won, for Aren was faltering. But suddenly Cahira had a line to his throat and . . .

And then Aren straightened, a light seeming to explode from deep inside him. It shimmered all around, as if the very essence of his spirit had burst forth and surrounded him. Cahira hesitated in astonishment, for she had never seen such a force. Blinded by rage and bloodlust, Bodvar charged, but Aren fell back and swung his axe in a mighty arc. Bodvar's eyes widened in shock and amazement, then grew dull and sightless. The Norskman fell slowly back and died.

Aren stood over his old friend and the light dimmed, but everyone in the cavern had witnessed its force. Elphin ran to Cahira and cut the bonds around her ankles, then helped her up, but she went to Aren. He turned slowly, stunned by the battle he had won.

She placed her hand on his face, streaked with blood, and cried as she looked up into his amber eyes. "*This* is my treasure—to see your face again," she whispered. He smiled.

"My treasure, my love," he answered. But then his eyes seemed to lose focus; he looked confused. "And now . . . now I think I might faint."

"Where in the name of the gods am I?" Aren struggled to sit up, but his head throbbed mercilessly and he lay back on what appeared to be a bed of some sort. Light streamed through an open window, and he felt the breath of the sea on his face.

"You're in the bedroom suite of the Arch Mage's palace."

Aren shifted his eyes, painfully, and saw Cahira sitting beside him, smiling. Her blue eyes glittered with tears.

"Are we his guests?" he asked.

"Not that he knows about, I hope," she replied. She eased his hair from his brow. "And I doubt he's planning to serve us dinner."

"How did I get here?"

"We carried you," came Thorleif's voice. Aren twisted his neck despite pain to see his company gathered around, and he smiled. "And it wasn't easy, my lord, even for the four of us, with Rika helping and the bat giving orders—as if that made it easier! Khadun found this place. We figured we ought to get the Lady Mage a good step away from that wizard's tomb, and we brought you here. Guess it's a bed. Old and broken, everything is, but we fixed it up with our blankets and Cahira's old sheepskin coat."

Cahira nodded to Elphin. "It was good of you to bring my coat along. It was Damir's, and I would like to return it to him one day."

"I knew you would," said Elphin.

"I have to admit," spoke up Fareth, "this portion of the Arch Mage's palace is a mite grander than anything I'd imagined, cut like this. When I looked out the window, I almost felt dizzy for as high up as it is." He paused and shook his head. "And our poor queen dropped herself out of one of those windows! Terrifying!"

"A castle built into the mountain!" exclaimed Thorleif. "It's impressive, if there had been light down underground. But those catacombs gave me the shudders. The idea of all those bodies, stuffed into little boxes like that . . . We burn our dead on pyres—that's the right way to honor the fallen."

"The dead should be placed into the ground," countered Fareth, "so that they can become part of the soil, part of nature. Burning's just a waste."

"Our dead are stacked in rows, labeled as to the name, clan, and age of existence," said Khadun. "That way, all are recorded through the passage of time."

Felix adjusted his position on Aren's headboard. "Of course, my species doesn't have any of those options. When one of my kind drops from our perch, something invariably comes by and gobbles us up."

"I guess that's back to nature . . ." said Elphin, but Thorleif cringed.

"Can we discuss something more pleasant?" suggested Cahira.

"Good idea," agreed Aren. He sniffed, and caught the warm, familiar scent of stew. "Which is it today, the Norsk recipe, or the Woodlander's?" he asked.

"Well," began Ranveig. "It's something of a mixture, you might say."

Aren's eyes widened. "Indeed?"

"Talked it over, we did," admitted Fareth. "Have to admit that he's got some good methods for making broth."

"And those old roots he carries do hold flavor," admitted Ranveig. "We put those together with some of the Guerdian spices, and came up with something that'll be getting strength back to your limbs, my lord."

Aren sat up, and the throbbing in his head eased. "Are you two all right?" he asked, but Cahira took his hand and kissed it.

"We haven't had our heads bashed by an axe," she said. Then she stopped as tears welled in her eyes. "And you never will again if I have anything to say about it."

"I generally try to avoid it," he replied. "Now, what happened to Bodvar? I defeated him?"

"Don't you remember?" she asked in surprise, and glanced at the others.

"I remember that he hit me, for sure," he replied. "Unfortunately, he has a good aim where my head is concerned. I'm surprised it's still on my shoulders. I remember a strange fury building inside me, something I've never felt before—

that he would dare take you from me, that he would betray our people and our land."

Cahira's brow knit as she studied his face. "That fury gave you a great power, Aren. I've never seen anything like it. It burst out of you and . . . and you glowed as if light came from inside you."

"Could it be Damir's sword?" he asked.

"You weren't using Damir's sword, though I wish you'd consider it from now on," she replied.

"That light came from *you,* my lord," said Felix, and he hopped onto Aren's shoulder. "Damir ap Kora said it would be so, that you carried unimaginable power inside you if you'd only allow yourself to let it go. And you did."

Aren looked down at the bat, then back at Cahira. "What would that mean?"

"That Damir was right about you," she said. "But for now, we've found a way down to the wharf below, and just as you hoped, there appear to be several ships pulled up near the harbor."

"Thorleif and I found them," said Elphin, "and Khadun looked them over. Some of them look too small for an ocean journey. One, at least, appears sea-worthy—it could carry at least fifteen passengers, and we're only eight."

"Nine," said Felix, but Thorleif snorted.

"How do we move it?" asked Cahira.

"There appears to be equipment for just that purpose," said Khadun. "It shouldn't be too hard to get it into the water, with all of us hoisting it."

Aren started to get up. "Then hoist it we will."

Cahira grabbed his shoulder and eased him back down. "Not until you eat and rest. The sun is setting anyway, and I don't think you want to set sail in the middle of the night."

"Given I've never set foot on a ship, that *would* seem unwise." Aren paused. "Have any of you?" They looked between each other uncomfortably. "Wonderful," he said.

"I've paddled on little boats in the Woodland lakes," offered Elphin. The others eyed him doubtfully.

"I used river skiffs on my trade route," added Khadun. He paused and pulled a bound scroll from his tunic. "Maybe this will help."

He passed it to Aren, who unfolded it. "This is the scroll I found in Amon-Daal!" Aren said. "It's a very methodical description of how to maneuver ships at sea, as well as how to handle various currents and weather conditions—even how to chart a rough course to our destination." He paused and glanced at Khadun. "I thought these scrolls were considered sacred to your people and bound to the Chamber of Tomes for eternity?"

"Well . . . our necks are sacred to my people, too," responded Khadun. "And when a Norskman speaks of setting sail when he's never even seen a sea-going vessel, a smart Guerdian comes up with alternatives."

Aren laughed. "Guerdians are ever logical."

"We are," Khadun agreed.

Aren paused. "Any sign of the Woodland wench?"

"I assume you mean Shaen," said Cahira. "I've been with you, but Ranveig and Fareth saw her when they went with Rika to . . . well, to . . ."

"We hauled Bodvar's body away," said Rika without emotion. "I said a few words, in your absence."

"That was good of you," suggested Elphin.

Rika's brow angled. "I denied him entrance to the Norsk Hall of Ages, stated that he had been defeated by a greater warrior, and that his spirit is no longer free to follow the Norsk path."

"Ah," said Elphin, and he eased away.

"Can't say he deserves better," Fareth said as he idly stirred the stew he was cooking. "Wish we had something suitable to say to Mistress Shaen—though I guess she's just succumbed to the lure of the Arch Mage and can't help herself. Still, it had to be her own darkness that let him get hold of her this way."

"I wonder," said Cahira; and Aren looked at her.

"Is that not what you saw?" he asked.

"She spoke of him that way, yes. She said he spoke to her and called her, and that she was driven to serve him. But something about it seemed wrong. Theatrical. I can't explain why."

Felix looked at her. "Not all the mists have cleared," he said cryptically.

"We placed Bodvar in an old tomb," spoke up Rika, "but I saw the wench as we passed back this way. She was hovering near the chamber of the dark wizard's tomb, struggling to open the door with her bony fingers. I had thought to return, to sever her head and have her annoy me no further, but she saw me coming and fled. I didn't bother giving chase."

"She's trying to enter his tomb, then," said Cahira. "That isn't surprising."

"What could she hope to find there?" asked Elphin. "Isn't he buried deep beneath? And even if she could access his resting place, he's still just energy and bones, isn't he?"

"Yes," said Felix. "She won't get far, if she's trying to bring him around herself. But she has Bodvar's pack with her, and enough food for awhile. She'll be here when we return."

"If we return with a method of ending the dark wizard's reign, she may wish she'd stayed in Amon-Daal after all," predicted Aren, but he gave no further speech as Ranveig passed him a bowl of stew.

Cahira produced a flagon of ale. "It's the last of it," she told him. "So we will share, I think. Besides, you'll want all your wits about you when we get on that ship, so after this, it's tea."

They ate and laughed together, and Aren felt his strength returning. As the sun set over the blue-gray sea, weariness claimed him again, and he lay back on his bed. Cahira curled up beside him, and the others laid out their bedding and gear and scattered themselves about the room as the fire burned low.

And there, in the cavern of the dark wizard, Aren drifted into sleep.

* * *

"It's a lot bigger than I imagined. And tippy." Cahira stood on the edge of a half-broken wharf and eyed the ship Elphin and Thorleif had selected. "Are you sure about this?"

Aren held up the scroll Khadun had given him. "I read it this morning when I woke up—and while the rest of you were still snoring with smiles on your faces. I think I have an idea what to do." He jumped onto the ship deck and held out his hand for her.

Cahira sighed heavily, then stepped gingerly over the rail. The ship swayed, and she seized his arm for support. The company followed, some more cautiously than others. Ranveig and Fareth held dire and obvious suspicions, but Elphin and Thorleif both leapt onboard like boys at play. Felix soared gracefully from Fareth's shoulder to the furled sail, where he perched majestically. Khadun darted about checking the fittings and examining the woodwork. Fareth sighed resignedly, then hurled himself unexpectedly onto the ship, tipping the vessel dramatically to one side.

Cahira squeaked and clutched the ship's mast, but as the ship settled back she breathed a sigh of relief. She pointed to Ranveig. "If you could climb aboard with a little less drama, my stomach would settle better."

The Norsk cook maneuvered on tiptoes, an odd sight, but he made his way from the wharf to the ship with great care, causing no more than a ripple as he edged to a central position on the deck. "It's not so bad once you're on," noted Fareth.

Ranveig nodded, then called, "Rika! What's keeping you? Jump over here like the rest of us—not using Fareth's method, though I doubt you'd pitch this boat the same as he—and let us take off to sea!"

The Norskwoman stood on the wharf still as stone, her eyes uncustomarily wide. Aren looked down at her. "Would the ice princess like a hand?" he asked.

She glared at him with rare emotion. "The ice princess would like a horse and solid ground on which to travel."

"This is the best I can provide, I'm afraid." Aren held out his hand. "When have you ever been hesitant before a new challenge?"

"When I can't see the bottom of an unfathomable sea!"

"We'll be all right, Rika," Cahira gently assured her. "And when we reach the desert of Kora, it will be warm and sunny, and the scent of flowers will fill the air. It will be an adventure to get there, but think of the wonders we might see!"

Rika peered at her, her expression full of doubt. "I do not like the heat, and I prefer the scent of burning wood to flowers." She paused and sighed heavily. "But if this is my fate, then so be it."

She took Aren's hand and gripped his fingers tight, climbed unsteadily onto the ship. She gazed heavenward for a moment, then took a deep breath, then another to calm herself. "It is just as horrible as I imagined," she said at last.

"Here," said Elphin. "Sit between Ranveig and Fareth, and you'll be safe enough."

Rika moved gingerly to the center of the boat and plopped herself down between the two innkeepers, who looked eagerly around as if Aren might simply sound his horn and set sail. But as Cahira looked up at the vast cliff wall above, she cried out suddenly. "Look! It's Shaen!"

Aren turned and saw a small figure clad in white looking down at them from a narrow balcony. "I take it she made her way in," he said. He was tempted to wave, but instead he turned his back. "Let her watch, for we are beyond her reach now."

"But she's where she wants to be," said Cahira in disgust. "Hovering over the Arch Mage's tomb, fancying herself the mistress of his domain."

"A fancy, indeed," agreed Felix, hopping down from his perch and making his way to Fareth.

Aren examined the scroll, then summoned Thorleif and Elphin. "I'll need you two to manage this," he said.

"Yes, my lord!" Thorleif glowed with happiness, and Elphin looked almost as eager.

"What do we do?"

"Ready the lines—you two can handle that, and prepare to cast off. You, Thorleif, hoist the jib sheet, fix the rigging, then help Elphin raise the main. I'll man the tiller and keep our heading, depending on the tack, and the rest of you, stay clear of the boom."

Cahira burst into laughter. "Oh, well then! I know exactly what to do!"

His eyes narrowed. "You, to the bow, my lady."

"Why?"

"Because it says there's always a beautiful woman's figure affixed in that area. You and Rika are the only women onboard, and it's clear she won't be moving anywhere."

"This vessel is having a strange effect on you," she said. "Where's the bow?" He pointed to the front of the ship, and she made her way there and sat down.

Thorleif and Elphin obeyed, and he directed them according to the Guerdian records, and soon the old canvas unfurled over their heads. It caught the wind with a gentle sound, but one that oddly stirred Aren's heart, and the ship edged slowly away from the broken wharf.

Rika sat stiffly with her eyes closed. Felix perched on Fareth's wide shoulder, leaning forward with the wind in his fur. Cahira steadied herself on a low railing, but she looked happy.

The wind picked up with a sudden draft, and it caught the sail above Aren's head. It tossed his long hair and cooled his face, and he felt suddenly as if his soul were new. He maneuvered the craft as if he'd been born to its deck, and they sailed out upon the sea. The land faded from view, and a strange thought filled Aren's head as the vast water rolled before him. *I am going home.*

14

THE PRINCE OF KORA

"You, Aren son of Arkyn, were born to the sea." Cahira sat cross-legged on the ship's bow, and he sat close behind her, his blond hair rippling in the ocean breeze. Thorleif, after much pleading, now manned the helm, which Aren had relinquished only reluctantly after a day and night of maneuvering the vessel through blue water.

Fortunately, the seas remained calm, and the night was clear with a full moon to guide them. Aren hadn't slept at all, so Cahira had to lure him to her side to get him to rest. He had to be tired, but his amber eyes were shining and his face held a blissful expression as he gazed across the western horizon.

"It's magnificent," he murmured; then he wrapped his strong arms around her and kissed her neck. "Like you, my lady."

"Thank you." She turned in his arms and looked up into his beautiful face. "Why is it that a man who has spent his life on snow-covered fields is so at home on the waves?"

He smiled. "Snow is just frozen water," he told her helpfully.

She gave him a look of amused disbelief. "I see. Are there such vessels as this in your Norsk wasteland?"

His eyes narrowed a moment, as if he considered the possibility. "Sadly, no. Only sleds pulled by horses," he admitted. Then he sighed. "But it is familiar to me, like an old joy—one I had forgotten, but knew once, ages ago."

"That is odd," she said. "I have no such reaction—though I have to admit, I feel safer now than I did when we first cast off. You do seem to know what you're doing. I told Felix you were smart, but I had no idea even you could learn so much from a short scroll!"

"The scroll was helpful, but it seemed to rekindle something that I already knew." He paused. "An emotion accompanies this knowledge, too, as if traveling upon the open sea offers freedom from toil and hardship, hope for a new life, freedom from bondage."

"I know the Norsk life can be strenuous," she laughed, "but I see no bonds around you."

"No," he agreed. "Among my people, I am a lord, and nothing in our land has been denied me. My brother kept me as a slave, but only briefly, and even then I understood it was he who was truly in bondage. Yet this feeling is almost as real to me as the memories of the rest of my life."

"Then this voyage should prove interesting, indeed," decided Cahira. "I wonder what we'll find in Kora. In some ways they sound like an advanced culture, but Damir's father had to escape execution there, and I didn't like the sound of Guerdian traders going to that land and never returning."

"They might have simply been lost at sea," suggested Aren, "for it often rages. We've been fortunate so far." He sounded a little disappointed by this, and Cahira shook her head.

"I would just as soon you didn't call up the Sea Gods and issue a prayer for a thrilling challenge."

His jaw shifted slightly to one side, as if he'd indeed considered this. "I wouldn't think of it," he said. Kissing her forehead he added, "Not with you on board, anyway."

"You are not to keep this vessel once we return!" she commanded.

"Why not? When peace is restored, it might be possible to guide this ship along the mountains, perhaps guide it to Amon-Dhen."

"Did you see the waves crashing along those cliffs? Khadun said a passage north was impossible now. It would be impossible for you, too!"

"Maybe."

Cahira groaned. "If you must, you could always take Thorleif and Elphin and sail along the mountain path—but in summer, when it's safe and warm. Then sail about at your leisure. But not in storms!"

His eyes brightened, and he smiled. "We are already thinking of our future, you and I. And I can picture it, too, as you move about my Great Hall like a queen, and we venture together to your homeland, and you escort me through those places that are most dear to you."

"The Hungry Cat Tavern! And Madawc's cottage, which has many wonders within, even though it appears small from the outside." She paused in her imagining. "And the palace, of course—though you've already seen that, and its wonders are more superficial."

"Of much less interest than Fareth's tavern, no doubt." Aren smiled.

"We will visit Damir and Eliana, and you will meet their children. Their sons are much intent on learning a warrior's skill, and you can teach them the axe." She gazed up at him, and her heart overflowed with love. "Just as you did with the little boy outside your Great Hall. Just as you will do . . ."

"With our own children," he said softly, and his eyes were shining.

Cahira's throat clenched with longing. "That is the life I want, so very much," she whispered.

"And you will have it, lass, but not before you both face the darkness in the Cavern of the Arch Mage." Felix spoke behind them, and they both started.

"Thank you for that uplifting reminder, bat!" said Cahira. "As my guide, shouldn't you be offering words of encouragement rather than portents of doom?"

Felix maneuvered himself onto Cahira's knee and looked thoughtfully over the low, rolling waves. "You will not find what you seek across these waters in that distant land."

"He *is* comforting, isn't he?" offered Aren.

"What you seek is within you, both of you, in the greatest power that either of you possess."

"Are you telling us that this venture is pointless?" asked Cahira indignantly.

"No. I perceive that it must be done, that an answer will be found. But not in the temples of Kora. And it will not be, I think, the ending either of you expects."

"Where else do you suggest we locate one of their high priests?" asked Aren. "And what other answer can there be, what other end than bringing about the destruction of the dark wizard?"

Felix looked back at Aren, and issued a strange chuckle. "Follow your heart, my lord. That is what you do best, and what you have always done. It will not fail you now, even in the catacombs of the Arch Mage."

"Land! Land, my lord! Land!"

Aren groaned and opened one eye, but he seemed reluctant to move his head from his resting place on Cahira's lap. She gazed down into his face and ran her fingers through his tangled hair. "I believe Thorleif has spotted land," she said.

"Indeed?" asked Aren. "The last three times he shouted that alert, it was a tiny island with one wispy tree, an elongated rock with a few fat white gulls crowded atop it, and one jutting rock."

Cahira nodded. But as she looked around, her heart caught in her throat. "Aren, this time I think he's right!"

Aren sat up and looked westward, and his eyes widened in awe. A vast golden shore rose slowly over the waves before them. Tall, thin trees swayed in the distance, and a shimmer of gold and silver reflected the new morning sun.

They had sailed through another night, during which Aren slept at last, allowing Thorleif and Elphin the helm, and they would now arrive at the port of Kora with the rising sun. The weather had changed dramatically, though the distance they had traveled could not be that great. Yet here the air was soft and warm, even on the open sea, so Cahira's hope of finding a balmy oasis seemed promising indeed.

"By the gods, what a place!" Aren leapt up to seize control of the vessel, which Thorleif had angled dramatically in his excitement.

"What did I tell you, my lord? Land!" He paused to whistle. "And what a land it is!"

Felix seemed almost as excited as the Norsk youth. The bat bounded from his perch on Fareth's shoulder and landed on Thorleif's. He flapped his leathery wings wildly, then hopped about in uncontained glee. "Never thought I'd live to see such a sight! The realm of Kora, land of princes and magic, and riches beyond imagining!"

"Careful with those claws," ordered Thorleif, but he seemed ready to hop, himself.

Rika hadn't moved since they'd left the wharf, except once when she got up, crawled to the edge of the ship, and vomited. "Tell me this is almost over," she murmured.

"Soon," offered Elphin. "Look! They row small boats toward us." He glanced at Aren. "Are they likely to be dangerous, my lord?"

"We have the advantage, with our ship against rowboats, so I doubt it," replied Aren. "But have your weapons ready."

When Cahira seized her bow, he arched his brow. "But don't *look* like you're ready!" he said. She eased it back over her shoulder, and he smiled. "And you call the Norsk aggressive!"

Cahira adjusted her long braid over her shoulder, and stood in what she felt constituted a nonaggressive posture. "What language will they speak?" she asked.

"The language of Kora, I assume," replied Aren. "Which, unfortunately, I don't know."

"I speak some of that tongue," said Khadun.

"As do I," added Felix, and they looked at him in surprise. "Learned it from Damir ap Kora's sire, when he was teaching his young son."

"You've been around a long time, then!" said Cahira.

"Bats of my species are long-lived," he replied.

"How old are you now?" asked Thorleif.

"Ageless, boy—and my wisdom is endless!"

Thorleif rolled his eyes. "Always boasting, he is. Puts the worst of the drunken Norskmen to shame."

"But I have reason, boy," grumped Felix. "A drunken Norskman just has ale."

As Thorleif appeared ready to retort, someone called out from the approaching rowboat, and Felix leaned forward to listen. "He asks for the name of your captain, of your ship, and for your purpose in the Land of the Prince," the bat translated.

"Tell him," began Aren. But then his brow furrowed. "I haven't named my ship as yet. It should be majestic, stirring, invoking its wonder and speed . . . '*Cahira!*'" He glanced at her happily. "Such vessels are often named for a woman whose good will the crew wishes to invoke."

"You have my good will already," she laughed.

"And I want to keep it! Tell him my ship is called *Lady Cahira,* and that we've come to seek counsel from the high priests of this land." Aren paused. "Khadun, maybe it would be best if you translated this, rather than the bat. We don't know yet how they'll react to a talking animal."

"Good idea," agreed Felix. "I can't get my voice to carry that far, anyway."

Khadun went to the ship's bow and spoke to the oarsman. The man answered as Cahira waited eagerly. "What did he say?" she asked before Khadun had finished speaking. Aren laid his hand on her shoulder.

"Patience, my lady."

Khadun turned back to them. "He says that all ships here reflect the title of their captain, and this is clearly not so. He has seen you giving the orders."

"Tell him it's called *Prince of Ice*," called Cahira. "I like that better, anyway."

Aren frowned, but then he shrugged. "Dramatic woman," he muttered.

Khadun repeated this to the oarsman, then listened a moment. His brow furrowed. "He accepts the ship's title, as well as your name, my lord . . ."

"Good," muttered Aren. "I wasn't eager to change it again."

"Odd thing, though. When I told him we seek the priests' counsel, he told us to come no farther, and to turn our ship around."

"Why?"

"He does not say, but he spoke emphatically."

"Then tell him it was an error in translation. You meant to say we sought the counsel of the prince."

Khadun nodded and did so. After a moment, he looked back and nodded. "That is acceptable." He paused. "But he expresses reservations about you, my lord, and states that you cannot go before their ruler in your current condition."

"Aren't we clean enough for him," growled Aren.

"That's not it, exactly—though it would be a fair request in my opinion," Khadun said, and he seemed to repress humor.

"Then, what? Shall I have my hair trimmed, or don a new tunic for this monarch's inspection?"

"No . . ." Khadun paused again, and cleared his throat. "It's the beard, my lord. He says only the slaves of Kora wear beards, and it marks their station. No slave is allowed into the palace of the prince."

"Slaves? I've never heard that the land of Kora held slaves!" Cahira looked down at the boatmen of Kora in horror. "Perhaps the beauty of this land is surface only, as Damir warned, for all is not as it seems."

"In the time of Damir's father, there was a rigid system of

classes, nobility and peasant, but no slaves that I know of," said Felix. "But during the time of the Arch Mage, it was so."

"Wonderful," said Aren. "Tell our friend we seek an audience with this prince, Khadun. And assure him I'll be presentable at that time." Cahira felt a certain eagerness to see what Aren's face looked like shaved.

"Does this mean Ranveig and I have to shave, too?" asked Thorleif in horror. Cahira suspected that in the absence of a beard, Thorleif would look no more than twelve, so it was a adornment he wasn't likely to give up without a fight.

Aren shook his head, as if that would indeed be too cruel a request.

"Cahira, Khadun, and I will go, and Felix will come with us," Aren decided. He paused and glanced at Khadun. "I'm afraid this means you'll have to shave that impressive growth, too, Guerdian."

The prince cocked his head to one side. "Unnecessary, my lord. They recognize me as Guerdian, and as such, accept my beard as a mark of distinction."

"They why don't you tell them I'm a Norskman, and they can accept that as well?"

"Apparently your people resemble their slaves, though they say your size is unusual."

"Is it?" Aren sighed. "Very well." He paused as he ran his hand over his beard. "It will grow back, I suppose."

Cahira beamed up at him. "This should be interesting! Where are you going to make this transition, anyway?" she asked.

He huffed. "You're cheerful, aren't you? And if our glorious hosts requested that you chop off that lovely hair of yours? What then?"

"I'd be staying on this boat, instead," she replied happily. "But fortunately, that does not appear to be a requirement for my visit."

Khadun spoke further to the oarsmen, then turned to Aren. "They say we can leave our ship on one of their moorings rather than drop anchor, because the sands in this harbor are very fine, and anchors don't hold well."

"Very well. Then the others can come ashore with us," said Aren. "Anything else?"

"He says there's a harbor inn where our company can rest." At this, Rika brightened and looked hopeful for the first time since they'd left shore. "In fact, one of these men seems to be the inn's proprietor. Trouble is, we don't have enough gold pieces to afford accommodations, and still be able to get food and other provisions. He did suggest a trade, however." Khadun paused and looked uncomfortable, and Aren's eyes narrowed.

"What do they want?"

"They favor your axe—as a novelty of some sort."

"This is too much! I am not surrendering my axe to these pirates!"

Rika rose unsteadily, turning so that her back faced the rowboats. "Give them Bodvar's axe instead," she suggested.

"Do you have it?" he asked in surprise, and she nodded.

"It was his sire's weapon, and he, a good man. I refused to leave it on his offspring's treacherous breast when we stuck him in the tomb, so I took it."

"I didn't notice you had it," said Aren, "but I'm grateful you do. We'll give them that, then. I certainly bear the weapon no fondness."

Aren glanced at the oarsmen below and offered a weak smile, then nodded. "Tell them I'll just fetch it now."

He eased to Rika's side and fumbled with his belt, then casually dropped his axe to the deck. He uttered a "tsk," then bent to pick it up, and Rika slipped Bodvar's into his hand. Cahira watched with delight. "Not the most honest trade, my Lord Chieftain," she said.

"They want a Norsk axe, and that's what they're getting."

"Fair enough." She peered down at the boats. "Now what?"

Aren shrugged and glanced at Khadun, who called down to the oarsman. "He says we can drop our rope ladder, climb down, and jump into his boat. He'll take you, your lady, and myself, and the next boat will fetch the 'thin ones.' The last will bear the two innkeepers. The bat, I assume, can travel with whomever he wishes."

"The first boat, of course!" said Felix, and he hopped proudly onto Aren's shoulder. "Let's be off, my lord!"

Aren eyed the bat. "You're excited, for one who proclaimed this venture destined to fail."

"No, I said it wouldn't give you the answer you're expecting."

"Ah," said Aren. "Now . . ." He approached a large ship box, broke open its rusty hinge, then pulled out a worn rope ladder.

"Oh, that looks sturdy!" commented Cahira sarcastically. "Are we really supposed to climb down that?"

Aren tested the rope and shrugged. "It's a strong weave, of a fiber I've never seen before. It's old, but it should hold even Fareth and Ranveig."

He positioned the rope ladder over the ship railing, then waited until the rowboat docked alongside. He jumped down with agility and grace, then held out his hand for Cahira. As usual, he didn't trust her with ladders. She refused his hand and hopped down beside him. He arched his brow, but Khadun's grumbling prevented a comment. Aren helped the nervous Guerdian climb over the railing, then held Khadun's arm in support as the prince dropped into the rowboat.

"This boat is much smaller than mine," Aren called out to Rika. "But steadier."

"Big, small—they are all alike," she responded miserably. "Of course, if it's the only way to dry land, I suppose it must be done."

"I have to say," said Cahira to Aren, "your delight with boats has taken ten years off your age."

He eyed her doubtfully. "That would make me fourteen."

"Precisely!" she laughed.

Aren frowned, but his handsome face knit with interest as

he assessed the little boat they had boarded. The oarsman spoke to Khadun, and Khadun laughed. "He says if you'd like to take over the oars, you're welcome to it, as he's had a long day fishing already, and it would seem to delight you."

"Truly?" Aren's eyes brightened, and he moved quickly to take the other man's seat.

"'Fourteen,'" repeated Cahira, but her heart lurched with affection as he tried the oars. His face lit in a bright smile, and he maneuvered the small boat backward. After a few tries, he had the method down, and the boat glided skillfully toward the shore with only a few more words of advice from the oarsman.

Cahira glanced back and forth between land and the other rowboats. Rika had made her way gingerly into the second boat, but she now clung to Elphin, of all people, and perched tensely in the center of the craft. Thorleif sat as close to the bow as he could and leaned forward to look over the side. "There are fish in the water!" he cried with glee.

Felix snorted. "Where would you expect to find them, boy? In the air?"

Just as the bat spoke, a fish with what appeared to be wings leapt out of the water, glided a short distance, then dove back into the sea. Thorleif whooped, and Felix turned in the other direction, looking sullen.

Ranveig and Fareth sat in the third boat, and Cahira could hear them chattering eagerly about what food to expect at the inn. She thought she heard Rika mention something about 'ale or even wine.'

I am happy today, she thought. *Whatever comes, this moment is a treasure I will never forget.* And she knew that these were the best moments that life offered, more precious than jewels, and that no matter what came, the essence of these joys lasted, and their echoes would find their way into her soul, and there linger forever untarnished and new.

If the land of Kora was one thing, it was hot. Aren tore off his leather jerkin and tugged at his collar. He and Cahira stood on the pier awaiting the other boats—he had outpaced both in a race that he'd been conducting in his own mind without alerting the other oarsmen. He hadn't told Cahira, lest she call him *fourteen* again, but he suspected she knew, because she was smiling and her blue eyes glittered as she looked at him.

The others reached the pier and, one by one climbed out of the rowboats. Thorleif and Elphin jumped up, laughing, but Elphin restrained himself enough to assist Rika as she stepped unsteadily onto the pier. "My knees will never be the same, nor my stomach either," she offered miserably. "Get me off this pier and onto solid ground!" Elphin nodded quickly, then seized her arm and guided her up the pier. Many Koraji people had gathered to watch them—apparently, visitors weren't common, though they had many vessels moored in the harbor. Most appeared to be small fishing ships, and only a few looked large enough to make the journey Aren had traveled.

The first oarsman waited expectantly, so Aren glanced at Khadun, who spoke to him. "He mentions payment for your guest quarters, my lord. The axe."

Aren slung Bodvar's axe from his belt and handed it to the oarsman. He bowed as if delivering a treasure, but he couldn't restrain a slight sneer of distaste as he eyed the blade, still stained with his own blood. The tarnished axe seemed to thrill its new owner, however, and he held it up excitedly to the crowd, then chattered eagerly to Khadun.

"He says you must be a great warrior, with the blood of many necks staining this blade."

"Just don't tell him it's my own," advised Aren, and he forced a smile for the crowd. Cahira looked at the assembled people with distaste.

"They aren't quite what I imagined," she noted. "They're dark-skinned and black-haired like Damir, but I had pictured them being more . . . peace-loving. Yet here they are coveting a bloody axe!"

"I don't suppose they won control of this land by reciting poetry," said Aren.

Cahira frowned. "No, but song might have served them better, for it appears all they've won are slaves."

"And a man who takes another into slavery is himself in greater bondage than those whose freedom he has stolen," agreed Aren.

Khadun looked at him thoughtfully. "Your people have a wise leader," he said. "It is strange to me that such words come from a Norskman, but you are kind and speak from your heart as few of any race have done."

Aren bowed slightly, and the Guerdian's expression changed and his dark eyes twinkled. "The inn's proprietor has sent another on to inform the prince of your arrival, and he believes, having little else to do apparently, that the prince will see you immediately. Before he returns, however, the proprietor suggests that you come along to his inn to make yourself presentable."

"He means to shave," explained Cahira, as if that hadn't been painfully obvious.

"I know what it means!" Aren paused, muttering a few of his favorite Norsk curses, then said, "Fine. Take us to the inn."

They all followed the proprietor, whose name Khadun said was Tocho, which apparently referred to some large predatory desert cat; and he led them along a harbor front walkway paved with evenly cut stone. Khadun stopped often to admire the buildings and workmanship, and Thorleif seemed distracted by the sparsely dressed women who came out from shops to watch them pass by. Ranveig and Fareth stared with equal shock and wonder, and Elphin looked a little nervous. Rika didn't seem to notice, so pleased did she seem to be walking on dry land.

Aren found himself absently gazing back out to sea as he walked. As beautiful as the port city seemed, he felt strangely closed in, and the call of the water was strong. Beyond the walkway's end, he could see a large wall made of what seemed to be hardened sand, and beyond that loomed a wide stretch of desert stretching beyond sight to the south. To the west, the city had been built upon a hill, with streets cutting back from the busy shore and more lavish homes and temples on the higher ground.

"Tocho tells me that the sands often swirl with the wind and form violent storms," said Khadun, "and the wall keeps out those drifts, and has for generations. The working people dwell on this lower level, the fishermen and shopkeepers, but the prince's palace is at the top of the hill overlooking all. He says there are many other cities in Kora, and that the prince has several palaces, some even grander than this, but at this time of year the prince visits the shore. When he comes, he brings a large entourage, and Tocho says this is why there are so many courtesans on the streets."

"Ah," said Aren. "That explains the attire."

Cahira looked eagerly around, her eyes wide. "We don't have courtesans in Amrodel," she said to Aren. "though I know what they are." She paused, and her brow furrowed. "I'm not entirely sure what they do, other than . . . well, what we've done. But I've heard it is creative in some way."

Aren laughed. "I guess that depends on the courtesan."

As they walked along, Aren saw beautiful cats with soft fur the color of sand and eyes as blue as the desert sky. Their faces were masked with brown, along with their tails and the tips of their ears, and their legs. Their paws looked dipped into frothed cream.

He smiled. "Those cats would be happier in the Norskland," he observed.

Cahira looked over at him and grinned. "Thirteen," she pronounced.

"What?" he asked, but he knew what she meant. His gaze flicked to the cats again. "They have warm coats, and we churn a great deal of cream in my land," he explained.

"Maybe you should fetch one and bring it with you," Cahira suggested.

"Possibly," said Aren.

Most of the people here resembled Damir, tall and slender, with dark skin and eyes, and black hair that hung to their shoulders. The women were graceful and pretty, and the men were elegant, though far less strongly built than even a Norskman like Thorleif.

Some among them hung back from the streets, and these seemed lower in station. Perhaps these were the slaves Khadun had mentioned. From one hut, Aren saw a young man with a round face and almond eyes look out at him. Their gazes met, and the quiet desperation in the man's face pierced Aren's heart.

"Who are those people, those that are smaller in height, with almond-shaped eyes?" he asked. Khadun posed the question to Tocho, who shrugged idly.

"He says they are the Lahari, from the land of Nikunja far to the west. At one time, theirs was a separate kingdom, though much smaller, according to Tocho. But the prince of Kora seems to have taken them over—whether by battle or other means, Tocho does not say. These you see are slaves."

"But these people don't resemble mine—nor is that young man bearded."

Khadun spoke to Tocho again, then turned back to Aren. "He says that the slaves you resemble are few now, descendants of another age—presumably the same as the time of He Who Fell and before. Those are like you, tall and light-haired with pale skin, though through time they blended with the natives and resemble their ancestors less than your people do. He says they came from a vast land far to the east, beyond the mountains of my own land, and they were a wild and savage people." Khadun paused. "What he describes is a people much akin to the Norsk, though perhaps less civilized—and that's saying a lot. No offense."

Aren smiled, but his heart was heavy in his chest. "Slavery is the offense, Khadun." He paused and sighed. "I wonder if my own ancestors hail from that region you mention, and crossed the mountains to found my homeland?"

"Not likely, my lord. Those mountains are impassable. My people have tried."

Aren shrugged. "Maybe in an earlier age, the weather allowed for such passage."

"I doubt it," said Khadun. "According to all our records, the weather has eased, not grown harsher. It's unlikely your people came from there, unless they traveled south along the east side of the mountains, then down the mesa, and perhaps crossed the sea again northward."

"Or were captured, and brought here," added Aren. He glanced at Cahira, and she looked up at him sadly. She took his hand as they walked and held it in hers.

"You're thinking your ancestors may have been slaves, aren't you? And that they escaped north when the seas were calmer."

"It is possible," he answered.

"Maybe that explains the color of your eyes," she added, "tracing to a distant ancestor here, whose blood was tinged with that of other races."

"A race of slaves," he said quietly. "Savage, proud warriors from a distant land of ice."

Tocho led them to a harborside inn, with tiled tables outside the entrance. Guests sat drinking pink wine, and they looked at Aren's group in horror as he entered. "The beard, I expect," he muttered. He met one horrified male's gaze, held it, then nodded slightly. The man jerked back as if offended, and Aren chuckled.

Cahira glared at the man, huffing. "He looks away, but his wife, I see, casts a lingering eye on you. If I had that overly dainty man as a husband, my eye might wander, too!" She fingered her bow angrily, and Aren's heart warmed with affection.

Two women came out of the inn just as Aren and Cahira entered. They stopped aghast when they saw Aren, then spoke to Khadun. Khadun's face reddened and he shook his head vigorously. One of the women turned her gaze back to Aren and wet her lips suggestively, but Khadun spoke again, and she sneered, then passed by.

Cahira stared after her, but Aren eyed Khadun. "What was that about?"

"Well, my lord . . . They asked if you were available for

hire, and if you'd been trained—though stars knows what that means."

Cahira issued an indignant squeak, then seized her bow. Aren grabbed her hand lest she start a battle, and she sputtered angrily. "What *is* this place? Hire, indeed! What did you tell her, Khadun?"

"That she and her friend would have to look elsewhere," the Guerdian said. His dark eyes sparkled, and humor infected his gruff voice. "I said he wasn't trained at all, and that you already owned him, anyway."

Cahira appeared satisfied by this, but Aren's brow angled. "Oh, did you?"

Cahira tapped his shoulder. "That's all right. You're trained enough for me." She paused, and her brow knit doubtfully. "I wonder what you'd be 'trained' to do, anyway?" She shuddered. "I suspect this is one of the many things I don't want to know." She looked thoughtful for a moment, then glanced at him. "They both wanted to hire you?" Her eyes wandered to one side. "At the same time?"

"That's what she said," replied Khadun. "Lusty females, these Koraji maidens."

"Koraji vixens, more like," corrected Cahira. "Two . . ." She muttered to herself as they went into the inn. "But you only have one—"

Aren coughed to silence her. "*Cahira*."

She looked up at him. "What?"

"This *is* one of those things you don't want to know."

"Ah," she said. "For the best, then."

They took two more steps, and Cahira stopped suddenly, darted to the south wall of the inn's entrance, and stared with her mouth agape at a large, framed painting. She turned back, her cheeks furiously pink even considering the heat, and trotted again to his side.

"What is it?" he asked, moving in that direction. She caught his hand and pulled forcefully.

"You don't want to know," she said in a tight voice. "But I see now what is meant by 'two.'" As Aren bit back a laugh, she peered up at him suspiciously. "I think I've also just learned why Bodvar and Shaen referred to being on one's knees so often."

"Is this something *I* won't want to know?" he asked, but her expression changed and a tiny smile formed on her lips. She looked thoughtful. In response, his blood heated.

She said, "Actually, this is something you may just enjoy finding out."

Aren stood before a round, gold-trimmed mirror and gazed miserably at his beard. A bowl of warm water sat untouched on the stand, complete with shaving gear that could render a bear in winter bald. "Well? You'd better get started," said Cahira cheerfully. "We don't want to keep the prince waiting!"

He cast a dark look her way, then moistened his beard. The water was scented with some fragrant herb or other, and pink petals floated on its surface. "This is disgusting," he said.

Cahira laughed. "Don't be silly! You'll be a pretty pink warrior in no time!"

He glared, then turned his attention to the task at hand. Cahira leaned toward him eagerly as he lifted the blade. He lowered it again and frowned. "This would be easier if you weren't breathing down my neck. You're making me very nervous!" he complained.

"Oh, very well!" She puffed out an impatient breath, then seated herself on a plush, pillowed seat. Resting her chin in her hands, she watched him from there.

Aren nodded. "Thank you." He turned back to the mirror, and he began to shave away the beard that had concealed his face since boyhood. He turned his back so that Cahira couldn't see as he toiled, and she issued another impatient huff.

"How long can it possibly take? You'd think you had the Guerdian king's beard at the rate you're going!"

"Such things must be done delicately," he informed her, "lest this blade take more of my blood than Bodvar's axe."

Cahira shuddered. "Take your time. There's no hurry."

He laughed, then shaved away the last vestiges of his beard. He rinsed his face in the scented water, sneered at the fragrance, then looked at himself in the mirror. It wasn't the face of his boyhood that looked back at him, though the eyes were the same. His lips were more even and fuller than he remembered, and his chin was stronger, his jaw and cheekbones more defined.

It wasn't a face that kept secrets or hid emotion, and as he turned to see Cahira, he realized that in this they were the same. "Well, what do you think?"

She had lost interest in the sight of his back, apparently, and was intently studying a pillow, which seemed to have some sort of scene embroidered on its surface. She flipped the pillow over as if it embarrassed her—or perhaps she didn't want him to view it.

As she looked up, her mouth opened then snapped shut, then slowly drifted open again. Her eyes widened into blue pools of shock, and she hoisted herself up off the fluffy chair and approached him. She gaped in complete and utter wonder, then reached out slowly to touch his cheek.

"If you tell me I look like the nine-year-old boy you first saw, you will find it a grievous error, my lady." He paused. "I'm still a man. Just not so . . . rugged looking."

"You look . . . you look like a god!" she gasped.

This was better, and certainly more flattering, than resembling a nine-year-old boy. A smile crept across his face that he couldn't quite contain.

"Do you know what Koraji women do with gods?" Cahira asked, and her voice had dropped suspiciously low. Her expression was decidedly sensual.

"What?" he said. His own voice sounded rather tense. His groin tightened in a way that made him hope the prince of Kora was a man brief in speech.

"Quite a lot," she whispered. "I just learned it from a pillow."

He swallowed hard and drew a taut breath. "That must be quite a pillow!" he laughed.

"It is," she agreed. She took his hand, cast a lingering gaze at his face, then sighed. "I just hope that king isn't as long-winded as Khadun's father."

"I was thinking the same thing," he agreed.

She smiled, and they left the room together. Aren tried to grab the pillow that had captured her interest, but she edged it aside and smiled innocently. "We're late, I think."

Khadun and Felix met them at the inn's front door, and Felix perched on its wide, swinging sign. "What does that say?" asked Cahira. "Is it the name of the inn?"

"Aye," said Khadun. "It's called the Harborside."

"Not very imaginative," she decided, but shrugged. "Odd, considering the rest of their culture. They tend to be very . . . creative."

"About that pillow," said Aren, realizing the direction of her thoughts. But she held up her hand and shook her head.

"Later," she told him. "Do you know where we're going, Khadun?"

"Tocho gave me directions, lady," the Guerdian said. "Follow me."

They maneuvered along streets bustling with activity. Many shops lined the way, and Cahira looked eagerly into each one as they passed. "I'm going to purchase a new dress while we're here!" she enthused. "On the way back, I think. Do you think I should?"

Aren glanced at a row of dresses, all brightly colored and extremely sheer. "Yes."

She nodded excitedly, then scurried on. They crossed another street, and here, the cobbles turned white. After another level, each stone was etched, too. Each depicted some form of lovemaking, and indeed, these too appeared "creative." Cahira's gaze fixed on the stones they passed, and occasionally she uttered a high squeak of surprise. Once she even muttered, "I don't think so!"

Aren glanced at her, and she shook her head. "For Bodvar and Shaen, perhaps, but not for you and me," she offered.

Aren laughed. "For once, *I* don't want to know."

"Actually, that one was more Bodvar and—," she began, but Aren cringed and cut her off.

"Don't say it!"

Cahira nodded. "That's probably better. Is that the palace?"

He looked up. They'd both been too distracted by the etched stones to notice where they were going, but Khadun had stopped at the entrance to a massive white structure perched like a great crown on the hilltop.

"This is it," said Khadun. Two guards in white armor stood by a tall white metal gate, but neither spoke as the Guerdian passed. Khadun led the way up a long tiled pathway lined with lavish bushes of red and yellow flowers, and with taller trees bearing delicate pink blossoms.

"I think those were floating in your bathing water," observed Cahira happily.

Aren sniffed once and frowned. "The same."

"You may have to bring one of those plants back to the Norskland," she suggested. "So that all your brethren can bathe thus, then pillage while smelling of the pretty pink petals."

His frown deepened, but she laughed and looked so happy that his irritation abated.

They reached the doorway, and it swung inward. The hall was larger than Aren's Great Hall, and the ceiling more than three times higher. No doubt the absence of winter allowed for such extravagance—or perhaps the abundance of slaves to provide labor. Great windows opened onto the vast desert that stretched beyond and below like a golden sea to the east and southward. When he turned, Aren saw more windows open to the harbor, and a great sweeping balcony that faced north over the ocean.

"Impressive," he commented.

"I am glad you think so," replied a low, heavily accented

voice. Aren turned to see a dark man enter the far end of the hall. His first impulse was to reach for his axe, but that had been left on board his ship. He still carried the sheathed Dragonfly Sword, but containing his instinct for battle, he bowed.

The man offered a slight nod in response, then moved toward them. He appeared young, no more than twenty, but his stance indicated high rank and the confidence that comes with great power. He wore a short tunic over sand-colored leggings, and a long multicolored robe hung from his shoulders. Two armored guards like those that stood before the palace gates came up and took position behind him.

"I am Makya, Prince of Kora," he said evenly. "I was indeed stunned and thrilled to hear we had unexpected guests from the northlands." His dark eyes shifted to Cahira and he smiled. "And one a maiden of Amrodel! How rare, and how beautiful!"

His voice was so oily that it was hard to imagine he bore any relationship to the far more direct and powerful Damir ap Kora, but this man surely was a cousin of some sort. Makya somewhat resembled Damir physically, though he was less handsome, his skin was darker and his smile harsh. He had an arrogant, affected manner, and Aren disliked him at once.

Aren forced himself to bow again. "We are honored to behold this great land, so different from our own."

Makya stared at him. "I am led to understand you are a leader of some sort. A 'prince,' is it?" He spoke the words with faint mockery, and Aren's jaw set.

"I am Aren son of Arkyn, chieftain of the Norsk," he said. His voice was colder than he'd intended.

"Has that name meaning in your tongue?" asked the Koraji, his tone condescending.

"It means 'flight of the eagle."

"Does it?" piped up Cahira. "How perfect! My name means 'warrior.'"

"Fitting," Aren, replied.

The prince laughed. "How ironic! In our language, my own name means 'eagle slayer.'"

"How amusing," muttered Cahira.

"'Son of Arkyn,'" Makya repeated. "Another surprising coincidence! That is the same fashion in which our first slaves named themselves, attaching the names of their fathers to their own."

"Indeed," said Aren. "Though in the north we had not heard that the land of Kora still endured the practice of slavery. In fact, we believed it long abolished."

"For a time, the practice faded from our culture. My sire restored it during his reign," said Makya. "In ancient times, a renegade priest challenged the practice, as a defiance against the prince he had thought to usurp. . . ."

"*Cheveyo?*" breathed Cahira in astonishment. "Could this be the one that we know now as the Arch Mage? But I never heard of him doing anything noble!"

"Cheveyo," repeated Makya, and the name came bitterly to his lips. "That name is no longer spoken among my people, nor has it been in the long years since his exile. He is known as Matchitehew Otaktay for his many crimes, and I do not think, my lovely maiden, that his deeds could be considered noble. Only the slaves admired him, and sought to follow him in a brutal uprising."

Cahira glanced at Felix. "Did you know this?"

"'Tis news to me, lass."

Makya noticed Felix for the first time, and his eyes narrowed. "This creature has the aura of a priest."

"He's just a bat," said Aren darkly. But his dislike of Prince Makya soared to almost unreasonable heights.

Makya laughed. "To one of your kind, maybe. But to my eyes, he is something quite different, and more dangerous. Priests are forbidden in this land, for they incite discontent and violence."

"Felix wouldn't do that!" said Cahira. "He's my guide, a creature of the Woodland . . . and a product of my own spell-casting. He's no threat to Kora."

Aren glanced at her in surprise, then smiled as he remembered the words she had spoken when they first rode from the Norskland: *I only lie if I dislike someone intensely.* Apparently, she felt the same as he did about Makya, and felt the need to prevaricate about Felix's nature.

"Keep him with you," ordered Makya, his voice soft but steely.

"Where did your priests go?" asked Aren. "It is for their advice we came."

Makya's eyes flashed, but his smile remained. "The priests of Kora are all banished or dead," he said calmly. Then he bit his lip as if aggrieved. "Though I once trusted them as my dearest advisors, I learned to my great sorrow that in their greed for power and importance, they sought to overthrow me and take control of this realm. I was shocked and heartbroken, of course, so the only solution was exile."

"You had your priests killed?" Cahira looked at him in horror. He offered a sorrowful expression that failed to reach his eyes.

"Banished mostly, my lady. Yes, some were killed, but their deaths grieve me terribly. Despite my heavy responsibilities as prince, many have said I have too compassionate a nature."

"I know a woman just like you," said Cahira. "She is also terribly sensitive and compassionate."

He looked at her from beneath heavy eyelids, as if questioning her sincerity, but Cahira kept her expression straight. Aren restrained himself from laughter.

"But . . . I wonder why two of your kind would need the advice of our priests?" Makya asked after a moment.

"Because the dark energy of Cheveyo, the Spirit Warrior, has risen again, and soon his power will be complete," said Aren flatly. "We found mention in a tome kept by the Guerdian King of a spell that might unravel the enchantment he placed on himself, and with the Guerdians' help, we hoped we could destroy him."

"And destroy him you must!" exclaimed Makya, who

seemed genuinely horrified by the prospect of the dark wizard's return. "His evil is unfathomable, his lust for power beyond compare."

"Then perhaps you know of where we might find a priest in exile," Aren said. "For that may be the only way to stop him."

Makya's face instantly puckered with anger. "That is not possible. Even if I knew their location, there is no way to reach them. They are hidden deep in the jungle, with defensive spells so thick that they are impossible to breach. In any case, I doubt such a spell as you need exists. I am not a Mage, but because of my station, I have studied the Art. There are spells that can reverse spells of equal power, but I'm afraid anything Cheveyo cast would be far too great. No, I'm afraid you must find another way to destroy Matchithew. The Koraji cannot help you—though in this, we wish you well, for he will threaten us gravely should he arise again."

Aren bowed, then met the prince's dark eyes. He sensed no guile in Makya's response, though this was clearly not a man to be blindly trusted. "If that is so, I must ask your leave, Your Highness," said Aren. "My company is weary. We hope you will allow us to linger for a day or so before we depart."

"Of course," said Makya. "You are my guests in the city, and may come and go at your leisure."

"I thank you," said Aren, and he turned to leave.

"Son of Arkyn," called Makya.

"Your Highness?"

"There is a man known to me, by name only. He is called Damir, and he was the son of my father's brother. Do you know of him?"

Aren hesitated. He had no idea what news reached Kora now, and while it would be unwise to lie, it might be equally dangerous to speak the full truth. "I know of him, yes," he finally admitted.

"It is said that he has become king in the land of Amrodel." Makya's gaze shifted to Cahira. "So you must know him well, lady."

"I know him," she answered carefully. "He is a good man, and beloved in my land."

"A Mage, is he?"

"Like his mother, yes."

"And his father," said Makya.

"What else would you know of him, Your Highness?" asked Aren. With effort, he kept his voice light.

"Nothing else," said Makya. "We are cousins, he and I."

"I knew his father came from this land, but little more than that," said Aren.

"Our king is extremely private," added Cahira. "His father died when he was very young."

"Yes," said Makya. "How tragic!"

As they started to leave, he spoke again, softly. "You know, in my land, because of his magical energy, he would be a priest."

"What of it?" asked Cahira, her blue eyes narrow.

"Nothing, my dear lady," answered the prince. "But it is fortunate for him that his life has carried on afar."

"I'm sure he thinks so, too," Cahira said.

"Priests, I find, have a penchant for causing trouble," continued Makya. "We have had to take extreme measures to convince them such acts are . . . ill for their health."

"What do you mean?" Cahira asked.

Makya smiled, and Aren's blood chilled. The prince walked smoothly to an oblong marble stand by the great wall. He fingered a large ornate urn that sat upon the stand. He glanced at them, his smile broadened, and his dark eyes turned to black. Slowly, he lifted the top off the urn. Cahira gasped, but Aren just stood immobile, gazing in horror at the sight Makya revealed.

"A man's head . . . ," whispered Cahira, and she turned away.

Makya idly displayed the head of a young man, dark-skinned but perhaps once fair, his features contorted in agony, shriveled into a hideous mask. "He was one of my most troublesome adversaries, though he was young, as you

can see. Eighteen, I think. I took a slave wench he fancied,
as is my right. She made an amusing concubine for a time.
But she actually attempted to leave my palace in the company of this very priest! I caught them, of course, and after a
lengthy interview with my guards . . ." Makya directed their
attention to another urn and his brow rose. "I'm afraid
they'll never be quite together again—but almost."

Aren's throat constricted, but he forced himself to speak
evenly. "A strange choice of decoration," he said. Makya
laughed.

"It is necessary that we keep reminders—however
distasteful—that will serve to dissuade further disruptions."
Though he termed the grotesque collection 'distasteful,'
Makya lingered over the sight. "To preserve the peace in this
fair land, drastic measures are sometimes required. The
priests were cruel and indiscriminate in their attacks against
my people. They used their power against us to dominate
and change our way of life. They had to learn the way of
pain, I fear."

"You mean 'torture,'" said Aren.

"If you would take such measures against them, even to
save yourselves, I do not see that you are any better," said
Cahira fiercely, and for an instant, Makya's anger flared.

"The priests were mad with power. They threatened my
reign, demanded control over this land!" Makya slapped the
cover back onto the urn, stood beside it like a conquering
lord. "We must attach a heavy price to such disobedience, as
all rulers do. Even you, I imagine, 'Lord Chieftain.'"

"My people are violent, and we love battle," said Aren,
and his fingers twitched as he envisioned attacking Makya
then and there. "But we do not carry the heads of our enemies, nor torture them, for those are not the acts that bring
glory or honor. They bring shame, instead."

"You have your ways, we have ours," replied Makya lightly.
"But I hope when you return to your northern lands, you will
tell my cousin that a visit to Kora might be . . . unwise."

The Prince smiled and departed the room, followed by his

guards. Cahira and Aren looked at each other, then left as quickly as they could.

They exited the palace gates, then hurried across the street, where they stopped. Cahira stared up at the palace, and then she shuddered. "What an evil man! To keep someone's head . . ."

"I have seen much of violence," agreed Aren quietly, "but I have never seen such malice in any enemy's eyes. He has no will to fight, but he delights in pain inflicted upon others."

Cahira drew a long breath. "Maybe he really is like Shaen, though their methods are different. But in the end, all they seem to want is the pain of others."

"And they want others to see the pain they've caused," said Aren, "to know they have 'power.' If power it can be called."

"That is the nature of darkness," spoke up Felix softly. "It is not strong in and of itself. It seeks out the light it perceives in others, and tries to quench it. So, even those as weak as Shaen or this prince can cause great damage."

"I've always imagined visiting Kora because it sounded so grand," said Cahira, "but now I can't wait to leave." She paused. "Do you think he's telling the truth about the unraveling spell?"

"I'm not sure, but he had little reason to lie about this," Aren said. "I believe he fears the dark wizard's arising even more than we do."

"He speaks the truth," cut in Felix, and Aren glared.

"Then why didn't you say so when we formed this plan, bat?"

"There are other questions that will be answered here, lord," answered Felix quietly. "And your heart led you to this land, did it not?"

"It did," replied Aren.

"Then trust its voice, lad. It has not failed you yet."

Cahira looked around, and her brow furrowed. "I don't understand this place. It is undeniably beautiful, with the white cobblestones, the magnificent buildings. The flowers are beautiful, and their fragrance is sweet; and I hear the songs of birds like to none in the Woodland. The people are fair of face . . . And their artwork . . ." She hesitated, then glanced at Aren. "It depicts scenes of very creative lovemaking. And yet . . ."

"And yet, it feels sterile," said Aren, "as if what was once an intense interest and joy in the pursuit of bliss has turned dark, instead, and is now reduced to renting slaves for physical gratification."

"This land has floundered," agreed Felix. "Once, it offered many pleasures, but those were not dark in nature, for the people celebrated the passionate union between lovers and the force of life itself—even as bats of my species do."

Aren glanced at Cahira, but she listened to the bat with interest. "These people may have celebrated life once, but no longer. This land is empty of real feeling, and even their art is just an exhibit of power." She glanced at the tiles decorated with scenes of lovemaking. "It is strange that these same acts can come from the heart, or be used as a weapon. This land would suit Shaen well, for that is how she approaches the art, too. I suppose Cheveyo was the same."

"Not entirely," said Felix. "His sensuality was renowned, and as he grew ever-darker, that sensuality grew more and more removed from his heart. But when he met the Woodland Queen, he could not deny what he felt for her."

"But he destroyed her!" said Cahira. "How could he destroy her if she had touched his heart?"

"Ah, lass, don't you know? He destroyed her *because* she touched his heart."

"I don't understand," said Cahira.

"Don't you?" Felix asked. "Sometimes, the heart is already so wounded that it becomes too painful to touch."

"It sounds to me as if he was the one who wounded others," said Cahira.

"Aye, that's true." The bat sighed. "But sometimes unseen wounds run the deepest."

Aren glanced at the tiles beneath his feet, and his gaze fixed on a depiction of a man and woman locked in an embrace. The woman's head tipped back as if she rode waves of rapture, and the man had given all of himself to her pleasure. "The people of Kora felt true passion once, it seems . . . These depictions are remarkably . . . accurate."

Cahira peeked down at the tile that captured his interest, and she blushed. "They do, at that." She shifted her weight from foot to foot, then glanced at Felix and Khadun, who looked embarrassed. "I suppose it all depends on why you do things, not what . . ." Her voice trailed off, and she turned her gaze to Aren. She looked at him thoughtfully, but her eyes seemed to darken, and he recognized the slow burn of her desire.

"Fair point," he said, and cleared his throat.

She glanced at Felix and Khadun. "We're going back to our room now. Aren needs rest, because of his injury."

He opened his mouth to inform her he was fine, but she shot him a warning look. "I am somewhat weary."

Felix issued a long sigh. "If that's what you call it. Guerdian, escort me to the tavern. I need to set myself up with young Thorleif, and see that those lads are in hand. I wonder if they have ale in Kora. I believe their proficiency is with the grape."

"Have a good time," called Cahira. And with that, she seized Aren's hand and they hurried back to the inn. As they passed a row of shops, she stopped without warning, darted inside, and left him standing in the street.

A short while passed, and several women in progression propositioned him with words he didn't understand but recognized too well. All alone, he was at the mercy of the lustful hordes, and he was in no mood to placate any of Prince Makya's willing subjects with even a polite rejection. When the third female approached, he laid his hand on his sword and issued a low growl that sent her scurrying away.

Cahira emerged from the shop as he re-seated the sword

in its sheath. "What were you doing? Fighting with someone?" she asked in surprise.

He started to answer, but his mouth just fell open and
stayed that way. Cahira had clothed herself in a dress that
made her Guerdian attire look puritan. Soft swathes of
sheer, multicolored fabric crossed over her round breasts,
just barely, then folded low over her hips, falling to her
thighs at a beguilingly uneven angle.

"Do you like it?" she asked innocently.

"Lady, I fall at your feet," he replied.

"I think, according to the pillow, it is supposed to be the
other way around."

"The pillow?" His voice came out a squeak, and she seized
his hand and led him purposefully back to the inn.

By the time they reached the guestroom, Aren's knees felt
weak and his arousal swollen against his leggings. He'd
edged his tunic lower, lest his condition catch the eye of any
other female, and when Cahira opened the door, it wasn't a
moment too soon.

She closed the door behind him but didn't speak. Instead,
she placed her forefinger in her mouth, and her little pink
tongue swirled around as if she imagined some great sweetness. He swallowed and tried to smile, but even his face felt
tight from wanting.

She reached out to his loose collar and trailed her fingers
from his throat to his chest. "You are a beautiful sight, Aren
son of Arkyn," she said softly, and her voice was lower than
normal, rich with desire.

"As are you, my lady," he answered.

She glanced down at her new dress and smiled. "This
dress is just what the female on the pillow was wearing."

"On the pillow?"

"It depicted an interesting position—the same that I saw
downstairs, in the inn's painting, although that one was a
man with two women."

Aren exhaled a taut breath while Cahira fiddled with his
shirt then undid the laces. "It was a small picture," she con-

tinued, "so I might have to make some of it up as I go along."

"Do so at your leisure, my lady," he answered, and she peered up at him through lowered lashes.

His shirt came apart before he knew what she'd done or how she'd done it, but suddenly it hung open, revealing both his chest and the arousal he had sought to conceal. She looked at him greedily, then bit her lip.

Reaching up and touching his mouth, she stood on tiptoes to kiss him. She swept her tongue between his lips then swirled it over his, then sucked its tip. His whole body hardened, but she drew back and her blue eyes were shining.

Her breasts rose and fell with quick breaths, but she fixed her attention on his chest and kissed him there. He felt her tongue flick out to taste him, and he slid his fingers into her hair. She kissed him more greedily now, across the expanse of his chest, then lower. To his surprise, she sank to her knees before him, then looked up at him as if—as if she looked up at a god.

He touched her face gently, and her lips curved in the most alluring smile he'd ever seen. She turned her attention to his painfully obvious arousal, then trailed her hand lightly along his shaft. Aren drew a hoarse breath as she outlined its shape with her palm. She pressed her lips unexpectedly against the taut fabric, and he felt the dampness of her tongue seep through the cloth.

He bit back a cry of pleasure as she moved her mouth along his length, and as her quick fingers unlaced his leggings and drew them apart, his cry became a moan. She slipped her fingers around his length and drew it out so that the warm air felt cool against its heat. Then she looked up at him again, her eyes blazing with passion, and she touched her tongue to the tip.

His gaze locked with hers as her pink tongue swirled slowly around the blunt end of his shaft. Slowly, down and up, and across the tip again. His breath came ragged and hoarse, and he longed to drop to the floor and take her; but she gripped his shaft at its base so that her wrist pressed with agonizing perfection against his tight sac. Then she lowered her mouth slowly over his length and sucked gently, then with more vigor. She moved up and down with enthusiasm. He saw her little toes curl as she made love to him this way, and she leaned forward as her passion took hold of her. Her firm backside arched, and he thought he might die of pleasure.

He clasped his hands in her hair as she continued to take him greedily, with a desire he'd never before come close to experiencing. She made love to him with a witch's fiery passion, and she loved him with the grace of an angel. He felt her swift breaths against his hot skin, and soft murmurs escaped her lips as she slid deeper into bliss.

Aren's whole body throbbed and grew tighter and tighter as she loved him. She drove him into bliss, into an unendurable ache, until his breaths came as ragged moans, raw and uncontained and primal. She sucked and licked until his body quivered and his fingers clenched, and then she peered up at him again, through her long, lowered lashes, and there was a fire of challenge burning in her beautiful eyes. That look was his undoing, and his rapture took control of him until his mind shattered in ecstasy and spiraled like a ship upon a raging sea.

She carried him through this rapturous crest, and after, as its waves gentled and eased. His body quaked with fiery aftershocks of pleasure, and she stilled in her sweet ministrations and looked up at him. She smiled with the bliss of triumph, as if the wonders of the world had all been revealed to her.

Aren sank to his knees, gathered Cahira in his arms, and kissed her with a fullness and hunger he'd never known. She drew back, beaming with happiness, and kissed his cheek. "You can learn a lot from a pillow!" she informed him.

He nodded, but he couldn't find the words to tell her what she had done to him, how deeply she had owned him, and how much pleasure she gave. He picked her up and carried her to the bed, and she gazed at him in sweet wonder.

"We are not finished, my lady," he said softly, echoing her own words when he had first shown her this bliss. "Thanks to your sweetness, the waves we ride next will be slower and last longer, but be deeper still. Would you go there with me?"

She smiled, and her face glowed with love. "Aren, I would go anywhere with you. Over waves, and through storms, and into the heart of the sun, I will follow. Because where you are is the only place I have ever wanted to be."

15

ANCIENT TIES

He took her with long, slow thrusts, driving deep inside her body until she quivered and moaned and called out his name, over and over until it seemed she was part of him. And when she thought she could take no more without shattering into fiery shards, he stopped and withdrew from her body. She cried out in the agony of denial, but he met her gaze and held it; then, with power and focus, he rolled her over onto her stomach and took her again.

From this angle, he reached deeper and drove harder. Cahira clenched the silken sheets tight, and he clasped her hips in his hands. He made love to her harder and faster until she writhed beneath him, sobbing in pleasure until nothing existed but what they felt. And after the fire that burned in her soul was as hot as it could get, he led her to a cataclysmic release and joined her on its crest where they blended together into one.

He stilled and lay quiet, then finally withdrew from her body and gathered her into his arms. They didn't speak, for no words could touch what they had shared. Cahira drifted into sleep listening to the strong beat of his heart, and she wandered into a dream where all the world was light. And in that light she saw a man, bent over and sobbing, his agony torn from deep inside him. He existed alone, dark amidst light, in a pain so excruciating that not even death could end it. A dragonfly hovered around him, protectively, it seemed, but he didn't see it, for he faced the ground. Beneath him lay two figures embedded in the sand.

Cahira wanted to go to the man, to comfort him like a child, but he raged against help and against light, and it seemed that his own darkness would devour him. But from the area of his heart, though he doubled over and wept, she saw a tiny flicker of light.

As she sank deeper into sleep, he faded from her vision and disappeared. But when she woke the next morning, the vision lingered and filled her with pity, though she did not know the reason.

Cahira opened her eyes. Aren had already risen and was nowhere in sight. She hopped up, packed her erotic new dress carefully in her bag, then dressed in her traveling clothes. She slung her bow over her shoulder, then went out into the main area of the inn.

Her friends had gathered and were eating breakfast together, though no other guests appeared roused at this hour. The inn's proprietor, Tocho, stood by as two servants delivered breakfast, but he looked bleary and somewhat resentful to be called upon so early. The servants were lighter-skinned than the others Cahira had seen, and in their faces she could see what appeared to be vestiges of the proud Norsk race. But they were smaller and weaker of build, and the bright fire that burned in Aren's people had faded almost to nothing in these slaves.

Cahira tried to catch a serving maid's eye, but the woman passed her by and didn't look up. She did glance back at Aren, though, with lingering sorrow and a trace of admiration as one looks upon a star or a hero. Cahira longed suddenly to help, but the woman left and didn't look back.

Aren looked up and smiled when he saw Cahira. She took

one look at his glorious face and shuddered with memory. Her legs felt suddenly shaky, and her breath came out a gasp. He waved her over, and she sat down at his side, unable to look away from his face.

"Why didn't you wake me?" she asked, trying to sound casual.

"You were sleeping so soundly, love," he replied. He passed her a fat roll, and she seized a round pat of butter.

"What are we doing this morning?" she asked as she stuffed half the roll into her mouth.

"I'm not sure," said Aren. "We were just discussing what appear to be our very limited options."

Felix positioned himself near the center of the table, swallowing a large bite of cheese before addressing the others. "Your visit here was not in vain, my lord, though maybe you do not see the path laid before you."

Aren angled his brow, and his jaw shifted as he took a long draught of a fragrant tea. He set it aside and grimaced. "This is disgusting."

"But they don't brew ale in Kora," said Ranveig sadly as he held up his own small blue cup. "Just this, and wine. Weak wine."

"It's too sweet for my taste," Fareth agreed. "But their cheese is passable. Disappointing, the food is, because I'd figured they'd make some fine, exotic dishes in this land. Damir ap Kora knew a few recipes, and they were tasty indeed. I offer them up at my tavern now and again, as a special treat for my guests. But I've seen nothing to match those here."

"Because their labor is forced," suggested Aren bitterly, "their meals are not crafted with delight or appreciation. All is soaked in oppression. I feel it."

Rika looked around. "I detested the heat at first. But after a few hours, the skin adjusts. I thought that it might be pleasant to venture to such a land as this during the darkest months of our winter. But now I too feel this oppression you speak of, and while it lasts, this land will hold no appeal for our people."

"A shame," said Elphin, "for it could be a fair land. What did you think of the prince, my lord?"

"That he was an evil man," Aren warned, "and one not to be trusted."

"Unfortunately, he couldn't help us, even if he weren't so detestable," said Cahira. "So we're at a loss as to what to do next."

"Perhaps I can help." A young man spoke up quietly from where he bent to refill a pitcher of tea. Cahira looked at him in surprise. He was not one of the slaves that resembled the Norsk. Instead, he was smaller, with olive-dark skin and eyes that angled exotically at the corners. His face was rounder than those of the Koraji natives, and his fingers long and lithe, as if he might be musical given the chance.

Aren looked as if he recognized him, then nodded as if accepting more tea. "Do you know where we can find a priest?" he asked in a low voice, careful that no one else could overhear.

"No priests," said the man. "All dead, or gone far."

"We have seen what remains of one that died," said Cahira. "Makya keeps a severed head in a jar."

The man didn't seem surprised. "He has done much evil besides that. No prisoner dies easily when taken by the prince's guards, for they excel at torture. They killed the priests swiftly, for they feared magic, but for those less fortunate—such as slaves caught trying to flee—the end is grim, indeed. Many slaves walk without eyes now, or lie unseen, crippled in huts. Even among the Koraji people, there is fear should they act in discordance with the prince's will."

"There is great evil in Kora," said Fareth quietly. "I knew that Damir's father fled this land, but I had not heard it was so grim."

"It has grown darker with each passing year," said the slave. "As the priests went into hiding, Makya's arrogance grew, and his control over this land is now complete. He chooses the most evil of his people to become his guards, those who enjoy inflicting pain. In times past, the guards were the noblest of the Koraji people, brave and skilled yet kind, defenders of those weaker. It is not so now. As soon as he ascended to his father's throne, Makya had those nobler guards murdered and mutilated—for, like the priests, they attempted to refuse him. The new guards are ruthless, and their cruelty knows no bounds. All fear them."

"A warrior should not be a murderer," said Thorleif in disgust. "There is no glory in such deeds, only the barrenness of the soul."

"You speak wisely, boy," said Felix. "But where darkness holds sway, such deeds will occur."

"I thought the darkness was just the effect of the Arch Mage," said Elphin, "but that doesn't appear to be the case."

"Darkness is ever-present," Felix said. "It exists in all lands, but only when the light of the heart is extinguished does darkness become an overwhelming tide."

"Like with the Arch Mage," added Cahira.

The young slave looked between them. "Word has passed between those of us trapped in this city that you seek news of Cheveyo, the Spirit Warrior who once defied this land, then himself fell into ruin. Great was he once, and dark his fall."

"We do," said Aren. "How can you help us in that search?"

"I can take you to a place of mystic ruins, where the priests once gathered for rituals. It is forbidden now, but some still meet there in secret, in defiance of the prince."

"What use would that be?" Aren asked, though he seemed interested.

"It is the last place Cheveyo stood when he defied this land and sent his wrath westward over the sands. It lies south and east of here, nestled in a cove, not far, only slightly farther south along the course you traveled on your voyage."

Cahira's heart took an odd leap. "We should go, I think,"

she whispered, feeling it was so. Aren looked into her eyes, and a strange light shone in their amber depths, one she had not seen before.

"I know." He nodded to the slave. "By what name are you called?"

"I am Ang Gelu," the man replied. "I am of the Lahari people from Nikunja. We were overrun by the prince's armies, those guards you see in white, and they slaughtered many, then took many more as slaves. Some of my people survived by hiding high in the mountains to the north of our land, but I remained behind to defend those fleeing, and was captured." He stretched out his arm to show that it was rent with a deep scar. "I did not give up without resistance, but armed with a bow and a knife, there was little I could do against the weapons of the Koraji."

Rika eyed Ang Gelu's scar, then stretched out her own arm and pulled back her sleeve. "I have just such a scar," she told him in a low voice. "I got it when I slew my husband's killer."

Ang Gelu turned his soft gaze to Rika, and he looked at her in wonder. "My own wife fell that day, and my child, but I could not avenge them. Instead, I was taken as a slave. I honor you, fair lady, for what you have done."

Rika blushed. "I fought one rogue, and no army," she said. "And perhaps my scar is not as deep as your own."

"You are a slave no longer," pronounced Aren, and his low voice trembled. "Come with us."

Ang Gelu smiled. "You are already looked upon with suspicion by the prince's guards," he said. "If you steal a slave, that suspicion will double."

"I doubt they'll pursue you to the dark wizard's tomb." Aren paused. "Do you know anything about sailing ships?"

"From my homeland, no—but I have learned something of the craft by necessity here, as we are sent out to fish when the seas are too rough for our masters. They care not if we drown, you see." He paused. "I don't care for the occupation, but sometimes, it's better than dwelling here in servitude, and more than one of us has simply gone to sea and not come back—has been lost to the waves by choice."

"The sea has meant freedom before, and it will mean so again," said Aren.

Ang Gelu nodded, then indicated Aren should drink from his still-full teacup. Aren did so, though he looked pained, and Ang Gelu refilled it. Cahira drank her tea, too, to give the servant yet another reason to linger.

"They say the slaves of old made their way to freedom," Ang Gelu said, "but the seas were kinder then. On stolen ships they ventured forth, and at that time, the bravest among them returned and saved others. It is to the place of their last village that I take you now."

"Did Cheveyo defend them?" asked Cahira. "It seems so unlike what we know of him."

"That was his promise," agreed Ang Gelu. "And for a while, it seemed it was a promise he meant to keep. But his rage at the prince and the priests who had betrayed him became his sole obsession, and he forgot those he had sworn to protect. They loved and trusted him, but as you will see, their trust proved their undoing."

"We will go to the ruins," said Aren, but then he looked around. "But is there anything we can do for these other people? I would not willingly leave them in bondage."

"Not all would leave, even if you gave them a destination, for long years in servitude make unseen shackles, and the soul grows weary with their weight," said Ang Gelu sadly. "But there are some as desperate as myself who still wear the bonds bitterly, who would gladly depart."

Aren glanced at Cahira. "It may be that I wield Damir ap Kora's sword after all."

"What are you planning to do?" she asked in surprise.

He leaned toward Ang Gelu, and the others all leaned in to listen. "Gather all those who would depart and have them meet us on the pier. Row slowly, as if planning to fish, then gather at my ship."

Ang Gelu smiled. "More would come than can fit in one vessel. Yours can hold . . . fifteen at most."

"Then we'll steal another." Aren paused and glanced at Cahira. "Plunder is in my blood," he offered pleasantly.

"It suits you, my lord," she murmured.

"We'll divide our company. Rika, Elphin, and Ranveig will go with Ang Gelu, and seize control of a second ship." Rika interrupted with a slight groan, but the thought of battle must have appealed to her enough to brave the open sea again. "The others will come with me to ours. I think we can assume there will be a fight, so bring whatever weapons you can find, which should be concealed until needed."

"Yes," said Ang Gelu. "I have refashioned my Nikunji dagger, though I've found no opportunity to wield it yet."

"I fight with a skillet," said Fareth, "so you're already better armed than I."

"Would you like a better blade?" asked Ang Gelu, but Fareth shook his head.

"No, lad. Gotten used to my heavy pan, I have."

Cahira smiled. "And you're beginning to look rather dangerous, Fareth. I hope when this is done, you remember its original purpose."

"Aye, lass, first things first."

"How are the guards armed?" asked Cahira. "Do they have bows?"

"They are ill-trained with bows, though they do have a few crossbows in their armory," replied Ang Gelu. "They mostly wield swords. But with those, they have deadly proficiency, and their armor is woven with magic—part of the reason the priests rebelled against the prince in the first place. The soldiers will be difficult to strike down."

"Is there a weakness in that armor?" Aren asked.

"At the neck, and below the arms," said Ang Gelu.

"Easy targets," commented Rika calmly. "My axe is meant to hew necks."

"And I can hit either," said Cahira. Already, she felt her *ki* rising, and her heart pounded with excitement.

"When were are clear of this harbor," Aren continued, "we'll make for the ruins you've mentioned. I doubt they'll expect us to take that direction. But I think I can convince them not to follow, anyway."

Ang Gelu clasped Aren's hand then hurried away. He bowed to Tocho, who yawned and paid no attention. Aren rose and stretched idly, but his amber eyes burned. This was his true calling, Norsk warrior that he was—to stand and fight against evil, to cast off the bonds of oppression and defend those who were weaker. More deeply still, Cahira understood that something in his soul demanded this battle, to set the slaves free if he could. In doing so, he hoped to right an ancient wrong that still troubled his soul.

At least forty slaves were gathered on the pier, more than Cahira had imagined. Some held small sacks of their belongings, and a few carried the sand-colored cats with brown paws that Aren had admired earlier. One woman carried a covered basket, and Cahira smiled when five little kittens peeked out, their blue eyes wide and round.

Aren mustered the group, and he directed them all to his ship and another moored close at hand. The second craft was slightly larger, but Ang Gelu said its speed would be the same, and that it could hold at least thirty passengers. The slaves clamored into rowboats which, though weighted down with extra people, moved quickly toward freedom.

Cahira waited with her heart in her throat. She and her friends positioned themselves between the escaping slaves and the city, waiting for the guards to recognize that an exodus had begun. A third of the slaves had departed when a great bell rang from the hilltop.

"It begins!" called Aren, and he shoved all but one rowboat from the pier. The guards charged down from the palace, but the first slaves already climbed from the rowboats on board the ships that would carry them to freedom.

Aren nodded to Cahira. "Are you ready, love?"

She climbed up onto a high post on the pier and set an arrow to her bow. "I am."

He winced at her position, at her vulnerability, but he didn't try to stop her. "Be careful up there!" he begged.

"And you down there," she called.

"I'll have to make more arrows on the trip back," she muttered to herself. "There should be wood enough. If only I could find—"

Felix glided easily to the post and took position on her shoulder. "Gather gull feathers when we reach the ruins—there should be plenty there."

"Good idea!" She caught her breath as the first guards charged onto the pier.

"Steady yourself, lass. Let your *ki* build first, then sight—"

"You sound like Madawc! I know what I'm doing."

But she wavered before drawing upon her energy, because Aren stepped out in front of the others and drew the white Dragonfly Sword from its sheath. He swung it around like an axe, then tried a slicing motion.

"He might have considered practicing with it earlier," Felix grumbled.

"Looks like he's got the hang of it now." Cahira sighed as Aren leapt forward and, in one slash, sent a guard's sword flying into the harbor. "I told you. He's smart."

"Learns quickly, he does," agreed Felix. "Now . . . focus!"

Cahira cast one last lingering look at Aren, but she knew nothing would hinder him now. The white sword glittered like diamonds on fire, and it blazed in his hand as he drove the guards back.

The wharf was wide enough for him to have help. Rika leapt onto a pier arm that ran vertically, and to Cahira's surprise, Ang Gelu appeared next to the Norskwoman, his curved dagger swinging. Khadun wielded his short spear, driving a guard back with a quick jab; Thorleif and Elphin chose the opposite pier arm, and Ranveig and Fareth moved in behind.

More guards poured down from the city, and at last Cahira turned back to the power inside herself, and she summoned her *ki* to its fullness. It rayed inside her like a bottled storm, nearing a crescendo. A familiar hesitation, a doubt, rose to greet it, one that had often defeated her full power in the past. But when she glanced down at Aren for a moment, he looked up at her and smiled. An invisible cord ran between them, pulsing with energy beyond her *ki*, beyond the vast strength of his soul. It bound them forever, and from it, her true power soared. It burst around her and whirled, and she lowered her head and directed its force from her core to her arm and into her bow.

She fixed her sights on a guard as he leapt toward Ang Gelu, and she let fly with her arrow. It struck true, despite an impossible angle on the shot, and the guard reeled and dropped into the harbor. Cahira heard Rika call out in praise, but she turned her attention to another guard who charged toward Elphin. "You will not touch him," she whispered, and again her arrow found its mark. The guard tumbled forward, and Elphin kicked him off the pier with a great splash.

The guards seemed to realize that Aren was an invincible foe, and so they targeted his friends on the pier arms first. But Aren bounded toward them.

Rika and Ang Gelu fought matched guards, and Elphin and Thorleif handled two more. But Aren drove against the entire onslaught, and they broke before him like waves upon the bow of a great ship. Ranveig and Fareth fought on either side of him. Cahira watched Fareth slam his skillet into a guard's white helm; the sound reverberated loudly and the man fell senseless, and Fareth shoved him over the edge into the water, then resumed his battle stance.

Cahira chose targets closer to land, thinking to stop the oncoming tide. A burly guard lifted a crossbow, and she frowned.

"There's a good one to stop, lass," advised Felix.

"Just what I had in mind," she replied. She took aim and

fired, and the bow dropped from the guard's hand. He reached for it, and she shot his other hand, and he stumbled away in terror.

"Well done, lass! No need to kill if you can scare 'em off!"

"Madawc's advice exactly."

"And wise it is, too!"

Cahira sought another target, but the guards were beginning to retreat, and she waited. Aren strode out before them, the Dragonfly Sword shining in his hand. He held it up in the air.

The Koraji prince himself had come down from the city, surrounded by guards. Cahira took aim, then hesitated. *I can do this. I can kill him*, she told herself. She glanced at Felix, but he offered no advice. "He's an evil man," she whispered, "and if I do this, I may save many."

Still, Felix made no comment, and she knew this was her choice to make.

Cahira lowered her bow and sighed heavily, and the prince disappeared behind his guards. Her chance was lost. She bowed her head.

Felix touched her gently. "His time will come, lass, but he is not yours to face. Had you shot him, another would rise in his stead, and this land would be no better off. It is not he but the culture that bred him who has failed this land's promise. A leader may come one day who can cleanse this country of its ills, who will heal all that has gone wrong. But until that leader's heart is healed, this city will fail, for its spirit is tied to his."

Cahira didn't ask who he meant—that leader was the man of last night's dream, crumpled soul-deep in agony. "For the sake of this city," she said, "I hope he finds his way."

"In time, lass, he may. He may."

A guard captain faced Aren, but dared not approach. "You may escape today, Norskman, but the prince has seen you and you will not be forgotten. Our ships will hunt you down and drive you from the sea!"

To Cahira's surprise, Aren laughed. "Follow me if you

will!" he called. "For I go to the lair of Matchitehew—and
we could use your help if we are to stand against the dark
wizard's wrath!"

The guards backed away in horror, and Aren waved to
Cahira. She jumped down from her post, and Felix glided
beside her to land on Aren's shoulder. "Took to the Dragonfly Sword after all, did you, lad?"

Aren whipped the blade easily around and examined it.
"An interesting weapon, I must admit. I will pay Damir ap
Kora my compliments when next we meet."

They had kept one rowboat at the pier to escape, and now
Ranveig and Fareth climbed in. The pair sat in the boat's
middle, while Elphin and Thorleif took positions near the
bow. Ang Gelu helped Rika gently down, and she seemed relaxed at his side. Khadun hopped down from the dock and
seated himself behind Thorleif, and Aren followed. He
turned and swung Cahira into his arms, kissed her deeply,
then settled her on the deck between his legs. Seizing the
oars, he rowed masterfully toward freedom.

The slaves already aboard the larger ship helped Rika,
Ang Gelu, and Elphin up a rope ladder, and Ranveig struggled on after. Then Aren rowed to his own ship, swung himself up and onto the deck not bothering with the ladder, and
he and the other slaves drew up the rest.

He gave orders, and Thorleif released the mooring and
four slaves helped him with the sails. Aren manned the tiller,
and the ship lolled gently in the wind as the sails unfurled. In
brief moments, the ships gathered speed and the golden port
of Kora faded from view.

Ang Gelu directed the two craft eastward for an hour, and
they also feigned a direction out to sea to throw off any possible pursuit. But now they angled sharply south and approached a vast swath of golden-brown desert. Aren stood
at his ship's helm as a cove came into view. Cliffs rose like a
cutoff bowl with a rim sweeping east and west into the
desert dunes, casting long shadows through their midst. As

they drew closer, Aren saw the ruins of an old hamlet dug into the shelter of the cove.

Ang Gelu furled his ship's sails and dropped anchor, and motioned from his ship's helm for Aren to do the same. They were still a short distance from shore, and in their hurry to get away, they'd brought no suitable skiffs along for landing. But something in that sheltered cove called to Aren, while at the same time filling his heart with sadness. *I have to go there and stand in those shadows*, he thought, though he did not know the reason. Thorleif lowered anchor, and Aren went to the railing.

"How do we access these ruins?" he called.

"Those who would venture there must swim," answered Ang Gelu casually. Aren heard a low groan he guessed came from Rika.

"I will swim," said Aren, "and any who wish to come with me. The rest may stay on these ships and await our return. We will not be long."

"I am staying right here," said Khadun. "Guerdians do not swim." He paused. "We sink."

"As your hearts decide," said Aren, tearing off his shirt.

Cahira tugged off her boots and bodice, wearing only her snug leggings and sheer shirt. "I'm coming with you," she said. "I can swim—Elphin taught me and my sisters when we were young."

"And for that reason, I'm coming, too," called the Woodlander from the other vessel. "Who will join us?"

"I will!" said Thorleif. He ripped off his tunic, baring a chest that seemed to have expanded since their journey began. Felix whistled.

"You, boy, have grown!"

Thorleif beamed. "I have, at that." He dove into the water and made for the shore. Elphin jumped in after him, and the swim became a race. Felix cackled, then soared over their heads, with the presumed intention of judging the winner.

"Such children," muttered Fareth; then to Aren's surprise, the innkeeper carefully removed his large tunic, folded it neatly, and set it aside. He tugged off his boots and positioned himself by the ship's stern.

"Be careful, Fareth!" called Cahira nervously. The innkeeper snorted.

"You're not the only one who swam in our Woodland lakes, lass!" He threw himself off the dock, curled into a ball, and splashed loudly into the water.

Beside Aren, Cahira held her breath, but Fareth's head soon bobbed to the surface. He sucked in a quick breath and began swimming to shore with long, masterful strokes. Aren looked to Cahira and shrugged.

From the other ship, Ranveig eyed Fareth, then tore off his own jerkin and cast it aside. "Big men swim faster," he announced, then splashed into the water after Fareth.

Rika crept miserably to the railing beside Ang Gelu.

"You don't have to go, Rika," called Aren. "There's no need."

She elevated her head. "I told you that I'd follow you into the lair of the wizard and beyond. I will follow you now." And with that, she closed her eyes tight and flung herself overboard.

"Rika!" Aren waved madly to Ang Gelu. "I don't think she knows how to swim!"

The ex-slave dove in after her, then emerged supporting her shoulder. Her eyes were wide in terror, but he spoke quietly to her, and calm returned to her lovely face. Slowly and methodically, he directed her toward the shore, and after a short while she was swimming evenly beside him.

"Well, my lady?" Aren turned back to Cahira. "It is left to us."

Cahira climbed over the railing, her bright eyes lit with challenge. "We meet again in a race for honor," she announced. "And this time, victory will be mine!"

"I cannot believe you beat me!" Aren pulled himself up on the shore and found Cahira waiting for him, hands on hips, her face pert and her black hair dripping. He shook the water from his own hair and stared at her in amazement. Her light shirt was soaked through and plastered to every curve of her body, and when she pulled it away to dry it, he sighed. "You could have lingered there a moment longer," he said.

She smiled. "If it were only you, I might consider it, but it's a little much with everyone else."

"Fair point," he agreed. "These leggings are tight enough, and the sight of you this way—"

"Fair point," she interrupted, then looked around. "This place fills me with a strange sorrow, though in many ways, it is more beautiful than even the city of Kora."

"I feel the same," said Aren quietly. "Let us learn the reason, shall we?" He took her hand, and they joined Ang Gelu on the sandy bank.

"The ruins lie at the cleft, yonder," the ex-slave told them.

They all walked over the low dunes, and at first Elphin and Thorleif jostled each other like boys, and Ranveig and Fareth discussed the preparation of freshly caught fish. Rika questioned Ang Gelu about swimming strokes, and Felix circled about like a gull. But then the group fell into silence, and the bat returned to Aren's shoulder. Everyone seemed to sense the strange aura of sorrow that emanated from the ruins, and as they approached, Aren's heart grew heavier in his chest.

"What is this place?" he murmured. "Why do I feel it so?"

Cahira squeezed his hand, and to his wonder, he saw tears in her eyes. "I feel it, too," she whispered.

Ang Gelu led them among ruins, then turned to wait as Aren's group gathered around. "This was the last village of the First Slaves, as they are now called. From here, long ago, many escaped north and freed themselves from their bondage."

"Why did the Koraji prince let this village endure?" asked Cahira.

"For a time, the presence of the high priest, Cheveyo, was enough to guard it, though he himself gave it little thought." Ang Gelu gestured to the eastern dune where it sloped up like a bowl edge. "When he was at last driven into exile, and the vast army of the prince came after him, he stopped here, on that very crest, and unleashed his power. A great storm of fire and ash it was, and it destroyed all in its path."

"He destroyed this hamlet, then," said Aren, and for an instant he could almost see the great blinding wave of the wizard's wrath. He wandered around, unsure what he sought, but as he examined the remains of old buildings, his suspicions of the Norsk people's origins were confirmed. He bent and ran his hand along an old foundation. "This is the same structure we use for our Norsk huts."

"And here," said Ranveig, "these broken pots are like those we use today. No other race uses the kiln and wheel as we do."

Aren sighed. "There is a race east of the mountains that bears resemblance to our own. From there may come our true origins. But I would guess these people were taken from them, and somehow became slaves in Kora."

"In my land, there are legends of this time," said Ang Gelu. "We speak of a race of mighty warriors, which, ages ago, plundered even as far as the desert that runs eastward from here to the far mesas. At that time, it might be, their farthest explorers clashed with the forces of Kora, and the prisoners taken became slaves."

Cahira looked wistfully around. "These were your ancestors, as you guessed. But I feel as if . . . as if I stood here in my childhood. But not here. . . ." She moved around the ruins, a mystical expression on her face. "I see a small village with shops and a central fire, and huts where mothers carried babies, and children played in the water. And little ships came and went . . ."

"Aye, I see that too, lass," said Fareth. "A little stand here, for corn and roots . . ."

"And here," said Ranveig, "another with freshly caught fish."

Rika moved between them. "Here was a fire with a great

iron pot." As she spoke, they saw the remains of just such a pan in ruins at her feet. The Norskwoman backed away and looked to Aren. "What is this place?"

"I don't know," he whispered.

"Boys played in the sea," continued Thorleif in a small, far-off voice.

"And caught fish, and bet on who would catch more," added Elphin, and his words seemed strained with emotion.

Felix looked sad. "It is the past you see." He paused as they turned to him. "Your own past, all of you, from a time when your spirits were young and new." He turned to Aren. "But two among you were stronger than the rest. One brave lad ventured across the sea, taking his kinsmen north to a new land where they could become like the wild, brave ancestors he had heard of in song." Felix glanced at Cahira. "And one who waited for him, as she gathered the others for escape and marshaled them into action. But they made one mistake. They trusted another for deliverance, and by his power and grandeur, they were deceived."

"*No.*" Cahira shook her head, but tears filled her eyes and Aren's blood ran cold. She backed away from Felix, then moved from the village toward the eastern dune. She stumbled on a low rock, then caught herself as she fell. Her face went white and she screamed, then scrambled back from the rock.

Aren ran to her, and she pointed, but it was no natural rock that had tripped her. There, embedded in hard sand that had become like stone, lay two petrified shapes, entwined but not touching, the figures of two young lovers lying immobilized in time.

He stared down at the figures, then sank to his knees beside them. The girl lay on her side, her hand outstretched. The boy lay face down, his head turned toward her as if he had crawled to reach her side as he died.

"Cahira," Aren breathed. "This is *you.*"

She looked up at him, her eyes wet with tears. "And you."

Felix flew down to settle near the dead boy's head. "Touch their hands," he said softly, "where they would meet. And then clasp your own."

Aren felt cold, but he touched first the boy's forehead and then his hand, and Cahira did the same. Then they looked into each other's eyes, and he knew, fully and clearly now, why he'd always seen the blue of the first dawn in her eyes. She lifted her hand and placed it in his, and when they touched, the petrified figures sank into the sand and disappeared.

Cahira sobbed and pressed her forehead against his hand, and Aren looked up at the sky. Tears streaked his vision. But then he looked eastward on the horizon, and he saw the shadow of a man who once stood there, a man who had been great. A man he had trusted.

Aren breathed a soft word in a voice that was no longer his own. *"Why?"* The shadow faded and disappeared, and in its place, a lone dragonfly hovered, neither real nor illusion. Then it flew off into the east, turning northward before it disappeared.

Aren rose to his feet and drew Cahira with him, and he looked north and east across the sea. "I know what I have to do now, my love." He faced her, then gently kissed her brow. She didn't speak. She knew as well.

"We will return and face Cheveyo."

16

THE DARK MAGE RISES

"You, who were slaves, are now free," said Aren. The two ships had drawn up to the Arch Mage's dock, and the passengers now gathered together on the broken wharf. They looked to Aren as if he were their king, and treated Cahira with the deference given a queen.

"You have delivered us from bondage, my lord," said an elderly man. "We can never repay you, for the gift of freedom is beyond price. But if there is anything you would ask from us, it will be done."

Cahira waited for Aren to say he expected no reward, but to her surprise, he hesitated. "Two of those kittens," he said, and he motioned toward the woman carrying the basket Cahira had noticed earlier. "A male and a female."

The woman beamed and handed him the basket. Aren looked over the five kittens, and turned to Cahira. "Which ones, do you think?"

Cahira peeked in the basket. One kitten with a grayish-brown nose peered back at her. "I like that one."

"That is a male, lady," said the woman. "But don't take

him. His eyes are a bit too golden in shade. Generally we prefer those with blue eyes."

Aren huffed. "We'll take him." He reached into the basket and played with all the kittens. The smallest, with a dark brown nose and tail, licked his finger, then seized his hand with tiny claws. "This one has good spirit!"

"That is a female, lord," said the woman. "She's rather . . . wilder than the others, but she will make a good pet."

Aren beamed with happiness, and Cahira had to restrain herself from pronouncing him *twelve*. He lingered a bit longer with the kittens, patting them and delighting as they squirmed around in play, but then he sighed. "Keep the kittens with you for now, madam, for I go into the wizard's lair. Khadun will guide you northward along the cavern passages. He will bring you to his city of Amon-Daal, and the joy of that land should be healing to your hearts and give hope to your souls."

"My father will be glad of their presence," added Khadun, "for our population has been depleted in recent years, and many dwellings lie empty."

Several ex-slaves regarded Khadun with interest, and Cahira saw hope in their eyes. After Kora, the Guerdian land would seem like paradise. But a few turned to Aren. "We would live with you, my lord, for our people were once kindred."

Aren bowed. "Then go also with Khadun, and from there, seek the Norskland. If I survive, that is where I will return. But there are other lands, other cities, to which by your natures you may yet be drawn. The port city of Amon-Dhen may prove welcoming to some, for the blend of races that dwell there. In Amrodel there may be a home for those who would seek the shelter of trees after lives in a desert."

"And for those who would sample the finest ale," piped up Fareth, "we'll soon be brewing our own Woodlander recipe as well as the darker Norsk stout! Seek out the Hungry Cat Tavern if you're in the Woodland—"

"And the Snow Pony Inn when you reach Eddenmark," added Ranveig. "With luck, we'll be there to greet you!"

Aren turned to the two innkeepers. "You, my friends, may also wish to depart, and go with Khadun to Amon-Daal. There is no need for you to brave wizard's lair."

Cahira said nothing, but she knew their response. Elphin looked at Aren and voiced it: "We stand with you, my lord, as you have always done with us."

"None of you can stand against the wizard, Elphin," Aren warned.

"We know that, my lord. But we will stand with you all the same."

"Through the Hall of the Wizard," said Rika, and she smiled.

"We are your brethren," agreed Fareth. "Our shadows all faded in those desert sands, and we have risen to stand with you now. We'll not leave you."

"This task falls to you, my lord," said Thorleif, "but we stand with you, whatever comes, to fall as you fall, or to go on to whatever reward yet awaits us."

Ang Gelu stepped forward and faced Aren, after pausing and glancing at Rika, who pretended not to notice. "I have lived the life of a slave, and for the hope and dignity you have restored, I would also stand at your side."

Aren nodded, clearly moved. Looking between them slowly, one to the next, he bowed. "My friends, I am honored to have you with me."

He faced Cahira and she smiled, though her eyes were full of tears. "And I am with you," she said, "always."

Aren looked up at the south face of the wizard's cliff. Many levels and balconies once lined that wall, but most had caved in and fallen into disrepair. One near the top had once been grand, formed in a great arch with intricate reliefs, but it had crumbled, too, and instead of a once splendid palace, the wizard's lair appeared like a giant tomb.

To the right of the old opening, and lower, Cahira saw the

narrow passage that led to the Arch Mage's tomb. Something moved within, a flash of color, then disappeared. "Shaen, at least, awaits us," she said. The sight of her nemesis depressed Cahira's mood, and the joy of the past days vanished.

Aren turned to the former slaves and bowed. "Go now, and follow Khadun. Hurry through the catacombs, for I do not know what devastation this battle may bring. Go with peace and with hope, and may your hearts find strength for the journey."

They bowed to him in turn, and some wept, and others kissed his hand. They all bowed to Cahira and the others as well, then departed. Cahira watched them file up the winding path until they disappeared into the western catacombs.

"Do you think Shaen will do anything to stop them?" she asked.

"Her interest is here," said Aren, and he gestured to the tomb.

Cahira glanced up, and Shaen appeared again, this time deliberately. She had changed from her Guerdian dress and now wore a long, flowing gown of what appeared to be green velvet. It had wide sleeves, and her hair hung artfully loose around her shoulders.

Fareth looked up at her and snorted. "Somehow, she's managed to garb herself like the ancient Woodland queen—or at least, like she was depicted in our palace murals."

Thorleif shuddered. "That's a bit disturbing, somehow. Dressing like a dead lady? How did she get the clothes—pick them out of some old tomb?"

"Most likely," said Aren.

Felix sat positioned on Thorleif's shoulder, where he'd spent the greater part of the voyage east. Oddly, the boy hadn't complained, and Cahira had seen him sharing both his flask and his bread with the bat. "Might have plucked that gown off a pile of bones, true," the bat said brightly, "but more likely she found some old store that the Arch Mage kept for his lover. I'd guess Shaen's been prowling all over the place, prying into every nook seeking remnants of the woman she longs to supplant—to *become* Aryana."

"What happened to Aryana?" Aren asked quietly. "What was her fate?"

"Well, she died!" said Felix with a huff.

"I know that," said Aren. "How?"

" 'Tis said she stood in that very arch, that one you see crumbled, in that room where she had faced her lover's betrayal, and learned that he intended to, somehow, absorb her energy and take her power into himself. He commanded that she submit, and instead, she backed out onto what once was a wide balcony. She recited a spell that is forgotten by all but a few, gave up her life, and let herself fall into the raging sea below."

"That is a grim fate," said Aren, gazing into the high, crashing waves.

"Aye, but it is said that as her body fell into the water, a lavender dragonfly arose from the surf, and that sign inspired the Woodland Elites. They surrounded the Arch Mage, and their power surged and threatened to overcome him, for he weakened when she was lost. With what remained of his dark alliance, he went down into the catacombs and placed himself in an enchantment that could only be broken by the return of her *ki* to his tomb."

"Then it must return, at last, and free him from his slumber," said Aren. "Cheveyo, I think, has waited long enough."

They ascended the winding stairs and entered into the dark catacombs, where they quietly set out their gear. Fareth and Ranveig positioned their equipment by the far corridor, and the others set their packs beside it. Ranveig looked around. "Once you're done with the wizard," he said thoughtfully, "we'll have to come this way to reach the passage back to Amon-Daah—assuming this battle doesn't bring down the whole cavern, that is."

"I will try my best to avoid it," Aren promised. He placed his Norsk axe carefully with the rest of the gear and sighed. "I suppose this will be of no use during this battle."

Cahira patted his shoulder. "When we visit Amrodel, we will ask Damir to place an enchantment on your axe, to keep it from all harm."

Aren considered, then nodded. "A good plan. I will do that."

She smiled and gazed into his eyes, savoring the last calm before the storm they must soon enter. His beard had started its regrowth on the journey home, and though the sight of his face had stunned her with its beauty, she realized she had grown to love the beard like the man. "Keep it trimmed though, will you?" she asked suddenly.

His brow furrowed, but then he laughed. "As my lady wishes," he replied, giving a bow. Then he looked at her as if he could hold the moment forever. "I love you, Cahira. That love is forever. We have that, no matter what happens in that cavern."

"I will follow my heart," she whispered, "as I follow you."

Aren's company left all but their weapons, then prepared to join him on the walk to the Arch Mage's tomb. He looked between them, and he smiled. "When we enter that room, those blades will be of no use against the wizard," he reminded them, "nor Fareth, your skillet, either."

"I feel better just holding it," said the innkeeper, and Cahira smiled.

"Somehow it makes me feel better, too," she said.

"As for myself," spoke up Rika, "my axe is for the Woodland wench, Shaen, lest she annoy me in any way."

"Fair enough," said Elphin.

Felix hopped from Thorleif to Cahira's shoulder. "Well, lass, this is it! All paths have led to this place, and the time has come."

Cahira took a deep breath, then straightened her spine. She slung her bow over her shoulder, then looked into Aren's amber eyes. "I am ready," she said, and then they all walked westward to the tomb of the Mage.

The air grew hot and still and hung heavy with silence except for the sound of their footfalls. Aren walked beside

Cahira, but they both faced ahead, sure of what they had to do. They reached the door to the tomb, where Bodvar and Aren had fought, and stopped. The door was ajar, the rusted latch broken. An old mace lay cast aside by the wall.

"Well, she certainly picked *that* off a body!" commented Thorleif. "And she found her way in, anyway."

Aren turned to Cahira. "You know what to do now."

"I will wait for your signal."

Aren nodded to Fareth, who pulled back the heavy door. Aren walked in, and the others followed, all except Fareth, who remained at the door.

"Aren!" Cahira heard Shaen's delighted voice call from within the room, and she frowned. "Allow me to welcome you to the chamber of the Arch Mage!"

"In his absence, you might speak in his name," said Aren casually. "But I would prefer to gain welcome from the wizard himself."

"By all means," Shaen agreed, and smacked her lips. Cahira had always found that habit grating, and no more than this moment. Shaen spoke again. "But I think we both know that his welcome requires a 'key.' Or should I say, the *ki* of a pretty Mage?"

Cahira felt sure that Aren rolled his eyes, for he didn't respond to Shaen's comment. "Fareth," he called, and the innkeeper turned to Cahira.

"It is time, lass. Are you ready?"

Cahira peeked at Felix, and the bat nodded. "His energy will respond to yours as soon as you walk in. Stand tall, and it will not harm you."

"I understand," said Cahira. She drew a breath, then closed her eyes. In her mind, she saw the image of a dragonfly. She opened her eyes, then walked to the threshold.

A large, granite sarcophagus sat at the center of an oblong room. Tall columns reached to the domed ceiling, and at the far end of the chamber, a narrow window opened to the sea beyond. Shaen stood at the head of the sarcophagus, dressed in a long, flowing gown, and with a silver circlet on her head that seemed fit for a queen. She beamed with triumph as she saw Cahira in the doorway.

"Welcome, Cahira. Come in. *He* awaits you."

Cahira turned her gaze to Aren. He stood facing the sarcophagus, his sword still sheathed. The others stood behind him. He looked to Cahira and smiled, then nodded gently. She took a breath, then entered the cavern. As soon as her foot touched the first wide stone, the room rumbled. The walls shook, and the sarcophagus began to break apart. The floor cracked, and a column crashed down. Shaen screamed and backed away, but the others remained silent and motionless.

Cahira went to Aren's side and took his hand as they waited. The mountain itself seemed to shake, and a low groan erupted from the chasm at their feet. The sound grew until it became a deafening roar—stones shattered, and the sarcophagus burst free, crashing down into the yawning gap. From the pit came a great cloud of ash and debris puffing upward like a cloud.

"It is like my nightmares," Cahira whispered, but she couldn't close her eyes to blot out the terror.

The dust turned black, as if soaked in evil, and sparks of energy burst everywhere as a new cloud followed the first, violent energy lashing out like flames. Cahira trembled, but did not look away. She heard Shaen's sharp breaths from across the room, gasps and small shudders that signaled the woman believed her time at last was at hand, and yet she seemed overcome by that reality.

Amidst the ash and whirling debris, a dark form emerged. Blacker than night it appeared, but as it rose, Cahira saw that it had human shape. It appeared as the figure of a man, and as the cloud parted, the shape became clearer. He wore a great black cape, which rippled in the whirlwind around him, revealing a lining of dark red satin.

It was her nightmare, become real before her eyes. Yet now the details were also clear. "Not blood and flame, but red cloth!" she exclaimed. Her voice was swallowed by the throbbing roar that filled the cavern.

Aren must have heard her, however, because he nodded as he watched the creature before him rise. In her nightmares, the figure appeared hooded, but now she saw that it was the back of his head she faced, and what she'd thought to be a dark hood was instead long black hair that fell past wide shoulders.

The wind stilled, the cloud of dust dissipated, and the roaring eased. But when the creature tipped back his head, his voice came louder and more chilling than any sound preceding. He roared like a beast, wounded and ravenous, blinded by pain. The sound of his rage took was a name, and he called out with all the fury of his soul: *"Aryana!"*

The name of the Woodland queen echoed through the room. "Aryana Daere is dead," said Cahira. Her voice was calm and even, and when she spoke, the rumbling in the room stopped. "She fell an age ago."

The Arch Mage turned his head, slowly, toward the sound of her voice. Cahira caught her breath—she looked upon a face of such surpassing beauty that only one other compared. But a vast wisdom lit Aren's amber eyes, and his beauty was strong and clear like the sun rising at dawn. The being that stood before her reflected the dark of night lit by a single star.

Beside her, Aren drew a harsh breath and then, despite the darkness and terror of the Arch Mage's rising, he suddenly laughed. "Well, you were right, Cahira. He is hideous!"

Cahira found herself smiling, despite the terrifying power that emanated from the great Mage. She looked at Aren, and peace returned unexpectedly to her heart.

"Cahira . . ." The Arch Mage spoke, his voice low and wondrous, faintly accented with the lilt of Kora.

From the corner of her eye, Cahira saw Shaen step trembling toward the risen Mage. "Matchitehew," she breathed. "Don't be afraid. I'm here."

The Arch Mage stepped down from the broken rock, approached Cahira. "I sent for you. You came," he said.

"I came, but not because you called." Cahira held herself tall as she faced him. "I came to end this dark force you have sent against my people, and the plague of negative energy that emanates from this cavern."

His dark brow arched and a smile flickered on his full lips. "You are . . . her heir?" He spoke slowly, like a man newly risen from a dream.

"Obviously," said Cahira. "Since you've risen up out of the shadows."

He bowed, but his smile remained, and his dark eyes seemed to grow in focus and depth as he looked into her face. He reached for her and touched her cheek—his fingers were cold, yet she felt life within him. "I see her face in yours."

Cahira pulled back. "You look for your old lover, but she is gone. I am but a distant descendant of her younger sister."

"Passable fair, her sister was, too," interrupted the Arch Mage idly. "Too fair, perhaps, for the seed of a lover entered her womb before I could summon her to my side." He shrugged. "But no matter." He held out his hand. "Come. I have waited long, and when I draw you into myself and take all that you are as my own, my destiny will be complete."

He spoke as calmly as if he'd suggested breakfast, and he turned away slightly as if he expected her to take his hand and accompany him to this marital suite where he would devour her soul. Cahira stood speechless, but Aren stepped forward.

"A fate less fair awaits you, Cheveyo." He laid his hand on the Dragonfly Sword, but he didn't draw it.

The Arch Mage turned back, his brow furrowed as he looked from Aren's face to Cahira, and back at Aren again as if puzzled. "Who calls me by that name?"

Aren moved in front of Cahira, and he bowed once, then faced his enemy. "I am Aren, son of Arkyn, chieftain of the Norsk."

The Arch Mage's brow angled. "What are Norsk?"

"My people live in the ice lands far to the north," said Aren. "But in your time, a few of my kin dwelt in your land as slaves. To them, you were known as Cheveyo, the Spirit Warrior, and for a long while, they placed great faith in you."

Cheveyo's eyes darkened like smoldering coals. "That name has no meaning for me now! The past died with it!"

"But for those who remember," said Aren, "it lives."

"He prefers to be called 'Matchitehew,'" said Shaen, and she moved more boldly toward the Arch Mage's side, positioning herself facing Aren. "It meant 'evil heart' in his land, but that is merely their perception of a power so much greater than their own. People fear what is beyond them." She paused and gazed up at him adoringly. "But I do not, for I accept it—and all the unique demands that go with such a vast force."

For the first time, Cheveyo noticed Shaen. His dark eyes flashed with anger when he saw the dress she wore. "You wear *her* dress!" he hissed.

Shaen placed her hand at her throat and smiled. "I wore it to honor you."

"You wore it to hide in her shadow," said Cheveyo. "You have failed."

"You were right about one thing, Shaen," Cahira laughed. "He is handsome. But it doesn't look like he'll be showering you with gratitude anytime soon."

"He doesn't understand yet how much I've done for him." Shaen reached out, but the Arch Mage eyed her hand as if it were something to be struck away. "It is true that I come from lowly beginnings, and I stand here trembling before you. But it was I who found the means of your awakening."

He eyed her doubtfully for a moment. "No one awakened me. It took an age for me to summon enough power to reach the Woodland, and longer still for a female Mage to be born, one related to my betrayer." He paused and sighed as if weary. "All that time passed without even one. Male Mages, female Mundanes! Then at last, three appeared in succession—Eliana, this maiden, and if this one failed, there was still Eliana's daughter. I am pleased not to have to wait for the third." He cast a dark look at Shaen again. "'Awakened,' indeed!"

"So much for that," said Cahira brightly. "I guess it wasn't your doing, after all, Shaen."

Shaen's lips tightened, but somehow she managed a smile. "Perhaps he isn't aware of exactly what transpired."

Cheveyo's brow angled and his dark eyes flickered. "I sent out a Mage from the land of Amrodel—a male who was weak and easily bent to my will. There were few in that land as malleable as he, unfortunately, and he was the best I could do." He paused and his lip curled in distaste. "Like a fool, he directed my great force into a creature. It had considerable brawn, but I could have done better with an ox or a bull."

"That creature was my brother," Aren said coldly, and Cheveyo glanced at him without interest.

"Yes, I'm not surprised, for you resemble him."

From the back of the cavern, Thorleif issued a derisive snort. "The chieftain looks absolutely nothing like Bruin the Ruthless. Lacking in perception, he is, my lord. Best to get this over and be done with him."

Cheveyo glanced at Thorleif, then turned to Cahira. "You brought more of these creatures? What use are they?"

"They have a wisdom greater than yours, if you think Aren is anything like his brother!" Cahira replied fiercely.

Cheveyo's brow angled. "The hair on their heads is pale, like the desert sands under a blazing sun. Their bodies are large, and their capacity for thought appears so . . . limited."

"You really are a fool," muttered Cahira. She nodded to Aren. "Thorleif is right—fight him and be done!"

Cheveyo laughed. "You cannot expect this"—he waved his hand absently—"descendant of slaves to battle me!" Yet when he spoke, his voice quavered slightly, whether at the prospect of battle, or at the mention of Aren's heritage, Cahira couldn't guess.

"They have come here to destroy you," offered Shaen. "He

carries a sword crafted by Damir ap Kora, who convinced poor Cahira that it would give its bearer the strength to defeat you."

"You are wrong about even that!" Cahira glared at Shaen. "Damir's sword responds to the light and power of the one who wields it. The strength is within Aren, and it moves from his heart *into* that blade."

Shaen looked blank, but Cheveyo eyed the sheathed sword with interest. "Damir . . . I know that name. Eliana whispered it far too often. Damir claimed her from me, thanks to the failure of that weak Mage and his brute, and her energy was lost to me."

"Her energy now lies frozen in Amrodel!" Cahira longed to seize her bow and simply shoot him. "You trapped all of them, put them to sleep!"

"Yes, of course," he replied, and she saw a vestige of his fabled cruelty and malice. "And there they lie, helpless, while you have made your way to my side. No such lover appeared for you, so I see that you stand here before me, a maiden untarnished and fair, and with the *ki* of a Mage." He paused. "Yet yours is a strange *ki,* like none I have known."

Cahira rolled her eyes and glanced at Felix. "If even the Arch Mage doesn't recognize the nature of my *ki,* it must be flawed indeed."

"Not flawed, lass," said Felix. "Rare."

Cheveyo glanced without interest at the bat, then fixed his attention back on Cahira. "The sword of Damir ap Kora will fail. Give yourself to me, and your power will live forever."

"You have no power over me." Cahira moved closer to Aren. "You cannot touch me, for I am guarded by Damir's shield, and even you cannot breach it while he lives."

"Ah . . . But even now, his life ebbs away," said Cheveyo, and his malice was evident. "Farther and farther he drifts, and soon it will be a sea too wide for him—or any of them—to cross."

"My son lies among them, you demon!" Elphin leapt forward unexpectedly, tears glittering on his face.

Cheveyo waved his hand, and Elphin reeled back as though he'd been struck. He fell against a column, staggered, then charged toward the Arch Mage again. Rika grabbed him and pulled him back. She looked into his eyes and spoke quietly, and Elphin relented.

"Matchitehew's will rolls over all in its path," bragged Shaen, as if it was her own power she glorified. "We cannot expect him to concern himself over the fates of those so much weaker than himself."

Cahira glanced at Cheveyo. He seemed to accept Shaen's words, but took no pleasure in them; and the shadow around him grew. "Just out of curiosity," Cahira asked, "have you been tormenting her dreams as you did mine and Eliana's?"

Shaen froze and her dark eyes burned, and Cahira knew the answer. Yet still did Shaen protest: "I hear him always! I am closer to him than mere speech allows."

"I know nothing of this female," said Cheveyo dismissively. "My *ki* is fixed on you, maiden, and before that, on the one Damir denied me, for you are strong and the power of life flows freely through you. That is my desire . . . to conquer that force and bend it to my will."

"I told you he'd want a female equal, and not one groveling in darkness," crowed Felix, and the bat sounded smug.

"He will need my support and my sympathy, I'm afraid," said Shaen, "when he realizes that Cahira has betrayed him."

Cheveyo's dark gaze shifted to her. "You lie."

"I would never willing cause you pain, my lord, but it is true," said Shaen, and she pressed her lips together as if deeply grieved. "Cahira has taken this Norskman as a lover. Like her ancestor and Eliana, she has betrayed you—but I'm afraid it was to be expected. These are willful women who think only of themselves, and their passions are so unpredictable!"

Cheveyo fixed his attention on Cahira. "This cannot be so. I sensed no such deed!"

"But you didn't sense Aren at all, did you?" Cahira asked quietly. "You can't, even now. You don't know what he is, nor how strong. And you have no idea why."

Her words hit the mark, and Cheveyo's eyes lit with anger. "He is nothing, no one! If he dared touch you, I would know it."

"He's done more than touch me. And you didn't know, because he is beyond your sight."

"You have learned to mask your *ki*. That is why you were able to hide from me."

"I lay in his arms, and his power protected me."

"That is not possible!"

Shaen moved toward the Arch Mage, emanating sympathy, and she placed her hand on his arm. "You must try to accept it, Matchitehew," she said with the gentleness of a sharp blade aimed at the heart. "I tried, desperately, to keep her safe from his dark seduction, but Aren played on her emotions—and she is such a determined, strong-willed girl! And I'm afraid she gave in to his primitive demands, and has indeed lost her virtue."

Cahira chuckled. "He gave in to a few of my demands, too."

Cheveyo looked at her in horror. "I demanded that you appear to me untarnished!"

Cahira returned his furious gaze. "You have no right to demand anything. And I am not 'tarnished' for joining with the man I love, for I have given him my heart—as once our queen gave her heart to you."

"I wanted nothing of her heart! Her power, that is what I sought," he insisted, but Cahira's brow arched.

"Yet you care when another dons her attire?"

"It is an insult to me," he replied hastily.

"You didn't love Aryana, then?"

"Not at all." He hesitated. "She was a beautiful creature, sweet to the touch, quick to my bed. But love? Never! There is no such emotion in me—only the desire for power."

Cahira stared at him, then shook her head in disbelief. "He's so . . . determinedly evil," she said quietly.

"What did you expect?" called Elphin from his position by the rear columns. "That the one known as 'Evil Heart' might be kind and sentimental?"

"No," she agreed. But then her brow puckered. "It's just that he's trying so hard."

Cheveyo frowned. "There is no good in me, maiden. It's a fool's hope to imagine otherwise."

"Are you trying to convince me, or yourself?" Cahira asked. His dark eyes flashed.

"Foolish woman! My very existence is proof of my power. My will dominates all in my path!" He glanced between her and Aren. "You may have lain with this brute, but you do not bear his seed in your womb, for your *ki* is as yet undivided, and a pregnant woman's energy wraps around her child. Where you place your heart is of no interest to me, an idle fancy doomed to fail."

"Perhaps we failed before," agreed Cahira. "But we have found each other again, and we still love desperately and without end. You may have all the power of the stars, but you do not have that, for you turned it away when it fell within your grasp." She paused. "Have you truly no heart, Cheveyo? I think you do. I think you broke Aryana's heart because your own was wounded."

Energy crackled around him, and Cahira felt his *ki* forming and swelling. "My heart is evil, maiden, black with no light, and in that darkness, I have grasped a power beyond anything you can imagine." He seemed to grow, and he towered over her. "As Damir's life ebbs, your shield fades. Did you know that he struggles to maintain it, and that in so doing, his energy recedes even faster than the others'? The more I threaten you, the sooner he will die."

Cahira shook her head. "No!"

"He's right, lass," said Felix. "Damir attached his life force to yours, and it is fading."

Tears welled in her eyes. "Then I will release the shield and fall," she whispered. "I cannot let him die."

"No, lass!" ordered Felix. "Not yet."

Cahira looked into Cheveyo's dark, angry face. "What can he do to me that I cannot withstand? I have found what I lost an age ago. I have enjoyed true love. He can't hurt me now." And before anyone could comment, Cahira gathered her *ki* and it welled inside her. *"Rhyddhau 'i, Damir, 'i angen ti dim rhagor."*

She felt Damir's resistance. Even now, weakened, he fought to protect her.

"Release me, Damir, I need you no more!" But still he refused.

A wild cry tore from Cahira, a force from deep in her heart. It welled and burst and the winds from the sea blew through the window and whirled around her. The energy she had summoned in Aren's Great Hall was as nothing compared to the power that surged around her now. Her cry shook the columns, and rocks fell from the domed ceiling. She screamed with a primal force until the cavern rumbled and threatened to collapse.

The energy sparkled around her, and through its glittering haze she saw Aren looking at her in wonder. *"I* choose," she said, and her voice came like that of a goddess. At the same time, a soft voice, faraway, spoke in her thoughts, and the sound was filled with joy. *"I release you, for your choice is pure."*

Damir's shield departed, and Cahira sank to her knees. But her own power remained strong, and she rose again to face Cheveyo.

His eyes glowed in triumph. He moved toward her like a desert cat descending upon its prey. "Now you are mine, and the power of my darkness will be complete!"

That was when she heard the slow glide of metal, of a blade against its sheath. The Dragonfly Sword was drawn.

17

BATTLE FOR A SOUL

Aren gripped the white sword, and it shone in the dim cavern like a torch. Cahira turned and walked to him as if entranced. The glittering aura she had summoned still glowed around her, and he knew that he saw her now as she truly was, ancient and wise, powerful beyond measure. The magical bond between them was visible now, and it reached from her heart to his, entwined both, and circled back.

She held up her hand and he raised his own, and their fingers entwined like the magic. "I am with you," she breathed. "All that I am, forever." As she spoke, her energy seemed to pour into and encircle him, and then she sank to her knees and smiled. "I am with you."

The cord of magic disappeared from Aren's view, but it was not gone. He looked down into her face, and love filled his heart. "For we were one before we were two," he replied.

He turned to face the Arch Mage, holding up the white sword as a flame of light crested its blade. Cheveyo met his challenge, dark eyes blazing. The wizard smiled, as if by defeating Aren he could conquer all the world. He backed up to the yawning pit where the sarcophagus had lain, and he reached his arm downward. From below, a black sword rose. He seized its hilt, and flames sizzled to life along the blade.

"So it begins," said Felix, but Aren kept his gaze fixed on Cheveyo.

"Dark against light," Aren said. "Will this battle prove which of us is stronger, or which is more complete?"

"My darkness endures no light, and you will fall before it. You are no Mage! Death awaits you, and despair forever after."

Aren smiled and strode toward the wizard. "But you, Cheveyo, face something far worse than death and despair. Doubt—the cruel, lingering agony of a single star that shines upon you, that you have never been able to destroy."

Cheveyo roared with fury, and he swung back his flaming black sword and slashed toward Aren. But the white sword did not fail, and Aren deflected the blow. He shoved Cheveyo back. The wizard dove at him again, and the two blades clashed like thunder in the cavern. The walls shook.

Over and over Cheveyo lashed out at Aren, relentless, like lightning in a storm upon the sea, violently raging against an impenetrable cliff. But nothing the wizard did, no power, no force, touched Aren, nor drove him back, nor even deflected the white sword. That shone brighter and brighter, and for its power, Cheveyo had no answer.

The wizard backed away, his sword a dark flame in his hand. *"What are you?"* he asked, his beautiful voice soaked with mingled anger and awe.

Aren held his sword up before his body. "Damir asked me that once, long ago," he replied. "And I told him what I tell you now." He took a step forward, and Cheveyo stepped back again. "I am Aren—"

"You are nothing, no one!" Cheveyo moved behind the black pit, and Aren followed. His gaze never wavered from the Arch Mage's dark eyes.

"—Son of Arkyn—"

Cheveyo bounded to the far side of the pit. "You cannot defeat me!"

Aren leapt after him. "—chieftain of the Norsk."

Cheveyo raged, then swung his black sword against Aren, but Aren met the desperate flurry blow for blow. As they fought, the flames along the black sword receded and dimmed, until it was just a dark blade. A small light formed in it, a reflection of the Dragonfly Sword.

"You are no Mage," repeated Cheveyo as he staggered back. "What are you?"

"Haven't I told you that twice already?" Aren asked, but then he looked into the wizard's eyes, and beyond fury, he saw an endless agony, and in the power that still burned inside Cheveyo's heart, he felt a great pain, as if a cry had begun an age ago, and its echo still lingered undimmed and undaunted, unanswered.

Aren held the wizard's gaze, and he knelt before Cheveyo. He braced the white sword in front of his knee, his hands on the hilt. "I am called Aren, but you know me from another time, in another guise."

"No . . ." Cheveyo's voice was ragged and torn as he bit back the bitterness he had swallowed ages before. "I do not know you."

Aren looked up at him and the horror in the Arch Mage's face grew. "I am called Aren, but within my soul lies a memory and a shadow, the shadow of a boy who sailed his small ship north over the sea and back, a boy who trusted your promise of freedom for those in bondage. Do you remember, Cheveyo? I was a boy who loved a girl, and who watched as you faced your enemies and sent your wrath against them, not caring that our little huts lay between, nor that we called to you and begged for your aid. . . ."

Cheveyo recoiled in shock and in pain, shaking his head as if Aren's words dealt him a blow more grievous than any blade. He dropped his dark sword and it clattered to the floor at his feet.

"My love died in your wrath, and I crawled to her side. Before I followed her into oblivion, I looked up at you, my hero, my friend, and I spoke one word . . . *'Why?'*"

"No!" Cheveyo groaned in agony, as if his heart was torn asunder. "You cannot be. It cannot be!"

Aren held his tortured gaze, and his heart was moved with a pity greater than any he had ever known. "I am Aren, son of Arkyn . . ." He bowed his head once, then met Cheveyo's eyes again. "And I forgive you."

The Arch Mage trembled, the room stilled, and silence filled the air.

Cahira knelt beside Aren, and she looked up into the wizard's face, smiling gently. "I am Cahira Daere, the last Mage of Amrodel. I was a girl who loved a boy, and I fell to your hand. And I forgive you."

Fareth knelt near Cahira and his gaze met the wizard's, and his face was kind. "I am Fareth of Amrodel, innkeeper of the Hungry Cat Tavern. I sold corn and roots in a hut by the sea, and I fell to your hand. And I forgive you."

One by one, the others followed, their voices low and haunting, a chant and a prayer. "I am Ranveig, son of Eirik the Fat, keeper of the Snow Pony Inn. I was a fishmonger, and I fell to your hand. And I forgive you."

"I am Rika, daughter of Rognvald. I was a mother of many children, and I fell to your hand." Her bright, warrior's eyes locked with Cheveyo's, and a soft smile gentled her beautiful face. "And I forgive you."

"I am Thorleif of Eddenmark, and I was a boy who played in the sea—I fell to your hand. And I forgive you."

Last, Elphin knelt beside Rika, and he bowed before speaking, his face wet with tears. "I am Elphin, horse-master of Amrodel and father to a Mage Child who lies in your grasp. I was a fishing boy who fell to your hand." His voice caught, but then his expression cleared and he met Cheveyo's shocked gaze with a smile. "And I forgive you."

Cheveyo stood immobile, his face stricken. Then, slowly, like a soft mist rising from the sea at dawn, a tear formed in his eye and fell down his strong, beautiful face. And then another, and another. He sank to his knees and his head bowed low, and he wept silently as they waited. Moisture misted Aren's own eyes, and beside him, Cahira softly cried; but she did not look away.

The Arch Mage looked up toward the ceiling—or beyond—and he spoke hoarse words in the tongue of Kora. "The Mages," he said with effort, "are released. They are free."

A piercing, horrified scream rent the room, and Aren leapt up and looked around to see Thorleif, his hand clasped over his heart as if he might faint.

"It's a man!" the young Norseman cried, and pointed to where Felix had perched. Aren gaped in wonder at the old man adjusting his dark green tunic and fiddling with his gray hair, seated on the broken column where the bat had been.

"Madawc!" Cahira leapt to her feet and ran to the wizard, then hugged him, laughing through her tears. "What are you doing here? Damir always said you could appear and disappear at will . . ."

"Lass! I have been here all along!"

She drew back and looked at him in wonder. "It was you! You were Felix!"

Madawc nodded, and it occurred to Aren that the bat had been very like the Mage all along. He should have guessed.

"That I was, lass, and no mistake!" Madawc nodded happily to Aren. "This young man called it well, there when we met, by naming me after the Great Mage Felix, Master of Beasts. Pulled it off well, I did. Not a one of you knew!"

"Well . . ." Elphin rose also and smiled. "Why do you think I kept slipping you ale, Elder?"

Madawc's eyes widened in indignation. "You had no idea, lad!"

"Who else would perch on Cahira's shoulder, call her 'Mage Child,' and give orders as you do?"

"I don't believe it." Madawc looked sullen, and even more like the bat into which he'd been transformed.

Fareth laughed heartily, then went to slap the old Mage's shoulder. "I'd have felt a mite better if I'd known—but how did you do it, Elder? And why?"

"I put myself through the transformation before he"—Madawc gestured pleasantly at Cheveyo—"could lay hold of me. Left my body to the Dark Tide, and took off in the body of a higher life form."

"You were the bat," said Thorleif, still stunned. "The bat." He got up and circled Madawc first one way, then the other, then stood before him and stared. "A bat."

Madawc cocked his head to one side. "I am an Elder, and a Mage, boy!"

Thorleif pondered this a while longer, then brightened. "How incredible. What's it like to fly? Do you soar and glide and perch on the tops of trees?"

Madawc's chest expanded slightly, and if he could have perched on Thorleif's shoulder, Aren suspected he would have. "The tops of trees, aye," the Mage agreed. "You all look smaller from on high," he added. "You especially, boy."

"Well, this is a wonder and no mistake!" said Ranveig, standing up to stretch.

"He seems exactly the same as before," said Rika. Then she went over to Ang Gelu and smiled. "Our lives are not always so strange."

The ex-slave grinned, and to Aren's surprise he took Rika's hand in his and kissed it. "I wouldn't have it any other way, fair lady." An almost imperceptible blush crept into the Norskwoman's fair cheeks and her smile turned shy.

"Another has joined us, I think," Aren noted, and he directed everyone's attention to the sorrowful darkness that surrounded Cheveyo. The white sword was glowing, and from its blade, a dragonfly emerged. Cheveyo saw it and his eyes widened. It hovered a moment; then, seeming to fly into his heart, the dragonfly disappeared.

"She has not left you, Cheveyo," whispered Cahira. "She never did."

The Arch Mage looked up, his expression ripe with doubt,

with the renewed fear of one whose frozen heart has begun slowly to thaw. "*She* brought you to me! She *knew*."

"Yes," said Aren. "I believe she did."

A loud snarl cut off any further words. Shaen seethed in the shadows, her face taut with fury. "*She?* The Woodland queen has done this? Just like Eliana, she's maneuvered herself into everything!"

"She protects her love," said Cahira in surprise. "Can't you see that? She couldn't leave him to suffer endlessly."

"He was not suffering," countered Shaen, unable to grasp what had transpired before her. "He suffers now, because you have sought to destroy him. You've used this little magic trick to deflect his power. He could have easily defeated you all!"

"Forgiveness is not a trick, and it's a far greater power than magic," said Cahira. But Shaen only sneered.

Madawc touched Cahira's shoulder. "She can't hear you, lass. She gave her heart over to darkness long ago, and with each choice she's made, the shadows have grown thicker."

"You know nothing of me!" cried Shaen.

"I know I never begged you to study with me!"

"We remember things differently, perhaps," the woman said. "But others encouraged me to believe I might share Eliana's *ki*."

The old Mage snorted derisively. "You coveted another's life, her existence—even her heritage," he countered. "You are intuitive, I'll give you that. Intuitive enough to know that Damir ap Kora was in love with The Fiend, and wouldn't give you the time of day."

"I never wanted Damir!"

"Didn't you now?" Madawc's eye brow angled. "You never once asked me directly if I sensed a Mage's *ki* in you, Shaen. You never asked if I would tutor you. You manipulated and lied and told me 'your friends believed . . .' I wondered what motivated you, because I had never seen another with eyes like yours—with no light within, with no life of your own. All I saw was what you coveted in those stronger than yourself, as Eliana surely was. And in my study, you thought you found a heart of darkness that had all the power you coveted and so bitterly lacked." He paused. "Cheveyo."

"I found evidence of him there, yes," admitted Shaen, and she cast an adoring look from beneath lowered lashes at the stricken Arch Mage. "I knew then that he was my true destiny, my love."

"And the fact that he looks like a dark brother of Damir ap Kora had nothing to do with it? Or that his fabled lover was Eliana's ancestor?"

"I never had true feelings for Damir! It became clear to me at once that Matchitehew was a far greater sorcerer," argued Shaen. Her eyes snapped with hatred, and she waved her hand at Aren. "As for this . . . brute! He cannot compare, though clearly he found some way to manipulate—"

Madawc chortled. "Are you really so blind? None of them, not a one, comes close to this young man's power!" He paused and laughed again, and Aren eyed him doubtfully.

"In this, she may have a point," said Aren. "When Cahira and I found the shells of our past, I knew what had happened. I saw Cheveyo as a shadow in my mind, and I knew his pain, and I knew what I had to do. But I have no 'power' as it were, no—"

"He is no Mage." Cheveyo's deep, hypnotic voice interrupted them and Madawc looked at him in surprise. Then the Arch Mage's gaze fixed on Aren, and he bowed his head. "He is a god."

Aren laughed. "I am no god."

"Aren't you?" asked Cahira with a smile. "I've said that myself."

"In your arms, perhaps," he agreed with a grin, "but the power of the heavens is beyond me."

"The power of the heavens is *in* you, Lord Chieftain. It has been all your life," said Madawc. "Damir saw this, and in some measure, he knew, just as Eliana did. They loved you for your kindness, and then they trusted their lives to you."

"If I have not failed them, that is all I ask," said Aren.

"Humble, isn't he?" said Elphin.

Thorleif eyed his chief, then made a noise with his lips. "Think you'll be wanting a temple in your honor, my lord?" He posed the question earnestly, but Aren groaned and frowned at Cheveyo.

"Did you have to phrase it quite that way?" he asked with a sigh.

"I speak the truth," said Cheveyo, evenly and yet in awe. "In my land, the high priests spoke in hushed voices of those far beyond, spirits ancient and wise. They return at whiles, manifesting in life forms as their energy directs—for simple purposes, it was said: for love of the land, its creatures, their people . . . and each other."

"I have heard those words before," said Cahira. "But not from you . . ."

"Why else does a man live?" asked Aren impatiently, but Madawc smiled.

"For too many reasons besides those, lord, and you know it." The old wizard eyed Thorleif, and shook his head as if tutoring a wayward young pupil. "The Koraji use the term 'god' differently than your people do, boy. Their priests believe that spirits are born continuously, new energy created out of older, and going onward everlasting. Spirits born from the original source of One—one that was really two entwined as one."

"Oh," said Thorleif. Apparently, it wasn't as easy for him to debate the old Mage as it had been the bat.

"Each soul is born with its twin," continued Madawc, "and the two souls are forever connected—sometimes painfully, sometimes in bliss. When Cheveyo says your Chieftain is a god, what he really means is that Aren is an ancient soul, deeply wise, and in command of his own power—as younger beings are not. Therefore, no power of Magery has any control over him."

"I see," said Thorleif, though he sounded confused, and his eyes shifted to one side. "Still, a temple . . ."

"No," cut in Aren firmly, but Cheveyo gazed at Madawc.

"How do you know so much of our teachings, old Mage?"

"I've studied your beliefs, for reasons of my own," said Madawc, and Aren thought the old man seemed a little embarrassed. "It's not so far from our Woodland beliefs, though we don't term older spirits 'gods.'" He paused. "Generally, the old are called 'Elder.'" He paused again, then glanced at Aren. "I am old but not ancient, and I still have much to learn."

"You seem wise to me, Elder," offered Cahira, and he smiled.

"And so I am, lass! But Aren gives more than I am able."

"I don't consider my actions as unusual or extreme," said Aren. He paused, and his memory turned to his brother Bruin dying—a fate Aren hadn't been able to reverse. "Nor have I always been effective in this regard."

Madawc huffed. "Well, you wouldn't consider it unusual, would you, because you're you! But the ancient, the wise, give pity without scorn, generosity without seeking reward. They give help and aid growth, as you did with the brother you loved, and in the end, you saved him from his darkness, whether you know it or not."

"He's right, you know," said Rika softly. "With his dying breath, Bruin named you his heir and chieftain of our people. He loved you, Aren, and he remembered it in the end."

"And you, lass," said Madawc to Cahira, "how you guided your father, whose spirit lacked focus and was so easily lost, how you patiently befriended Eliana and Damir . . . and even put up with an old man's endless lectures because you knew how much he loved to teach. What other Mage sneaked into taverns just to listen to people talk, to delight in their antics while asking nothing taking nothing, save a nip of ale?"

"Me?" asked Cahira in surprise.

Aren touched her hair and eased it over her shoulder. "If I am a god, you are a goddess, my love."

Her brow furrowed. "That doesn't sound right at all."

"Nor to me, either."

"It's for this reason that none of us, even Cheveyo, could read your *ki,* lass," continued Madawc. "It was far beyond ours, because you didn't really need it. You never wanted to shift reality, did you?"

She chewed her lip. "Well, no, not really. I liked archery, though."

"A simple joy, and a direct one," said Madawc. "No ancient soul bothers about shifting reality, because they have seen from a great height, have seen life's many seasons and unending tides. They accept themselves as they are, both positive and negative, night and day."

"But Aryana said Aren is pure light," said Cahira.

"Did he not prove that here?" asked Madawc. "When he defeated Cheveyo, then offered forgiveness instead of a blade?"

"Yes," agreed Cahira, "but Elder, I do not believe Cheveyo is 'pure darkness,' as the prophecy also said."

"Ah, but Aryana did not refer to Cheveyo. The true battle was fought between a man who follows his heart and perceived good in his enemy, and one who has separated from her heart utterly and who lusted for a dark man, never caring how he suffered, even seeking to prevent his redemption. Those two fought for Cheveyo's soul. It was this battle I came to witness, for though I am old, I have much to learn."

Aren turned to Shaen and bowed. "So we met in battle, after all, you and I."

Shaen blazed with hatred, and she wailed an almost inhuman cry. "You have not won! I know what matters most to you, and I will take it!"

Before Aren could react, Shaen ripped Ang Gelu's wide, curved dagger from his hand, lunged and plunged the blade savagely into Cahira's stomach.

Cahira doubled over in agony and blood spilled to the stone floor. Aren reached for his sword, but a blast of dark fire rent the cavern and consumed Shaen. With a last bitter screech of hatred and lingering malice, she succumbed and died. Aren crumpled to the floor sobbing, cradling Cahira in his arms. She gasped in brutal pain.

No one moved, all staring in stunned silence, even Madawc, but Cheveyo came over and knelt before her. He laid his long brown hand over the gaping wound, then spoke soft words in the language of Kora. The blood stopped and the wound closed, then disappeared. Cheveyo sat back, drained, but when he looked up, his tortured soul seemed to have begun healing.

Cahira touched her stomach, but there was no trace left of the wound. "And you call *me* a god?" Aren asked in wonder.

Cheveyo smiled, and the cold, dark beauty of his face gave way to the promise of that vast tenderness he had so long denied. "I was a high priest of Kora, Aren. This skill is taught in our temples." He looked reluctantly back to Cahira's stomach. "Her womb is ripe," he said, and Cahira blushed furiously.

"Oh, thank you so much for announcing that!" she said.

"Is it?" Aren asked.

"Can we discuss this later?"

Madawc went to inspect Shaen's remains. "So, this is the fate she chose," he said, and he shook his head. "I guessed it would be so."

"Did you know the lass was evil, Elder?" asked Fareth.

"I suspected for a long while," answered Madawc. "It was her eyes that drew my notice, as I said to her. Such strange eyes! Taking in all light, and revealing nothing. She was so quick to smile, so quick with a compassionate word, and yet, when she thought no one could see, I would catch her casting a furtive, hidden glance at Eliana, and later Cahira, with such hatred! Jealousy was always her real motivation, not desire or love as she claimed."

"I noticed those looks she gave Eliana, too," said Cahira. "What will become of her soul?"

"All spirits endure, whether good or evil," said Madawc.

"Shaen will go on, a bitter, spiteful energy filled with malice and envy. One day, perhaps, some light in her core will rekindle her heart, and she will find her own path anew. Until that time, her capacity for treachery remains great, even if it's just as a malevolent spirit in the wind. She died cherishing the belief that Cheveyo was her destiny, and perhaps she intuited that another woman will arise to claim him. She attacked you to injure the one who defeated her—Aren—but she aimed for your womb."

"That was vile indeed, and for this reason, I can find no sorrow at her passing," said Cahira.

"My favors had been sought by many," said Cheveyo, "but I have never encountered one so relentless. She was not to my taste at all, for she was weak and without understanding." He paused again. "Though a strong female is no longer to my taste, either, considering . . ."

The Arch Mage started to sit back, but a low, haunting voice filled the room—a woman's voice. "*Cheveyo . . .*"

He sat forward, then rose to his feet. "You!"

Aren looked at him in surprise. "I believe that is Aryana!" he said.

Cheveyo glared. "I know who it is! What do you want, vile maiden?"

Cahira looked over at Aren and rolled her eyes.

"Your appreciation is too much to ask, I suppose," said the voice.

Cheveyo pointed his finger at nothing and glared. "You brought them here! Guided them with your little purple wings and your soft whispers!"

Thorleif looked to Aren, then seated himself on the fallen column. "This is odd beyond measure. No one at home will believe it, you know. He's arguing with an insect—a dragonfly—and one he can't even see!"

Aren shrugged, and Cheveyo paid them no heed. "You left me this way, alone and in such darkness . . ."

"A darkness you crafted yourself! And 'left you?' You threatened to devour my *ki* and render me powerless! I have waited all this time for you to let go of your anger and pain, but no man has ever been as stubborn as you, Cheveyo!"

"Indeed, maiden? Your own nature bears more than a hint of that quality."

"I will return to you," she said softly, and her voice held a hint of teasing. "In another guise than you have seen me before."

"Choose any guise you want, maiden, for I will not be here to see it!" He stormed to the edge of the pit and his black cape rippled in the ocean breeze. Aren stood up but Cheveyo held up his hand. "No interference is welcome here. I will return now to my slumber, and let none of you think to wake me again."

He started to recite a chilling spell, but soft laughter echoed around his words. "You cannot escape me, Cheveyo," she said. "I will come to you and rouse you, whether you will it or not. I have already selected my parents, and will soon begin my growth anew."

"As what?" asked Thorleif to the invisible air.

"As the daughter of gods," said the voice.

"I think we're going to have a baby," said Aren, and a smile grew on his face as he considered the prospect.

"And I guess it will be a girl," added Cahira. "Well, well!"

"I must go now into meditation to prepare," said the voice.

"Can we name you 'Aryana,' for simplicity's sake?" asked Cahira.

"As you wish," said the voice, and it faded, then disappeared like a sigh.

Cheveyo's face lit with indignation, and he continued his chant. A soft gray cloud rose up from the pit and enveloped him, then cradled him gently, and lowered him from their view.

Aren went to the edge of the pit, but he saw only darkness below. He sighed heavily, then laid the Dragonfly Sword flat, and dropped it into the pit after Cheveyo. "He will need it more than I," he explained when Cahira peered in after it. The light of the white sword faded from view, but Aren knew that the time of Cheveyo's night had passed, and he would lie in darkness and pain no longer.

"Was that truly Aryana's voice we heard?" Cahira asked Madawc.

"It sounded like her voice, aye," said Madawc.

"'Sounded? I haven't exactly heard her before—more a whisper in a dream," said Cahira. "Has she spoken to you?"

"Once, long ago," said Madawc.

"Why have you said nothing?"

"It was not a time I like recalling, lass. I was a young man, and broken-hearted," admitted Madawc, "though you might not imagine such a thing being possible."

Cahira looked at him kindly. "I could, easily, Elder. You are a man of great heart. I guess it was when Damir's mother returned to the wood with her new husband."

"Aye," said Madawc. "And a shock it was, too, for I had thought to ask for her hand upon her return. There she was, the prettiest lass to ever grace the Woodland, at least in my eyes, on the arm of that great, swarthy Mage of Kora. Yet the happiness on her face told me her choice had not been in error."

"What happened? What has this to do with Aryana?"

"I wished her well, and then, lad that I was, I returned to the cottage of my Elder—my own cottage now—and I wept like a child, as if my heart had been ripped from my chest. As I lay there in the depths of my despair, a creature came to me. A dragonfly, it was, and it landed on my pillow. I thought to swat it, but its voice reached my ear."

"She came to you, then? Aryana?"

"Aye, 'twas she, and she told me then that a great destiny would soon unfold, and spoke of my part in it. She said that my true love dwelt in Kora, a woman as like to myself as a sister, and yet as different as night from day."

Cahira nodded thoughtfully. "That might be said of myself and Aren, too."

"Aye, and Eliana and Damir. And the queen herself, and Cheveyo. We are each one, yet separate."

"We were one before we were two," whispered Cahira, and Aren squeezed her hand.

"She told me she would return one day, and become the last child of my tutelage," continued Madawc. "This means, I assume, that the young one you'll soon be carrying will spend time in my study," he added. "And when the time comes when Cheveyo returns to the land of his origin—and he will—she will go with him, though the fires and furies between them may yet run strong. And I will go with her—in a form like to that I chose for my venture with you."

"As a bat? Good!" Cahira bit her lip. "I missed him—you—a bit, I'm afraid." She paused. "Then you may meet your own love, at last!"

"So the queen foretold," he responded quietly. Then he huffed. "An old lass she will be then, and probably very fat."

Cahira's brow puckered. "Does this mean our daughter is destined to reunite with Cheveyo? In twenty years or so?"

Madawc nodded. "That path seems laid before her, aye."

Cahira glanced at Aren. "What will we teach her so that she can hold her own with such a man?"

Aren smiled. "We will teach her to follow her heart and heed its voice, love. And her heart will make clear her path, wherever it leads."

"He will be armed with the Dragonfly Sword if he rises again," Cahira considered.

"And want it even less than I did," said Aren. "His confidence must waver now, and he will doubt his power now that he's fallen once in battle. But to use that sword, he must find that power again—within himself, and not drained from another."

"If he rises again," said Madawc, "it won't be at his own command, but at the call of another. Need will drive her to this cavern, though I cannot foretell the reason. And she will not stand alone, for this I do see: A circle of young companions will surround this tomb, the children of Damir, and your own sons as well. I will be with them, I think. . . . Aye," he added, and he smiled.

"We will have sons?" Cahira clapped her hands and leaned forward eagerly.

"Two, at least, I see," said Madawc. "One with hair as black as night, and eyes like his father's."

"Good! How beautiful! And the other?"

"Like his father in looks, but with your eyes, lass. And both headstrong and proud."

"Both Mages?" she asked, but Aren took her hand and kissed it.

"Do you really want these answers now, love, or will you let life's simple joys unfold on their own?"

Her lips twisted to one side. "I suppose you have a point."

Aren kissed her hand, then turned to the others. "Our quest here is fulfilled, and the wizard's darkness has come to an end. We will travel first to the Guerdian city and retrieve our horses, and rest from our labors. Then we can go on with our lives as we wish, and as our hearts direct."

"A Guerdian dance would suit me well," said Madawc, but then he winked at Aren. "Fine place to start on a little one, too."

Cahira blushed but Aren squeezed her hand.

"What then, my lord?" asked Thorleif.

"Cahira and I will ride to Amrodel, and those of you who wish may join us."

"And then?" she asked.

"And then, Lady Mage, I would ask the king of Amrodel for your hand, and for his people to ride north with us, where I will host them in my Great Hall. There, before all, we will wed, you and I . . . if you agree."

She put her finger to her lip and her smile widened as he drew her into his arms. "Will you warm me through the long winter nights?" she asked.

"I will warm you," he replied, "through the days as well. In the meadows of summer, and as the golden leaves of autumn fall."

"Then, my Lord Chieftain, since you have had my heart all along, I give you my hand as well."

Epilogue

THE RETURN HOME

They rode over the low, green plains east of Amrodel with the rising of the morning sun. They'd spent three days in Amon-Daal, among the happiest in Cahira's life. The Guerdian king had given them a larger room, which he said was now reserved for the "Prince of Ice and his Princess," and they had made love for hours on end, lingering over each sigh, each touch, and leading each other to new and ever-sweeter levels of passion.

Their company had danced in the courtyard with their hosts, laughed, ate and drank together at the Guerdian tavern, though both Elphin and Thorleif avoided the Guerdian wine this time. Rika and Ang Gelu were clearly falling in love, and went about holding hands. A strange sight, it was, because Rika stood at least a head taller than Ang Gelu, and yet somehow they were so much the same, both proud and practical, with clear minds and strong hearts. Ranveig and Fareth had formed a friendship as well as a prospective business partnership, with a plan to set up a 'Woodland Ice' tavern in the port city of Amon-Dhen, and perhaps several variations along the trade routes soon after. Madawc had agreed to lend his magic into various tavern fixtures, making them an exotic lure to travelers, and he had enlisted Thorleif to do what he termed the 'brawny work,' which had pleased Thorleif's pride to no end.

They had ridden from Amon-Daal westward, stopped for a night at the Lusty Boar Inn, where Aren's people greeted him with joy, though none seemed surprised he had managed "the witch's quest," nor that he had conquered Cahira and claimed her as his bride. Their welcome was accompanied by several challenges, and Cahira had sat cheering as Aren defeated a string of brawny warriors in arm wrestling. She'd seen him as he had been, young and strong, the leader of a strong people who loved life and welcomed its trials with the courage and joy of the sun upon snow, and her happiness was boundless.

They rode south to the port city of Amon-Dhen, where Cahira investigated its many shops, and selected a large assortment of tiny clothes for the baby she now felt certain grew within her. She had felt no signs of pregnancy yet, but she and Aren had certainly given it ample opportunity.

In Amon-Dhen, they walked hand in hand along the shore as he studied the waves with a critical eye, then at last pronounced them navigable, much to her dismay. He had already planned a trip back to the mountains, where he planned to retrieve "his ship," and sail it northward to the port city. Thorleif and Elphin eagerly agreed to go with him as crew, and Cahira miserably insisted she, too, must accompany him as the bow ornament, since he felt her capacity to obey his commands was limited and she still hadn't learned his many nautical terms, thanks to paying no attention to his instruction while focusing on the glow of his eyes as he laid out his journey.

Cahira gazed at him as they rode along together. The horses Pip and Zima had formed a bond during their stay in the Guerdian stables, and now walked easily together, though Zima still stole Pip's meals when Pip wasn't looking, and he did little things to antagonize her, like stretching out his nose just enough to edge past her. He did this now, and Zima lengthened her stride to pull past him. They were about to break into an unsolicited trot, but Aren halted Pip and pointed into the west.

"It seems a great host awaits us!" he said.

Cahira looked up and saw a vast line of riders, and some walking on foot, coming toward them from the orchards that lined Amrodel's eastern border. The morning sun shone on the approaching host, and to her surprise, she saw many golden-haired Norsk among the dark Woodlanders. Cahira spotted Damir and Eliana riding at their fore. She cried out in joy, then galloped Zima over the meadows to meet them.

Aren and the others followed, and the gallop became a race. Damir and Eliana had dismounted and they waited together as Cahira charged toward them. She leapt from Zima's back, shouted, "I win!" to Aren, then ran to Damir and Eliana and hugged them as tears flowed down her cheeks.

Elphin dismounted, too, and walked as if spellbound into the crowd. His wife, Cahira's sister, went to him, their son in her arms. Neither spoke. They just looked at each other, tears shimmering in their eyes. Elphin took his son and hugged him close, and Cahira knew his journey was now truly complete.

Damir looked down into her face, and his dark eyes glimmered with tears. "You did it. I knew you would, little one. Even without my shield at the ending. . . ."

She fidgeted, then shook her head. "Cheveyo said you were dying. I had to let it go."

Eliana looked at Damir, aghast, then turned to Cahira. She touched Cahira's cheek, then hugged her again. "Then I thank you doubly, my friend, for that is a loss I could not endure."

Aren came up beside Cahira and stood quietly, but Eliana's green eyes filled with tears as she looked at him. She went to him and beamed with the pride of a mother whose son has returned in a triumph long expected, but cherished nonetheless. "Aren," she whispered, "you're so tall. And so handsome." She patted his cheek as if he were a small boy again, though she had to stand on tiptoes to reach him. Aren hugged her, then smiled gently.

"Lady Eliana, it heals my heart to see you renewed and well." He looked to the small boys standing beside Damir, and the little girl holding a cloth frog, and he smiled. Bronwyn stepped shyly toward him and held her frog out to him.

"You woke us, great hero," she said formally. "For all gifts, there must be sacrifice, so I present to you this token of my esteem."

Aren knelt before her and took the frog. He adjusted its tiny frock coat, then held it against his heart. "A hero could not take a child from its parent," he told her gravely. "He might ask, instead, for a like gift to be made for his own child, so that when that child is born, she has a fine friend for her bed."

"Mother and I will make another frog, as my Green Frog's brother, perhaps!" said Bronwyn happily, and she retrieved her toy from Aren's hand.

He smiled and stood, but tears returned to Cahira's eyes as she watched him with the little girl. She had been unusually emotional of late, and Eliana looked at her in surprise.

"Are you all right, Cahira?" she asked gently.

Cahira sniffed and nodded, but Damir's two sons approached Aren, looked up at him in wonder, then directed their shining gazes to his Norsk axe. "You're even bigger than the others!" said the eldest boy, Tarian, and the younger, Damek, nodded vigorously.

"That's a fine axe!" he added eagerly. "We have swords that our father made—they're magical, you know. Better than axes, I think."

"I have seen that," said Aren, but he seized his axe from his belt as their eyes widened in glee. "But to wield an axe, you must be quick"—he swung it in an arc—"and be alert for foes, for they could be anywhere!"

The boys nearly hopped with excitement, then whirled to Damir. "Can we make axes, sire?" they asked together, "with sharp blades and long handles?"

Eliana groaned. "Dull blades, and short handles, maybe."

Aren set his axe back to his belt and looked around in wonder as several Norskmen emerged from the crowd. "My people are among yours?"

Damir nodded. "When we first woke, I thought Amrodel had been invaded. We went downstairs and found two Norsk warriors seated at our table."

"They were drinking their own ale, though," added Eliana, "which they offered to share."

"And my queen accepted all too eagerly," said Damir.

"They were very pleasant," said Eliana. "We went to the Hungry Cat to find out what was going on, but Fareth was gone." She looked to the innkeeper and beamed in admiration, and Fareth bowed.

"Alouard told us you had gone with Elphin and Fareth," said Damir, "and Shaen."

"Why possessed you to take her?" asked Eliana. "And where is she, anyway?"

Cahira glanced at Aren, and they hesitated, but Madawc stepped forward. "She's dead," he said without emotion. "Got herself blasted by the Arch Mage, she did, but it was her own doing, and no less than she deserved, for it was she who had first sought to rouse him, for her own evil purposes." Several Woodlanders reacted with grief at this news, but Eliana nodded.

"Somehow, I'm not surprised," she said. "But what are you doing in Cahira's group, Elder?"

"We wondered where you were," added Damir. "Alouard told us he went to check on you about a week ago, and your body had disappeared." He paused. "By the way, I think your cottage has been infested with bats."

"You didn't injure the creatures, did you?" asked Thorleif in horror.

"No," said Damir.

"Well, don't, lad!" added Madawc. " 'Twould be an act of barbarism, that would."

"We'll explain later," offered Cahira, and Damir nodded, then faced Aren and smiled.

"So you faced the Arch Mage, after all, did you?"

"I did," said Aren.

"Then he is destroyed," said Damir.

Aren hesitated. "Well, actually, I gave him your sword."

"Ah." Damir paused. "Did he wield it, or is it embedded in his black heart?"

"Neither," said Aren. "It lies upon his breast, awaiting a time when my daughter, my sons, and your children will seek to rouse him once more."

"Why would they do that?" asked Damir evenly, but he glanced at his two sons as if they might find any number of reasons.

"Do you really want to know that?" asked Aren. "I know I don't."

"About 'your daughter,' " began Eliana, and her green eyes glittered.

"That is what she really wants to know," said Damir, and several Woodlanders leaned in to listen.

Aren looked uncomfortable, but Cahira puffed out a quick breath. "Aren and I have fallen in love. Actually, Damir, he hopes to ask you for my hand, which I expect you to grant—and according the ancient Woodland queen Aryana, who appeared to us as a dragonfly and then later as simply a voice, I shall soon give birth to a daughter!" She withdrew one of the small garments she'd purchased in Amon-Dhen.

Eliana beamed and fingered it, then turned to Damir. "Pay up!"

Aren looked between the two in surprise, as Damir feigned innocence. Eliana turned to Aren and offered a polite smile. "Damir and I placed a friendly wager on the outcome of your quest," she admitted. She paused, and her gaze shifted to one side. "None of us wagered on you giving the Dragonfly Sword to the Arch Mage, however."

"That was unexpected," agreed Cahira, and Aren nodded.

"But most importantly," Eliana continued, "I placed a bet that you would come back together."

"I thought it might take a little more time than it did," said Damir, and he cast a sidelong glance at his wife. "After all, it took us many years to follow that path to its rightful conclusion."

"They had a spat or two," Madawc spoke up, "but most of that was manipulated by Shaen—and the natural clashing of their strong wills. But all such issues were resolved in the"—he paused, and smacked his lips— "usual fashion."

Cahira blushed furiously, but Aren took her hand and smiled. Behind Damir, several Woodlanders and Norsk exchanged coins. Alouard stepped from the crowd.

"We have a few more wagers to settle here, sire," he told Damir, and Damir rolled his eyes and sighed.

"*I knew that.* Let us make our way back to the Hungry Cat, and you can settle them there."

"Good idea!" said Fareth, and he turned to Ranveig. "Give you a good look around, I will."

Ranveig appeared both eager and serious. "About the matter of 'tater' storage, I have some questions. . . ."

Aren looked at them and smiled. "Our people, it seems, have found a common ground after all, yours and mine," he said to Eliana. "As once we dreamed they would."

"It was touchy here at first, apparently," Amrodel's queen replied, "though Damir and I weren't around to witness it. The Norsk came charging into the Woodland to find out what had happened to Aren. Alouard explained the situation to them as best he could, but they insisted on viewing the enchanted Mages before they were convinced." She paused. "It was the sight of our children that moved them, he said. And they took up the guard around us, and around all the others who lay in the Arch Mage's spell. Our people, who had been so afraid, felt protected with the Norsk suddenly defending them, which made their days easier as they waited for the darkness to lift."

"Which it did," said Damir quietly, "though you say the Arch Mage is not destroyed?"

"Cheveyo released the spell," said Cahira, "because of what we learned in Kora."

Damir's eyes widened. "You went to the land of my ancestry?"

"As it happens, it appears my own ancestors spent time in that land," explained Aren. "It is a fair land and glorious, but the prince is evil, and I fear for its fate while he rules. There is a darkness and malevolence upon Kora now, and its people suffer beneath a growing oppression."

"Forty less than before," crowed Cahira. "Aren freed those slaves who would join us—Ang Gelu is one." She glanced to Ang Gelu, who bowed before Damir. "But there are many more, and I fear the prince's grip will tighten."

"The troubles there weren't a product of the Arch Mage's darkness?" asked Damir.

"I think not," said Aren, "for Prince Makya hates and fears Cheveyo even more than he fears you."

Eliana groaned. "Wonderful! This prince isn't a threat to my husband, is he?"

Aren shook his head. "Not yet. Makya has no magic. But he has power. He is someone of whom to beware. Though they are related, he's as unlike Damir as stagnant mud differs from the sea. In fact, Cheveyo resembled your husband far more."

"I knew it!" said Eliana, and she peeked at Cahira. "Was he terribly handsome?"

"In a dark, arrogant, and agonized way, yes," Cahira said. Then she sighed. "But if he's to take up with my daughter, I supposed I'd best get used to him."

Everyone stared at her, and Aren shrugged. "The dragonfly talked a lot," he explained. "But now that Cheveyo has given up his anger, has faced the tortured past that haunted him, there may yet be hope."

Madawc nodded thoughtfully. "A tiny crack begins in an eggshell, and slowly it expands until the egg shatters and the gold within is revealed. So it will be with Cheveyo, I think."

"That reminds me," piped up Thorleif, "I'm hungry. We had a good meal back in Amon-Dhen, but I'd like to see this tavern of yours, Fareth."

"As would I," said Aren, smiling at Cahira. "I would like to learn where my lady wife once spirited away sips of ale and busied herself wagering on the escapades of others."

"'Wife?'" asked Eliana, and she clasped her hand over her heart as if she might explode with happiness. She nodded to Damir. "You owe me for this bet, too, Damir."

"We aren't actually married yet," admitted Cahira, and Eliana's lips twisted.

Aren spoke up. "After we visit the Woodland, I would have you, and all those who would make the journey, ride north with me, where I will take the hand of the Lady of the Wood in marriage."

Damir smiled. "It pleases me you waited to formalize this bond," he said, "or I'd be carrying a keg of Norsk ale to a spot by the Woodland lake." He glanced at Eliana, laughing, and she looked disappointed. "As it is, our wagers require us to venture to the lake with perhaps a small flask—and she will serve me berries and other delights."

"I would like to swim with you again," Cahira said quietly to Aren, whose amber eyes darkened.

"I hope the Woodland lakes are warmer than those in the Norskland," he replied. "Such an expedition as you mention is best done at night." She nodded vigorously, and he bent to kiss her cheek.

"Are *children* to be invited to your wedding ceremonies?" asked Eliana's daughter politely.

Aren turned to Bronwyn and smiled. "Your presence will be a great honor, little one. And if you come to my Great Hall, you can play with our new kittens. I sent them on ahead when we left the Guerdian city, so they could settle in."

Bronwyn clapped her small hands in delight. "Kittens!"

"I would welcome a visit to your land again," said Damir. "Summer has come, and I trust the snow drifts are smaller in size?"

"They have washed away into meadows," said Aren. "And the land lives anew. But I will move my people south again, now that the darkness has lifted. We will dwell in Eddenmark, and I will craft a new hall, with room for many children and many guests."

"I will be at your side, my love," Cahira said softly. "Where I have always wanted to be."

They all went back to their horses and rode into the Woodland, and into the sweet embrace of a life yet to come. Cahira felt the happy tide rising around her, and as she looked at the beautiful, strong Norsk warrior riding beside her, she knew the light she had found in his heart would drive away any darkness that even challenged them. Now, and forever, they were safe in each other's hearts, for the truth she had guessed as she first lay in his arms had risen above all else: they had been one before they were two.

AUTHOR'S NOTE

Because fantasy stories generally use unusual place and character names, I often wish authors would include descriptions of how they imagined the names to be pronounced. In most cases, the races in my books are loosely based on real historical cultures. The Norsk, obviously, are based on the Norse people of northern Europe. The Woodlanders of Amrodel are meant, more or less, to be similar to the Welsh, and their land resembles Wales. The language Cahira speaks when reciting a spell is my rendition of Welsh (which I don't speak, so it's the best I can do). The land of Kora bears some resemblance to the culture of the ancient South American Indians, though their landscape is more like a desert oasis. The city of the Guerdian people is built like an Anasazi cliff-dwelling such as Mesa Verde, but their own culture is more Egyptian, as are their names.

Some of the character names I've chosen are fairly obvious, like Elphin and Eliana and Bodvar, but others might be more difficult and could be pronounced many ways. I hear them specifically, however, and so I've listed a few of the more obscure ones with the pronunciations as I imagine them.

> **Aren**—*AH-ren*, not *Aaron*
> **Cahira**—*Ca-HEER-ah*
> **Shaen**—has two syllables; not *Shayne*, but *SHAY-en*
> **Rika**—*Ree-kah*
> **Thorleif**—*Thor-leaf*
> **Ranveig**—*Rahn-veek*
> **Khadun**—*Khah-DUNE*
> **Damir**—*Dah-MEER*
> **Cheveyo**—a Native American name meaning "Spirited Warrior," and is pronounced *Cheh-VYE-oh.* (At least, that's the way I hear it!)
> **Ang Gelu**—a Nepali name, pronounced *Ahn-GAY-luu*

I hope you've enjoyed my story! You can e-mail me at nidawi@mac.com, or visit my Web site at:

STRANGE BREWS
STOBIE PIEL

Eliana Daere is the greatest herbalist alive. Only one man exists whom she fears—one man who constantly thwarts her will, one handsome, insolent and gifted sorcerer. But Damir will never turn down her offer of an alliance, and when he drinks of the Wine of Truce, Eliana will spring her trap.

He's never trusted Eliana Daere. Her beauty has haunted him since their school days, but she has reputedly aligned herself with the enemy. That is why Damir finds Eliana's offer hard to swallow. When she falls into his hands, he feels no remorse about teaching her a lesson—a gentle one. He will craft a seduction so potent that, in the end, she will have to admit to her own desire. It is a strange brew that brings them together, but nonetheless the sweetest he has ever tasted.